No C̶h̶i̶l̶d̶ ̶o̶f̶ ̶M̶i̶n̶e

Sus...
no...
One Day at a Time, the mo...
Bristol. She lives in Gloucestershire. Her website address is
www.susanlewis.com

Susan is a supporter of the childhood bereavement charity,
Winton's Wish: www.winstonswish.org.uk and of the
breast cancer charity, BUST: www.bustbristol.co.uk

Praise for Susan Lewis

'Spellbinding! You just keep turning the pages,
with the atmosphere growing more and more
intense as the story leads to its dramatic climax.'
Daily Mail

'A multi-faceted tear-jerker.' *heat*

'Utterly compelling.' *Sun*

'Expertly written to brew an atmosphere of
foreboding, this story is an irresistible blend
of intrigue and passion, and the consequences
of secrets and betrayal.' *Woman*

Susan Lewis

No Child of Mine

arrow books

Published by Arrow Books 2013

2 4 6 8 10 9 7 5 3

LANCASHIRE COUNTY LIBRARY	
3011812675716 4	
Askews & Holts	12-Apr-2013
AF GEN	£6.99

Addresses fo   be found
at: www.randomhouse.co.uk/offices.htm

The Random House Group Limited Reg. No. 954009

ISBN 9780099550785

A CIP catalogue record for this book is available from the British Library

The Random House Group Limited supports The Forest Stewardship Council® (FSC®), the leading international forest-certification organisation. Our books carrying the FSC label are printed on FSC®-certified paper. FSC is the only forest-certification scheme supported by the leading environmental organisations, including Greenpeace. Our paper procurement policy can be found at www.randomhouse.co.uk/environment

Typeset in Palatino 11.5/13pt by Palimpsest Book Production Limited, Falkirk, Stirlingshire
Printed and bound by CPI Group (UK) Ltd, Croydon CR0 4YY

To James, just because . . .

'Hello. And who are you?'

The little girl's deep brown eyes stared unblinkingly at Alex Lake; she seemed almost ethereal, Alex was thinking as she stooped down in front of the swing, as though she might have stepped from an Impressionist painting. Her creamy cheeks were smudged with tiny rosettes of colour, and the wiry cloud of dark hair that rose and dipped in whimsical curls made her seem so delicate – and perfect. How old was she? Alex wondered. Three? Four? Definitely closer to three.

'What's your name?' Alex asked with a friendly smile.

The child didn't answer, simply continued to stare into Alex's eyes and clutch the chains of the box swing. Her legs were dangling over the tarmac, too short to reach it so she was unable to make herself rock back and forth, and there didn't appear to be anyone close by to push it. There was a hypnotic quality about her that Alex was sure she'd felt even before she'd spotted her. It was what had pulled her attention from the children she was with, her niece and nephew, who were still a few yards away swishing gleefully down the slide into their mother's arms.

'My name's Alexandra,' she told the little girl, 'but most people call me Alex.'

The girl blinked and Alex smiled at the slowness of it, and felt strangely moved by the fine blue lines in her lids, and the extravagant curl of her lashes.

Her mother, or nanny, must be one of the group of young women sitting on the grass nearby. The instant she spotted a stranger talking to her child she'd no doubt come running, fighting down panic and appalled with herself for having turned away, even for a moment.

A moment was often all it took.

'She's very shy, I'm afraid.'

Alex looked up to find a man smiling down at her. With the sun behind him she couldn't make out his features, but he was dressed in a lime-coloured polo shirt and khaki chinos, with a tan leather belt sitting just below his ample waist. He wasn't tall, maybe five eight at the most. As she stood up she could see his neatly combed hair more clearly; his eyes, the shape of half-moons, though friendly, contained a look of wariness. Only to be expected from a parent who'd found a stranger talking to his child, she thought.

'She's also very pretty,' Alex said, wondering where he had suddenly come from. She hadn't noticed him anywhere, and there weren't many people around for him to get lost amongst. Then she spotted a woman sitting alone on a blanket several yards away, her hands buried in the grass behind her, her face turned up to the sun.

Probably the mother, Alex decided.

'Come along,' he said, lifting the child off the swing and setting her on her feet. A small Paddington Bear, with boots but no hat, fell to the ground. The little girl quickly picked it up and tucked it under one arm. When her head stayed down Alex looked at the feathery curls and felt something stir deep inside her – a desire to scoop her up and make her laugh, the way she did with her sister's kids. There was also an awakening of unease that Alex didn't like at all.

Something wasn't quite right with this child.

She watched the little girl's hand go into the man's, a precious jewel slipping into a shell that completely engulfed it.

The man's smile was affectionate and cheerful as he said, 'Best get her home, I suppose,' and turning her around he began walking her away.

Alex stood watching them, expecting them to stop at the sun-worshipping woman, but they simply went straight past. A few yards further on the little girl glanced over her shoulder, and feeling a catch in her heart, Alex lifted a hand to wave. Working in child protection could be a hazardous thing, making her see crimes where none were being committed.

Or were they?

'Shame on you,' her sister Gabby teased, coming up behind her.

Alex looked puzzled.

'Trying to pick up a bloke by making friends with his kids,' Gabby explained with a nudge.

Alex's smile was weak. Glamorous and vivacious though her sister was, her humour was often a bit off. Her gaze returned to the child and the man who'd almost reached the park gates by now. Surely she wasn't watching an abduction? No, it couldn't be possible. The girl had given her hand without being asked; she'd clearly known him – and if she belonged to anyone else in the park they'd almost certainly be screaming blue murder by now.

Yet for some reason they didn't seem to belong together.

'You're getting that look about you,' Gabby warned.

'What look?'

Gabby rolled her eyes. 'Not every man you come across is a child molester,' she reminded her. 'And that one looked pretty respectable if you ask me. Quite dishy, in fact.'

Alex was surprised. 'Did you think so?' she replied, having failed to see it herself.

Gabby shrugged. 'I suppose I didn't get that good a look, and he was a bit on the short side – though taller than you.'

'Not difficult,' Alex said with a smile. At five foot two she was at least four inches shorter than Gabby, and also unlike Gabby she had fine, ash-blonde hair, sea-green eyes and a petite frame that her father had always said just didn't seem big enough to contain so much energy, or such a big heart. 'Not forgetting all that attitude,' her mother would snipe, though that had mostly been when Alex was in her teens.

She was twenty-eight now and Gabby was thirty-three, with inky dark hair, toffee-coloured eyes and a smile that used to be dazzling, but lately had started to lose some of its lustre. Having two kids was tiring. In many ways she was coming to resemble their mother, a dubious fate that would never befall Alex. Nor would she ever come to look like their father, for the simple reason that, unlike Gabby, she had been adopted into the family, rather than born.

Both their parents were dead now – their father having succumbed to cancer two years ago, while a heart attack had taken their mother ten months later. Alex still missed them, especially her father, but not as much as Gabby did.

'Right, better go and round up those rascals,' Gabby declared.

As she started off to the maze of climbing frames where Phoebe and Jackson were twirling and leaping about like monkeys, Alex turned to look for the man and child again. Unsurprisingly, they'd disappeared into the world beyond the park, and yet, oddly, it was as though something about them was lingering invisibly in the air; or perhaps it was settling inside her like a curiosity, or a concern – it actually felt, she realised, like an affinity with the girl.

As a social worker she knew better than to become fanciful where children were concerned, or let her feelings run away with her, but there were occasions when she simply couldn't help it. And for some reason this was seeming like one of them.

She was thinking about the man again and what Gabby had said, that she suspected every member of the opposite sex of being a child molester. It wasn't true, not even close – why would she, when most men she knew would never harm a hair of a child's head? However, she knew better than to be taken in by appearances; some of the worst offenders she'd had to deal with weren't from the sink estates on the edge of town, or other sorts of deprived backgrounds. Attributes such as charm, sophistication, and high levels of education often provided an effective mask for those with depraved and monstrous intent.

Her real father hadn't been that kind of a monster, but he'd been one all the same.

'Auntie Lex, Auntie Lex,' her niece and nephew cried, bounding towards her.

Laughing as they threw their arms around her waist, Alex hugged them back and smiled at her sister who was ambling on behind, loaded down with bags. Since Gabby was married to such a wonderful man, Alex knew she'd never have to fear for her five-year-old niece and nephew.

'Can we stay at yours tonight?' Jackson begged. 'Please, please, please.'

'Oh, Jackson,' Gabby groaned, 'please don't start that again. You know we're driving back to Devon tonight. You want to see Daddy, don't you?'

'Yes!' he cheered, and punching a fist in the air he zoomed off like an aeroplane.

'Auntie Lex,' Phoebe said, putting her head back to look up at Alex.

'Yes, my darling?' Alex responded, cupping her niece's flushed, sweet face in her hands.

'Who was that little girl you were talking to?'

Turning to stare across the empty parkland to where the traffic was coming and going beyond, Alex said, 'I don't know, Phoebs. She didn't tell me her name.'

Chapter One

'Hi honey, I'm home.'

Alex had never actually watched the nineties TV series of that name, nor was she old enough to have plucked the phrase from the fifties. However, she often sang it out when she walked in the door because it was what her parents used to do, and it had usually made them laugh – or at least smile.

It generally had the same effect on Jason, but not this evening apparently, because he didn't seem to be at home. Unless he was in the garden braving another attempt at putting the new shed together. It was going to be hard to get anything as polite as a smile out of him if that was the case. In spite of him being a fully qualified builder his last effort had ended with a hammer boomeranging off the back wall of the house, while he performed a weird sort of Friday prayers next to the compost heap.

Since then, the offending shed parts had been banished from sight, and were quite likely, Alex suspected, to stay that way until they were ready to behave like the reasonable, easily assembled components they were supposed to be, according to the website they'd ordered them from.

Dropping her heavy work bag and grey denim jacket at the foot of the stairs, she quickly checked the time on her watch and groaned inwardly to see how late it was already. She had less than an hour to shower, change and grab a snack before needing to head out again. After the day she'd just had she wouldn't have minded simply crashing in front of the TV for the rest of the evening, or outside on the patio in their smart new loungers with a bottle of half-decent wine. On the other hand, she was excited about tonight – so excited, in fact, that merely thinking about what lay in store was enough to dispel her exhaustion and infuse her with so many exhilarating waves of energy that she could sing, dance, even turn cartwheels across the lawn if required.

That would have given old Millie Case a bit of a chuckle, if she'd still been in the cottage next door. Sadly, Millie had been moved to a care home a few weeks ago, her Alzheimer's making it impossible for her to carry on living alone.

Quickly adding a visit to Millie to her list of must-dos at the weekend, Alex entered the kitchen to find it empty. However, both top and bottom halves of the stable door were open to the patio, and the buzz and roar of the lawn mower careering up and down the back garden explained why Jason hadn't heard her come in. Inhaling the delicious scent of freshly mown grass, she was about to go and commend his manly horticultural skills when the phone on the dresser started to ring.

Tucking the receiver under her chin, she opened the fridge to take out some wine. 'Hi, the Vicarage,' she answered. Though the house no longer belonged to the church it had retained its name since her father, the rector, had bought it, and its position of splendid isolation at the top end of the village (with Millie's cottage attached) made it one of the area's more desirable homes. Not that it was particularly large, or well modernised – in fact it could boast none of the grandeur of most renovated vicarages around the country. It was the views that made it so sought after, both out across the open fields behind, and down over the random sprawl of village rooftops in front. Alex was always mindful of how lucky she was to be living here now that her parents had gone, but knew that the day would soon come when Gabby would want to sell.

What was she going to do then on her paltry salary?

No time to think about it now.

'Hi Alex, is that you?' a voice demanded from the other end of the line.

'Yes, it's me,' Alex replied, gliding effortlessly into her evening persona of joint founder/director/producer of the Mulgrove Village Players. Alex the child-protection worker would fall away magically when she shook out her hair and removed her specs. Or so she liked to think. In reality, the problems of the day never really went away, they simply went off backstage for a while, very often to work themselves up into something superbly melodramatic ready for a middle-of-the-night session when she was unable to sleep. 'How are you, Hailey?' she asked chirpily.

'Oh, you knew it was me,' Hailey gushed delightedly.

Alex couldn't help but smile. Hailey was the most self-effacing writer with talent she'd ever come across – not that she'd come across many writers, but there had been a few. 'Is everything OK?' she asked, half-filling a glass with perfectly chilled Chardonnay. A sudden cloud threatened. 'Please don't tell me you can't make it tonight.'

'Oh, no, no,' Hailey cried hastily. 'I mean, yes, of course I'll be there. I'd never let you down, you know that. I was just checking to make sure I have the time right. Seven thirty at the village hall.'

Suspecting Hailey really just wanted to speak to someone who'd understand how nervous and excited she was, Alex, in her role as director, said, 'I know you won't be late, and having you there will make the world of difference to everyone.'

'Oh, don't say that,' Hailey protested. 'I'm just glad that it all seems to be going so well. I never dreamt that I'd ever actually have one of my plays produced.'

'So you see, dreams do come true,' Alex told her, grimacing at her own corniness, while feeling amazed all over again that timid little Hailey Walsh from a neighbouring village had managed to come up with such a boisterous comedy. OK, it was cheesy in parts, and very definitely over the top, but if the hilarity during rehearsals was anything to go by, the show itself would have their friends and neighbours rolling in the aisles. 'I'd better ring off now,' she said, glancing at the clock on the wall, 'or I'll be late getting there. See you at seven thirty.'

'On the dot,' Hailey assured her, and Alex didn't doubt it.

No sooner had she hung up than the phone started off again. Checking the caller ID she clicked on with a merry, 'Hello, Mulgrove Vicarage, Alexandra Lake at your service.'

Chuckling, her Aunt Sheila said, 'Hello dearie, how are you? Is this a good time?'

'Actually, no,' Alex admitted, spotting Jason

4

taking a call on his mobile. 'Unless it's urgent. Is it?'

'No, just ringing to let you know I've received my tickets.'

'For the opening night? Fantastic. So you'll be able to make it?'

'I'm certainly going to try, but you know how busy I am here. I can't think when I last had a day off, and I'm far too old for it all really.'

Knowing that the day her aunt gave up her beloved horse refuge would be the day she keeled over, Alex said, 'Seventy is the new fifty, I'm told, and anyway, you don't look a day over forty.' It wasn't true, because actually her adoptive mother's sister looked ancient, but where was the harm in saying it if it made her feel good? 'Do you know if Gabby's got her tickets yet?' she asked.

'I haven't heard from her so far today, but I'm sure she has. Oh, hang on, don't go anywhere, this might be her now and I'll be able to tell you.'

As she waited, Alex took a sip of wine and felt proud of herself for not minding that her sister and aunt spoke on a daily basis. Once upon a time it would have made her feel fretful and excluded, but she'd learned in recent years to have better control of her insecurities. No doubt they were still raging away somewhere in her psyche, getting themselves nicely fuelled up by the issues she had to deal with in her day job. However, not since she was a highly strung teenager had she got herself into an emotional state over not mattering as much as her sister. Their mother had always denied it, of course, saying that if she hadn't been told she was adopted she would never have come up with such nonsense. And occasionally Alex had wondered if that might be true, but even if it were, there was no doubt in her mind that Gabby was more special to her parents simply because she was theirs.

'No, not her,' Sheila announced, coming back on the line. 'I'll let you go then, if you're in a hurry. Toodle pip and all that.'

After saying her own goodbye Alex hung up the phone, and seeing that Jason was still on his mobile she blew him a kiss through the open window and ran upstairs to take a shower. It was only when she turned it on that she remembered one of Jason's regular plumbers had come on an emergency call out that morning to disconnect it. Heaven only knew what demon or gremlin had been at work in the system during the night, but for some reason water had started gushing out of it at six a.m. with no one turning it on, and apparently the plumber hadn't managed to sort it yet.

Resigning herself to a lengthy wait for the bath to fill to a mere few inches she stuck in the plug, spun the crusty old brass taps, and went back along the landing to the master bedroom to dig out some fresh clothes. This had always been her parents' bedroom until her mother, newly widowed, had moved down to Devon to live with Sheila and be closer to Gabby and the children. The furniture was all theirs, the old-fashioned wrought-iron bedstead with its slightly bent foot rail and limp feather mattress, the his-and-hers wardrobes with the maddening system of front-to-back hanging rails, and the odd collection of walnut chests and pine cabinets. The carpet was a busy mix of red and green swirls, while the curtains were a dusky shade of gold. It would win no awards for interior design, but with its dual-aspect windows bringing in so much light Alex loved the room anyway, and Jason, who'd only lived in modern houses until he'd moved in with her a year ago, always claimed that he loved it too.

Unfortunately his children couldn't stand it, but since their mother had convinced them that they couldn't stand anything to do with Alex Lake, or Mulgrove, or in fact anything outside of Kesterly-on-Sea, the nearby coastal town where they lived and Alex worked, it would have been a bit of a miracle if they'd fallen for this ramshackle rural idyll at first sight.

'It's like *dead* creepy,' Tiffany, Jason's thirteen-year-old, had murmured disgustedly before she'd even set foot in the door.

Taking up the theme, ten-year-old Heidi had shuddered theatrically as she'd gulped, 'It really scares me.'

'Has it got ghosts?' eight-year-old Tom had whispered, his eyes bright with the thrill of it.

Though Alex had never felt anything in the least bit sinister about the house, she would readily admit that to some it might give the impression of containing other-worldly residents reluctant to move on. Its association with the church, which was opposite the house halfway down the hill going into the village, clearly added to its sense of mystique. But for her the only real ghouls that existed anywhere near the Vicarage were the ones inside her head – so she couldn't actually claim they were real. However, she was certain they weren't imagined either, because the nightmares that had troubled her ever since she was a child she knew came from the time before the rector, her adoptive father, had rescued her.

Shaking off the thoughts before they had a chance

7

to start darkening her mood, she ran back down-stairs to find out if Jason was off the phone yet. What had happened back then was all a very long time ago, and who needed to be dealing with a twenty-five-year-old horror when she had fresh ones coming up practically every day?

'At last,' Jason declared, pocketing his mobile as she finally made it outside to greet him. 'You're back later than I expected,' and scooping her into his arms he planted a bruising kiss full on her lips. 'Mmm, that's better,' he murmured suggestively as he pulled back to gaze at her with his intense blue eyes. At five foot seven he didn't tower too far over her, but at thirty-eight he was a full ten years older, and with the grizzle of grey in his wiry dark hair, and lines around his eyes, he often looked it. However, there was no getting away from the fact that he was heart-stoppingly hand-some – at least to her mind he was – and not even the unsightly scar that puckered his right cheek would change her opinion on that. He'd got it in an accident as a child, which he'd told her all about the night they'd met at a party, in Kesterly, eighteen months ago. Not the traditional sort of chat-up line designed to sweep her off her feet, but she'd fallen for him anyway.

'Good day?' he asked, kissing her again.

'Depends how you define good,' she smiled. 'How about you?'

'On a scale of one to ten it's just tipped off the top end.'

She eyed him carefully.

'I mean seeing you,' he said with a laugh.

'OK, as long as it's not something to do with the call you just took, or I might be jealous.'

Since she wasn't jealous by nature he never took her quips seriously; however, on this occasion he grimaced awkwardly and turned to start packing up the mower.

'So who was on the phone?' she prompted as he carted the empty collection box over to a springy pile of cut grass.

'I think you can guess,' he replied, not turning round.

Her heart immediately sank. 'Gina,' she stated, trying to keep the frustration out of her tone. No call from his estranged wife was ever a good one. 'So what did she want?'

Sighing, he said, 'Apparently her car's broken down so she wants me to drive Heidi to her dance class.'

Taking no more than a split second to work out what that was going to mean for the evening, Alex's eyes flashed with anger. 'I swear she does it on purpose,' she cried. 'She'll know what we had planned for tonight . . .'

'How would she?'

'Anyone could have told her, or knowing her she's been on the theatre's Facebook page checking up on everything we're doing. Jason, you can't let us down tonight. It's a tech run, for God's sake.'

'I know, I know, but what am I supposed to do? Heidi's passionate about those classes and she's due to perform at assembly on the first day of term, so I can hardly make her skip a lesson now when there's less than a week to go.'

'But she can already dance the piece perfectly.'

'Says you. She doesn't think so, and as she's the one who's performing . . .'

'So are my troupe, tonight, specially for you so

you can sort out all the technical stuff for our opening night the *weekend after next.'*

Looking as guilty as he felt, he said, 'Can't you change it to tomorrow? There . . .'

'No, Jason, I can't change it to tomorrow, not at this short notice. Half the company will already be on their way, and the village hall's not exactly at our personal disposal.'

Not bothering to point out that she and Mattie Graves, one of her old schoolfriends, virtually ran the village hall – or theatre as it would be tonight – he said, 'I'm really sorry, honest to God I am, but I have to take her.'

'And wait and bring her back, which means you won't be able to get to us until nine at the earliest, by which time we'll have finished our run-through and everyone'll be too tired to do it again. Great. Just bloody brilliant.'

'I'll find a way to make it up to you,' he called after her as she stormed inside.

'You said that the last time,' she shouted back. 'And the time before that, and the time before that.'

'Think how big the diamond's getting,' he tried to joke.

Under any other circumstances she might have laughed – right now she was too furious even to try.

Ten minutes later she was stepping out of the bath and reaching for a towel when her work mobile started to ring. Seeing it was Wendy, her manager who had a habit of calling out of hours with issues that could easily wait, she let it go through to messages, and wrapped her hair in a towel as she padded through to the bedroom. The sun had moved round by now and was spilling in through the front window, casting a soft crimson glow over

10

the gaily upholstered love seat that hugged it. This was where she and Gabby as children used to sit with their father, gazing out over the church and village as he told them stories about angels and imps, trees that could talk and the miracle bird who could make all the bad things go away.

She could do with the miracle bird now to transport the dreaded Gina to the far end of Purgatory.

If only.

'Am I allowed to come in?' Jason called out sheepishly from the landing.

Though Alex didn't normally cover up in front of him, she was still too cross to want to risk arousing him with her nudity, so grabbing her robe she said, 'It's your room too.'

The latch clattered as he released it and the hinges gave a faint squeal before he popped his head in, apparently still not entirely sure it was safe to enter. 'I'm sorry,' he said, helplessly.

Sinking down in front of the mould-spotted mirror of the dressing table, she glanced briefly at his reflection as she replied, 'You always are, but it never changes anything, does it? She still keeps calling at the last minute with some demand or other, and you just up and jump every time she cracks the whip.'

'Oh, come on, you're not being fair. I don't do it for her. It's Heidi . . .'

'Who has two aunties and an uncle living within half a mile of her, any one of whom could easily take her.'

'They've got kids of their own . . .'

'And you've got another commitment this evening. Just tell me this: what is the point of a tech run without a technical director?'

Grimacing, he said, 'I've been to most of the rehearsals so I've got a fair idea of what's required already.'

'But eight busy people are making it their business to come to our village hall this evening in order to stage a rehearsal especially for you.'

'I swear, you can't make me feel any worse than I already do. Maybe if you could delay for an hour. I might be back by then . . .'

'No you won't, because as I've already pointed out, you'll have to wait with Heidi while she has her lesson, and you know very well that Gina will have something else for you to do when you get back there.'

'If she does then I'll just tell her . . .'

'No, Jason, you won't tell her anything, because you never do. You let her rule you through those children, and as far as I can see that's never going to change.'

'What am I supposed to do, pretend my children don't exist?' he cried, throwing out his hands in frustration.

'Now you're being ridiculous. All I'm asking is that you stick to your word when you give it, especially when other people are going out of their way to put on a rehearsal that *you* asked for.'

Looking guiltier than ever, he pushed his hands across his face and back through his hair. 'We talked about this before I moved in,' he said. 'We agreed, you understood that the kids have to come first . . .'

'But this isn't about them, it's about Gina, surely you can see that. As I said, she's always ringing you at the last minute, using you like a handyman or a babysitter, or someone she's still married to. And if she doesn't ring herself she gets Tiffany or Heidi to

12

do it for her, turning the screws even tighter, making you feel like you're neglecting them, or that you don't care – or even that you just upped and abandoned them, when we all know that it was their mother who broke up your marriage, not you. She's the one who was having an affair and got you to leave your own home so she could move him in, and now he's dumped her for someone else she's trying to get you back . . .'

'But she's not going to win . . .'

'Says you.'

Taking a deep breath in an effort to calm things down, he said, 'Look, I don't want to fall out with you . . .'

With an incredulous laugh she cried, 'It's already happening, the same way it always does when you go rushing off to tend to her little emergencies. But if I continue this I'll be playing straight into her hands, and frankly one of us doing that is enough. What time are you leaving?'

Glancing at his watch, he said, 'I guess I ought to be on my way. What are you doing about food tonight?'

'We're going to the pub after rehearsals so I'll hang on till then. If you're hungry now there's a pack of sandwiches in my work bag, which is around here somewhere. Prawn and mayo.'

'Oh yippee, my favourite,' he responded, with a wryness that made her swallow a smile. She wasn't quite ready to forgive him yet, but nor did she want them to part bad friends, particularly when she knew what a struggle he had with not being a full-time dad. It really wasn't his fault that his marriage had broken up, though obviously she couldn't help feeling glad that it had, or he wouldn't be in her life.

13

'Looks like you've got a message,' he said, pulling out her mobile as he rummaged about for the sandwiches.

'It's work,' she said, taking it from him and quickly checking to make sure it wasn't anything urgent. As she'd expected, it was from Wendy, reminding her that her annual CRB check was due, which could easily have waited until the morning, but hey, why wait when she could ring someone at home? Her other phone started to ring. 'Ah, thanks,' she said, as Jason passed it over.

'Two lives, two phones,' he teased. 'I just hope you don't have two lovers.'

Catching his eye in the mirror, she narrowed her own meaningfully as she said into her personal phone, 'Hi Mattie, everything OK for this evening?'

As her co-producer began giving her a blow-by-blow account of everything she'd done in preparation for the rehearsal, and Jason left, Alex pulled out a drawer to look for fresh undies. When Mattie got going she generally wasn't required to say much more than 'great', 'fantastic', 'you're amazing', which she was delivering in abundance as she pulled on some tatty jeans and a strappy T-shirt and pushed her feet into a pair of old ballet pumps. Having known Mattie for most of her life she was used to her friend's obsession with detail, which, though exasperating at times, made her pretty indispensable too, because no one else Alex knew came even close to possessing Mattie's magnificent organisational skills. And Mattie loved being involved in the theatre almost as much as she loved being Alex's friend, though they'd never been as close as normal best friends, mainly because Mattie couldn't cope with anything too personal.

By the time Mattie rang off Alex was more or less ready to leave, so checking a text that had come in during the call she started down the stairs. As soon as she saw who the message was from her heart melted.

Hello Auntie Lex, I came second in the sack race and Mummy won a goldfish on the bows and arrows which she let me have. Love Jackson.

You're brilliant, she quickly texted back to her sister's mobile. *What are you going to call the goldfish?*

Before a reply came through the phone started to ring, and seeing an unfamiliar number she clicked on, saying, 'Hi, Alex Lake speaking.'

'Oh, yes, Alex,' the voice at the other end stated, as though she'd momentarily forgotten who she was calling. 'It's Heather Hancock here. I've just heard that Jason's not going to be at the run-through tonight, so I guess it's been cancelled.'

'Actually, it hasn't,' Alex told her, trying to keep the irritation out of her voice. How did Heather Hancock, reporter-at-large for the *Kesterly Gazette*, already know that Jason's plans had changed? As if she needed to ask. Her good chum Gina had obviously been in touch for a bit of a gloat.

'Nevertheless, something else has come up that I really ought to go to,' Heather was informing her. 'I'll be in touch to rearrange.'

'Hang on,' Alex cried before she could ring off. 'That will be before the opening, I take it.'

'Of course, if I can fit you in.'

Bristling, while reminding herself to try to sound friendly, Alex said, 'The deal was you'd give us some publicity upfront if we let you come to the tech run.'

'Actually, I don't think there was a deal,' Heather interrupted, sounding bored. 'I just agreed to drop in on a rehearsal if I was passing and had time. Tonight was always going to be difficult, and now I know Jason's not going to be there . . .'

'But he's not in it, so what difference does it make?'

'As I said, something else has come up. I expect you've heard about the show due to open at the Kesterly Playhouse. Obviously, something of that calibre has to take precedence, especially when one of the cast used to be in *Emmerdale*. The public will want to read about her.'

Throwing the put-down straight back at the local hack, Alex said, 'How gracious of her to spare the time to talk to a provincial paper that no one ever reads.' She winced. *As usual she'd gone too far*.

'If that's what you think then there's really not much point in me covering your little amateur production at all, is there?' came the tart response. 'Best go, see you around,' and the line went dead.

As furious with herself as she was with Heather Hancock, Alex stuffed her phone in her bag and tore open the front door. What was she thinking, letting that supercilious old cow get under her skin when her little theatre group needed all the free publicity it could get if they were ever going to land any bums on seats? Were it not for the fact that Heather Hancock was a friend of Gina's, as well as a known self-adulator, she'd never have risen to the bait.

So merrily off down the hill the evening went, hardly pausing for breath, and all courtesy of Jason's wife who was no doubt already being informed by her best chum of just what a pathetic and nasty piece of work Jason's girlfriend actually was. (Alex doubted they'd put it so politely, but it was as far as she was prepared to go in lambasting herself.)

Remembering that her nephew had probably texted back with his goldfish's name by now, she dug out her phone while locking up the house and after checking she started to laugh.

Fantastic. I've always wanted a goldfish named after me, she texted back. *Can't wait to meet her.*

If only all kids could be as happy and loved as her sister's twins.

The little girl was shaking so badly that she was terrified of not being able to keep quiet. Her mummy had told her she must, so she was trying, but it was hard, so hard, and everything was dark. There was a little boy here too, snuggled in tightly against her. She could feel his fear pounding through her. It was making it difficult to breathe.

There was lots of screaming outside, and roaring in anger; loud thumps, crashes, heavy footsteps and the smashing of glass.

The little girl squeezed herself into a tight ball.

The boy was standing up. He was older than her, taller, braver. He was opening the door, telling her to stay where she was, and then he was gone.

She wanted him to come back.

She didn't want to be on her own. The bad man might get her.

Her mummy would come for her soon.

She'd promised.

A door slammed and everything fell silent, but she was still too afraid to move.

Where was the boy? Why hadn't he come back?

The darkness was like a monster, trapping her in its lair. It was closing in on her, wrapping itself around her; her terror was so fierce it was eating her up.

Her mummy must have forgotten where she was. Still shaking, she stood up and went to the door.

Suddenly there was noise again, and she shrank back. The bad man was out there, he'd come to take her away so she'd never see her mummy again.

Using a fist to stuff down her sobs, she cowered into the shadows, squeezing herself in behind a giant box. She could hear lots of people and no one sounded like her mummy.

Tears were streaming down her cheeks, but she had to keep quiet.

She wanted her mummy.

Why didn't she come?

It was a long, long time later, after everything had gone quiet again, that she stood on tiptoe, straining towards the latch. It was too high; she couldn't get out. She tried and tried, but her arm wasn't long enough. She could see her hand in a chink of light, pale and small, fingers outstretched. The latch was above it, but she couldn't reach.

'Mummy,' she sobbed. 'Mummy.' She was crying very hard now, and wanted to scream, but she couldn't make any sound come out. She tried and tried, but all that happened was a silent rasp of terror, and still nobody came.

As Alex's eyes flew open she knew right away, though on a distant level, that it was a nightmare, but the terror, the need to scream was still with her. Her heart was like a pounding fist; sweat was pouring from her skin. It felt so real. She must break free of it, tear through the force of its horror and properly connect with where she was, and who she was now.

It took a while, longer than usual it seemed, but eventually the dreaded demons of her past began falling away. If only it was just a dream, something created out of a small reality and blown into nonsense, but she knew the child was her; and that the little boy, who she'd never seen again, and never would, was her brother.

Moving carefully, so as not to wake Jason, she pushed aside the duvet and went downstairs to make herself some tea. She knew from experience that it wouldn't be possible to go back to sleep for a while, so there was no point in trying.

The dismaying, and most disturbing part of the dream – this was the first time she'd had it for months – wasn't so much what was happening in it, though God knew that was the worst of it – it was that her unconscious mind felt compelled to go back to that horrifying time.

When would she ever be free of it?

Why couldn't she let it go?

She understood now that she'd been too young when the nightmares began for her adoptive parents to explain what was causing them. It wasn't a tale a child should hear at any age, and certainly not when she was barely five. It wasn't until she'd reached her teens, and still unable to escape the night-time terrors, that her father had finally decided she must be told the truth. They weren't, as she'd always been told, an abstract reconstruction of something she might have seen on TV as a child, or read in a book, but a more or less accurate representation of the truth, as she'd known it, aged three.

For a long time after she'd heard the details she'd

wanted to pluck the horror of it out of her mind, cast it away, stamp on it, destroy it in any way she could. How was she ever going to live with the fact that her real father, the one whose genes she bore and whose blood ran in her veins, had carried out such a brutal attack on her family while she'd been shut up in a cupboard? Her grandparents, her aunt, her aunt's boyfriend, her mother and her four-year-old brother – all of them had been victims of his crazed attack.

If only her brother had stayed with her that night he might still be alive too.

As it was, his little body was the first the police had stumbled upon when they'd broken down the door to get into the house; the others were in the sitting room, dining room and kitchen.

It was a day later, the rector had told her, while he was at the crime scene, gaining an understanding of the trauma the police officers had experienced in order to help them, that a little girl had been found alive and uninjured in a hidden compartment of the attic. Alex had no memory of being taken from the cupboard, or of anyone carrying her outside to a car, but she knew now that the first arms to reach for her had been the rector's. And in the absence of any known family to hand her over to, he'd insisted on taking her home to his wife.

She knew that would never be allowed these days, but back then, when the rules governing child protection hadn't been so stringent and men of cloth were more highly respected, there had been no objection to the trustworthy young priest and his wife taking her in. As they were registered foster carers she might have ended up with them anyway, so the authorities had simply arranged the paperwork to suit. She'd been three years old then; four and a half when they'd officially adopted her and five by the time Douglas Lake had become the rector of Mulgrove and they'd moved to the Vicarage.

By then her real father, who was known to have carried out the killings, still hadn't been found. Police believed that his human-trafficking associates, mostly Asians and Russians, had smuggled him out of the country back to his native Romania, but no trace had been found of him there either. The reason for the killings, Alex had been told, was that her mother, who'd come from Liverpool and got herself into an early, disastrous marriage, had threatened to go to the police when she'd discovered the truth of her husband's business.

He'd never been traced, and because there were fears that he might one day come back and try to find her, Alex's identity had always been fiercely protected. No one outside her immediate family (apart from Jason now) knew that she was the little girl who'd escaped the Temple Fields killings. In fact, they'd happened so long ago that no one ever really thought about them now, apart from her.

At the time of learning the truth about her roots she'd begun tormenting herself with how different her life might have been if she'd grown up with her real mother and brother. Not that she didn't love Myra, her adoptive mother, but she'd always known in her heart that Myra hadn't been happy about having the daughter of a maniacal murderer foisted upon her. She'd tried to be kind, of course, and to ensure that Alex didn't go without, at least in a material and welfare sense, but she'd never managed to make Alex feel as special as Gabby. And the way she'd later broken the news to Alex that, actually, she wasn't the only survivor of that terrible night, had been so matter-of-fact as to be downright cruel. Why had she not realised how shattering it would be for fourteen-year-old Alex to learn that her mother had come through it too, in spite of the near fatal knife wounds to her back and chest? She'd been hospitalised for almost a year, Myra had told her, but after her discharge she'd simply disappeared.

'Didn't she come to see me?' Alex had asked, her voice hoarse with the shock.

Myra had shaken her head. 'I'm afraid not, my dear,' she'd replied, managing to sound both sympathetic and disapproving – though whether she'd disapproved of the question, or of Alex's real mother, Alex had never been sure. 'She met with the rector and it was agreed that you were safe and settled with us, so it would be for the best if she left you here.'

'But she must have wanted to see me?'

'Oh, I'm sure she did, but she was afraid – we all were – that if she came she'd lead your real father straight to our door. So after signing the adoption papers she left the area and we never heard from her again.'

In her pubescent state Alex became almost obsessed with her real mother. It was as though she could feel her beating through her heart, speaking to her on the wind, watching her from somewhere just out of sight. She could see her gazing back at her from the mirror, and sense her understanding the crazy thoughts that charged about her mind. She'd realised then why she wasn't like the family she was with, especially when it came to religion. Not that she didn't believe in God because in a way she did – He was definitely good in emergencies, in that there had to be something to hold on to when life had pulled up the ladder, whipped out the rug, or smashed all the dreams. And as far as she could tell He'd always had a big part to play in births, marriages, deaths and for old ladies who didn't seem to have much else to do. However, she'd never been able to see Him in quite the same way as the rector did. Nor had Gabby, come to that, though she'd done a far better job of hiding it. And Alex wasn't entirely sure that Myra had ever had that close a relationship with Him either, considering how mean she could be at times. Alex had never challenged her on it, however, mainly because she and Myra were already finding more than enough to row about by then.

Though the rector had agreed to try and find her mother, sadly, frustratingly, his efforts had come to nothing; it was as though she'd vanished off the face of the earth. 'She won't be Angela Albescu any more, I'm sure,' he'd said regretfully, 'but I can't find any trace of Angela Nicholls either, which was her maiden name.'

Alex had never voiced the fear that her mother had gone to be with her father, and God knew she didn't want to believe it, but in the job she did now she saw it all the time, women forgiving men for the most unthinkable atrocities.

'She probably has a new family by now, a bit like you,' Gabby had once suggested, trying to comfort her. 'And if she has, maybe she doesn't want you to find her. I mean, if she's got other children and no one knows who she used to be – not that she did anything wrong, but you know what I'm saying . . . Anyway, she probably won't want anyone

23

finding out about her past, and they'd have to if you turned up on the doorstep.'

Though it had hurt Alex deeply when Gabby had said that, and still did in her bleaker moments, she had now come to accept that her mother, whoever and wherever she was, really had chosen not to be reunited with her. If she had she'd have made some kind of effort to find her by now, either through the police, or social services, or even the church. Maybe it would have helped if Alex had been able to add the name she'd been born with, Charlotte Albescu, to the register giving permission for birth parents to be in touch. However, this was impossible, as the fear always remained that her serial-killer father might come looking for her, instead of the mother she'd barely known.

'Ah, there you are,' Jason said, yawning as he came into the kitchen. 'Are you OK?'

Touched that he'd got up to find her, she said, 'Yes, I'm fine,' and giving a murmur of pleasure as he came to massage her shoulders she let her head fall back against him.

'Please tell me you're not still mad at me,' he said, stooping to kiss her.

Having forgotten their spat earlier, and the fact that she'd already been in bed and half asleep by the time he'd come home, she said, 'No, of course I'm not, but you were late in.'

'Would you believe, I fell asleep reading to the kids? That's what comes of working hard. Anyway, tell me how it went this evening.'

Switching her mind to the rehearsal, she said, 'Yeah, pretty good. I think we stand a chance of everyone being line-perfect by opening night.'

'Great,' he approved, going to reheat the kettle.

'So if you're not worrying about that, what are you doing up at this hour? Please tell me you didn't have one of those nightmares again.'

Sighing, she said, 'As a matter of fact, I did, but it's OK, I'm probably ready to go back to bed now.'

Turning to lean against the cabinets, his bare arms folded across his chest with the hard muscles showing their tattoos, he looked at her closely. 'So what do you think might have prompted it?' he asked, his tone letting her know that he wasn't about to be palmed off.

She inhaled deeply and let her eyes fall to the mug she was holding between her hands. What she was seeing in her mind's eye had nothing to do with her as a child, and yet strangely it seemed to feel in some way connected. 'If I told you there was this little girl,' she began, 'I expect you'll say there's always a little girl, or boy . . .'

'Because there always is in your case, it goes with your job.'

She nodded absently. 'I saw this one in the park, a couple of weeks ago,' she continued, 'you know, when I went with Gabby and the twins. She had quite an effect on me for some reason, and I haven't been able to get her out of my mind since.'

Sounding ironic, he said, 'Don't you already have enough kids to be worrying about, without adding another that you don't even know?'

She was too deep in thought to catch the tease. 'There was something about her,' she said, picturing the child's solemn yet angelic little face. 'I know this is going to sound odd, but I felt as though I knew her, even though I'm sure I've never seen her before.'

He nodded. 'You're right, it does sound odd.'

Her eyes came up to his.

'Sorry,' he said, clearly realising his humour had missed the mark. 'So why do you think she's sticking in your mind?'

She shrugged. 'Maybe it's the man she was with. There was nothing wrong with him . . . I mean, he didn't behave strangely or anything, but as they walked away I got this horrible feeling . . . Well, that I was watching an abduction.'

Jason blinked.

'I wasn't,' she assured him, 'because I've checked the records, and anyway, if a child, especially of that age, had gone missing it would have been all over the papers by now. But something wasn't right in that situation, or relationship, I just know it, and now I can't seem to stop thinking about it.'

'Did you actually talk to her?' he asked.

She nodded. 'Kind of. She didn't answer, but the man, who I assumed at the time was her father, said she was very shy.'

'But now you're not sure that he was her father?'

She shrugged again. Then, realising this wasn't going to help her to get any more sleep tonight, she got up from her chair and went to put her arms around him. 'You're right,' she said, resting her head against his chest, 'I already have enough children to be worrying about, so definitely not a good idea to start looking for problems for another when I don't even know who she is.'

Chapter Two

'Lay one finger on my kid and you're fuckin' dead,' the greasy-faced bruiser of a woman roared as she struggled with the police officers restraining her. 'I said back off . . .'

'Shut it, Laura,' DC Carroway cut in sharply. 'Do what you have to do,' he barked at Alex.

'Get away from him,' Laura Crowe raged, as Alex moved towards Daniel, the nine-year-old boy who looked no friendlier than his mother. 'One finger on him and you'll never use the fucking thing again.'

Checking to make sure Carroway and his colleague had a firm hold on the woman who was capable of tearing someone twice Alex's size limb from limb, and wouldn't have had second thoughts about doing it, Alex was just reaching for the child when to her horror he whipped out a blade.

She stepped back quickly, wincing as the mother cackled.

'That's my boy,' Laura crowed. 'Stick the bitch and get the hell out of here. Go on, you stupid bastard, run!'

Before the boy could move Paul Bennett, another officer, was on him, knocking him to the floor and banging his wrist against a chair leg to force him to drop the blade. As it clattered to her feet Alex grabbed it and flung it through the open window, hoping another policeman would pick it up. 'You need to come with me, Daniel,' she told the boy sternly. 'You know the procedure . . .'

'Fuck off,' he spat, his face still pressed to the ground.

'Don't talk to the lady like that,' Paul Bennett snarled, his fist tightening on the boy's hair. 'Now, when you're ready to be nice . . .'

'You can fuck off too,' the boy seethed through his yellowed teeth.

His mother guffawed loudly. 'You're a bunch of fucking wankers,' she rasped crudely. 'You got no business forcing your way in here like this. We ain't done nothing. You got the wrong people, as usual, you waste of fucking spacers.'

'Must be making you wonder what your old man's been telling us,' Carroway jeered at her. 'Do you reckon he's grassed you, Laura? We know you were with him when the arcade job went down. Driving the car again, weren't you? And without a licence. You're a bad girl, Laura Crowe. No supper for you tonight – and think of the example you're setting for your little boy there . . .'

'Get your effing hands off me, you dickhead,' she snarled at him. 'You're filth, the lot of you. That's why we call you the *filth* . . .'

'Where's your sister these days, Laura?' Alex butted in, trying to steer things in another direction. Inside she was every bit as unnerved by this woman as she'd been the first time their paths had crossed, but she'd never let it show.

Laura's snake eyes blazed with malice.

'She got sent down last month,' Paul Bennett

informed Alex. 'So if you were thinking of taking the boy there . . .'

Alex had been, but clearly it wasn't an option. It didn't matter; Family Placements had already arranged a backup. 'You're going to have to come with me,' she said to Daniel.

'I told you not to touch him,' Laura hissed. 'He's a good boy. He ain't done nothing wrong . . .'

'A good boy who's been taught to pull knives on social workers,' Paul Bennett scoffed. 'That'll get him through his SATs nicely, won't it?'

As Laura's fury erupted again, so viciously that it seemed to stain the very air, the arresting officers tightened their grip and bundled her roughly out to the waiting car.

These sorts of scenes were always made more difficult by regular CID who, unlike their child protection colleagues, had scant interest in whatever child was being taken into care. They were only concerned with the parents, who in this case had apparently been behind the armed robbery of an amusement arcade in the centre of town a few days ago. Knowing there was a possibility the boy would be in the house when they came to arrest the mother, someone had thought to contact social services to tip them off, so Alex, accompanied by her colleague Ben, had hotfooted it over here. Ben was still outside in the car, no doubt starting to feel faint at the sight of a gathering crowd. Everyone dreaded coming into the Temple Fields estate, though Alex kept reminding herself that no social workers had ever actually been harmed here, in spite of the threats and abuse that were so often hurled their way.

As the foul-smelling room emptied of officers, Alex's attention remained fixed on Daniel. He was a slight boy with oily hair that straggled into his eyes, and such a bony frame that it was no wonder his clothes appeared far too big for him. He was doing his best to look pissed off, mean, ready to carve up whoever took him on. His defences were bristling so fiercely that Alex knew already how unlikely it was she'd get through them to make him understand that she meant him no harm.

He should know it, given that this was far from their first encounter, but mistrust of authority was inbred in him.

For several minutes they listened to the ruckus going on outside as neighbours came to taunt the police and Laura swore unholy vengeance on the arseholes who'd never learned to wipe shit from their hands. This last, Alex knew, was a repulsively racist jibe directed at Sanjid, the uniformed officer who was the driver of one of the marked cars. He might well be used to such abuse from this estate, nevertheless it still made Alex cringe to hear it.

Her eyes remained on Daniel. What was he really thinking? Deep down in there somewhere he surely had to be scared, or at least confused, worried, floundering about out of his depth in a world that would terrify most other kids. A sense of deprivation and violence was all-pervasive on this estate, dragging the residents into bitter feuds that regularly erupted between the criminal families. Being born into the infamous Crowe clan, this poor lad had never stood a chance.

Knowing there was no point trying to treat him like most kids his age, Alex said, 'Lucky you're not any older, or they'd have arrested you for the little stunt you just pulled.'

'Fuck off,' he snorted, and wiped the back of his

hand over his mouth in a gesture that seemed way beyond his years. Who had he picked that up from? His stepfather, currently remanded in custody for the robbery? His psycho uncle, two years into a life sentence for clubbing a pizza-delivery boy to death? Perhaps it was the older kids around the estate who clustered about street corners in menacing gangs, rarely going to school, or work, or anywhere that might in some way improve their lot.

In a tone borrowed from some kind of gangster movie, Daniel said, 'If you think you're taking me anywhere . . .'

Alex cut him off. 'You can't stay here alone, you know very well the law doesn't allow it.'

'I can take care of myself.'

'I know you think so, and I'm not arguing, I'm just telling you what has to happen.'

His shifty green eyes flicked briefly to hers. He was hunched inside a shabby blue T-shirt, making her think of a small bird caught in a trapper's bag.

'Come on,' she said, trying to sound friendly, 'we've been here before, so you know the ropes.'

His thin lips curled with contempt. 'I'm not going with that sicko again,' he snarled. 'He's a paedo, a bumfucker . . . My dad's going to kill him when he finds him.'

Alex sank inside. She didn't doubt for a minute that Frankie Crowe would do his worst were he ever to get hold of Daniel's last foster carer. God, what a screw-up that had been, but who knew until it was too late that Ralph Tanner and his church-going wife had registered as foster parents with only one purpose in mind? The question still unanswered was how the hell they had managed to get clearance when the vetting process was supposed to be so stringent. It was everywhere else, but Dean Valley County Council did not have an outstanding track record where carers were concerned, which inevitably meant that the children who came under its protection didn't do so well either. Indeed, if Daniel hadn't spoken up when he had – and tragically so few found the courage to when they were being abused – the Tanners might still be accepting more already disturbed kids into their care.

'Where are they taking my mum?' he growled menacingly. 'When's she coming back?'

Alex shrugged, because she knew how to be cool with kids like Daniel. 'I don't know. It'll depend on whether she's remanded in custody, or let go on police bail.'

'She didn't do nothing wrong,' he shouted. 'I was with her that night, so I know she wasn't where they're saying she was. Go and tell them that, bitch.'

Knowing he probably didn't even know which night they were talking about, never mind where his mother had been for most of it, Alex said, 'I'm sure you'll get your chance to speak up when the time comes. Until then, it's my job to get you somewhere safe . . .'

'I told you, I'm not going nowhere, especially not with those sado-wackos who tried . . .'

'You're not going there,' she assured him.

'Look at me, sister, *I* is not going anywhere.'

'The police already have a Protection Order, so I'm afraid you don't have a choice.'

'Fucking bastards,' he retorted, but he seemed to be more intent now on what was going on outside.

'Talking about Her Majesty's police again?' Paul Bennett sneered as he came back into the room. 'Sorry,' he said to Alex, 'should never have left you alone with this little shit.' He advanced on Daniel. 'Have you got any more weapons tucked away there, dude?' he demanded.

'Get away from me, scumbag,' Daniel hissed.

'Charming, isn't he?' Bennett commented.

'Who's that out there?' Daniel asked nervously.

Paul eyed him meanly. 'What are you afraid of, Danny boy?'

'I'm not scared of nothing.'

Bennett grinned. 'It's who you think it is, boy, so I'd say it was time to make your choice. Either go with Alex here, or stay and have a nice little chat with the lowlife who reckon your old dad's been trying to dump one of theirs in the crap. Let me think, how was it they treated their last hostage? Oh yeah, that's right, he doesn't talk or walk so well any more, does he?'

'Please,' Alex cut in sharply. 'There's no need . . .'

'Step back into your sandals,' Bennett warned through his teeth.

Alex moved forward and put her back to the detective. He might think he was in charge here, but the boy was now her responsibility. 'Do you want some help packing?' she said to Daniel.

'I told you, I'm not going nowhere,' he shot back.

'Then I'll have to pack for you,' she sighed.

'I'll wait and make sure he doesn't scarper,' Bennett told her as she started out of the room. 'Don't reckon you're in a hurry to be going out there though, are you, Danny boy? Not when the baddies might get you.'

'They don't scare me,' Daniel snorted, though it was evident from the way his eyes kept darting to the door that they did.

In truth they were unnerving Alex too, since the

grudges some of these families had against social services, never mind each other, went back a very long way, and not many of them would care that she personally might not have been involved in their issues.

She could think of at least three families right now who'd very much like to make her pay for removing their kids. It was the main reason she always hated coming on to this estate, it actually terrified the life out of her at times, but it was her own fault, no one had forced her to apply for a job in the North Kesterly hub. She could always have gone to the southern region, which didn't have anything like as many poor housing developments, or the same kind of racial tensions – plus it was a lot closer to home – but she'd always known she'd come here. This was where she'd been born – admittedly in a house that no longer existed, and that had actually been a part of old Temple Fields – and consequently she felt as though she shared roots with these people (not that any of them knew it). The whole reason she'd become a social worker was to do what she could to help protect the children of this estate.

It was no surprise to her to find Daniel's bedroom in such a sorry state, with a coarse blanket draped from the window acting as a curtain, bedding that looked as though it hadn't been changed since new and a carpet with more cigarette burns and stains than it appeared to have pile. The posters on the walls were mostly of bruising men in leather and black shades brandishing machine guns, or machetes, or seeming ready to inflict all manner of gruesome torture on the world at large. Touchingly though, there was one of an early Harry Potter movie. In a scorched saucer next to the bed she found an old needle with a candle and belt close by, evidence that someone – hopefully not Daniel – had been shooting up in here.

Leaving it for the police to discover, she shook the pillowcase free of the pillow and began filling it with clothes gathered from the floor and bed, along with a magazine about dinosaurs, an iPod and earphones, and a comb that was in such a dismal state that she decided to chuck it. She hesitated over the laptop and computer games since they had almost certainly been stolen, plus the computer might contain information useful to the police. Leaving it where it was, she braced herself for the bathroom to seek out a toothbrush and maybe a flannel. What she found was so grimy that she couldn't even bear to pick it up, and deciding to buy Daniel replacements on their way to his temporary foster family, she started back down the stairs.

There was still some sort of commotion going on outside, insults being thrown, police trying to keep things calm. Alex guessed that her colleague, Ben, was probably ducked down behind the steering wheel by now and shaking in his fancy cowboy boots.

If anyone was in the wrong job, it was definitely Ben.

'Have you finished up there?' Bennett called out. 'The rest of us have got a job to do.'

'We're ready to go,' Alex told Daniel as she moved to the doorway.

'You take me out there, they're going to shoot me, man,' Daniel declared.

Grim and violent though this estate was, shootings were actually rare, so Alex wasn't particularly alarmed by the claim. However, she played along with it, saying, 'With the police standing right there? I don't think so.'

'They ain't scared of no police . . .'

'Daniel, if you're that afraid of them then why on earth would you want to stay here? Once the police go you'll be on your own . . .'

'I told you, I can take care of myself.'

'So you like to think, but even if you can, it isn't an option, so come on. The car's at the gate, I'll be with you and Ben's a really fast driver.'

'He's chicken,' Bennett jeered as Daniel continued to hold back.

'No way,' the boy spat. 'I just want to stay alive, all right? And those fuckers out there, they told me already what they're going to do to me if they get their hands on me.'

'But they won't get near you,' Alex insisted. 'Now please, let's go, or I'll have to ask the police to carry you out.'

It was evident from his expression that he'd rather be shot than humiliated. 'Where are you taking me?' he demanded.

'Way over the other side of town,' Alex assured him. 'Nowhere near here so you'll be perfectly safe.'

'For how long?'

'Will you just get the fuck out to that car,' Bennett interrupted fiercely. 'This isn't for negotiating, son. You've got to go with her, like it or not, and I want out of this dump as fast as I can before the stink suffocates me.'

Casting the detective a scathing look, Alex reached for the boy's hand, and was quickly rebuffed. However, he walked past her out of the room, and once she joined him in the hall they stood together for a moment, steeling themselves to make a run for Ben's car.

As Alex opened the door the hubbub died down for a moment, then someone from the crowd shouted, 'You should be ashamed of yourself, bitch, coming round here breaking up decent people's homes . . .'

'Why aren't you out there saving the likes of Baby P?' someone else shouted. 'We don't need you round here screwing with us.'

'Get that kid somewhere safe,' a male voice cautioned, 'or Bill Prince's lad's going to have him.'

'There's nowhere safe for the little runt,' another voice sang out. 'Nor for you, Alex Lake.'

She didn't look up because she already knew it was Shane Prince, one of the nastiest pieces of work she'd ever come across, and she'd come across plenty. With his loud mouth, arrogant swagger and own impressive criminal record, he now considered himself head of the Prince clan while his father, brother, two uncles and older sister did time for a whole slew of crimes. Alex doubted his mother recognised his authority, but hey, what did she know about what went on inside that sorry family. What she did know was that they were the sworn enemies of the Crowes, and of social services, and that if she caught Shane's eye now he'd make some sort of lewd gesture like raising his fist or rubbing his crotch.

'Hey, Daniel, give your old man a message from me,' Prince shouted, as Alex moved the boy swiftly down the path. 'He try pinning anything on me then it's you we'll be going after. You tell him that, motherfucker, and you remember it good.'

Piling Daniel into the back of Ben's car, Alex

jumped in after him and even before the door was closed Ben was speeding out of the street, almost taking the corner on two wheels. She didn't imagine anyone was coming after them, but it couldn't be ruled out, so she was quite happy for Ben to keep his foot down. Daniel was obviously relieved to be out of Shane Prince's firing line too. Would they really harm a child as small and defenceless as Daniel appeared? The answer was yes, they undoubtedly would. The poor kid had next to no chance now of ever escaping his background, or of going forward into the future as a healthy, optimistic, undamaged young man with a world of opportunities to choose from. As he sat there next to her, sunk into his puny frame, she could only feel the futility of her compassion, the overriding sadness of being unable to change things in the way she'd hoped when she'd taken the decision to follow this path.

'So where are we going?' Daniel prompted, sounding far less bolshie now he was out of his father's home and on his way to the unknown. 'I told you, I ain't going to . . .'

'The Tanners,' Alex interrupted hastily, 'are where they should be, partly thanks to you for speaking out.'

'Yeah, like I was going to let them do all that stuff to me and get away with it,' he retorted fiercely. 'Bet it'd be right up your street,' he said rudely to Ben.

Ben's kohl-lined eyes came to his in the rear-view mirror.

'The people you're going to live in Westleigh,' Alex declared, quickly steering Daniel away from his inherited homophobia with the promise of a much classier area than the one he came from.

Apparently unimpressed, he growled, 'I'm only going till my mum gets back.'

'That's right,' Alex confirmed, while knowing that if Laura was remanded in custody it was going to be a much longer stay than he thought, and probably not in Westleigh.

'Have you dealt with that text yet?' Ben asked from the front seat. 'The one you got earlier from the drama queen?'

Alex glared at the back of his head, annoyed that he was bringing this up in front of Daniel. How stupid could he be when he knew very well that Kylie Adams, one of the teenagers in her caseload, had threatened to run away and never come back if Alex didn't get her a different placement by Friday.

'It's in hand,' Alex reminded him shortly. For God's sake, he'd been sitting right there when she'd spoken to Kylie's foster carers, who were now asking for the girl to be removed as soon as possible. Being a self-harmer as well as an arch-manipulator and despiser of other girls her age, Kylie required special handling. Alex was now in the process of arranging for her to go into residential care. That way a team of social workers would always be on hand to keep an eye on her and do everything they could to rehabilitate her.

Grabbing her phone from the bag she'd left in the car while dealing with Daniel, she checked to see if any more texts had come in from Kylie and found that one had. The contents were grim.

Just slit open my veins. Bleeding everywhere. Fucking hate this world and you and them and every fucking one.

Quickly scrolling through to Kylie's foster carers, Alex made the connection and was told that Kylie was on her way to hospital.

'I'll be there as soon as I can,' she assured the distraught-sounding woman at the other end. Audrey Bishop was a long-time agency carer with a rare good record for handling disturbed and violent teenagers.

Clearly Kylie was too much even for her.

Clicking over to another call she said, 'Hi Fiona. We should be at the Fenns' place in fifteen minutes, maybe less.'

'Great,' Fiona replied. She was in Family Placements at the South Kesterly hub and had organised Daniel's emergency care, since there hadn't been anywhere available in the north. 'Have you got the Emergency Protection Order yet?'

'No, he's still under police protection,' Alex replied, 'but legal are on it, so it should be sorted any time. I forgot to ask earlier, are there any other children in this family, birth or otherwise?'

'The birth kids are at uni, but the Fenns are caring for a seven-year-old boy at the moment. Oliver Barratt. He's a Munchausen victim and misses his mother terribly, but we're still not sure when, if, he'll be allowed to go back to her.'

'Is she in therapy?' Alex asked.

'Of course.'

'So how long has the boy been with the Fenns?'

'Almost a month now, and they adore him.'

Starting to worry about how Daniel might treat a child as vulnerable as Oliver sounded, Alex decided she'd have to deal with that if the problem arose, and after ringing off she made a quick call to the office, then to the legal department to find out how they were getting on with Daniel's EPO, and lastly to a lawyer who was representing one of her teenagers in a mugging case. By the time she rang off they were pulling up outside an end-of-terrace Georgian town house in Westleigh.

As they got out of the car Alex couldn't help wondering if Daniel had ever been anywhere like this before, with its gravelled driveway, immaculate garden beds and impressive double front door with spiralled boxwood topiaries either side of it. Realising that if he had, it would probably have been to help rob it, she immediately started worrying about what souvenirs he might help himself to while he was in the Fenns' care.

'Fancy place,' Ben commented as he hauled Daniel's bulky pillowcase from the boot. 'Bit too good for the likes of that little shit,' he added under his breath.

'Why don't you wait here?' Alex suggested stiffly, and taking Daniel's belongings she hoisted her own bag on to her shoulder and was about to steer her charge to his temporary destiny when Ben sniped, 'Happy to, Your Highness. I didn't want to come on this job in the first place.'

Refraining from informing him that she'd never have used him as backup given the choice, she went to put a hand on Daniel's shoulder, had it shrugged off and so turned to the front door as it opened.

'Alex, hi,' a smiling, bespectacled Chinese girl said warmly as she came out to receive them. She was a social worker attached to a prestigious nationwide agency who only had the highest-quality carers on their books (all too few of them based in the Kesterly area, unfortunately), and so was paid way more than her council-employed colleagues. However, she was so good-natured Alex would never hold that against her.

'Hi Mei,' she said breezily. 'This is Daniel.'

'It's nice to meet you, Daniel,' Mei told him.

Ignoring Mei's outstretched hand, Daniel looked down as he scuffed a toe of his worn trainers through the gravel.

Realising that he was far more upset about what was happening to him than he'd ever let on, Alex said, 'Why don't we go inside? It looks a really nice place, doesn't it?'

'I wanna go home,' he muttered.

'Hello, are you Daniel?' a friendly voice asked from the doorway.

Alex looked up to find an elegant woman in her early fifties coming towards them. 'Hello, I'm Maggie,' she said to Alex, holding out her hand to shake. To Daniel she said, 'I've just made some ice cream and there's far too much for us to eat on our own. Will you come and have some with us?'

Tensing for the 'eff off', or 'no effing way', Alex was pleasantly surprised when Daniel said belligerently, 'What do you mean, you made ice cream? I thought it came from a shop or a van.'

'Maggie makes the most delicious ice cream,' Mei told him gushingly.

Alex could tell that Daniel wasn't warming to Mei.

'I can vouch for that,' a tall, jug-eared man with half-moon specs and a snowy white beard declared as he came out to join them. 'Hello, young man, I'm Ronald, but you can call me Ron if you like, most of my friends do. I hear you're going to be staying with us for a while.'

Daniel eyed Ron Fenn warily.

'You can have your own room if you like,' Maggie informed him. 'Or if you and Oliver get along together . . . Speaking of whom, where is he?'

As a small, frightened figure with a mop of shiny dark hair appeared in the doorway, Alex felt torn between pity and dismay. He was so tiny and looked so defenceless that she found herself worrying again about how well Daniel would treat him. She dreaded to think of him being cruel or trying to corrupt Oliver in some way. It was likely to happen, though, it often did amongst children in care – the weakest were preyed upon, used, even abused, and eventually turned into feral little creatures fighting for their lives.

On the other hand, Daniel was just a child too, and in every bit as much in need of kindness and understanding as Oliver, whether he wanted it or not. It looked as though he might get it here, but just for a while, until he was moved elsewhere. What would happen to him then?

Knowing she'd have to worry about that later, she put a hand on his shoulder and followed the Fenns inside. As soon as he was settled, she'd get Ben to drop her at the infirmary to check on Kylie, then she'd have to get the bus back to the office since she'd left her car there. Hopefully she'd be in time for a strategy meeting with an Ethiopian family who, mercifully, were welcoming the support of social services.

Sadly, not everyone was so receptive; many were actively hostile, especially in her area. But as frustrating and even devastating as her work could be at times, she'd never give up on the children who needed her protection.

Not ever.

Erica Wade was staring from the window of her tired-looking house on North Hill. It had once been a grand Victorian dwelling with smartly painted walls and windows, a garden of pleasant flowers and a welcoming driveway. It stood in its own grounds, surrounded by tall hedges, and dwarfed from behind by a towering maple. It was the kind of place a reasonably distinguished family might once have felt proud to call home.

Though Erica's grey eyes were directed towards the end of the short drive where a dilapidated gate was open and partially lost amidst the crowding bushes, she wasn't seeing it. Nor was she registering the brave, sun-seeking blooms springing from a tangle of shrubs and weeds that skirted the over-grown lawn. A dropping cherry tree was casting dappled shadows over an open-fronted playhouse and doll's pram, but she wasn't noticing that either.

Once in a while her gaze seemed to catch on one of the cars or lorries tearing up and down the hill outside, as though trying in a ghostlike way to travel away with them. Almost no one walked past the house. Her neighbours came and went from the stately B & B next door, never staying for more than a night or two. The same with the purpose-built holiday apartments the other side, and across the four-lane road.

It wasn't possible to glimpse the sea from here, the house was on the wrong side of the hill, but it took no more than a minute to walk to the top and from there the vistas down over Kesterly Bay and out into the estuary were impressive. It was one of the many spots from which tourists and scenic photographers took their shots of the old-fashioned holiday town. The wide stretch of the beach sat between two rocky outcrops over which the tide flung itself in exuberant sprays; and the newly refurbished pier stretched off towards the horizon like a walkway to the great beyond.

Erica never went to the top of the hill, or to the end of the pier.

Her sore, grey eyes remained blank as they tracked a pair of swallows swooping in and out of the garage attached to the house. They'd built a nest inside and were making a mess all over her car. It didn't matter, she never used it anyway, and Brian usually kept his parked in front, on the drive.

The skin stretched over the fine bones of her face was pallid and lined, seeming to add ten years to the mere thirty she had lived. She didn't feel alive any more, or not often. Sometimes, after she'd taken her medication, she felt as vibrant and free as the butterflies skittering and settling amongst the wild roses, verbena and milkweed. There was a time when the butterflies had inspired her to write a melody, but she didn't have a piano to play it on any more, or the will to try. She'd been able to name the butterflies then, and probably still could if she tried – orange sulphur, comma . . . She didn't really want to. It would mean engaging with them and she couldn't allow herself to do that, even though her mind was like one of them, hovering over thoughts and vistas, noting them but never allowing anything to reach into the gnarled and shadowy depths of her feelings.

The postman had dropped some mail through the door a while ago. He was one of the few who came, along with other deliverymen with her online orders, and a local councillor canvassing for an election. They used to have quite a flow of visitors, mainly children coming to learn the piano, but that was when they'd lived in their other house, the one they'd bought just after Jonathan was born. It was miles from here, way up north close to the Scottish border. She'd had friends then, just a few, who'd carried on coming after Jonathan's death, but she'd found it too hard to pretend that life could go on the way it had before. She'd had to ask the parents of her pupils to make alternative arrangements, and then she'd withdrawn from her friends too. And before long the only person she was seeing in a day was her husband, Brian.

She didn't include Ottilie because Ottilie was only three. She might be four soon, Erica couldn't be sure because she had no idea of the day or month.

She wished she didn't have to see Ottilie at all; everything would be so much easier if she didn't.

She could sense the child's eyes on her now; they were making her feel jumpy and sick. Her heart was starting to jerk; the swallows were soaring inside her head; her eyes were full of butterflies. Ottilie was watching her from the open door at the far side of the room, waiting for her to turn around. Sweat trickled down her back. What did she think was going to happen? Did she think at all? Of course she did, but it was hard to know what went through her mind since she barely spoke. Her eyes were the colour of beech bark, her hair as soft as cashmere, wavy and as dark as the earth. It wasn't often that Erica looked at her daughter. It was too confusing, and she, Erica, was too weak, too broken and afraid of what she might do if she touched her.

Get away from me. Get away from me. GET AWAY FROM ME YOU FILTHY LITTLE BITCH.

Was it her voice that had spoken, or one of those inside her head?

Ottilie had never known her brother; she hadn't

been born by the time he'd died. She'd come along a few months later like some sort of compensation, or maybe she was a punishment. That was how it felt, like a life sentence for what she, Erica, had done – or failed to do.

It was Brian who bathed Ottilie and put her to bed. Got her up in the morning and gave her breakfast. If he didn't Ottilie would go unwashed, maybe even unfed, though if she was hungry she'd learned to help herself to food from the fridge. Sometimes Brian read her stories, or played games with her, the kind of games that Erica could never take part in. She'd put on her music while they were happening, Brahms or Debussy, and lose herself in the thrall of her favourite sonatas until the kindly substances reached her brain and quietly closed it down. She hated the games, despised them as much as she despised her husband, her mother, her father, her whole rotten life.

Seeing Brian's car turn into the drive she drew back from the window before he could see her. They slept in separate rooms now and only communicated when they had to. He knew the truth and so did she; it was a secret that bound them together, so tightly that she had no idea how she managed to breathe in its grasp.

As she walked across the room she could feel the ghosts parting, past residents of the house always lurking, perhaps they were trying to shame her. Could they hear the voices inside her head? Maybe the voices were theirs. Did they listen when she spoke to Ottilie? Did they scoff at the things she told her in rambling or frenzied whispers? She wouldn't look at Ottilie now, she couldn't; her nerves were jumping, her eyes were waterfalls of tears. She knew

Ottilie's head was bowed. Was she waiting for her mother's touch, or preparing to shrink from it? Her limbs were tiny, too small for her age, and white; precious few rays of sun found their way on to this wretched child. She almost never went out, not even into the garden to play with the toys her grateful daddy had bought her.

He took her out though, once in a while, but they never went far, or for long.

'He's home,' she said, passing the child and going through to the kitchen. He'd want his usual whisky and soda and in this Erica was happy to please him, provided he brought what pleased her. Sometimes he'd put his little girl on his knee and tell her about his day, the children he taught at the school where he was the deputy head, those who'd excelled at drawing or sums or spelling; and those who'd had to be scolded for not trying their best.

They were aged five up to eleven. Jonathan would be seven by now, if he'd lived.

They didn't have any photos of him around the house. In many ways it was as though he'd never existed, except his memory lingered around her conscience and tormented her soul with the same testing presence she felt from Ottilie.

Ottilie trailed her into the kitchen. Erica wished she would go away. She felt like a nemesis. *Get away from me. Get away from me. GET AWAY FROM ME YOU FILTHY LITTLE BITCH.*

Except Erica didn't care if Ottilie saw what her father brought home and gave to her mother. She wouldn't know what it was, and even if she did she wouldn't understand.

He wouldn't forget, he couldn't, he knew what would happen if he did.

It was her only power, her only escape.

As the door opened she tried not to look at him, but her desperation was too great. Seeing it, he drew an envelope from his pocket and tossed it on the table, his eyes full of contempt. Then, turning to Ottilie, he opened his arms for her to come to him.

Ottilie stayed where she was, her faithful bear pressed to her mouth. Her eyes were round and frightened; her tiny frame seemed as though it might be blown away in a draught. Had Erica not been swimming in relief she might have smirked in triumph to see that Ottilie was heeding her mother's frantic advice, doing as she said like a good little girl. *Don't go to Daddy. Don't go to Daddy. STAY AWAY FROM DADDY YOU FILTHY LITTLE BITCH.*

Brian would be furious if he knew.

But why would she want to go to Daddy?

'Come here,' he said shortly to Ottilie.

Ottilie looked up at her mother, waiting to be told what to do, but Erica only pushed her out of the way as she went past, eager to get to her room. Ottilie turned to watch her, then feeling her father's arms lifting her she went limp and drew her faithful bear back to her face.

Chapter Three

'OK, Alex, pet, brace yourself.'

Alex turned so swiftly from the whiteboard where she was writing up her movements for the day that she almost collided with Tommy Burgess, her team leader.

'Hey, what's making you so nervy?' he laughed, straightening her up.

Rolling her eyes, Alex said, 'I was miles away and didn't hear you coming.' She was very fond of Tommy with his Geordie accent, hippy hair and rugby player's physique, not least because he was such an effective buffer between her and Wendy, the department manager. There was a time when Wendy used to be reasonable, and definitely supportive, particularly over issues that attracted criticism or scrutiny from on high, or even bad press, but since her promotion a couple of years ago she'd become remote, superior, and definitely more interested in impressing the powers that be than in what was happening on the ground.

Tommy was grimacing as he read what she'd written on the board. *Collecting Daniel Crowe from carers, Westleigh; returning to TFE.* (TFE was Temple Fields estate.) 'Rita was saying this morning that she'd rather take a stroll through the Gaza Strip than a drive through Temple Fields,' he commented.

Alex's eyebrows rose. No one ever wanted to go to the estate, but her colleague, Rita, was especially unnerved by it, mainly because everything scared poor Rita. Much like Ben, she was in the wrong job. 'Oh, it's not that bad,' Alex sighed, 'or come to think of it, it probably is. Anyway, I'm definitely not looking forward to dealing with Laura Crowe again. They've only gone and released her with all charges dismissed. How did that happen, I'd like to know?'

'They maybe got her off on some kind of technicality, or she's done herself a deal more likely, but all we need to bother about is the boy. Have you found out yet how the weekend went at his placement?'

Waving as Tamsin Green, another of her colleagues, hurried out of the door shouting cheerio to the world at large, Alex said, 'I'm taking the view that no news is good news.'

'Great policy.' Then abruptly, 'Amina, what are you doing back here?' Amina was Kenyan by birth, and the youngest and newest member of the team.

'Forgot to take the file,' she cried, rushing to her desk in a fluster. 'That would really work, wouldn't it, standing up in court with no paperwork? Alex, did you know you've got a flat tyre?'

'You're kidding!' Alex exclaimed. 'I don't have time to mess about with bloody tyres.'

'Speak nicely to Gus,' Pete Minchin called out, referring to the mechanic who had a workshop at the back of the business park where their hub was located. Pete was their expert in disabled kids and one of only four males, the others being Victor, an amateur wrestler who came in very handy when a bit of muscle was required, and Ben, of course, who didn't go in for flexing any muscle at all.

'OK, I'm gone,' Amina announced, heading back to the door. 'Wish me luck everyone, cos we definitely don't want some idiot judge sending Harvey Critchley back to his scumbag uncle.'

Raising a hand to signal his support, Tommy followed Alex to the break-out area where a couple of health visitors from the offices downstairs were making tea and she was peering through the window at her car. 'It's not mine with a flat,' she announced with a sigh of relief. 'Amina must have spotted someone else's, same colour, same make. Anyway, rewinding, what am I supposed to be bracing myself for, and if you're going to get me to write up someone else's reports . . .'

'No, no, not that,' he jumped in quickly. 'Well, we are behind with Sally's assessments now she's off sick . . .'

'Just don't go there, please, you know it's impossible to read her writing, and besides I've got a backlog of my own that I never have time to catch up on.'

'But you'll find it, I know,' he assured her with his most charming smile. 'Maybe later, when you get back from a little visit to one of the Crowes' neighbours.'

Alex immediately drew back. 'No, Tommy, no, no, no,' she declared, holding up her hands like a cross. 'You cannot dump the Prince family on me.'

He looked pained. 'You know I wouldn't if I could help it.'

'They're Victor's,' she reminded him.

'He broke his shoulder at the weekend.'

'You're kidding me.'

'Afraid not, so that means with Christie and Jane

both on leave, we're only sixteen strong at the moment instead of our usual twenty . . . Will someone get that phone! So I'm afraid, with everyone else up to their eyes . . .'

'And you think I'm not?'

'I know you are, but someone has to do it.'

'But why me? I've already got the flaming Crowes.'

He was looking as regretful as he could.

Her eyes narrowed as she suddenly understood. 'Wendy's shoving it my way, isn't she?' she demanded. 'Well, you can tell her from me . . .'

'Ssh,' he cautioned. 'She's in her office.'

'Then I'll tell her myself.'

Yanking her back, he said, 'Best not do it right now, the chief's in there with her and you won't do yourself any favours if you start laying into her in front of him.'

She appeared amazed. 'I don't lay into people,' she protested.

He laughed. 'No, right, and especially not Wendy.'

Conceding the point, she said, 'OK, I might make the odd exception in her case, but only because she always does this to me. Everything no one else wants always ends up on my desk.'

'You could take it as a compliment,' he suggested, 'because she knows that whatever it is, you can handle it.'

Seeing right through him, she said, 'Do you know you're wasted here? You should be negotiating peace in the Middle East or out there charming kids off the street.'

'Given the choice I'm happy where I am,' he retorted drolly. 'So let me bring you up to speed on the Princes . . .'

'I haven't said I'll do it yet.'

'But we both know you will. So, we've had a call from the family GP to say he's worried about Polly Prince – again.'

'Oh, you mean the delightful fourteen-year-old daughter who tried to burn down Shirley Little's house the last time she was taken into care?'

He winced. 'That would be her, and I guess it wouldn't be a good idea to try and place her with Shirley again. But that's not your problem . . .'

'No, mine is getting off that estate alive when her thug of a brother realises I've come for his sister.'

'You're only going in for a chat,' he reminded her. 'Nothing heavy this time around, no taking her in. We just need you to assess the situation.'

'And who's coming with me, because I definitely can't go alone?'

'Indeed you cannot, which is why I'm not recommending you go when you drop off Daniel later. We can't spare anyone to accompany you today, so it'll have to wait until . . .'

'Bloody anonymous callers, they really hack me off,' Ben complained irritably as he sauntered past on his way to make tea. 'That's the second time someone's rung in about some kid on North Hill.'

'What about the kid?' Tommy asked.

'That's just it, nothing. All this woman will say is that we ought to go over there and check it out. Not why we should, or what she thinks the problem is, she just wants to waste our time.'

'Have you made all the usual calls?' Tommy demanded.

Looking offended, Ben said, 'Of course, and I'm telling you, there's not a problem. The mother's a music teacher, for God's sake, and the father's the deputy head at Kesterly Rise. According to our friends in the south hub, he's very highly thought of, and I found him perfectly polite and helpful when I spoke to him.'

Tommy was frowning. 'Did he have any idea who the anonymous caller might be?'

'Yes, apparently she's a bit of a nutter who tried to cause trouble for him at his previous school. He was pretty upset, actually, because he thought he'd managed to shake her off by moving here, but it seems she's managed to track him down again.'

As Alex moved away, back to her desk, Tommy said to Ben, 'Well, just make sure you do everything by the book, you can never be too careful,' and waving him on he went after Alex. 'Polly Prince,' he said, returning her to the subject. 'I'd go with you myself if I wasn't going to be on this training course for the next two weeks.'

Alex looked stricken. 'You're away for two whole weeks?' she protested.

'Tell me that's not true!' Saffy Dyer piped up from the next desk. 'Tommy, you can't abandon us for that long, we'll be in chaos by the time you get back. Or jail, if Wendy's planning on running things.'

'Ssh,' Tommy warned, glancing over his shoulder as several others laughed. 'She's in there,' he told Saffy, keeping his voice down.

'Let it rip,' Alex advised Saffy. 'Anyway, it's me she's always got it in for, and this proves it, landing me with the Princes.'

'Oh, bad luck,' Saffy sympathised.

'Sort someone out to go with you,' Tommy told her.

'Hang on, before you go, has the doctor told the family that he's been in touch with us again?' Alex asked.

'He knows the procedure, so I'm sure he has.'

'Great,' Alex muttered. 'So when I drive on to the estate to take Daniel home, if any of the Princes see me they're going to think I'm about to make an unannounced visit and probably rip my car to bits before I can even get out of it.'

Not denying the possibility, Tommy said, 'The best way round that is to set up an appointment with them before you go to get Daniel. That way, if they do see you today, they won't be expecting you to drop in on them.'

'Oh, that makes me feel so much safer,' she retorted drily. 'So who's up for coming with me?' she asked, looking around, and gave a splutter of laughter as everyone ducked.

As Ben came walking back with his tea, Alex's eyes went to Tommy.

He was smiling blandly.

'Don't even think it,' she warned. 'You sent him with me the other day . . .'

'There wasn't anyone else,' he murmured, pressing down on her shoulder to stop her going off like a firework.

Since Tommy was fully aware of what a liability Ben could be in certain situations, not to mention how he always managed to get out of the paperwork, Alex felt reasonably confident Tommy wouldn't inflict him on her again, at least not for a while. 'I have to go,' she said, starting to pack her bag.

'OK, don't forget we've got a core meeting this afternoon for Hamish Gingell,' Tommy reminded her as he started back to his office. 'Ben, have you entered that call in the log, the one about the kid on North Hill?'

'Just doing it,' Ben shouted back impatiently.

'Are either of Hamish's parents going to be there?' Alex called out before Tommy could disappear.

'The mother, apparently. Dad's gone AWOL again.'

Not especially surprised to hear that, since Hamish Gingell's father was a long-distance lorry driver who had at least five other children around the country, each of them known to social services for one reason or another, Alex scrunched back her hair, made a quick check of her mobile phone and started for the door. The chances of Hamish being returned to his mother in the near future were not looking good, since he had not yet shown any signs of abandoning a longfelt desire to reunite his little sister with her Maker.

On reaching the door she suddenly remembered she needed to set up a visit to the Princes' home, so with a quick pirouette she was back at her desk, searching the computer for a number.

'Hello, is that Mrs Prince?' she asked politely when a female voice answered the phone.

'Who wants to know?' came the snappish reply.

'I'm calling from social services . . .'

'Fuck off,' and the line went dead.

'Mm, that seems to have gone well,' Saffy commented drily.

Alex raised her eyebrows. 'I have a way with me,' she responded with a bit of a swagger. 'And did I just hear you say you'd come with me when I go? That is so cool, I knew I could count on you.'

'Believe me, I'd be there if I didn't have this telly thing hanging over me,' Saffy lied, 'but you know how it is . . .' Being of Somali origin, Saffy was currently helping an undercover TV researcher to expose the rumoured practice of genital mutilation in the local Somali community. Since Alex couldn't imagine anything more abhorrent being visited on a child – well, she could, because she'd seen it all too often, but it was right up there along with the worst – she was more than ready to accept that Saffy's priorities were in the right place.

Ten minutes later she was in her car, driving out of the dreary old business park, when she spotted a young family heading into one of the out-of-town furniture stores. Her heart immediately lifted. A small girl with a long blonde ponytail was riding her daddy's shoulders, while the mother was pulling funny faces at a baby in a buggy. It was a warming and welcome reminder of the millions of happy homes there were in the world, places where children were safe and loved and couldn't, thank God, even begin to imagine the kind of horrors those in Alex's care so often had to face.

On reaching the seafront she cast a quick glance out to the horizon and guessed she might just manage to pick up Daniel before the storm hit. There again, it might do its worst, and wait till she was delivering him to his front door to start chucking about a few thunderbolts: nature's symphonic accompaniment to the highlight of her day.

Turning inland past the public swimming pool to join the road that snaked up over the southerly head-land to the leafier suburbs of town, she began compiling a list in her mind of all the case notes and assessments she needed to write up when she returned to the office. Annie Ashe, once a drunken, obese, horribly depressed single mother of two, now a totally reformed character, stood a very good chance of getting her kids back. Family Support Services had worked wonders with her; her weight had now dropped from a massive twenty-four stone down to fifteen – and she was still dieting, she'd assured Alex yesterday with a beaming smile that was apparently receiving some dental attention. And she hadn't touched a drop of the hard stuff since the awful day Alex had been forced to move her children into care. Annie hadn't fought the decision, she'd been too crushed and disgusted with herself even to try. She'd known she wasn't coping, and the tears she'd shed when she'd admitted that she had no idea when she'd last cooked a decent meal for Becks, her son, and Vicci, her little girl, never mind got them to take a bath, had made Alex more determined than ever to turn things around for her.

Now, she was very close to recommending that the children could return to their mother on a full-time basis, rather than just for weekend visits, and the fact that Annie had recently found the confidence to apply for a job as a part-time cleaner was going to work massively in her favour.

Then there was Tyrone Miller, whose so-called uncle (in other words mother's new boyfriend) was a slimeball of the first order. Alex was sure the boy was being kept locked in his room when he wasn't at school, but neither Tyrone nor his mother would admit to it, and so far Alex had been unable to prove it.

Always her biggest problem, being able to prove the offences she felt sure were being committed.

As she began running through Jessie Moore's case – a twelve-year-old bundle of fury and loathing whose mother had died a couple of years ago and whose guardian aunt kept throwing her out on the street – she heard her personal mobile ringing and started to dig around for it in her bag. With a quick glance she saw it was Jason, and hoping there were no police around she clicked on.

You think rules were written just for you to break, she could almost hear her mother, Myra, sighing.

'Hi, everything OK?' she asked, slowing to go over a speed bump on Tannet's Hill.

'Yeah, I'm cool, you?'

'Busy day, but coping. Please tell me you're still on for the tech run later.'

'Absolutely. As luck would have it I'm going to end up close to home for my last appointment today, so I'll probably be there before you.'

Being a builder with his own small business he'd presumably been asked by a neighbour to take a look at something, which was great, if it turned into cash, because he hadn't been inundated with it lately. 'That's brilliant,' she told him. 'It'll give me a chance to drop into the care home to check on our dear old ex-neighbour Millie on my way back, seeing as she was asleep when I went on Sunday. Did you get a text from Gabby about the weekend?'

'I did. Are you sure you want to go all the way to Devon the day after opening night?'

'It's only a forty-minute drive, depending on traffic, and I don't want to let her down. Does it work for you?'

'Sure, but I'll have the kids that day, remember.'

Alex's heart sank. She'd forgotten, or more likely wiped it out of her mind.

'Provided it's all right with Gabby,' Jason continued, 'I guess there's no reason why we can't take them too.'

Thinking there were quite a few reasons, such as how mean his eldest could be to the twins, she refrained from saying so and replied sweetly, 'That would be lovely. Don't you have them one night this week as well?'

'Thursday,' he confirmed. 'Is that OK, do you mind?'

'Of course not,' she lied. 'I'll think of something special to cook for them. Or maybe we'll bring them into town for a pizza.'

'They'd like that. Now, I guess I should let you go. Call me when you're on your way home. Actually, there's something I want to talk to you about after the tech run. Nothing bad, so don't start getting worked up about it.'

Laughing, she assured him she wouldn't, and after ringing off she spent the next few minutes trying to imagine what it might be and not doing a very good job of stopping her thoughts from hiking off down the matrimonial aisle. However, the issues of her day were soon crowding to the front of her mind again as she indicated to turn into the Fenns' drive and found the way partially blocked by a very sleek Mercedes. Managing to squeeze her Punto in off the kerb behind it, she scooped up her bag and went to knock on the front door.

'Coming!' a voice called from inside, and a moment later Maggie Fenn was ushering her in. 'Sorry about the lack of parking,' she said. 'That amazing beast belongs to my brother, Anthony. He leaves it here sometimes while he goes fishing with friends, over on the Taw. They take it in turns to drive. He's a barrister,' she added proudly. 'In London.'

Touched and amused by her pride, Alex said, 'So how did you get along with Daniel at the weekend?'

Maggie brightened. 'Actually, very well indeed,' she declared. 'In fact, we're feeling rather sorry to see him go.'

Alex wasn't quick enough to hide her surprise.

Maggie Fenn smiled. 'He's very good company,' she told her quietly. 'My goodness, the stories he can tell . . . Oliver has really taken a shine to him. You'll see.'

Not sure she wanted to imagine Daniel's stories, while delighted to hear that he'd got along with Oliver, Alex said, 'I have to admit, this wasn't exactly what I expected to hear, but it pleases me no end.'

Maggie gave her a wink and turned to look up the stairs as her husband came halfway down. 'Maggie, I think you'll have to go to Oliver,' he said. 'He's getting himself into a bit of a state up here.'

'Oh dear, poor love. He's been dreading this moment,' she told Alex. 'How's Daniel bearing up?' she asked Ron.

'He's in his room finishing off his packing.'

Maggie turned back to Alex. 'Would you like to come up?' she invited.

Not entirely sure Daniel would want her to, Alex tried to find an excuse, but Maggie Fenn was already leading the way.

'We popped down the coast a way, yesterday,' she was saying as she climbed the stairs. 'Ron thought the boys would enjoy a spot of fresh air and they certainly seemed to.'

'It sounds as though you've given them a fabulous time,' Alex commented, admiring the family photographs that covered the walls. Most seemed to be of the Fenns' son and daughter, but there were others that Alex guessed were various foster-children from down the years.

'Anthony was a big hit with them while he was here,' Maggie was telling her as they joined Ron on the landing. 'They had a fine old time trying to beat him at table tennis, and they did, I might tell you. Ah, Daniel, there you are, dear. Here's Alex come to take you home. Are you all washed up and ready to go?'

Daniel's pasty little face looked strained and cross as he avoided Alex's eyes and grunted a reply.

'It's been lovely having you to stay, little soldier,' Ron Fenn said, ruffling his hair. 'You've brightened things up for us, especially Oliver.'

Daniel's head went down, but Alex could see how stiff he'd become. The effort to hold back his feelings was almost too much for him, and knowing he'd hate to lose control in front of everyone, she tried to bolster him with a reminder that his mother was at home looking forward to seeing him.

Daniel swallowed and nodded.

'Have you got your things up together?'

He gave an awkward shrug of one shoulder, then suddenly he was pushing rudely past them all and thundering down the stairs.

'I'll go after him,' Ron said. 'You'd better check on Oliver,' he reminded Maggie. To Alex he said, 'Daniel's bag is ready, if you can bring it down.'

'We've given him a new one,' Maggie told her quietly. 'We have so many, and it seemed a shame that he only had a pillowcase. I hope that's all right.'

'Of course,' Alex assured her. 'I'm sure he was chuffed to bits to receive it.'

'Just go right in,' Maggie insisted, as Alex hesitated at the door Daniel had come out of. 'I imagine it's in need of a bit of a tidy-up, but that's boys for you, isn't it?'

As Maggie headed off along the landing, Alex let herself into the bedroom and almost laughed to see how chintzy it was. Not the kind of thing Daniel would be used to at all, and as for the great big bed, he must have thought he'd died and woken up a king.

Spotting a Nike sports bag next to an old armoire she felt pleased for him that he had such a smart memento of his time here, and going to pick it up she was about to leave the room when it occurred to her that he might have helped himself to something he shouldn't have. She wasn't keen on the idea of checking to make sure all the bag's contents were his, but she'd be failing in her duty if she didn't unzip the top and have a quick rummage round. To her dismay, though alas not to her surprise, she found a silver-framed photograph of the Fenns on their wedding day wrapped up in a freshly laundered shirt.

Setting it back amongst the other photos on the windowsill, she zipped the bag up again and carried it downstairs.

Daniel was standing by the front door with Oliver and the Fenns, and as she drew closer she realised he was trying to comfort Oliver.

'You're gonna be a good bro now, OK?' Daniel was saying. 'You're not going to take no messing from no one, because I'm gonna be looking out for you, right?'

Oliver's little head nodded up and down, but his shoulders were shaking he was crying so hard. 'Can't you stay, please?' he begged.

'You haven't got to say things like that,' Daniel

scolded. 'I've got to go and take care of my old lady, you know what I mean? She can't get by without me, but Maggie and Ron, they're going to take care of you. They're good people, do you hear what I'm saying?'

Stepping forward Alex said softly, 'Are you ready, Daniel? Shall we get in the car?'

Averting his eyes, Daniel walked over to her Punto and plonked himself in the passenger seat.

'Bye,' Alex said to Ron and Maggie, 'and thank you. Sounds like he's had a very special time.'

'I think we all did,' Maggie replied, smiling fondly in Daniel's direction.

Going down to Oliver's height, Alex took his hand as she whispered, 'Thank you for looking after Daniel. He needed to find a friend and you strike me as being one of the best ones to have.'

He turned his tear-blotched face to look at her, but was too overcome to speak.

As she got into the car Alex could sense how bereft Daniel was feeling, but as she reversed out he didn't speak, or move a muscle, he simply kept his eyes fixed straight ahead, not even glancing at Oliver or the Fenns.

What a terrible shame it was, Alex was reflecting as they headed back towards the Temple Fields estate, that he couldn't just stay with the Fenns and Oliver, how different his life would be, how much better his chances. However, she had no right to think that way, when his mother, for all her faults – of which there were many, most of them criminal – had never given the authorities any reason to doubt that she loved her son. She might have a different way of showing it, with all her loud-mouthed belligerence and failure to send him to school or keep him clean, but that didn't make the bond she shared with him any less genuine or heartfelt. She simply hadn't had any of the advantages life had thrown the Fenns' way, starting with the family she'd been born into.

Now here she was, all tattoos, piercings and peroxide hair, striding down the path to meet her boy, looking ready to thump anyone who got in her way.

'Come on, you little bugger,' she growled, tugging Daniel out of the passenger seat. 'Bet you've missed me, haven't you?'

Daniel nodded, and gave himself stiffly to the rough shake and hug that conveyed her pleasure to see him.

'Where's your stuff?' she demanded.

'Here,' Alex answered, going to take the bag out of the boot.

Laura pulled a face as she saw it. 'What the bloody hell's that when it's at home?' she snapped. Then, rolling her eyes, 'Oh, for fuck's sake, you haven't been out robbing again, have you, Daniel? I've told you about that.'

'He was given it,' Alex said quietly.

Laura scowled at her. 'Yeah, right,' she retorted, snatching it from her. 'Well, we won't be needing the likes of you no more, thanks very much, so you can be on your way. Come on, Dan,' and grabbing his arm she began marching him off down the path. At the front door she turned back, saying, 'Cops got the wrong person, didn't they, same as they always do. I told 'em, it's that fucking Prince family they ought to be going after and leave the rest of us the fuck alone.'

As the door slammed behind her Alex could only

wonder what was going through Daniel's mind now, whether he was glad to be home, if he'd tell his mother where he'd been, or who he'd been with. He'd no doubt be furious when he found out he no longer had the silver photograph frame, but she couldn't have allowed him to walk away from the house with something that wasn't his. Especially not after the Fenns had been so kind to him.

Getting back into her car, she quickly pushed the button to lock all the doors, and started the engine. Laura's little rant against the Prince family had been all the reminder she'd needed of how keen she was to get off the estate before any of them spotted her.

Twenty minutes later, after pulling into a car park behind the town hall to jot down some preliminary notes about Daniel's pickup and return to his mother, she decided to make a quick check of her voicemails.

'Hi, Tommy here, thought I'd better let you know that the Princes' GP has been the victim of a mugging. Obvious suspects being questioned, we both know who they are, so don't hang around the TFE when you drop your boy off, OK?'

Thankful she hadn't, Alex clicked to the next message and her heart sank with shame as Maggie Fenn said, 'I'm hoping you might pick this up before you go too far. We gave Daniel a photograph he liked of us and he seems to have left it behind. Of course, it might have been deliberate, but if it wasn't, perhaps you'll have time to come back and collect it.'

Erica Wade was at the kitchen window watching Ottilie wandering about in the back garden, her skinny legs bare beneath the dress she'd put on inside out and her play high heels jammed on to the wrong feet. She clip-clopped up and down the path, carrying her bear, and stopping every now and again to inspect a leaf, or a caterpillar or whatever else she found. She didn't need any friends, she was used to entertaining herself.

Erica's eyes strayed to the luxury shed that Brian called a studio. The door was secured by no less than three coded padlocks; the large square window with its darkly tinted glass didn't open at all. Unlike Ottilie, Erica had never been inside the shed, but she knew it contained leather sofas, a fur rug, a computer and all kinds of camera equipment, because she'd seen everything being delivered. Brian belonged to a club, exclusive, specialised and nationwide. For all she knew it might even be global. The members exchanged photographs and videos for the purpose of education or entertainment. The subjects were always children, boys and girls, all colours, all ages.

Sweat was starting to form on her skin, bubbling up like blisters, trickling, tickling like bugs. Her breath was short, her eyes were clouding and blank. As she swayed she caught the edge of the sink to steady herself. It wouldn't be long now. Whoever she was waiting for would come and then everything would be all right.

Who was she waiting for?

She couldn't remember.

Ottilie came in clutching a fistful of flowers. She laid them on the table, then kicked off her shoes and pulled a chair to the sink to fill a cup with water. After putting the flowers in the cup she held it in both hands and looked up at her mother. There was a smudge of dirt on her cheek, a stray leaf in her hair. Her large brown eyes were watchful and worried.

Erica turned away, so Ottilie put the cup down on the table before dragging the chair back to its place so she could clamber up and sit on it while she looked at the flowers. She stayed there for ten minutes or more, her legs dangling, her hands clasped in her lap as she gazed at the squashed mix of daisies, grass and weeds.

At last the Sainsbury's delivery arrived.

Erica's breath came more easily. As soon as she'd packed everything away she could take her medication and sink slowly, blissfully back into the void.

When she opened the front door she heard Ottilie padding down the hall behind her.

The delivery driver was the same woman who'd been a few times before. She looked friendly, but worn, as though life was trying to drag her down.

Erica suddenly wanted to laugh. She should try living here, being screamed at by voices in her head and scorned by a man who was sick.

The woman said hello to Ottilie, but Ottilie only looked at her.

'Cat got your tongue?' the lady teased, as Erica carried the bags through to the kitchen. It was what she always said when she saw Ottilie. *Cat got your tongue?*

Ottilie only blinked.

'Would you like a lollipop?' the lady offered, drawing one from her pocket. As far as Erica was aware she'd never done that before.

Ottilie's eyes went to it warily, then reaching out a hand she took it.

'She's so sweet,' the lady commented, as Ottilie continued to stare at her.

Erica didn't answer. She needed this woman to be gone. She must close the door now, put the shopping away and go upstairs.

Brian could see to Ottilie when he came in. He always did anyway. *Brian always saw to Ottilie. Brian always saw to Ottilie. She's so sweet. Brian always saw to Ottilie.*

'Are you OK?' Alex murmured breathlessly.

With his eyes still closed, Jason said, 'Mm, I'm great. How about you?'

She smiled, and wrapped herself more tightly around him, loving the feel of her naked skin against his. These moments when they lay entwined after making love were, in their way, even more precious to her than the act itself for how safe and cherished he made her feel. He'd become so central to her life over the last eighteen months that she could hardly remember now what it was like before she'd met him. Nor did she particularly want to when she was so happy. Looking back almost always made her feel sad.

The tech run had gone brilliantly earlier, everyone had been on great form so they'd sailed through it, making Jason laugh till he ached and Alex want to squeeze and kiss every one of them in pride. Being on such a high no one had felt ready to go home, so they'd all tramped off to the pub where impromptu rehearsals had inevitably broken out, along with wild ideas for publicity, costume changes and how they were going to cope with the paparazzi when they hit the West End.

Four days to go and Jason's mate Grant had already delivered half the technical gear they were going to need for the opening night, and knowing Grant as well as she did, Alex had no worries that the rest would turn up in plenty of time. Her biggest concern was the set; however, Steve Perry, the local artist and landscaper who'd designed it, had simply told her to chill, his blokes were on it and no way were they going to let anyone down. Then Mattie had announced that every last ticket for the opening night had now been sold.

How amazing was that?

Terrifyingly amazing actually, but brilliant too. This was going to be the Mulgrove Players' third production in as many years, and Hailey's *Gender Swap* was definitely attracting as much if not more interest as *A Midsummer Night's Dream* and *Blithe Spirit*. Alex just hoped her Aunt Sheila and Gabby did manage to come, especially when they'd missed the previous two shows. It would mean so much to her having them there, provided the performance went well, of course, but she wasn't going to worry herself about that now. They had three more rehearsals scheduled before Saturday night so if anything did go wrong, there was still plenty of time to put it right.

'You know, you still haven't told me what you wanted to talk to me about,' she reminded Jason as he raised an arm for her to rest her head on his shoulder.

'Mm?' he murmured sleepily.

'You said earlier, on the phone . . .'

'Oh yeah, that's right.' Taking a moment to bring himself round, he rolled on to his side so he could look at her in the moonlight.

She'd all but stopped breathing. If this turned out to be what she thought it was she knew exactly what her answer would be, though obviously she understood that they wouldn't be able to go public or buy a ring or anything until he'd got a divorce from Gina.

'I've been thinking,' he said, tucking her hair

behind her ear, 'that I should do this house up a bit for you. No, hear me out,' he urged, as she lowered her eyes to cover the crush of disappointment. 'I know you don't want to spend money you don't have when you're going to sell it, eventually, but I could get all the materials at cost, and the labour, or mine anyway, would come for free.'

Managing to smile into his eyes and love him for the generosity of his offer, she put a hand to his face as she reminded herself that it really wouldn't have been right for him to propose until he was legally free to do so. 'You're amazing, did I ever tell you that?' she said softly.

Clearly pleased with her response, he said, 'Whatever you do have to spend you'll easily make back on the sale, because presenting it in better shape is sure to get you a better price. So what do you say? I reckon we could make a big difference for a couple of grand, which you and Gabby could split between you.'

He had no idea that she didn't have a share in the house, because she'd never told him, or anyone, that her mother, Myra, had left it to Gabby. And she didn't want to tell him now when she knew it would make her feel hurt and humiliated all over again to see his shock, and his pity when it came. God knew she'd felt enough of that when the solicitor had told her about the will; watching his embarrassment had been almost as bad as being made to feel as though she didn't matter, or that she was less deserving, or that she'd been an intruder all her life. Since then, she'd allowed everyone, Jason included, to go with their own presumptions that she was joint owner, and Gabby, who'd always claimed to feel terrible about it, had never contradicted them. Nor had Gabby ever charged any rent, so it made sense to Jason that all he and Alex were sharing was the bills.

'So?' he prompted. 'Are you up for it?'

Turning on to her back, she said, 'Well, I'd have to talk to my sister about it, obviously . . .'

'Sure, but I reckon she'll go for it, don't you? I mean, why wouldn't she? And I was thinking, I could contact Millie's family to see if they'd like the cottage next door tarted up a bit too. We could do that easily while we're here. Obviously we wouldn't give them such a great deal as we'd offer you, but it would give us some work and hopefully turn everyone a handsome profit at the end of the day. Have you heard from Millie's relatives lately? I take it you're still in touch with them.'

'On and off,' Alex replied. 'And honestly, I'm not sure they'll want anything done to her cottage. Whatever they make on it will probably have to go towards paying for her care, so it won't make any difference to them how much it sells for.'

Remembering the truth of it, he said, 'Of course, I'd forgotten about that. I suppose that's why they don't come to see her. Nothing in it for them.'

Though Alex slanted him a look, she had to admit she'd had the same thought herself at times. 'People have busy lives,' she reminded him, reaching for her robe, 'and it's a long way to come, all the way from York.'

'They could easily ring to find out how she is,' he pointed out.

'They do, occasionally. Anyway, she doesn't always remember who they are.'

'Yeah, but she does sometimes. How was she when you went in earlier?'

'Actually, she was quite alert, for her. She knew

73

who I was straight away and devoured half a packet of chocolate biscuits in less than ten minutes. Of course she wanted to know when Dad was coming to see her, and as usual she seemed more surprised than upset when I reminded her that he's no longer with us.' He'd left the house to Myra when he'd died, with a clause expressing his wish for it to be shared between Gabby and Alex when Myra went. So at least he had considered her worthy of something.

'Anyway,' she said cheerfully, 'it's a great idea about giving this place a bit of a makeover, but please don't mention it to Gabby when we see her at the weekend. I'll talk to her when we're on our own. You know how upset she gets about having to discuss anything to do with Mum and Dad. She hasn't even been able to bring herself to sort through their clothes or papers yet.'

Yawning as he flipped back the duvet and started for the bathroom, he said, 'Well, at least it's all stuffed in her bedroom, so it's out of the way, but she'll have to get round to it at some point. Unless you do it for her.'

Alex shrugged and started to pick up the clothes they'd discarded on their way in. 'I will if she wants me to,' she said. She wasn't about to admit that she'd already been through every box, bag, suitcase, pocket and purse in the hope of discovering something about, or maybe even from her real mother. She'd found nothing, apart from a letter that she'd written herself, aged fourteen, telling her real mother how unhappy she was and begging her to come and get her. Of course, she'd had nowhere to send it, and until she'd unearthed it from the bottom of an old handbag of Myra's, she'd forgotten she'd even written it. She might have wondered if it had upset Myra to read it, had the envelope not still been sealed, with the single word *Mummy* written on the front. She supposed the fact that it had never been opened proved that Myra, contrary to what she'd often claimed, had never really seen her as a daughter.

However, she'd tried, Alex would never deny that, and given how deeply she'd seen some children suffer, she knew better than to feel anything other than profoundly grateful for the stable and mostly loving upbringing she'd had.

Chapter Four

Ottilie was sitting at the top of the stairs, her bony knees pressed tightly together, her cloud of wispy hair knotted like seaweed around her pale, pixie face. Her dress was back to front and the buttons were skewed. She'd meant to put on some knickers but had been unable to find any in the drawer.

Her best friend, Boots, was tucked into her lap. He was a bear so he was brave. Sometimes he made her brave too, but not all of the time. It had been his idea to come out on to the landing and so far everything was all right. Ottilie's mother was downstairs somewhere, but Ottilie didn't know where. She couldn't hear her and she hadn't seen her since she'd come to tell Ottilie it was time to get out of bed.

Get out of bed, Ottilie. Wash your face, Ottilie. Listen to me, Ottilie.

Her daddy had gone to work the way he always did in the mornings, except when he took her to church. The last time they'd gone to church she'd worn a green and purple dress that was new and lots of people had looked at her and said nice things to her, but she didn't say anything back.

'She's very shy,' Daddy always told them.

Mummy never came to church. Mummy didn't

go out at all, she was asleep in her room most of the time, and Daddy said that it was for the best. It was good for Ottilie to stay at home too, he said, but she could always play in the garden. She did sometimes, when it wasn't raining. Daddy had bought her a playhouse and a pram, a swing, a slide and a see-saw, because she was a very good girl. She wasn't allowed on the swing or slide unless Mummy or Daddy were there to make sure she was safe. Mummy never came out with her, but Daddy sometimes did. He'd bring his camera and take pictures of her playing, then they'd go into his studio, where he put them on his computer so she could see them like she was on TV. Boots was in some of them, but Daddy wouldn't let her put him in front of her face the way she liked to because then he wouldn't be able to see her and she was very pretty, he said.

Daddy kept all kinds of dressing-up clothes in his studio for her to play with when he was in the mood to have her over there. He'd show her pictures of other little girls wearing the same sorts of things so she would know how to lie, or sit, or kneel when he was taking pictures. Sometimes he would just sit in his chair stroking the tiger that lived in his pocket as he watched her. She didn't like the tiger, but she didn't tell him that because it made him cross.

She wanted to go downstairs now, but Boots was asleep and she couldn't be brave without him, so she stood up and walked towards her room. She had a pink bed with daisies and fairies on the cover, and stars on the curtains. There were books on the shelves that Daddy read to her, and pictures on the walls that she'd drawn herself. She even had a TV all of her own. Boots liked it in here, and so did she, but only when it was just the two of them. She didn't like it when Daddy came in, unless it was just to tuck her up or ask if she wanted something to eat.

Hearing a noise on the landing she looked up, and her heart fluttered like a little bird as her mother appeared. She was scared and wanted to cry, but didn't in case it made Mummy cross. She wasn't sure what she'd done wrong, but Mummy had a funny look about her, and she was swaying. She did that sometimes, and even fell over, bumping her head and making herself bleed.

'Go to your room,' Mummy said, in a voice that didn't really sound like hers. '*Go to your room. GO TO YOUR ROOM YOU FILTHY LITTLE BITCH.*'

Ottilie hated it when her mother screamed like that; it always terrified her. She fled past her and into her bedroom.

'Stay there,' Mummy said, her voice shaking like the windows when they rattled in the wind. 'And don't come out until I say so.'

As Erica snapped on the TV and closed the door, Ottilie climbed on to the bed with Boots to wait.

She was very good at doing as she was told.

'Alex, it's Wendy.'

'Oh, hello,' Alex said sweetly into her Bluetooth, 'how lovely to hear you.'

'Yes, I'm sure,' Wendy retorted drily. 'I have some news for you. Lizzie Walsh has agreed to go with you to the Princes.'

Had Alex not been driving she'd have punched the air with a *Yes!* Since a small army, a machine gun or laughing gas was out of the question as backup for that visit, Lizzie Walsh was absolutely the next best choice. (Apart from Tommy, naturally, but he was already off somewhere being trained to fill in forms that should hopefully make the government's life easier.) In fact, contacting Lizzie – the most experienced and cool-headed social worker on the team, but only part-time these days – had been right at the top of her to-do list today. So it would seem that someone (Tommy, without a doubt) had already tipped Lizzie off. 'Tell her I love her,' Alex gushed. 'Or don't bother, I'll tell her myself. Yay! So, lucky us, we've won the star prize, a day trip to the Temple Fields estate to visit the Princes.'

With a sigh Wendy said, 'Alex, I know you think it's beneath you to go into that estate, but I'm sure I don't have to remind you that it's an integral part of our area that needs careful handling.'

Wishing she could punch the stupid woman who had absolutely no idea about anything – least of all that Alex herself had been born in Temple Fields, OK, not on the estate, but close enough – Alex decided not to dignify the ignorance with any sort of response. (And since when had she ever given the impression that it was *beneath* her?)

'Are you still there?' Wendy enquired patiently.

'Yes, I'm here,' Alex replied, indicating to turn in the direction of Westleigh. She had just enough time now to pop into the Fenns to pick up the photograph for Daniel, before dashing back across town to the family court where Annie Ashe was hopefully going to learn that she could have her children back from care. After that she'd call in on Kylie to find out how her self-inflicted injuries were healing, and then, with any luck, she'd make it back to the office in time for a core meeting about Lucas Green, whose severely depressed mother was leaning on him too heavily.

'We'll need an assessment on Polly Prince by the end of next week,' Wendy was saying. 'Lizzie is in on Tuesday and Wednesday, so I suggest you schedule the visit for one of those days.'

'Well I guess that would make sense,' Alex responded sardonically.

'Very funny. Polly will probably need to be taken back into care, but if I were you I wouldn't broach that while you're there.'

'Really? Do you think it might get me into trouble?'

Wendy sighed.

'So any news on Shane Prince's whereabouts yet?' Alex asked cheerfully. 'Please tell me they've remanded him in custody for the mugging of Dr Trevors, so I don't have to worry about being treated to his uniquely friendly manners when I turn up at his house.'

'I haven't heard back from the police yet,' Wendy replied, 'but I'll let you know when I do. Oh, one other thing before you go, I need you to cover for Ben on Friday.'

Alex nearly exploded. 'You're kidding me, right? I'm completely inundated . . .'

'It's all about prioritising,' Wendy interrupted in a tone that went straight up Alex's back. 'The families who can wait will just have to wait a little longer. I'll give you a call as soon as I've sorted out . . .'

'What the hell's wrong with him?' Alex demanded. 'He's always taking time off.'

'He's attending his grandfather's funeral. Is that good enough for you?'

It might have been if it weren't the third time in as many months that Ben had been to his grandfather's funeral, so either the old bloke wasn't staying buried, or Ben was an out-and-out shafter. 'So can't you get some agency staff to cover?' she cried.

'What a luxury that would be, but with all these cutbacks I'm afraid it's out of the question. Now, I think we've dealt with everything, so I'll leave it with you to sort out a mutually convenient time with Lizzie to visit Polly Prince.'

After ringing off Alex felt sorely tempted to call Jason, simply to let off some steam, since he was the only one who'd fully understand why Wendy's comments about visits to Temple Fields being beneath her were so fatuous and miles wide of the mark. However, he'd have far more important things to do with his day than spend time trying to bring her back from orbit. And actually, she could do it herself, with a few deep breaths and another reminder, albeit grudging, that though Wendy, along with the rest of her colleagues, knew she'd been adopted, they had no idea that she was the child, all grown up now of course, of the notorious Temple Fields killer. Alex guessed if anyone even thought about that tragic little girl these days, and after so long she doubted anyone did, they'd simply assume that she'd either been taken in by someone else from the family, or swallowed up in the care system. And indeed the system had processed her protection and eventual adoption, because no one else from her family had come forward to claim her. This was something she viewed with mixed emotions, since she wouldn't have wanted anyone from her father's side to try and grab her into the bosom of their care. However, there had been, and still was, a great-aunt on her mother's side (her grandfather's stepsister), who might have taken her in had she not been afraid of the murdering Gavril

Albescu, or one of his accomplices, finding out and trying to dispatch her too.

Alex had only discovered about this aunt five years ago, through the Internet, and it had taken months for her to pluck up the courage to write her a letter. It turned out she needn't have bothered, because the reply she'd got had told her, quite bluntly, that her aunt felt it best for the situation to remain as it was. *Nothing good can come of us meeting now,* she'd written in a rather childlike hand. *There is nothing I can tell you about your mother's whereabouts. She never stayed in touch, and I can only feel glad of that while your father is still at large. I don't suppose after all these years that he remains a threat, but I see no point in running the risk. We have our separate lives and families now, and I feel certain that the rector and his wife have proved kind and loving parents to you.*

Of course, if your mother does ever get in touch with me and is wishing to re-establish contact with you, I will tell her where to find you.

With my best wishes for your health and happiness
Helen Druffield

With that letter all Alex's hopes of forging some kind of connection with her real family had died. She'd taken the rejection hard at the time, realising that in her great-aunt's eyes she was tainted by her father's genes, and perhaps was viewed as some sort of bad-luck charm to those of her mother's family who'd survived, and who'd apparently rather not have her amongst them.

Turn around and come back, Alex, she told herself. *You know self-pity's a pointless place to go.*

Finding free access to the Fenns' drive this time, she quickly parked up on the gravel outside the front door and even before she could knock Maggie Fenn was coming out to greet her.

'Do you have time to come in?' Maggie invited, her kind eyes looking as anxiously hopeful as a child's in a toyshop who has no money.

'I'm afraid I'm in a bit of a rush,' Alex replied guiltily. 'I'm due in court . . .'

'Yes, of course, of course. I know how busy you are. Here's the photograph.' It was wrapped in brown paper and carefully tied up with black ribbon.

Touched by how smart she'd made it look, Alex said, 'I'll make sure he gets it.'

Maggie's smile faltered. 'Thank you,' she replied.

Unable simply to walk away, Alex said, 'Is everything all right? You seem a bit . . .'

'No, no, I'm fine. Truly. I just . . . Well, they came to take Oliver back to his mother yesterday, so I've got a bit of an empty nest I'm afraid.' She took a breath and shook her head, pulling herself together. 'You know his mother has Munchausen's . . . Actually we have to call it something else now, don't we?'

'FII,' Alex answered. 'Fabricated or Induced Illness.'

Maggie nodded. 'I do hope he'll be all right.'

Putting a hand on her arm, Alex said, 'Don't worry, his social worker and the family support team will keep a very close eye on him.'

Maggie braved a smile. 'I'm sure they will. And before we know it I expect I'll have another troubled little soul or two to be running around after. Let's hope so, eh? Oh, I don't mean . . . I'm not wishing them to be . . .'

'It's OK, I know what you mean,' Alex assured her. 'Now I'm afraid I really do have to run, but I'll give you my details in case you want to call for a chat at any time.' As she scribbled her numbers on a slip of paper she wasn't quite sure why she was doing it, especially when Maggie Fenn wasn't even in her area. However, she couldn't just abandon the woman, giving her nothing when she was clearly so upset.

'Send Daniel our love when you see him,' Maggie said, taking the details. 'And if you happen to run into Oliver at all . . . I know he doesn't come under your office . . .'

'Don't worry, I'll tell him,' Alex promised with a smile, and still feeling awful for having to rush off she ran back to her car, knowing already how unlikely it was she'd be able to get across town in time for the hearing.

However, an hour later she was listening to the senior magistrate saying to Annie, '. . . so I'm afraid Mrs Ashe, that in light of this recent incident you've left us with no alternative but to keep the current custody arrangements for your children in place.'

Sensing Annie's confusion and panic Alex quickly reached for her hand.

'What does he mean? What's he saying?' Annie cried as the magistrates started to leave the court and the lawyers began packing up their papers. 'No, don't go! Come back, you can't keep my children. Alex! You have to stop him. Please, make him come back.'

'Ssh, ssh.' Alex tried to soothe her. 'I'm really sorry, Annie. I didn't . . .'

'But you said he'd let me have them . . .'

'That was before what happened in the street.'

'But that doesn't have anything to do with it. Make him come back!' she shouted to one of the clerks. 'Tell him he's got it wrong. He can't keep a mother from her children. It's not right.'

'Come on,' Alex whispered, slipping an arm around Annie's ample frame and feeling a surge of pity for how much weight she'd lost this last year, all in a bid to win back her children. They would be just as devastated when they found out it wasn't going to happen – like their mother, they'd invested all their hopes in today.

'I've done everything,' Annie was sobbing after they'd said goodbye to the lawyer who'd been appointed to her case. 'I keeps my house up together now, I been learning to cook, I've got me little cleaning job, what more do he want? Oh, Alex, Alex, I can't go home without my babies. I just can't.'

Easing her gently into the passenger seat of her car, Alex went quickly round to the driver's side and got in next to her. 'Annie, look at me,' she said, reaching for Annie's shaking hands.

Annie raised her fleshy, tear-ravaged face to stare out at the drizzling rain. 'It's that stupid cow Maureen Day's fault,' she growled angrily. 'If she hadn't started mouthing off at me the way she did I wouldn't of thumped her, but she deserved it, Alex. The names she called me, they was horrible, disgusting and none of it was true. I was never on the game and I never, ever beat my kids. You know that, don't you?'

'Of course I do, and you shouldn't have listened to her. You know she's a troublemaker.'

'Everyone does, so why didn't the bloody magistrate understand that? I was provoked . . .'

'You were also drunk, Annie, and you know that one of the conditions you had to meet was to join AA.'

'I did join AA and I goes regular. It was only the once, Alex, I swear it. It all just got too much. I was that nervous about today and all worked up about everything, then she started going on, shouting out terrible stuff so everyone could hear . . .'

'It's OK, I can understand how it happened, but unfortunately getting yourself arrested was only ever going to result in setting your case back.'

The anguish, the unbearable strain of it suddenly overwhelmed Annie again and as she sobbed with despair Alex held her as comfortingly as she could, while wishing, as she always did at these moments, that there was more she could do.

'Come on,' she said when Annie was finally a little calmer, 'I'll drive you home now and make you a nice cup of tea – and remember, no matter how bad the pressure gets, don't reach for the bottle, OK? If you feel overwhelmed, or worried, or you just need to chat, you have my number, so call me.'

After delivering Annie back to her council flat on the edge of Temple Fields, Alex drove on to the children's residential home in Cliff Down, about four miles away, to check on Kylie. On being told that her charge was in the middle of a therapy session, she left a note so Kylie would know she'd been, and returned to her car to check what was next in her diary. A Nigerian family who'd recently arrived in the area. Though she hadn't yet met either of the parents, she'd spoken to the mother several times on the phone and if the woman's surprise and concern at finding herself on the social services' radar was anything to go by, then this meeting today should go well. It wouldn't be the first time she'd had to school newcomers to the country in how things were done here – i.e. physical punishment of children and staff was not allowed, even if it was the norm where they came from.

What she found when she got to the Adebayos' freshly painted home in the affluent area of Bradshaw was father and son kicking a football around in the neatly mowed back garden, while mum and daughter were baking a traditional Nigerian colour sweet cake in the kitchen. Though Alex guessed this perfect domesticity was being staged for her benefit, when she left half an hour later she felt fairly satisfied that they were good parents who simply hailed from a different culture and were now eager to adapt to the new one. When she wrote them up she'd recommend another visit in a couple of months just to see how things were going, and if all was well there would be no need to bother them again.

By the time she'd made two more visits, one to a young mother and baby, both addicted to heroin and both in foster care; the other to a fifteen-year-old boy who'd recently been returned to the family home after being removed for beating up his mother and sister, it was gone six o'clock. So, turning the car in the direction of home she switched on her personal mobile, ready for her own life to sweep like a gentle tide over the shores of her hectic day. Unsurprisingly, with opening night virtually upon them, she was inundated with messages and texts from cast and crew, though, to her relief, nothing was requiring her immediate attention. Everything was going so well, and to time, that her biggest concern now was the fact that *nothing was going wrong*. However, she must remember that it was still only Thursday, so plenty of time yet for some monster of an issue to raise its ugly head, which would absolutely not be brilliant, just normal.

Before driving on she called up her work messages, in case of emergencies; the first was from Family Support giving feedback on the various cases she was leading; next came a lengthy update from Wendy on what she'd been listed to do to cover for Ben. (Nothing about Shane Prince's custody status, thank you, Wendy; and not so much as a thank you either, or 'I hope this isn't too much, if it is do let me know and we'll work something out.') The last message was a reminder from Millie's care home that Millie was due for an assessment next week, if Alex or a member of Millie's family would like to be there.

Firing off a quick text to Millie's niece saying she'd be happy to try and fit it in if none of the family could make it, Alex drove home and finally pulled up outside the Vicarage twenty-five minutes later – just in time to click on her work mobile as it rang.

'Alex, Neil Osmond here,' the voice at the other end informed her. 'Sorry it's taken me this long to get back to you. What's up?'

Neil Osmond from CAIT – Child Abuse Investigation Team. Why had she called him? Slapping her head as she remembered, she said, 'I have a big favour to ask. I think I already know the answer, but here goes anyway: I have to pay a visit to the Prince family next Tuesday and I was wondering if you, or someone from your department, might be able to come with me. Us, actually, Lizzie Walsh is coming too.'

With the expected sigh of regret, he said, 'You know I'd love to help, but having a police presence is going to create the wrong impression, like you're saying some sort of crime has gone down, and as far as I'm aware it hasn't?'

'Not that I know of,' Alex conceded. She wasn't surprised by this response, since she knew that the police never liked to get involved unless they had to, but she was disappointed anyway.

'I'll tell you what,' he continued. 'If you let me know when you're going, I'll make sure a couple of uniforms are in the vicinity. That way, if you need to dial 999, someone'll be on the doorstep.'

Knowing it was the best he could offer, she said, 'OK, thanks. I've got your email so I'll be in touch when it's set up.'

'Hang on, before you go. I might as well talk to you about this now, while you're on the line. We took an anonymous call earlier about a kid living on North Hill. Do you know anything about her? The family name is Wade.'

Screwing up her nose as she tried to connect with the distant ring of a bell, Alex said, 'What was the caller saying?'

'Just that she thought someone ought to go over there and see to the kid that lives there, which is why I'm passing it on to you.'

'OK, I'm not actually in the office at the moment, but I'll check it out when I go in tomorrow,' and after jotting the name down she ended the call, and seeing Jason at the door she melted into a smile.

'You're late,' he said, as she walked into his arms. 'I'm just on my way to go and pick up the kids.'

Having forgotten they were coming for the evening, Alex felt herself instantly deflate. The one night this week that there was no rehearsal, and she had to spend it with them. She didn't want to be mean, but it was the last thing she felt up to right now, and she knew damned well that they'd rather be anywhere than with her. 'What are you doing about food?' she asked, hoping he had planned to take them into town for a curry or a pizza. He might not like it if she cried off, but they would, and tonight was all about them, wasn't it?

'I popped into Tesco on my way home,' he told her, starting towards his car. 'They'll be happy with beans on toast and a Magnum each.'

And what will I be happy with, she was thinking irritably as she opened the front door. Though she could no doubt come up with several answers, she decided that maybe she should start viewing this as another opportunity to make Jason happy by doing her best to win them over.

'No bloody way am I going down there,' Tiffany raged, her thirteen-year-old attitude punching its weight about the kitchen like a fist and carrying up to the landing where Alex was at her desk. She was meaning Devon, of course, and the barbecue at Gabby's on Sunday. 'You're always trying to make us and . . .'

'Shush, keep your voice down,' Jason scolded, 'and stop that swearing.'

'I'm not going,' she hissed. 'I hate it down there. It's boring and I can't stand horses, nor can Heidi, can you?' she demanded of her ten-year-old sister.

'No, they really scare me, Dad,' Heidi responded earnestly. 'One nearly trod on me last time, and it would have really hurt if it had.'

'But it didn't, and anyway, we're not going to her Aunt Sheila's, we're going to her sister's and you like it there. They've got a pool, remember . . .'

'The pool's really cool,' Tom, his eight-year-old, piped up. 'We could have races . . .'

'Shut up!' Tiffany seethed through her teeth. 'We're not going, and that's that.'

'But you can't stay here on your own,' Jason pointed out.

'We can stay with Mum,' Heidi retorted.

'But you're with me that day . . .'

'Yeah, *you* not her,' Tiffany spat, 'or her stupid family.'

'Ssh, she'll hear you.'

'And like I care? I'm telling you right now, Dad, I'm not going, so you might as well get it into your head . . .'

'Don't speak to me like that, and you'll do as you're told.'

'If you make me go I promise you, I won't speak to anyone all day.'

'You didn't speak to her just now when we were having our tea,' Tom reminded her. 'That was rude, really, wasn't it, Dad?'

'Very,' Jason agreed. 'Alex was doing her best to be friendly . . .'

'Shut *up*!' Tiffany shouted. 'She's your girlfriend, not ours, so I don't see why we have to have anything to do with her. You ought to tell her you want to come and live with us again. You don't belong here . . .'

'Tiffany, stop this.'

'Why should I? She's not interested in us, it's all just a show, the way she goes around pretending to care about kids, when she didn't think twice about taking you away from us, did she?'

Hearing Gina's words – fabrications – coming out of Tiffany's mouth, Alex sighed quietly to herself and tried to carry on writing up the notes of her day. However, it wasn't easy to block out what was going on downstairs when it was so loud, and anyway, she guessed that as far as Tiffany was concerned she was supposed to overhear.

Of course both she and Jason knew that Gina deliberately wound Tiffany up before her father came to collect her, determined to set her off like some pubescent Rottweiler to spoil the day, but what could they do? Gina was the girl's mother, and they were very close, so no one was going to have a bigger influence on her than that. And if Jason tried to exert his own authority it usually erupted into an unholy row, much as it was building towards one now.

'If it weren't so difficult for the kids it might almost be laughable,' Alex remarked to Gabby when she rang later to say that she'd be coming to the barbecue alone on Sunday. Jason had caved in as usual and agreed to stay behind with the children. This was only good in that it meant the spiteful Tiffany wouldn't be able to have a go at the twins. The flip side of it was that Gina, via Tiffany, had won again.

'You know what's funny,' Gabby commented with a laugh, 'is there you are supposed to be an expert with children, but you just can't seem to get it right with them.'

There went Gabby's humour again, managing to strike all the wrong notes.

'Where are they now?' Gabby asked.

'He's taking them home, and I'm sitting here with a great big glass of wine, more thankful than you can imagine to have the house to myself for a while. Please tell me I wasn't that bad when I was Tiffany's age. OK, I know I was probably worse, so maybe this is payback time.'

With another laugh Gabby said, 'Well, you did grow out of it and I'm sure she will too. Now, changing the subject, how are the rehearsals going?'

Feeling her shoulders relaxing a little as a less stressful scenario presented itself, Alex said, 'Yeah, good. Actually, too good, but let's not start scaring ourselves with that. You are still coming to the opening night, aren't you?'

'Absolutely. Martin's going to babysit, and I'm driving Aunt Sheila. You know how nervous she is behind the wheel in the dark.'

Even though wanting to show off in front of her sister and aunt was a bit ridiculous, Alex reminded herself that it was only natural to want to impress your family with your achievements, and she felt sure they were going to love this latest production. 'You can stay over if you like,' she offered. 'I can easily get your old room ready, and Aunt Sheila can have mine.'

To her surprise, Gabby said, 'Actually, that might be a good idea. I'd be able to have a drink at the party after if I do. You are having a party, I take it?'

'Of course, at the pub, and everyone will be dead pleased to see you.'

Seeming to like the idea even more, Gabby said, 'Tell you what, I'll talk to Martin. If he's OK with it, and Sheila is too, I'm definitely going to take you up on it.'

Even more thrilled than she'd expected to be, Alex decided not to remind Gabby that her old room was stuffed full of their parents' belongings, since it might change her mind about staying. She'd just make sure it was all safely stored out of sight by the time Saturday came round. In fact, feeling so uplifted by the prospect of entertaining her sister and aunt, she decided to make a start right away.

She didn't bother opening any boxes or bags as she began moving them out, there was no point when she already knew what they contained. She simply transported as much as she could into drawers and cupboards in her old room, and pushed the heavy suitcases under the bed. She felt glad now that she hadn't torn down Gabby's old posters of Take That and the Backstreet Boys, or thrown out any of the concert memorabilia that she had once prized so highly. Gabby might enjoy going through some of it again, if she had time, a little meander down memory lane that would make her laugh and possibly even share with Alex some of the secrets she'd had back then. At the time, being the younger sister, and a bit of a nightmare, she'd been strictly banned from Gabby's room, and told absolutely nothing at all. Had Gabby but known it Alex used to sneak in anyway when Gabby was out, not because she was interested in all her stupid stuff, as she'd called it back then, but simply because it wasn't allowed. Anyway, it wasn't as if Gabby could have secrets that were ever going to top her own, because Gabby hadn't found out she was adopted, had she? Or that her real father was a psychopathic maniac who'd wiped out most of his family and was *still on the loose*. Or (though this had come later) that her real mother had survived and hadn't bothered to come and find her.

'Hey, what are you doing?' Jason said, arriving at the top of the stairs to find her trying to force the wardrobe doors closed in her old room.

'Hiding my parents' stuff,' she explained. 'Gabby's probably coming to stay on Saturday night. Isn't that great?'

'Yeah, I guess so,' he replied, lending a shoulder. Once the doors were shut and firmly locked, he turned to take her hands in his. 'How much of all that did you hear, earlier?' he asked, his eyes showing his concern.

She shrugged as she tried to make light of it. 'Enough to be able to tell Gabby that you're not coming on Sunday.'

Nodding, as though having expected as much, he said, 'I'm sorry, but I guess with all things considered, it's probably for the best.'

Unable to disagree, she slipped her arms round his neck and kissed him on the mouth. 'I could always take Heidi and Tom,' she suggested, 'if you wanted to stay here and have some quality time with Tiffany.'

He gave it some thought, but in the end sighed and shook his head. 'It's a lovely offer, but I don't think they'd go without her, and even if they did she'd manage to kick up somehow. No, it's best if we leave it this time.'

Secretly relieved, she kissed him again and felt the pleasure of being at home, just the two of them at last, with the little of what remained of the evening all to themselves. 'So what will you do with them while I'm gone?' she asked.

Turning to gaze across at the darkened window, he said, 'I haven't taken them to my parents' for a while, so I guess we'll go there. We might even stay over. She'll like that.'

Surprised, Alex said, 'Don't they have school the next morning?'

'Yes, but they can always take their stuff with them. Let's see what Gina says.' As he drew her closer and pressed his mouth back to hers she gave herself completely to the moment, determined not to let Tiffany's imagined smirk of satisfaction have more than a fleeting appearance. Not only had the girl managed to come between her father and Alex for the day on Sunday, it was looking as though she'd be able to pull it off for the whole night too.

Two up to you, Gina, she was thinking as she followed Jason back out to the landing. Except he was here, with her, most of the time, she reminded herself as she tightened her hand on his, and instead of feeling angry with Tiffany, she should remember that the child was the victim of a broken home. It naturally made her difficult, confused, unable to focus on anything but herself, much the same as many of the children in Alex's caseload. And yet Tiffany wasn't the same, because she had more love than many of Alex's troubled children could ever dream of, and a decent home in a pleasant and safe part of town with a large extended family who'd always be there for her if anything were ever to go wrong.

She had no idea how lucky she was, but children who were properly loved and cared for never did. And why should they? It would be wrong for them to be afraid and worried about anything more than the minor issues that came up in their worlds. Yet at the same time, how could Alex not feel more concern for the tender little souls who were out there suffering even now and who, God help them, had no one to turn to, or to save them, apart from a system that in some cases was tragically too late?

Ottilie was sobbing so hard she could barely catch her breath. She was sitting on the floor behind her bed, clinging to Boots, shuddering and gasping, desperate and afraid. A horrible thing had happened to her; she was bruised and bleeding, she didn't know what to do.

Erica was cracking apart inside and aching with loathing. Voices were echoing all the way through her, resonating across the years, wrapping themselves around her like choking hands. *You shouldn't have been born. I should never have had you. I SHOULD NEVER HAVE HAD YOU, YOU FILTHY LITTLE BITCH.*

Last night, or was it earlier, Erica had climbed up the walls, across the ceiling and back down to the floor. Round and round, up and down, she'd been unable to stop. Waves had come crashing in from the sea, sweeping her away on a terrible tide. She'd tried to hold on, but there was nothing to hold on to. She'd screamed and screamed as Brian shook and punched her, except it wasn't Brian, it was her stepfather, trying to kill her. His fists were like rocks smashing into her. She was naked and wet, drowning, drowning, gasping for air. He roared at her, over and over, grabbed her hair and forced her to look at him.

She'd passed out with her body convulsing to the tune of her heart, but she'd woken up, safe in her room, where her stepfather never came.

Suddenly she was back in Ottilie's room. Something had pushed her forward, a force inside that didn't belong to her, and now she was grabbing Ottilie and shaking her. 'That's enough,' she shouted. 'That's enough, do you hear me? *Stop crying.*'

Ottilie's head went down as she buried her face in Boots. Her tiny frame continued to jerk with the sobs she was trying desperately to hold in.

'What are you doing?' Brian demanded.

Erica rounded on him. 'Get away,' she hissed. 'Don't you dare come near us.'

'You're terrifying her,' he shouted.

For an instant Erica appeared astonished, then her head went back as she laughed.

He grabbed her hand, but she snatched it away. 'I'm terrifying her,' she cried, her eyes glittering wildly. '*I'm* terrifying her.'

'Look at her,' he challenged.

Ottilie was cowering even further behind the bed, her hands covering her head, blood trickling down one leg.

'I didn't do that to her,' Erica snarled. '*You* did that to her, you fucking pervert . . .' The punch to her jaw silenced her.

'Get a grip on yourself,' he growled.

Erica laughed again, loudly and shrilly.

Shoving her on to the landing, he dragged her to her own room and pushed her inside. 'Just remember,' he said, his face an inch from hers, 'if it weren't for Ottilie you'd be in prison now, so stay out of my business. Do you hear me? Keep taking your drugs, do as you're told and *stay out of my business.*'

Going back to Ottilie's room he scooped her into his arms and held her close. Her limbs trembled against him, sending tremors to every part of him. 'Ssh, ssh,' he soothed, stroking her hair. 'Everything's going to be all right. There's nothing to be afraid of.'

Ottilie continued to shake and shudder.

'I showed you on the computer how the other girls do it,' he said kindly, 'and they didn't make a fuss, did they?'

Ottilie kept her face averted as more tears streamed down her cheeks.

'I expect it hurt them the first time too, but you saw how much they like it now. You're going to like it too, my angel, I promise you. And it makes Daddy happy. You do want to make me happy, don't you?'

Ottilie couldn't answer. She didn't understand.

'There's a good girl,' he murmured. 'Now we'll go and put you in the bath shall we, get you nice and clean, and then you can come and sleep in my bed tonight. That'll be nice, won't it? You can bring Boots too, if you like, because I don't expect he'll want to be left on his own, will he?'

Chapter Five

Alex winced at the noise that assailed her as she pushed through the swing doors into the office. Everyone was talking at once, and apart from those tied up on phones, it didn't take long to work out that the others were all jabbering about the same thing. A rumour had reached their shores that Dean Valley Council was planning to merge the Kesterly hubs, thereby creating one supercentre for the area's social services, to be based in the southern district – and up to *twenty* jobs would go.

Hearing the news Alex felt a judder of nerves go through her. Though the new location would be good for her, in that it was closer to home, it wasn't going to mean very much if she ended up as one of the twenty. God, what a horrible thought. She loved her job, in many ways she *was* her job, so it would be like a character amputation if it were taken away. She couldn't imagine doing anything else, and certainly didn't want to; even less did she want to abandon any of her kids. It was unthinkable, simply undoable, especially when some of them had already been abandoned once, even several times, in their tragic little lives. Then there was the question of how she'd earn a living if she was forced to go. Social work was all she was qualified for, so she'd have to seek a place with another council, somewhere else in the country. But what about Jason? He wouldn't want to leave his kids, or his clients, and no way could she go without him.

Typical, Alex, get yourself all wound up about something you don't even know is true.

'There's a union meeting the Saturday after next,' someone shouted from the back of the room. 'We'll have to go.'

Dumping her bag on her desk, Alex was about to ask where the meeting was when the doors to the office banged open and an incandescent woman with wild red hair and even wilder eyes began ranting at Tamsin Green.

'If you think you can do so much fucking better,' she raged, shoving two grubby boys forward, 'then be my guest. Here they are. I'm sick to fucking death of you lot coming round my house, criticising everything I do, sticking your fucking noses in where they're not wanted, and I'm sick of these little bastards too.'

Clearly enjoying the moment, the boys began pulling faces and making gestures to say she was off her head.

Tamsin was rushing towards them, trying to calm the woman down and ushering her into a meeting room, while grabbing the boys too, and ignoring the V signs they were making behind their mother's back.

'Nothing like a soothing ease into the day,' someone quipped, making everyone laugh.

Finding she was still worked up about the possible loss of her job, Alex quickly reminded herself again that absolutely nothing had been confirmed yet, and anyway, even if it was true, she might not be amongst those chosen to go, so best to come down from the ceiling. She was good at what she did, was dedicated, and hardly anyone ever complained about her – apart from Wendy, who complained about everyone. No, she would be fine, she felt sure of it, especially when there were some in this hub who were known by everyone to be in the wrong job – which reminded her she was supposed to be covering for Ben today. What a joy!

Picking up her bag she carried it over to his desk and dumped it down again. Whatever new cases came in during this spell on duty, she'd already made up her mind that they could *not* be added to her caseload. She just didn't have the time to take on any more, so they'd have to go to someone else. Though she knew she'd stand more chance of offloading if Tommy was around, she was fully prepared to fight Wendy if she had to, in fact she might just enjoy it. On the other hand, if redundancies were in the offing, there was every chance Wendy would be involved in deciding who had to go, so it might be a good idea to try the impossible and stay on the right side of her.

Did Wendy actually have a right side?

After settling herself between the two other duty workers, Carmel and Janet, she was about to fire up the computer in front of her when the phone started to ring. Somehow, mysteriously, the other two managed to disappear, leaving her to deal with whatever fresh problem was waiting to cough itself down the line and into her world.

'Hello, children's services,' she sighed into the phone. She hadn't even had a coffee yet, so one of the absconders had better bring her one or this would be the last call she was taking.

There was a moment's silence, giving her hope that it might be a telemarketer with a stammer who she could simply hang up on, but then a woman's gravelly voice came down the line. 'I'm trying to find out if anyone's been to check on the little girl on North Hill yet. I rang before, and I spoke to the police yesterday. They said they were going to pass it on to you.'

Immediately feeling guilty for having forgotten all about Neil Osmond's call last evening, Alex said, 'Can you tell me who you are, please?'

'It don't matter who I am. I just wants you to make sure someone's going to check on that kiddie, because I'm telling you, something's not right in that house, and if the kind of thing that's going on there is what I think it is, then it's up to you lot to get her out of there.'

Digging into her bag for a pen (wasn't it just like Ben to go off leaving his desk locked?), Alex said, 'Can you tell me what you think is going on?'

'You know what I'm talking about, I don't want to have to put it into words.'

Understanding as much as she needed to from that, Alex said, 'So what evidence do you have to suggest that something's not right?'

'I just know. I can see it, feel it, every time I go there.'

'So you know the child, and the family?'

'No, I don't, but I can tell you their name's Wade and they live at number forty-two North Hill. I've seen the kiddie, and like I said, something's not right with her. She don't speak, for one thing, and the mother's strange. I've never seen the father, so I can't tell you nothing about him, but I think he lives there.'

Though the woman didn't sound like the kind of anonymous caller who was out to make mischief for an ex-spouse, or neighbour they'd fallen out with, it was never that easy to tell, so Alex said, 'It would help a lot if you'd give me your name. I realise that . . .'

'It's not going to happen. People get funny about those what call in social services and I got enough crap going on in my life without adding to it. I just want to know that little girl's safe, that's all.'

'But why exactly do you think she might not be?' Alex pressed.

'I told you, it's just a feeling I get when I go there.'

Waving out to Saffy as she left the office, Alex said, 'Do you go there often? How well do you actually know the family?'

'I already said, not at all. I just makes deliveries now and again and that woman what lives there, she's not normal – or she isn't in my book, anyway. Listen, I told you all this before when I rang. I spoke to a bloke the last couple of times, he said he'd look into it, but I don't reckon anything's happened, that's why I called the police, but they told me I had to call you.'

The pieces were starting to fall into place now: Ben complaining about an anonymous caller who'd rung up about a kid on North Hill; Ben saying he'd made all the follow-up calls and there was no need to take it any further. Ben describing this woman as a nutter. Though she didn't sound like a nutter to Alex, maybe she'd said something while talking to Ben to tip him off in that direction. Or something had come to light during his follow-up calls. Hadn't he said that the father worked at Kesterly Rise Primary? She could easily check, and would, once this call was over. 'Do you know the little girl's name?' she asked the woman.

'No, I told you, she don't speak, and the mother never says much either.'

'Have you ever seen any injuries on the child?'

'Well, no, not so's you'd notice, anyway.'

'Does she look undernourished or uncared for, maybe unwashed, messy hair, dirty clothes, that sort of thing?'

'No, in that respect she seems quite normal. Maybe she is. I'm just telling you what my gut is telling me. Something's not right in that house and I reckon it ought to be looked into.'

'OK. Would you happen to have a telephone number for the family?'

'As a matter of fact I have, not that they ever answer it.'

After jotting it down, Alex said, 'And is there a number I can call you on if . . .'

'No, I already said, I don't want to get involved. Just go and see the girl, prove me wrong if you like, I'd be happier if you did than if you didn't,' and the line went dead.

Immediately trying 1471, Alex wasn't surprised to find that the woman had withheld her number, so turning on the computer she brought up the duty log for the past couple of weeks.

It didn't take long to find Ben's notes for both calls, and details of the background checks he'd carried out. From these Alex quickly learned that Ottilie (sweet name) Wade was three and a half years old, and that the family had moved to Kesterly from Northumbria just over a year ago to make a new start after the loss of their son, Jonathan, to an asthma attack.

Ben's notes went on to detail a phone conversation he'd had with Brian Wade, the deputy head of Kesterly Rise Primary, during which Wade had told him of accusations that had been made against him, back in Northumbria, following his son's death. An anonymous caller – female – had rung the headmaster of the school where Wade was teaching to warn him that Wade was dangerous, shouldn't be around children, and that his new baby (presumably Ottilie) was now at risk. The school hadn't contacted their local social services over this, or the police, the reason being that the caller – according to Mr Wade – was known to be a paranoid schizophrenic. Apparently she'd targeted several other teachers over the years, accusing them of anything from theft, to child abuse, to attempted murder. In Wade's case she'd gone a step further in accusing him of killing his own son.

Clicking on to the next page of Ben's report, Alex read that the schizophrenic woman, whose name she hadn't yet come across, had apparently managed to track Wade down to Kesterly Rise where he was now employed, and had once again begun her campaign of harassment. 'Mr Wade is extremely keen for us NOT to contact his wife about this,' Ben had written, 'as it's likely to cause her a great deal of unnecessary distress at a time when she's finally managing to get over the loss of their son.'

So that would be the reason no one had gone to the house, or tried to speak to the mother. Wade had convinced Ben that he was the victim of a deranged woman, and that his wife was as fragile as an egg.

Sitting back in her chair, Alex let out a long breath as she looked at the child's name scribbled on a pad beside the computer, and waited for her mind to clear in order to start this over again. The thing that was bothering her the most for the moment was the fact that the woman who'd just rung in had had a local accent. Of course, this didn't preclude her living in Northumbria, it just didn't seem all that likely, especially when she made deliveries to the house.

Setting that aside for now, she began going through the database to find out the name of Ottilie Wade's health visitor. To her surprise, Ottilie's name brought up no results. (Hadn't Ben noticed this?) However, the child was registered with a GP in Kesterly South, Dr Timothy Aiden, who Alex didn't know, but had heard of. After leaving a message with the receptionist for the doctor to call when he'd finished surgery, she dialled the number the anonymous caller had given her for the Wades' home.

After letting the phone ring for some time she was on the point of hanging up when it stopped. She waited for someone to say hello, but nothing happened, so she said it herself.

There was no response, but she felt certain someone was there. Guessing from the faint sounds of breathing that it was a child, she said, very gently, 'Is that Ottilie?'

Again no response, but she could still hear the breathing.

'If that's Ottilie,' Alex said, 'can you go and get your mummy please? I'd like to speak to her.'

More silence, but Alex could sense the child still listening. 'Ottilie, who's at home with you?' she asked, concerned now that the child might be alone.

No reply.

'Is someone else there? A grown-up?'

At last someone spoke, but the woman's voice

was distant and cross as she said, 'Ottilie, stop playing with the phone,' and a moment later there was the clatter of the receiver going down.

Immediately Alex dialled the number again, but this time it was busy, and it stayed that way for the next several minutes, until on the last attempt it simply rang and rang with no one picking up.

Digging out the number of Kesterly Rise Primary, she went through to the office and asked to speak to Brian Wade.

'Hang on,' the voice said at the other end, 'I'll see if I can find him. Can I ask who's calling please?'

Alex told her, and propped the phone under her chin to carry on working as she waited.

Brian Wade was in a first-floor classroom, over-looking the playground. He was perched on a small desk with his laptop on the windowsill in front of him showing images of the children below playing. Using the mousepad he zoomed and panned, clicked to capture or record, then moved on.

As a founding member of the exclusive Internet service he and two other like-minded individuals had formed a few years ago, he'd quickly learned the vital techniques of online security. Having a partner who was chief executive of a global enterprise that specialised in identity and access management, virtual copyright protection and video surveillance, obviously helped. This partner regularly advised all new members on how to make their online activities as secure as the most sophisticated software would allow, and ultimately all but untraceable to their identities in the real world.

For the site, each member had a virtual name. Brian's was Tiger.

As Tiger he was a frequent contributor to his own site. In fact, he had enjoyed some considerable success with the sale of the videos and photographs he had posted. Having such ready access to children put him at an advantage, of course. Even so, it was his submissions of Ottilie that had made his teaser links the most viewed – and the full material the most expensive to download.

She was such a pretty girl, he couldn't be prouder of her if he tried – and it was no surprise at all that she'd found so many fans.

She'd soon have many more, once he got round to shooting the footage his eager members were waiting for, the footage he'd already titled *Riding the Tiger*. In truth, he wasn't particularly interested in the money, at least not for himself. All proceeds went into Ottilie's savings account; after all, it was only right that they should be hers.

Shooting the video of the next time wasn't going to be easy. However, it would help, he felt sure, if he kept showing her how good other little girls were who made movies with their daddies. It had worked a dream with the photographs; she'd become much more compliant after that, almost competitive he thought, if she were capable of such a feeling at such a tender age. She'd certainly seemed to understand how important it was to be a good girl for Daddy and make him happy. Soon she would learn other ways of winning his favour, and in no time at all he was sure she would become very good at it indeed.

It was a pity these early attempts were making her cry and unsettling her mother, but at least there had been no blood last night, and the bruising and swelling from the first time were already going down. It was true what they said of little girls, they were very spongy at that age, far more malleable – and adaptable – than most would imagine.

Continuing to watch the screen, he felt the jolts of pleasure inside him building towards a feverish pitch. There were so many fresh, uninhibited little souls tearing about the nets and hoops in the playground, swinging from bars and tumbling into tangled heaps, that it was almost too much to bear. He shut his eyes and allowed himself the indulgence of a blessed few moments. The whistle would sound soon and the children would return inside; before that he needed to secure his computer and avail himself of the staff facilities.

He was on his way back to his office, laptop tucked under his arm, hands still damp from being washed, when the school secretary called out to him.

'There you are,' she declared, catching up with him. 'There's someone on the line for you. Alex Lake, from social services. She didn't say what it was about.'

Feeling a prickle of unease grazing over his skin, he quickly reminded himself that it could be about any one of the children at the school, and even if it wasn't, he simply needed to behave as he had before, with calm and composure, and be in no particular hurry to take the call. Haste could be interpreted as anxiety or worse, panic, and he really didn't want that. On the other hand, he didn't want to appear indifferent either. 'Thank you,' he said pleasantly to the secretary, 'could you tell her I'll call back at the end of the school day?'

He'd probably be too busy by then to remember, and being as frantic as social workers always were these days, she might just forget she'd even asked him to be in touch. Like everyone else, she'd probably be getting ready for her weekend, and given what an exhausting job she had, he could imagine that she was very much looking forward to having a couple of days off.

He had to admit, he was looking forward to it himself.

'Bugger!' Alex swore as she looked at her watch. It was already five o'clock, and being POETS day – piss off early tomorrow's Saturday – she didn't imagine there'd be much chance of finding the deputy head of Kesterly Rise still at his desk. However, it was always worth trying, and as she punched the number into the phone she began clearing up her desk.

Either the secretary hadn't passed her message on, or Mr Wade had been too busy (or reluctant) to return her call. While she, being so tied up with other things, had let the time tick on well past four, when she'd intended to try again if she hadn't heard anything from him by then.

As the line clicked through to the school's answering service, she decided not to leave a message and carried on stuffing things into her bag. She needed to get out of here fast now, or she'd end up being the only one left with Wendy, who, irritating person that she was, was refusing to be drawn on the rumours of a merger with the southerly hub and subsequent job losses.

Wouldn't it be great if Wendy turned out to be one of the twenty to go and Tommy was promoted in her place? Actually, Alex didn't really want to see anyone out of work, even Wendy, so she was going to hold out for the next best thing, which would be for Wendy to be hauled even higher up the ladder in order to make room for Tommy to become overall manager.

Though there was a rehearsal scheduled for this evening, it wasn't due to start until eight, so deciding she had time to make a detour over to North Hill, she turned her car in that direction as she left the business park. For some reason it was irking her that Brian Wade hadn't bothered to ring back, so if it achieved nothing else, an unscheduled drop-in would remind him that even busy men in his position needed to respond to social services. After all, she might not have been calling about his personal issues, which he no doubt felt he'd already adequately dealt with when talking to Ben (though not to her satisfaction, it had to be said). She could have been trying to talk to him about one of his pupils, so for that reason alone he should have found time to pick up the phone.

Unsurprisingly, the traffic along the seafront was at a standstill, so setting up her Bluetooth to start tackling her personal calls she was about to contact Jason when he rang.

'Hi,' she said cheerily. 'Please don't tell me there are any technical problems, not at this late stage.'

'OK, I won't, because there aren't,' he responded. 'Everything else we need is being delivered first thing, so we should be able to start rigging by ten.'

Feeling a bloom of pleasure opening inside her, she said, 'Brilliant. You're a genius. Are you home already?'

'Just got here, and I have some news I thought you'd want to hear. I spoke to Heather Hancock from the *Gazette* earlier, and she's going to come to the opening tomorrow.'

Amazed, and thrilled – then worried – Alex said dubiously, 'That's fantastic – I hope. I mean, it'll be great to get a mention in the local paper, or even on their website, provided it's good, of course.'

'How can it not be when everyone who's seen a rehearsal has said how hilarious it is? You've done a fantastic job with Hailey and the script, and with the staging, and the cast are naturals.'

Feeling that this might be true, Alex said, 'They'd love to hear you say that, and actually they are pretty good for a bunch of amateurs. No, they're better than good – they're great. Anyway, the point is, it should be a fun evening, if nothing else, lots of laughs and a wild old party after. Is your mum coming, by the way?'

'Absolutely, and Janice and Rick,' he added, referring to his sister and brother-in-law. 'They're bringing a load of mates, remember, and the guys from rugger have all got tickets. They're really looking forward to it.'

'The booze-up after, more like,' she teased. 'Now please tell me that Heather Hancock isn't bringing her best mate Gina, because I'll go . . .'

'It's OK, Gina definitely won't be there,' he assured her. 'My sister offered to bring the kids, but Gina's doing something else with them tomorrow night, so we're in the clear.'

Managing not to express her relief too energetically, since it was so great it would have sounded offensive, she said, 'Are you still taking them to your mum's on Sunday?'

'Yeah, it's all fixed. We'll go in the morning, in time for lunch, and stay over so she can make a really big fuss of them.'

Since she could hardly begrudge his mother time

with her own grandchildren (only her son), Alex said, 'I'm sure they'll love it, I just wish I could be there too.' There was no point in telling him how much she'd prefer it if he was coming with her to Gabby's on Sunday; he couldn't make it, but would if he could, so she needed to accept it and move on. 'I should ring off now,' she said, as she finally turned on to North Hill. 'I might be back a bit later than I expected. I'll let you know when I'm on my way, but you should go on and eat if you're hungry.'

A few minutes later she was on the wrong side of North Hill (the one without sea views), turning left into the drive of number forty-two. Though it wasn't a large house compared to the massive, double-fronted B & B on one side and the purpose-built holiday flats on the other, it still managed to exude a certain Victorian grandeur, she thought, as she came to a stop in front of a double garage that had clearly been added on in more recent times. At first glance the place didn't appear neglected: the paintwork was fresh enough and the tall sash windows were clean. However, the branches of a giant maple towering up from the back of the house almost smothered the roof and upper storey, which surely had to make the place quite gloomy inside.

Buffeted about by a brisk wind, she ran to the front porch and finding a button next to the door she gave it a push. Satisfied by the chimes that rang inside she listened for any sounds of someone responding, but as the seconds ticked up to a minute nothing happened.

She peered through the letter box. There were no lights on that she could see, but it wasn't dark out, only stormy, and besides if there was anyone at home, they could easily be in a room at the back of the house. Or out in the garden.

She rang the bell again and turned to look down the drive to where the open gate was trapped by a tangle of overgrown bushes and the traffic beyond was speeding imperviously by. She couldn't imagine there being much of a community around here, not with most of the properties being run as businesses and staffed by itinerant foreigners. The nearest shops were over the other side of the hill, close to the seafront, and the only park she could think of in walking distance was Nibletts, which was more of an old-age pensioners' garden than a children's play-ground. She wondered where Ottilie went to nursery – since she hadn't managed to find one yet with Ottilie's name on its register she was becoming concerned that the child might not attend one at all. That certainly wouldn't be good.

Since this was part of what she was here to find out, she gave the bell another prod and stepped back to look at the upstairs windows. There was no sign of anyone, and since there were no other cars in the driveway, and the side gate turned out to be locked, she guessed she'd have to accept that she wasn't going to get any answers today. So, taking out an official slip she rested it on top of her satchel and scribbled a note asking Mr and Mrs Wade to call her at the office or on her mobile number as soon as possible.

After posting it through the door she ran back to her car, and hearing her personal mobile ringing, she quickly grabbed it from the passenger seat as she sank down behind the wheel.

'Hi Gabby, everything OK?' she asked, tugging loose her seat belt and starting the engine.

'Not really,' Gabby wailed. 'Martin and the kids

have all gone down with some bug. They're in a terrible state, I hardly know what to do with them.'

Realising exactly where this was going, Alex felt so crushed that it was a moment before she could say, 'Do you know how they got it?'

'Probably from school, you know how these things go round like wildfire. Anyway, I'm sure they'll all be fine again in a couple of days, but it's going to mean that I can't make it tomorrow, I'm afraid. And I don't think the barbecue on Sunday's likely to happen now either. Poor Martin, he can hardly stand up he's so weak.'

Since her brother-in-law was a GP there wasn't much point in asking if they'd called the doctor, so all Alex could say was, 'Well, please wish them well from me, and I'll miss you tomorrow. I guess Aunt Sheila won't be coming either.'

'She's as upset about it as I am,' Gabby assured her, 'but there's always next weekend, isn't there? I know it's not the same as opening night, and there probably won't be a party . . . Oh hang on, we're going to a wedding next Saturday. The daughter of one of Aunt Sheila's friends is getting married, Kathy Austin. I don't know if you've ever met her.'

'I don't think so,' Alex replied, feeling ludicrously dismal as she pulled out of the Wades' drive to rejoin the traffic. What difference did it make whether they were there or not? She was going to be so rushed off her feet she probably wouldn't even notice, and anyway, she'd hardly have time to talk to them. And what if it turned out to be a disaster? She was going to feel pretty thankful then that they weren't around to witness her humiliation, or try to make things better afterwards by insisting that everyone thought it was brilliant when they patently hadn't.

Instead of driving along feeling sorry for herself, she decided, she was going to shed her disappointment like a skin right now, along with her concerns about a little girl she hadn't even met – and all the other kids who made up the tragic circus of her caseload – and float merrily off into the weekend with no more thoughts about anything apart from the play, the party after and the fact that Jason was going to be there for her, even if nobody else was.

Erica was sitting on the bed watching Ottilie at her play desk, trying to fit the large, irregular pieces of a wooden jigsaw together. The ringing on the doorbell a few minutes ago had distracted her, but only to make her turn to her mother to see if she was going to answer. When Erica didn't move Ottilie had gone back to her puzzle and hadn't looked away from it since.

Brian had called to warn her that a social worker had been in touch again. 'If they call the house, or come round, you know it wouldn't be wise to speak to anyone without me there,' he'd added, the mildness of his tone belying how terrified he must have been.

Terror for Erica was the void that was swallowing her up from within, pulling at her skin, her bones, crushing her heart, her very soul, sucking the blood from her veins. She could see hands growing from trees outside, waving, clawing the windows, smashing the glass to get in. Faces were in the sky, floating about her feet, emerging from the walls, their voices screaming in her head. *You killed your boy, you killed him. Kill her too. Do it now, before he comes home.*

Save her. She's not you. Let her go.

Coward! Slut! Wicked, evil child. Open your legs; bend at the waist; do as you're fucking well told.

She's not you.

Kill her.

She tried to focus her gaze on Ottilie's bent head, the wispy dark curls, and the tilt of concentration. A terrible rush of anger was swelling up inside her. She clutched her head, scratched at her face. 'Stop,' she screeched at the voices. 'Stop, stop!'

Ottilie dropped to the floor, curling tightly into a ball with her bear.

Erica reached down and hauled her back to her feet. 'You shouldn't be here,' she spat in her face. 'You have to go. Go on, go,' and shoving her towards the door she snatched up the jigsaw and hurled it against the wall.

Ottilie ran to the stairs. Her tiny legs were shaking so hard that she fell, tumbling over and over, bumping against the banister, scraping on the carpet until she reached the bottom in a crumpled, helpless little heap behind the front door.

Outside the wind was blowing savagely around the house as Brian Wade pulled into the drive and got out of his car. At the top of the stairs Erica looked down at her daughter, aghast at the snakes crawling, writhing, slithering open-mouthed towards her.

Chapter Six

Alex was up, and at her computer, by six on the morning of opening night. No matter how crazy the day was going to be, and she was expecting it to get pretty manic, she simply had to finish off her outstanding assessments before Monday. She might also try giving the Wades another call, to show she meant business, but when she got round to it there was no answer again, and apparently they didn't have voicemail.

By the time Jason left at eight thirty she was about done with her paperwork, so standing up for a luxurious stretch she watched him from the landing window, running through the rain down into the village where he was about to start rigging the hall. Her heart gave a flutter of love and nerves. The way he'd embraced her theatre projects since they'd been together, taking them as seriously as she did and doing whatever he could to help, made her feel so close to him, and incredibly lucky to have met him. She sometimes wondered if she let him know often enough how she felt about him, and was suddenly sure that she didn't. This was something she was going to put right later, after the opening-night party, she decided, and seeing him turn at the bottom of the hill to look up and wave, as though sensing her watching him, she felt her heart fill up all over again.

He really was so wonderfully special.

Deciding to give the Wades another try she picked up her work mobile and redialled, but still no reply. So, scrolling through to Lizzie Walsh's number, she pressed to connect to her colleague instead. Their looming visit to the Princes on Tuesday wasn't really something she wanted to discuss today, but her diary for Monday was so full that there might not be another opportunity for them to speak before it was time to go.

'Hey, Alex, everything OK?' Lizzie asked sleepily. 'What time is it?'

'Almost nine,' Alex replied with a smile. 'Don't tell me you were out on a bender last night?' Since Lizzie was probably closer to fifty than forty and had five children, two dogs and a mother-in-law, but no husband, living with her, Alex didn't imagine pub-crawling or clubbing was really her thing.

'What do you think?' Lizzie chuckled. 'A girl's got to do something to obliterate the torments of the day. So what can I do for you? Oh, this is going to be about our fun day out on Tuesday, yes?'

'It is,' Alex confirmed. 'I hope you got my text expressing my undying gratitude for agreeing to come with me.'

'Well someone has to take care of you, and I's a bit of a rougher diamond than you is, girl, so a bit more cut out for it. So sweet little Polly's gone and got herself another STD, and the doctor's earned himself a few bruises for reporting it.'

'That's about the size of it, though I'm not sure the police have been able to prove that yet. Anyway, all we have to do is get a sense of what's going on in the house, if she's having sex willingly, or being forced into it.'

Lizzie laughed. 'That girl's been putting it out since she was twelve, and from what I hear she's on the game these days.'

'And she's only fourteen – what is the world coming to?'

Lizzie chuckled again.

'Well, if she is on the game and sharing out her nasty little disease,' Alex continued, 'then lucky her, she'll have to come with us.'

'Good luck with that,' Lizzie responded. 'You going to take the lead, right, I'll be there as backup. They less likely to mess with me, but you never know, that mother of theirs sure ain't someone you want to get on the wrong side of. Have you ever met her?'

'No, and I was really hoping to keep it that way, given everything I've heard about her and what a charming son she's produced. I'm still trying to find out if they've made any charges stick for attacking the doctor. I don't suppose you've heard anything?'

'Not a word, but I'll see what I can come up with between now and then. So what time, and where shall we meet? I suggest we only take one car.'

'Absolutely, so let's hook up at the Minster layby opposite Tesco, yes? Say about ten?' Alex suggested.

'Perfect. See you then.'

'Hang on, hang on, aren't you coming tonight?'

'Oh, hell yes, I was forgetting about that. Of course I'm going to be there. The whole office is coming. So break a leg, all of you. That should make for an interesting show,' she added wryly.

Laughing as she rang off, Alex went downstairs to the kitchen and found a bowl of muesli and fruit all laid out, with milk, yoghurt and even a spoon next to it. Smiling at Jason's dadish habits, she settled down to start eating, knowing that this was probably the only meal she'd manage today.

Everything was going so marvellously to plan.

Nothing to worry about, so no point trying to create a problem out of thin air. If something was going to go wrong it would find a way to erupt soon enough.

After making a coffee she took it back upstairs and checked her personal mobile. Someone surely must have a problem by now, or at the very least a question only she could answer.

However, to her amazement, and deepening concern, it seemed no one did, so just after ten she made her own dash through the rain down to the village hall, wondering what she was going to find. It turned out to be the set and lights going up a treat, the chairs being carried out of storage by a couple of the locals and three ladies from the WI already on site unpacking their trestle tables ready to lay out the refreshments their members were delivering later.

'I'm stunned,' she told Mattie, who came to greet her with a pencil in her mouth and a curly wig in each hand. Mattie was plump, plain and hopelessly awkward with people she didn't know. With those that she did, like Alex and most of the cast, she felt confident enough to come out of her shell, and it never failed to touch Alex to see how happy it made her to be so fully involved.

With a frown, Mattie turned back towards the stage. 'Isn't it weird? I'm beginning to think this production is blessed by the Muses themselves,' she declared.

'Oh God,' Alex shuddered, going after her as she started across the hall. 'Don't tempt fate, please. We've still got the rest of the day to get through yet. Does everyone know it's a two o'clock call for the dress?'

'I'm presuming so, but I've made a note to text reminders at eleven. Jason!' she shouted. 'Can the disco ball go any higher? The guys are going to walk into it where it is.'

'It's OK,' he called back, 'it's not staying there.' Catching Alex's eye he gave her a wink and hoisted himself up on to the DJ stand where one of his helpers was rigging the flashing lights.

'Any news from Scott?' Alex asked Mattie, referring to the DJ who'd put himself in charge of the music.

'Not yet,' Mattie answered. 'He's not due for another hour, though. He won't let us down.'

'He's only had one rehearsal,' Alex reminded her anxiously, 'and the timing has to be right or half the jokes are going to go flat on their faces.'

'Tell you what, let's worry when we have to,' Mattie advised, and grabbing a rail of costumes she began wheeling it backstage.

By two o'clock everyone who was supposed to be in the hall was in the hall, and by three Alex, Mattie and Hailey were in the middle row of the audience seating, watching cast and crew take their opening positions. The only hitch they'd encountered so far was Scott getting stuck in traffic, but he was here now, all set up and ready to roll.

Minutes later the opening scene was under way and it wasn't long before those seeing the piece for the first time – Jason's helpers, the WI ladies and the make-up artists hired in for the day – were starting to laugh. Alex might have heard the jokes a hundred times already, but they could still make her smile. However, the cast, clearly energised by their costumes and mounting excitement, were giving every sign of going straight over the top. It was to be expected; it often happened during a dress run, so Alex simply made a note to remind them to bring it down for the actual show, and continued to revel in how much they were enjoying themselves.

During the break at the end of the first act she jumped up onstage to discuss a slightly different approach to the third scene of the second act with Johnny and Sarah, the two leads. Since it only involved them and they were always highly responsive to her suggestions, it took moments for them to give it a quick try-out and agree. Then using the rest of the break to dish out technical notes and lashings of praise, she seized the tea the stage manager had grabbed for her, and sank down between Hailey and Mattie again to watch the second part.

Though it suffered from a few late cues and a couple of missed lines, on the whole there was little for her to be concerned about. 'Just don't anyone get in a car, walk down the stairs or do anything at all to jeopardise your brilliant performances,' she instructed the cast, who had gathered onstage for final notes. 'That's all for now. I don't want to start fussing you with niggly stuff, and that's all it would be. You know where it went wrong, so you know where to put it right. I'll see you all back here this evening, when I honestly think we're going to bring down the house.'

Loving their beaming faces as they started to mill

off the stage, looking ludicrous, hilarious and downright huggable in the gender-swap costumes, she turned to Mattie and Hailey and as the three of them squeezed hands and jumped for joy, Jason flipped out his iPhone to capture the moment.

By seven thirty the audience was starting to fill the hall and to Alex's delight, as she greeted them at the WI bar with laughs and warm embraces, it soon became clear that just about everyone was treating this as a special occasion, since they were all so smartly turned out. She herself was wearing a lemon silk shift dress with gold strappy sandals, while Jason, much to everyone's amusement, had chosen to don a tuxedo for the occasion. Completely over the top, of course, especially as he was working, but he looked so handsome in it that Alex experienced little shivers of pride every time she caught sight of him.

'Don't look now,' a voice muttered in her ear, 'Heather Hancock's just turned up.'

Glancing, all intrigue, at Mattie, Alex leaned back against Salina, Mulgrove's sensation-with-a-sewing-machine, who'd whipped up some amazing costumes for the production. 'Who's she with?' she murmured, needing to be sure it wasn't Gina.

'Actually, she might be on her own,' Salina replied, trying to be discreet about checking. 'No, hang on, there's a bloke with her, and let me tell you, he's not half bad.'

Unable to stop herself, Alex stole a quick look over her shoulder, and almost choked on her drink as Heather smiled at her so sweetly sugar might have dripped from her lips.

After giving her a wave, Alex turned back to

Mattie and Salina. 'Did you see that?' she murmured. 'I think she likes me.'

As the others spluttered with laughter, Mattie said, 'Brace yourself, she's coming this way.'

Alex barely had time to turn round before Heather was upon her, all corkscrew red hair, cobalt-blue eyes and bored, I'm-too-good-for-this-amateur-stuff sort of smile. 'Looks like a reasonable turnout,' she commented, kissing air either side of Alex's cheeks.

'Even better than we hoped for,' Alex confirmed. 'And lovely that you could make it.' Though they knew each other vaguely from school, since Heather was five years older they'd rarely mixed, at least not by intention. However, they'd occasionally found themselves at the same party, such as the one where Alex and Jason had met. Their paths had also clashed a couple of times more recently, firstly when Heather had managed to get some of her facts wrong in reports she'd done on one of Alex's cases. Since this wasn't something Alex was prepared to take lying down, she'd thought nothing of calling Heather up to put her straight and demand a correction. Heather had refused, so Alex had contacted the editor, and got her way. The second time Heather had failed to cover herself in glory, at least in Alex's eyes, was when she'd given a mean-spirited one-star rating to a new restaurant in town, which could hardly be blamed for the power cut that had taken out all the ovens on its first night. The Water de la Mer belonged to a friend of Alex's, and consequently she'd fired off a hotly worded protest to the paper, which had found its way on to the letters page.

She didn't imagine she and Heather Hancock were ever going to be best mates.

'Can I introduce you to Greg Sanders,' Heather

was saying in her best throaty voice, as she turned to put a hand on her very handsome escort's arm. 'Greg, this is Alex Lake, the director of tonight's *spectacle*.'

Wincing at the French pronunciation of the word which was clearly meant to belittle her production, Alex turned to Greg Sanders, who she knew was the *Gazette*'s sports correspondent. 'Lovely to meet you,' she said charmingly. 'I hope you're going to enjoy the evening.'

'I'm actually really looking forward to it,' he replied earnestly. 'I've been hearing great things about it.'

Wanting to snigger at the flinty edges now cracking Heather's smile, Alex was about to respond when Heather gave an odd little laugh.

'He has a very unusual sense of humour,' she declared. 'It takes some getting used to. Anyway, we want to wish everyone good luck – oops, sorry, we're not supposed to say that in the theatre, are we? But hey, this is a village hall, so does it count?'

Sensing Salina and Mattie bristling either side of her, Alex replied diplomatically, 'Let's just say we like to get into the spirit of things, and there are so many people here who've put so much into tonight it would be a pity to . . .'

'Oh, of course,' Heather interrupted. 'It's a real community bash, I understand that. It's why I'm here, of course. We want to do our bit at the *Gazette* to support the arts in our region.'

'Well, I'm very happy about that, and Mattie's sorted out some good seats for you, so if you'll excuse me I'd better go and check on what's happening backstage.'

Finding every bit as much chaos in the makeshift

dressing rooms as she'd left ten minutes ago, she set about bolstering everyone's confidence with a few slugs of Dutch courage and generally assuring them that nothing was going to go wrong.

Famous last words, she was thinking with her fingers tightly crossed as the curtains slid apart for the first act to begin, and creeping quietly out into the hall she went to stand in the aisle with Mattie and Hailey. Spotting Jason watching her from the lighting gantry, she gave him an anxious little smile and loved him for the way he came back with such an assertive thumbs-up.

To her dismay the first few minutes seemed to misfire badly, creating a sense of confusion in the room that made her wish she could shout cut and send the actors back to the top. She knew nerves were getting the better of them, and had actually expected it, but she'd hoped, prayed, it wouldn't happen.

Eventually, to her relief, they seemed to find the flow and as the audience got carried along with them, understanding at last what was going on – that blokes were having a taste of what it was like to be girls on a night out, and vice versa – the hilarity began to kick in. The first chat-up line, 'Do you believe in love at first sight, or do I have to walk by again?' though not original, was delivered so vampishly by Johnny as Jazzer (short for Jasmine), in his bouffant wig, mini-dress and five-inch heels, that he had to pause for almost a minute to wait for the laughter to die down.

The next showstopper came when binge-drinker Bonnie, played by Stuart Guard the local handyman, slurred his own chat-up line: 'I've heard you're better at sex than anyone, you just need a partner.'

Minutes later, the dance around handbags by four of the men virtually brought the house down. What made it even funnier was that the actors found themselves corpsing as they tried to play the next lines.

There was a story to the piece, naturally, which was part romance, part tragedy, but with so much laughter it wasn't always easy to follow. Realising she should have prepared for that, Alex whispered to Hailey that they might need to cut some of the one-liners for the next two shows, and was relieved when Hailey nodded agreement.

By the end of the evening everyone was clapping so hard that if Alex hadn't signalled the stage manager to keep the curtains closed after the seventh encore, they might have been at it all night. OK, the audience was made up mostly of friends and family, but she'd noticed plenty of unfamiliar faces in the crowd too, and every one of them had seemed to be having a good time. Even Heather Hancock had managed to crack a smile or two, she'd noticed, though mostly she'd been assuming her important-critic pose, with an ear cocked towards the dialogue and a pen poised over her page.

'I think you could call it a triumph,' Jason murmured drily in Alex's ear as he came to find her. 'Come on, let's get to the bar and meet your public before those scene-stealing actors get their kit on and start making with the limelight again.'

There turned out to be so many congratulations waiting to assail them, especially when the cast began drifting through, that it started to look doubtful they'd ever get out of the hall and across to the pub.

'Alex? Is that you?' a voice called from somewhere behind her.

Turning round, Alex gave a cry of surprise to see

Maggie and Ron Fenn caught up in the crowd. 'I didn't know you were coming,' she said, pushing through to greet them. 'How lovely to see you.'

'You too,' Maggie said warmly. 'I wondered if it was you when I saw your name in the programme. I can't tell you how much we enjoyed it.'

'That's fantastic,' Alex beamed, trying not to wince at Ron's vicelike handshake, while glancing up at the man who was with them. He was tall and very striking, almost fierce in a way, she thought, with such intense black eyes and strong features she wasn't sure whether he was handsome or not.

'Alex, this is my older brother, Anthony,' Maggie announced with a playful twinkle.

Realising from the tease in Maggie's voice, not to mention the look of Anthony, that he was definitely the younger of the two, Alex said lightly as she shook his hand, 'Aha, the fisherman with a liking for fast cars.'

Appearing surprised, and amused, he glanced at his sister as he said, 'Has someone been talking about me?'

'As if,' Maggie responded, with a roll of her eyes.

Enjoying the interaction between them, Alex said, 'Actually, I saw your car when I visited your sister's last week . . .'

'. . . and because she can't keep anything to herself she told you where I was,' he came in, 'along with my name, address, date of birth, profession . . . I can hear it now. Anyway, I have to compliment you on an excellent play. I'm very glad I came.'

'Thank you,' she responded warmly. 'We're having a party across the road at the pub if you'd like to join us.'

'Oh no, we don't want to inflict ourselves,' Maggie

replied, 'and we shouldn't hog you any more, either. I'm sure everyone wants to talk to you, but I couldn't leave without saying hello – and well done, obviously.'

'And thank you,' Ron added, half crushing her hand again.

'Just one quick thing,' Maggie said quietly, turning her back to the others. 'I don't suppose you have any news of Oliver.'

Alex shook her head sadly. 'If he was in my area . . .'

'I know, I know, and I probably shouldn't have asked, but he was such a sweet little soul. We've got a lovely little girl coming to stay from the end of next week, so I expect I'll fall for her too. It's a much more difficult business, this fostering, than I'd counted on, but I love it all the same.'

'It can be very rewarding,' Alex assured her, 'but it's definitely not for the faint-hearted.' *And wouldn't it be wonderful if we had more like you*, she was thinking. Catching Anthony's eye she felt herself reddening slightly as she smiled at him. 'Thanks for coming,' she said, shaking his hand again. 'It's not often we can boast a London lawyer in our midst.'

His expression was wry as he said, 'Some would consider that a bit of a blessing.'

Laughing as she waved them off, Alex was soon swamped by more hugs and congratulations from Jason's mother and sister, followed by Mattie's elderly parents, most of the village and just about everyone from work. She was on such a high that she barely had time to mind that neither Gabby nor Aunt Sheila had thought to send a text before or after the show to find out how it was all going.

They'd definitely call tomorrow, she assured herself, and if they didn't, well, she'd just call them.

'What's happened to Heather?' she asked Jason as he fought his way back to her. 'Is she still here?'

'No, I just walked her out. She didn't want to stay for the party.'

Quietly thrilled, Alex said, 'Did she say anything about the show?'

'Not really, but there again I didn't ask. So who was the chap you were talking to?'

She had to think for a moment. 'Oh, you mean Maggie Fenn's brother. I just met him, but Maggie took care of one of my kids for a few days recently. Why, you're not jealous, are you?'

Eyeing her dangerously, he said, 'Do I need to be?'

Laughing, she linked his arm to launch the exodus over to the pub. 'We're due back here at eleven in the morning to start the big clear-up,' she told him, 'but typically of you, you've managed to get out of it.'

'I'll come in earlier to derig the lights and stuff,' he assured her. 'So what are you going to do in the afternoon now that Gabby's barbecue is off?'

'Not sure yet,' she replied, knowing she'd have to think of something, or the come-down after tonight might sink her to a place she wouldn't much want to be. 'Are you still planning to stay over at your mother's?'

Ducking as one of their neighbours came to try and grasp him in a headlock, he said, 'Yeah, if that's OK.'

'Of course it is. I'm just wondering if maybe I should come too.'

He seemed surprised. 'Do you want to?' he asked cautiously.

In truth she wasn't sure that she did. 'It might be easier, me being with the kids, if your parents are there too,' she pointed out.

'But if they start acting up . . . I wouldn't want Mum to have to deal with . . .'

'No, of course not. It was just a thought, and now's not really the time to discuss it. So let's leave things as they are,' and hooking on more tightly to his arm she told herself cheerily that, hangover permitting, she'd manage to find a way of killing a few hours tomorrow that, hopefully, wouldn't have anything to do with work.

Millie Locke was reclining against a cosy mound of pillows, her glassy blue eyes fixed on nothing, while her trembling right hand fiddled idly with the emergency button at the end of a long cord. Her room in Beech Tree Lodge Care Home was a small, private space that might have been almost cell-like were it not for how gaily Jason had painted it, and the bright daisy curtains Alex had brought from the old lady's cottage. There was a small loo and washbasin in an en suite cubicle that Millie had to be hoisted to, a TV dominating an ornate chest of drawers that had also come from the cottage, and an elaborate doll's house with internal lights and minuscule hand-carved furniture that Millie had always taken much pleasure in.

'Hey Millie,' Alex said softly as she came through the open door. 'You're awake, that's good.'

Millie frowned, blinked and took a moment to locate where the voice had come from. When she found Alex her tired old face crumpled into a smile that made Alex's heart swell with affection. No matter what kind of state she found Millie in, and it could change dramatically from one visit to the next, the dear old soul almost never failed to recognise her, even if she couldn't always quite remember how she knew her.

'Alex,' she said huskily. 'There's lovely.'

'How are you?' Alex smiled, going to perch on the arm of the wingback visitor's chair. 'The nurse just told me that you fell out of bed.'

Millie seemed puzzled. 'Did I? When was that then?'

'Last night, she said.' Apparently someone had rung Carol, Millie's niece, but Alex didn't imagine Carol was unduly concerned, since Millie hadn't sustained anything more than a couple of bruises.

Not appearing very interested in her fall either, Millie gazed about for a while, presumably drifting through the wilderness of dementia that was clouding her ageing mind. Alex sometimes wondered if it was her father's death that had pushed Millie into this next, more debilitating stage of the disease – she'd been absolutely devoted to him, and had often said that the world wouldn't be worth staying in without him.

Now, having lost the use of her legs, along with the ability to wash herself and go to the bathroom, Millie was almost entirely dependent on the carers and nurses of this home, apart from when Alex came in. Though she wasn't in any way strong enough to lift or change the old lady, she occasionally helped her to eat if she was there at mealtimes, and wheeled her around the gardens when it was warm enough for her to be outside.

As Millie's rheumy eyes came back to her, Alex saw that they were starting to dance. 'My little stick of rock,' she croaked with a laugh.

Alex laughed too and wanted to hug her frail old bones. Ever since she could remember Millie had called her that, saying it was because she had special stamped all the way through her. In many ways Millie was like the grandmother she'd never had. She'd always been there, in the cottage next door, usually treating the world as the enemy, never seeming to mind who she upset unless it was Alex, or her favourite of all, Douglas. Gabby had never had much time for her, and their mother had never denied she found her a bit of a trial, but for Alex, particularly after she'd learned she was adopted, she'd felt a bit like a kindred spirit. She was an outsider too, who'd been drawn into the warmth of the rector's heart and embraced as extended family.

'What time is it?' Millie asked.

Alex glanced at her watch. 'Just after three,' she replied.

Millie nodded, though it didn't look as though anything had registered. 'So have you come to give me my breakfast?' she wondered.

Alex smiled. 'Not for the moment. You should be having your tea soon.'

Millie snuffled a little, smacked her gums together and looked down at the two small mounds her feet were making under the crocheted blanket. 'Where's your dad?' she asked, bringing her eyes back to Alex. 'Is he coming to see me?'

Reaching for her hand, Alex said, 'He can't, Millie. He died, don't you remember? About two years ago.'

Millie scowled, and started to look fussed. 'Don't be silly,' she chided. 'He was here yesterday. You're a bad girl to be saying things like that. You'll never go to heaven if you tell lies.'

Knowing better than to argue, Alex said, 'Have you been out of bed at all today?'

Millie's tight little mouth with its fans of deep feathery lines opened and closed a few times before she said, 'Not yet, no. They don't get me dressed till after breakfast. I think I'll have my hair cut today, and a nice perm. Got to keep yourself up together, haven't you?'

'Absolutely,' Alex agreed, wondering when Millie's white halo of angel fluff had last seen anything stronger than shampoo and a comb. 'Have you made yourself a boyfriend then?' she teased.

It took only a moment for Millie to chuckle. 'Oh no, my courting days is over,' she said, her head wobbling about in pleasure. 'But the boy who brings the tea, oh he's lovely he is. If I was ten years younger he'd be in trouble.'

Alex gave a gurgle of laughter. The boy who came with the tea probably wasn't even twenty, so quite how old Millie thought she was, was anyone's guess.

'Your mother's dead too, isn't she?' Millie stated vaguely after a while.

'That's right,' Alex confirmed.

Millie sat with that for a moment, and Alex wondered what she'd thought of Myra. She'd never said, at least not to Alex, but she must have sensed that Myra wasn't overly fond of her.

'I never understood how that woman could have given up a dear little thing like you,' Millie rasped softly. 'Never came back to find you, did she? Funny that. You'd have thought she would, when she left the hospital, you being the only one she had left.'

Alex's heartbeat was slowing. She'd assumed Millie was talking about Myra when she'd said, 'Your mother's dead too,' but now it didn't seem

136

so. Did that mean her real mother was dead? Not sure how she'd feel if she found out it was true, she said, 'Did you – did you ever know my real mother, Millie?'

Millie's eyes wandered as she shook her head.

'So how do you know . . . What makes you say she's dead?'

Millie blinked a few times and failed to reply.

'Millie?'

Several more moments ticked by before Alex realised tears were beading in the old lady's eyes.

Alarmed, Alex reached for her hand. 'What is it?' she urged. 'Millie, what's upsetting you?'

Millie's voice rasped with sadness as she said, 'I just wants to see your dad and my poor dear mam. She'll be here in a minute to take me home.'

Imagining Millie's mother as an angel coming to take her on to the next world, Alex smiled as a lump formed in her throat. There was no point trying to force Millie into seeing or making sense when she no longer had any idea what sense was.

'No bugger ever thinks about me, except your dad,' Millie complained as a tear ran down her cheek.

'And me,' Alex reminded her.

When Millie looked at her again she seemed surprised and pleased to see her. 'Alex,' she said happily. 'There's lovely,' and the visit seemed to start all over again.

Twenty minutes later Alex was sitting at the wheel of her car watching the comings and goings of the home and wondering if Millie had, albeit fleetingly, been talking about her real mother. She rarely allowed herself to think of her these days, it did no good, but if she was dead . . . She couldn't be, Myra or Douglas would have told her.

Wouldn't they?

And what difference would it make to her if she had died?

She didn't quite know how to answer that, apart from realising it would make her feel cheated, ridiculously lonely even, and deprived of a dream that she barely ever connected with, but it was there all the same.

Taking out her phone she clicked on Gabby's number, and inhaled a shuddering breath as she waited for an answer. Gabby would know if it was true.

As the machine picked up at the other end she remembered that Martin and the kids were sick, so leaving a quick message wishing them better and asking Gabby to call when she had a minute, she tried her Aunt Sheila instead. She'd be even more likely than Gabby to know if it were true, given how close she and Myra had been.

Suddenly realising how difficult she might find it if Sheila did confirm the worst, she rang off before the call connected. She had to make sure she was ready to hear it, prepared to cope with the fact that there would never be any sort of fairy-tale ending for her and her mother.

She was trying to make herself think rationally. It wasn't as if she'd be grieving for someone she knew, she reminded herself. Her mother had never been real in a sense that she remembered. She'd been a figment of her imagination, a dream to hold on to in times of loneliness and confusion, particularly during her teenage years. *Everything'll be all right once we're together,* she used to tell herself when she'd first found out her mother was still alive. *She'll be loving and kind and have a good reason for why she didn't come to find me before. And anyway it wouldn't matter what the reason was, because she'd come in the end and at last we would be together, where we belonged.*

She hadn't realised until now quite how powerful that small voice inside her still was. Over the years she'd kept trying to drown it out with a scornful, angry tirade that berated her mother for returning to a man who'd *massacred her family*, for God's sake. How weak and pathetic could she be to go running after someone who had caused her so much pain and suffering, who'd inflicted it on others too and who probably viewed her with nothing but contempt?

But her mother might not be that person. There was nothing to say that she was, no single shred of evidence from the research Alex had done, or veiled suggestion from Myra and Douglas, or even the glimmer of a possibility on the Internet. Nor had anyone, until now, ever hinted that she might be dead. So she really couldn't take Millie's word for it, especially when Millie was no longer in her right mind.

Moments later she was through to her Aunt Sheila, barely even asking how she was, or if it was convenient to talk, as she launched into what Millie had told her.

'Oh my, oh my,' Sheila sighed sorrowfully when she'd finished. 'I honestly don't know why Millie would have come out with something like that, except she's very muddled these days, as you would know better than most.'

'Her long-term memory isn't too bad,' Alex protested, 'and she seemed quite lucid for the few moments she was talking about her.'

'Well, all I can tell you is that I've never heard anyone say that she's dead. To be honest, I'm not sure how your parents would have known anyway. As far as I'm aware they weren't in touch with her, and I'm sure Myra would have said if they were.'

Alex's head fell back against the seat as she closed her eyes, then hearing voices in the background, she said, 'Sorry. I didn't realise you had company.'

'Oh, it's just Gabby with Martin and the kids. They came over for a Sunday roast and I think they might be about to leave.'

Stiffening with surprise, Alex said, 'Oh, I see. Well, it's good to know they're feeling better.' *Why hadn't they invited her to join them for lunch? Gabby had known she was on her own today, hadn't she? It didn't matter; she'd already decided by then to go and see Millie anyway.*

'Oh, I think they'll live,' Sheila chuckled. 'It did them good to get out of the house for a while, they've been all cooped up since Thursday.'

'Please send them my love,' Alex said through a wavering smile, 'and tell them the play went really well.'

'Oh goodness, I'd forgotten all about that. Did it really? How marvellous. I'm sorry we couldn't make it, dear, but I'm sure we'll get up there before it closes.'

'That'll be lovely,' Alex assured her. 'I'd better let you go now so you can see them off.'

After ending the call she turned the key in the ignition and started to drive out of the car park, knowing that if she didn't get herself moving right away she'd end up sitting there wallowing in some hideous wave of self-pity that had no more business in her head than it did in her heart. Her mother was someone she didn't even know, and might not even want to know if she did, so perhaps she should think about that instead of romanticising her on to some sort of pedestal. And as for Gabby and Sheila, she needed to remember that they had lives too, and she couldn't expect to be a number one priority for them, especially when Gabby had a husband and kids.

She'd call Jason when she got home to tell him what had happened. Or no, she'd just ask how it was going at his mother's and suggest that they do something special for his kids once the show had closed. Maybe they could take them to Center Parcs for a weekend, or even on a ferry over to France.

Chapter Seven

On Tuesday morning Alex had precious little time to spare before going to meet Lizzie for their dreaded visit to the Princes. Even so, she wasn't going to allow another day to pass by without making some sort of contact with the parents of Ottilie Wade. She'd left messages at the school again yesterday, and called at the house when passing to no avail, so if she didn't get anywhere again today she'd be turning up at Mr Wade's office tomorrow, or the classroom, she didn't mind which.

However, just as she was finishing up her report on the hellish Monday that had included her trying to tear one of her charges away from a drug-addicted mother, and another child letting the tyres down on her car while she was inside talking to his stepfather, her mobile rang and seeing it was from Kesterly Rise Primary she quickly clicked on.

'Ms Lake, it's Brian Wade,' a polite, cheerful voice informed her. 'I'm sorry I haven't managed to get hold of you before now, but how can I help?'

Quickly hitting the save button on her computer, Alex cut straight to the chase. 'We've had a call expressing some concern about your daughter, Ottilie . . .'

'Oh dear, not again,' he interrupted with a sigh.

'I can assure you my daughter's fine, and I must apologise for the trouble this is putting you to. The person who's making these calls . . . I take it I'm right in thinking it's a woman who didn't give her name?'

'Yes, but . . .'

'She never does. Well, you'll know that if you've checked your records, and I'm sure you have. It's a dreadful nuisance, for everyone, but I'm afraid I don't know how to make her stop. She's made accusations against me before, you see, when my family and I were in Northumbria . . .'

'Yes, I read that, but I can't seem to find any record of her name. Do you know what it is?'

There was a pause before he said, 'McCarthy, I think. Yes, Jill McCarthy. I don't know her personally, I have no recollection of ever even meeting her, so I've no idea why she decided to make me the target of her . . . I suppose we should call them delusions. All I can tell you is that losing our son was the worst experience my wife and I have ever been through, and these . . . *calls* were upsetting in the extreme. My wife has never been the same since Jonathan was taken, and if this crazy woman is going to start bringing it all up again I'm afraid I shall have to take some very serious steps to make her stop.'

Wondering what the steps might be, Alex said, 'I appreciate your concerns, Mr Wade, I really do, but I'm sure you know that I'm required to perform an assessment on Ottilie . . .'

'But I've already assured you my daughter is fine . . .'

'In which case you'll have no objection to me coming to see her.'

Sounding slightly strained now, he said, 'I've just tried to explain about my wife's fragility . . .'

'You have my sympathy, believe me, but I still need to see Ottilie. If it's going to be difficult for her mother perhaps you'd like to be there when I visit. May I suggest after school tomorrow afternoon, at four thirty?'

With a tremulous, almost irritable sigh he said, 'Ms Lake, I don't think you're quite understanding the damage this might cause to my wife.'

'With respect, Mr Wade, you know I have a legal obligation to see your daughter regardless of the harm it might cause your wife . . .'

'Can I remind you that your colleague, to whom I spoke on the previous two occasions, saw no reason to doubt my word, so I'm at a loss as to why you're being so persistent. This surely isn't what social services are about, coming into families and causing more problems when there is absolutely no need to.'

Keeping her tone reasonable and polite, Alex said, 'Mr Wade, your resistance to my visit is making it more necessary than ever that I make one. So, I'll be there at four thirty tomorrow. Please make sure Ottilie is too, or it could result in us having to involve the police.'

As she rang off she blew out a heavy sigh, releasing some of the built-up tension. She might have gone a bit far in mentioning the police, given that he was a deputy headmaster; however, there was no harm in reminding him that he was as obliged as anyone else to comply with the rules, especially where child protection was concerned. She was going to be interested now to see if he was at the house when she turned up tomorrow, or if he tried to cancel or postpone. He might even, she thought, as she ran down to her car, try contacting her superiors to get them to make her back off.

Good luck with that, she was thinking as she headed off to Temple Fields. No one at her office, no matter where they were on the ladder, took kindly to interference when there were question marks over a child. And even if he did manage to get someone on his side, she'd already made up her mind that she wasn't going to let this one go.

We'll find out then, Mr Wade, she was thinking to herself, as she clicked on to her Bluetooth to take a call, *which of us has the most power where your daughter is concerned. If she's fine, as you say, I hope it's you. If she isn't, you're going to find out very soon now that it's me.*

Twenty minutes later Alex was driving into the layby opposite Tesco, about half a mile from Temple Fields, where Lizzie was already waiting in her trusty old Ford estate. She was a strikingly sumptuous West Indian woman with sparkling brown eyes and an enormous chest that contained an enormous heart. Her experience of the more troubled estates of their region was far greater than most, since she and her family lived on the more desirable west side of Temple Fields in the midst of the largely black community. The Asian families had cornered the northern side, while the whites and smatterings of various other ethnicities had a stranglehold on the south-easterly sprawl of tower blocks, run-down terraces and battle-weary semis.

'So how are things?' Lizzie asked, sliding into the passenger seat of Alex's car. 'I should warn you, I've had a crap morning so far, so if the Princes have got any ideas about messing me around they're going to find themselves in a whole heap of trouble they won't have bargained for.'

Alex's eyebrows arched. 'Let them be warned,' she smiled.

'Indeed. Did you hear yet whether that waste of space Shane is in custody?'

'Yes, and I'm afraid he isn't, which should spice things up a little.' Alex was easing the car back into the traffic, and though she was making light of a possible encounter with Shane Prince, the prospect of having to deal with him as well as the mother and sister had given her a very poor night's sleep. 'I've just spoken to the police and they assure me there's a patrol car in the area, so if there's any trouble we just ring 999.'

Lizzie gave one of her famous scoffs. 'Yeah, and they's going to come running as fast as they fat little legs can carry 'em,' she retorted. 'But we're going to do just fine without them, don't you go worrying 'bout that.'

Taking heart from Lizzie's confidence, Alex drove on along the dual carriageway and minutes later they were entering the estate. As they reached the Crowes' sad-looking semi on Barton Street she pulled over and reached into the back for her bag. 'I'll just be a second,' she said, 'something I have to drop off,' and going to ring on the bell which she doubted could be heard above the throb of loud music and shouts of male voices inside, she eyed the letter box, tempted to push her package through and run.

'Who is it?' Laura Crowe's tobacco-coarsened voice yelled from behind the door.

'Alex Lake from social services. I have something for Danny.'

The door opened as far as the chain would allow. 'What is it?' Laura demanded suspiciously.

'A photograph his foster carers gave him. He left it behind.' She wasn't about to inform Laura that she'd assumed Danny had stolen it, since it wouldn't do much to improve their friendship.

As Laura's hand snaked out through the gap Alex handed the package over. 'Is Daniel at school?' she asked, knowing it was a discipline Laura hadn't bothered to master.

'Mind your own fucking business and piss off,' Laura snarled and the door slammed shut.

'Sweet,' Alex murmured and turned back to the car. She'd better call Bradshaw Junior later to find out.

The drive through the next few streets was as dispiriting as ever: seeing so many homes barricaded up to protect the terrified, law-abiding residents from their fearsome neighbours was always depressing. How did any of them ever manage to keep hope alive, she often wondered, when they'd been forgotten in just about every way? The tower blocks, deeper into the estate, were as dismally run-down as the low-rise flats, and since she'd visited them many times Alex had no problem imagining the ammonia stench of urine and faeces in the lifts and stairwells.

'So, here we are,' Lizzie announced with a marked lack of enthusiasm as they turned into Green Avenue to find no trace of green in the scrubby front gardens nor in the wasteland of a playing field at the far end – otherwise known as the junkie pit. 'Armageddon on a day off.'

Alex smiled past the unease of now being in a cul-de-sac. Though the only activity seemed to be rubbish skittering along the pavements in the wind, she could hear someone hammering and drilling behind one of the boarded-up facades, and music blaring out of somewhere. A few intrepid neighbours had dared to hang flower baskets next to their front doors, or balance the odd pot of geraniums on precarious-looking windowsills. Mostly, though, the street was a misfortune of makeshift repairs and shabby paintwork, with an odd assortment of wrecked and pristine cars parked along the kerbs and satellite dishes on every rooftop.

'What, no welcoming committee?' Lizzie commented as Alex came to a stop in front of the Princes' semi, where patches of pebble-dash still clung to the walls in a last desperate bid to show its former glory, and an upstairs window was made of an opaque plastic sheet. 'Oh, that's right, no one's expecting us – and now, with any luck, no sorry ass will be at home so we can turn our pretty little selves around and get the hell out of here.'

Though she'd have liked nothing better, Alex said, 'Try to think of Polly Prince and what a good thing it is that she has us to look out for her.'

Lizzie's eyes nearly burst from her head. 'Yeah, like that little slapper's going to be real grateful for us coming knocking on her door. She's going to say, oh hi Alex, hi Lizzie, how lovely to see you. I been wondering when you'd show up to rescue me. Shall I go get my stuff?'

Choking back a laugh, Alex pushed open the car door and after taking her bag from behind the driver's seat she waited for Lizzie to join her on the pavement.

'Reckon it might make more sense for me to stay here,' Lizzie said sagely, 'you know, in case we need to make a quick getaway.'

'Nice try,' Alex responded, registering the heady scent of marijuana floating by on the breeze.

With an exasperated sigh Lizzie prised herself from the passenger seat and, after reminding Alex how much she owed her for this, she led the way up to the Princes' front door.

Leaning past her, Alex gave three sharp raps with the knocker and quickly scooted behind her again.

'Yeah, you're real funny,' Lizzie told her drily. 'There ain't no one home, so come on, let's go.'

'Give them a chance,' Alex laughed. 'I can hear music.'

'That'll be the angels hovering about with them harps the way they do when they've got a couple of newcomers on their way.'

Stepping in beside her, Alex gave her a wink, and felt her heart lurch as a chain started to rattle the other side of the front door, followed by a bolt grating and a couple of keys turning. Eventually a small, scruffy boy dressed in shorts and jelly shoes appeared from inside.

'You go and unlock all them keys and bolts by yourself?' Lizzie asked incredulously.

He only blinked at her.

Guessing someone else had done it for him and was now standing behind the door, Alex said, 'Is your mummy at home?'

'What's it to you?' a croaky voice demanded from the darkness. It wasn't possible to tell whether it was male or female until a shaven-haired young woman in her mid- to late twenties stepped in behind the boy and put a hand on his head. 'What do you want?' she snapped.

'We're from social services,' Alex informed her, noting the puffy black eye and cut lip that appeared to be as recently applied as last night's make-up. 'We'd like to have a chat with Polly if she's in.'

The young woman eyed her coldly. 'Yeah, I bet you would,' she rasped, and to Alex's surprise, she swung the door wider and jerked her head as an invitation to follow.

The living room turned out to be as cluttered and rancid as Alex had feared, with old blankets thrown over a sofa, at least half a dozen full ashtrays spilling on to the floor and more empty beer bottles than she could count scattered about various surfaces. Unsurprisingly, the corner next to the hearth was dominated by a forty-two-inch plasma TV that had almost certainly fallen off the back of a lorry, and an impressive range of computer games and technology that had no doubt taken the same spill.

For all the detritus of human neglect and indulgence there was no one else in the room, and the music Alex had heard from outside had stopped. It gave her an eerie feeling, as though someone was lurking, waiting to eavesdrop on what might be said. Shane? Polly? Their mother? She guessed she'd find out soon enough.

'I'm Cindy, by the way,' the young woman informed them, 'Polly's sister. This is Ryan.'

Alex smiled down at the little boy, but he didn't smile back. Was he part of someone's caseload? she wondered. She'd check when she got back. 'Is your mother at home?' she asked Cindy. Since it wasn't possible for them to interview Polly without a parent or legal guardian being present, they might as well get that established first.

Cindy lit a cigarette. 'Yeah, she's upstairs in bed,' she answered. 'I thought it was Polly you'd come to see.'

Lizzie said, 'It is, but your mother . . .'

'. . . has to be there,' Cindy interrupted. 'Yeah, yeah. Go upstairs and get Nan,' she barked at Ryan. 'And while you're at it, tell that scummy little bitch Polly she can get herself down here too.'

Slouching off to do as he was told, Ryan slammed the door behind him. A moment later he could be heard yelling, 'Nan,' as he climbed the stairs.

Cindy said, 'So, do you want to sit down, or what?'

Glancing at Lizzie Alex said, 'Thank you,' and trying not to think of what might be creeping about in the cushions she settled on to the edge of the sofa, while Lizzie made the wiser choice of an upright chair.

'You got some nerve coming here after what happened to the doctor,' Cindy commented through a cloud of smoke.

Alex spoke carefully as she said, 'You know about that?'

'It'd be difficult not to when the pigs came straight round here and lifted my brother, wouldn't it?' Cindy retorted.

Trying not to glance at Lizzie, Alex said, 'Do you live here?'

'Sometimes. Depends. Why do you want to know?'

Alex smiled. 'Just making conversation.'

Cindy eyed her suspiciously and took another drag. 'You don't say much, do you?' she shot at Lizzie.

Lizzie raised an eyebrow. 'I got plenty to say when the time is right,' she informed her with a friendly smile, 'so don't you go worrying about that.'

Cindy sniffed and wiped the back of her hand

151

across her nose, a dozen or more silver chains rattling as she moved. 'So, what do you want to see Polly about?' she demanded. 'If you ask me you ought to hike the dumbfuck cow back into care, we'd all be a lot better off round here if she was out of the way.'

Hiding her surprise, Alex said, 'Why do you say that?'

'Why do you think? That fucking disease she's got. She's spreading it around like it's fucking Smarties. No one's safe, because the horny little slapper don't give a shit who she goes with. If it weren't for our Shane someone would have done something to stop her by now, but they're all so fucking scared of him that no one dares say nothin'.'

Before Alex could respond Lizzie said, 'I take it he's not here.'

'Does it look like it?'

'So where is he?' Alex asked.

'Don't ask me, ask her.'

Alex turned to find Debbie Prince, a bone-thin, exhausted-looking woman with bloodshot eyes, an oddly crooked nose and lips with more lines around them than she had teeth inside, coming in the door. Her hair was ratty and dyed red, her clothes hung loosely from her frame, showing a rose tattoo on her arms and another on her neck.

'What the fuck do you want?' she snarled, going to fetch her cigarettes from the mantelshelf over the gas fire. 'We got no need of the likes of you, so why don't you just bog off out of here and let us alone?'

'We're here to speak to Polly,' Alex explained, getting to her feet. 'I'm told she's at home.'

Debbie shot her eldest daughter a scathing look. 'So what if she is?' she snapped, lighting up. 'She's busy right now, so she ain't got no time to speak to you.'

What could a fourteen-year-old be busy doing on a Tuesday morning when she was supposed to be at school? Alex wondered. 'It's OK, we can wait,' she smiled.

Debbie Prince inhaled deeply and regarded Alex with her mean little eyes as she blew smoke from the corner of her mouth. 'Well, maybe I don't want you to wait,' she told her. 'Maybe I don't want you in my house at all.'

'Mum, cut it out, will you?' Cindy complained. 'They're not doing no harm and someone has to talk to the stupid little cow.'

'You can shut your fucking mouth,' Debbie told her sharply. 'You go on like that and next thing they'll be having her out of here and into some care home, and if that happens then someone's going to be very fucking sorry around here.' Her piercing eyes came back to Alex in a way that blatantly fixed Alex as the someone.

'The doctor informed us that Polly has an STD,' Lizzie piped up. 'At fourteen she shouldn't be having sex at all . . .'

'Who the fuck asked you?' Debbie spat, and her scathing addition of the n word brought the colour flooding to Lizzie's cheeks.

'Being offensive isn't going to help anyone,' Alex came in quickly. 'If Polly is engaging in sexual intercourse then we need to establish first of all whether this is of her own free will . . .'

'Oh, what, so you think we're fucking tying her up and raping her, do you?' Debbie snarled.

'We're not accusing anyone of anything,' Lizzie replied, 'but when a child of fourteen is known to have a sexually transmissible disease it's clear that something, somewhere is wrong. Wouldn't you agree?'

'What I know is that she's my daughter, which makes her my business, not yours. So take your fat ass off my chair, mama, and get the fuck out of here before my lad comes home and chucks you out.'

Glancing at Lizzie, Alex said, 'We really do need to see her, Mrs Prince. If you refuse we'll just have to come back with a Protection Order and I don't think any of us wants that.'

As Lizzie winced at the mention of a PO, Debbie Prince leaned towards Alex and blew a cloud of smoke in her face.

Waving it away, Alex said, 'You must realise this isn't helping Polly.'

'Why don't you do as I said and fuck off,' Debbie Prince told her. 'And you,' she snarled, rounding on her daughter, 'what the fuck were you doing letting them in here?'

Cindy's eyes flashed. 'Like she said, if we don't go along with them they'll just come back with a protection order and that means the cops. Do you really want them barging their way in here again?'

Debbie Prince's inflamed eyes stayed on Cindy as she took another drag of her cigarette. 'It's a pity that old man of yours didn't manage to knock a bit of sense into you when he had a go,' she said bitingly.

'What's wrong with what I said?' Cindy cried, throwing out her arms. 'Or do you want the cops in here, is that what you're saying?'

Ignoring the question, Debbie turned back to Alex. 'You still here?' she snapped. 'The door's over there; use it and do yourself a favour, don't bother coming back.'

Since they had no powers to force the issue, Alex waited for Lizzie to go ahead before following her into the hall. Guessing Polly would be somewhere in earshot, she turned back to Debbie and said, 'I hope you're getting treatment for Polly's condition, because if it goes unchecked her whole future, even her life, could be in danger, and it can leave terrible scars, especially on the face.'

Sounding weary, Debbie said to Cindy, 'Does that bitch never give up? Get her out of here before I lose my temper.'

Needing no further prompting Alex followed Lizzie out to the car, flinching as the front door slammed behind them.

'Well that went well,' Lizzie remarked cheerfully.

Alex wanted to laugh, but knew better than to be seen with a smile on her face until they were well out of sight.

'Nice parting shot,' Lizzie commented as they got into the car. 'The girl's sure to have heard, so hopefully it'll strike enough fear into her stupid little head to get herself treated.'

Not bothering to ask what kind of mother would allow such a disease to go untreated, since she'd come across plenty of negligent mothers in her time, Alex glanced up at the house as she started the engine. 'As soon as we're off the estate I'll call Wendy to get an Emergency Protection Order,' she declared.

Lizzie gave a low whistle. 'Well, that'll certainly set the cat amongst the pigeons, coming back here with the cops to drag the kid out.'

'What else are we going to do, just leave her there?' Alex demanded.

Lizzie didn't answer until Alex had turned the

car around and the house was behind them. 'Actually, you might want an SO,' she advised, meaning a Secure Order. 'Given how often the girl's absconded from her foster placements in the past, we have to make sure she gets proper medical attention and don't remain sexually active. The only way of doing that is to put her under twenty-four-seven observation.'

Relieved to have Lizzie's support, Alex was about to speak again when a bolt of fear struck to the core of her heart. 'Oh my God,' she murmured, hitting the brake.

Standing in a straggled line across the end of the cul-de-sac, hoods up around their shaven heads, arms folded or hands stuffed in low-slung pockets, were Shane Prince and his mates.

Lizzie took out her phone. 'OK, you're needed,' she said, when someone answered her call.

Alex glanced at her.

Lizzie was dialling again. 'Police please,' she said. 'Yes, it's an emergency.'

By the time she'd finished giving details of who and where they were, Alex had locked all the doors and was trying to decide whether to reverse back up the street, or drive straight at the yobs and not care who she hit.

'What shall I do?' she gasped, as they surrounded the car and began bouncing it up and down and pitching it savagely from side to side.

'Hit the gas,' Lizzie told her urgently.

Alex let out the clutch and slammed down the accelerator, but the wheels were off the ground.

The boys laughed and jeered. 'Fucking women drivers,' they heard one of them scoff.

There was a grating sound as someone dragged

something sharp along the paintwork, and a thumping as someone else tried to push in the back rear window. A face loomed up at Lizzie's window, his tongue out and his eyes crossed.

Alex almost screamed as someone banged the driver's door. She turned to find Shane Prince leering in at her.

'Alex Lake,' he sneered in delight.

She pulled back as his expression turned feral and he pressed a fist to the window.

'You stay away from my family, do you hear?' he told her. 'Stay the fuck away or you're going to find out what it means, messing with me.'

Scrabbling for the keys Alex restarted the engine. It roared as she tried to find the clutch. She was close to panicking. She heard the boys shouting, then suddenly, to her amazement, the car hit the ground hard and the gang was running in different directions. A moment later another, larger, gang of youths was swarming into the street, all of them black, though similarly dressed and just as scary.

'The cavalry,' Lizzie murmured.

Alex turned to her.

'We needed proper backup,' Lizzie explained, 'so I thought it best to call on a few friends. One patrol car wasn't going to do it, not with the likes of Shane Prince.'

'But Lizzie, this is how riots start,' Alex protested.

Putting a hand on Alex's, Lizzie smiled. 'You've still got a lot to learn,' she told her, and pushing open the passenger door she got out to meet their unlikely saviours.

Ten minutes later, after being introduced to the charming, but hideously scarred Nathan Cole, one of Lizzie's neighbours, and told that any time she needed assistance she just had to call, Alex was driving back into the layby where they'd left Lizzie's car.

'Well, I guess it could have been a lot worse,' she declared with a shaky laugh.

'It sure could,' Lizzie agreed drily. 'He's a good boy, Nathan. I mean, a bad boy, but good if you get my drift. I've known him since he was knee-high. In and out of care all his life. He's learned the hard way how to survive.'

Thinking of how tragically it showed in his face, Alex turned off the engine and reached for her phone.

'Ah, there go the cops, just in the nick of time,' Lizzie commented, as a patrol car sped past, siren wailing, lights flashing. 'Don't much want to think where we'd be now if we'd waited for them to join the party.'

Watching the vehicle disappear round the bend, Alex said, 'So you had Nathan and the others waiting nearby?'

Lizzie slanted her a look. 'Don't be shocked. You learn about these things the longer you're in the job. I knew they were our best chance of getting out of there if Shane Prince and his lot turned ugly.'

Still, the idea of a rival gang lurking in the shadows, ready for an unholy scrap that might have developed into something seriously threatening, remained unnerving.

'You still going for the EPO?' Lizzie asked as Alex dialled the office.

'She has to be got out of there,' Alex replied.

'So you're not put off by what Shane Prince said to you?'

Alex inhaled deeply and shook her head. 'No, I mean yes, but I can't let him intimidate me like that.'

'That's my girl. And remember, if you need to, you can always call on our Nathan.'

Doubting she'd ever do that, while realising it made her feel a little easier to think she could, Alex asked to be put through to Wendy and moments later she was practically shouting at her down the line.

'But we know from the doctor that the girl has an STD,' she insisted, 'and apparently she's still sleeping around . . .'

'You only have the sister's word for that,' Wendy pointed out, 'and you know what sisters can be like. All kinds of history and jealousy could be coming into play. And you didn't even see the girl, so how can I recommend any kind of protection order when we haven't even attempted a second visit?'

'Wendy, if you'd been there, if you understood how important it is to get her out . . .'

'That may be so, but you know very well that we have to be extremely careful when making these decisions. Just because the mother was uncoopera-tive doesn't mean she's not seeking medical help elsewhere, or that she's allowing the girl to be promiscuous. No, I'm afraid this is a situation that will have to be closely monitored over . . .'

'Didn't you hear what I said?' Alex broke in furi-ously. 'Shane Prince has already threatened me. I can't just go in and out of that house . . .'

'Lizzie can go with you, or Tommy when he's back. Now, I need you here as soon as you can make it. When is that likely to be?'

Somehow resisting the urge to throw the phone out the window, Alex said, 'Probably around three,' and before Wendy could dump any more on her she cut the connection. 'Sometimes I wonder why we bother,' she snapped irritably to Lizzie.

'I've asked myself the same question a thousand times over the years,' Lizzie sighed. 'But somehow we keep on going. So where are you off to now?'

As she remembered, Alex's eyes closed in dismay. 'Yarnham,' she answered, referring to the neighbouring estate, which wasn't much more edifying than Temple Fields. 'Do you remember Gemma Knight, the little girl whose mother was dying of cancer?'

'I do. Don't tell me, the mother's gone.'

'At the weekend. Gemma's grandmother's staying with her for now, but I have to go and pick her up and take her to her carers.'

'Does she know them?'

'Yes, she's been spending time with them ever since her mother was first diagnosed. It's just a pity the grandmother can't take her in, but the old lady's got a heart problem, and to be honest, I'm not sure about the son, Gemma's uncle. He's a real seedy type, never works, or washes by the look of him. She'll be better off with her carers.'

'Please, Alex, please, please, let me stay here,' Gemma was sobbing half an hour later, while clinging to Alex with all her might. 'I know Granny has to go home, but I can take care of myself. I know how to cook and clean and I'll go to school every day, I promise.'

With tears streaming down her own face, Alex held the child tight as she said, 'You know I can't do that, you're way too young.'

'Then let me come and live with you,' Gemma

begged. 'I'll be good, I swear it. I'll do everything you tell me to – you won't even know I'm there.'

Holding the girl's ravaged little face between her hands Alex tried to explain that she wasn't a registered carer, and nor could she be while she had a full-time job. Besides, Gemma was going to be very well looked after by the Brownings: she and her mother had got to know them together during her mother's lengthy decline.

'Your mummy wanted you to go to them,' she reminded Gemma gently. 'She'll know you're safe there, and you won't be far from the rest of your family, so you'll be able to visit them.'

'I don't care about them,' Gemma shouted, her glasses clouding up again. 'Why should I, they don't care about me?'

'You know that's not true,' Alex insisted. 'They want what's best for you too. We all do.'

Hardly able to speak through her sobs, Gemma said, 'Will you still come and see me?'

'Of course I will,' Alex promised, with a smile. 'You're one of my star charges, aren't you? There's no way I'm going to stop seeing you. And you have my number, so any time you want to call you know you can.'

It turned out to be small comfort in the end, because when they got to the carers Gemma simply couldn't let Alex go. In fact, if the angel of mercy from Winston's Wish, the child bereavement charity, hadn't shown up when she had, Alex suspected she and Gemma might still be clinging to one another now.

Instead, she was finally driving into Mulgrove at the end of the day so battered emotionally and engrossed in the notes she was dictating into her

BlackBerry that she almost missed Mattie waving out to her.

'Hi,' she said, pulling up next to the gift shop. 'Everything OK?'

Mattie pulled a face. 'You obviously haven't seen it yet,' she declared.

Alex's mouth turned dry. 'Seen what?' Fire had ravaged the Vicarage, the village hall . . .

'Heather Hancock's review. It was posted on the *Gazette*'s website a couple of hours ago, it'll be in the paper tomorrow.'

'Oh God, is it that bad?' Alex groaned.

'Afraid so.'

'Just when I was thinking today couldn't get any worse,' Alex retorted, putting the car back into gear. 'Anyway, thanks for the warning, I'll see you at the hall in about an hour.'

If you're into cheap laughs, village-hall romps and hairy men dressed up as airheads, then the Mulgrove Players' production of Gender Swap *is for you. There was plenty of hysterical rolling around the aisles during the performance I attended, but as most of the audience was made up of friends and family of the director and performers that was only to be expected. For the rest of us the experience of watching a bunch of buxom blokes dancing round their handbags, and butched-up princesses scratching their arses, ricocheted from excruciating to tiresome, to please, please let this be over before I start pulling my own teeth.*

Given the right direction, this piece might have spoken to our hearts and left us with more to think about than where your ten quid might be better spent. But alas it seemed to lack any sense of direction at all.

So, my friends, unless you're in the mood to find out

162

*what gives amateur theatre a bad name I urge you not
to waste your time going to see this sorry little fiasco of
a production.*

The review was so unnecessarily spiteful and
condescending that Alex could only wonder at just
how much venom Heather Hancock had stored up
inside her. And all because Alex had had the nerve
to challenge an unfair review of a restaurant over a
year ago and point out the mistakes Heather had
made in a front-page report on the standard of social
work in the area.

'We've got absolutely nothing to feel ashamed of,'
Johnny Grant declared to the assembled cast. 'It's a
brilliant production, you only have to go on Facebook
to read how much everyone loved it. And the audience was *not* made up of only our family and friends.
There were loads of people we'd never met before.'

Alex looked around at their dear, loyal faces.
'Have there been any cancellations since this came
out?' she asked Mattie.

'Three, but we've no way of knowing if they're
anything to do with this. Anyway, I've sold the
tickets on already, so we've still got a full house for
Saturday night.'

'Even if we don't, we'll go on anyway,' Sarah
Grant informed her. 'We've committed to three
performances so three performances we shall give.'

'Hear, hear,' the rest of them cheered with a small
round of applause.

'Actually, I owe you all an apology for letting this
happen,' Alex confessed. 'I knew before we invited
Heather Hancock how she felt about me, I just never
imagined she'd go public with it like this.'

'But how could she not like *you*?' Sarah protested.

Alex had to laugh at that. 'I just want you all to

understand that everything she's written here was meant as an attack on me – well, I think she's made that pretty clear – but it's written with a grudge, or a sense of vengeance in mind that means she was never going to allow herself to view our play objectively, never mind fairly.'

'Well, I for one want you to know,' Hailey stated hotly, 'that I've loved working with you and I'm proud of what you did with my script. It wasn't meant to be touchy-feely or schmaltzy, you understood that even if she didn't.'

'She would have slammed it whichever way we played it,' Johnny pointed out. 'So I say we just ignore her and forget she even exists.'

'No way am I buying the *Gazette* tomorrow,' Mattie declared.

'Me neither,' several others added.

Alex smiled. 'Well, I don't suppose I could ask for much more support,' she remarked, 'so thank you. And I think we should just keep looking at Facebook and take our lead from that.'

'Absolutely,' Steve Perry agreed as he walked in the door. 'Sorry I'm late, everyone. Got caught up on a job. I take it we're talking about the crap on the *Gazette*'s website? Well, wait till you see what's been going down on their Facebook page in the last half an hour, if you haven't already.'

Alex looked at him, intrigued.

Grinning, he spun out his iPad, tapped through to the relevant page and passed it round for everyone to see. 'Outrage, I'd call it, on an industrial scale,' he announced. 'Demands for retractions, explanations, even sackings. OK, a lot are from our nearest and dearest, but not all. Like these from a couple called Ron and Maggie Fenn, and this one . . . Just listen to this, it only got posted a couple of minutes ago: "I've no idea where Ms Hancock left her sense of humour on Saturday evening, but happily everyone else brought theirs and frankly I can't remember when I last laughed so much. Well done to Alex Lake and all the cast, it was a tremendous show that from where I was sitting everyone thoroughly enjoyed."' He beamed triumphantly. 'Anthony Goodman, QC,' he told them. 'Anyone know him? He was obviously here.'

Alex's heart tripped with surprise as she said, 'He's related to the Fenns, who are a couple of foster carers I dealt with recently.'

'My God, we had a QC in the audience,' Sarah gushed in delight. 'And now he's written this. That'll really put HH in her place.'

Handing the iPad to Alex, Steve said, 'He's not the only one speaking up for us. Here, take a look.'

'Do you reckon we might be able to get her to print a retraction?' Hailey suggested, clearly switched on by the thought.

Though Alex would have loved it more than anything, she said, 'Actually, I think the best course now is to maintain a dignified silence. She'll hate that more than anything, especially when she sees all this.'

'So where's Jase?' Steve demanded, pulling up a chair. 'Don't tell me he's gone to sort out those kids again?'

'Actually, I'm not sure where he is,' Alex replied, feeling slightly lost without him. 'He texted earlier to say he was going to be late, but nothing about what was holding him up.'

'I bet he's gone to tear that vindictive little bitch to pieces,' Sarah decided. 'They're old friends, aren't they?'

'He knows her,' Alex conceded, 'but it's his wife who's friends with her, not him.'

Johnny threw out his hands. 'So there we have it, the motive for all this crap. She's doing it for her mate.'

Not at all sure Heather Hancock would allow herself to be used in such a way, Alex could only shake her head in confusion. More than what was driving Heather Hancock, she'd have liked to know where Jason was, since his text hadn't mentioned anything about the review, so there was a chance he might not even know about it yet.

'At last,' she declared, when she finally got through to his mobile. 'I was starting to worry.'

'I'm sorry,' he said, 'I tried calling earlier, but I was on this job that just wouldn't finish and it was a total dead zone. I'm nearly home now though. Are you OK?'

'Fine, apart from getting over the shock of Heather Hancock's review. Have you seen it?'

He gave a weary groan. 'No, and by the sound of it I don't want to. Just ignore it. You know what she's like, she never gives a good review about anything. I suppose she thinks it makes her more interesting to stir up controversy or hurt people's feelings.'

'Well, she might not be wrong there, but if she looks at the *Gazette*'s Facebook page – and ours – she'll find out it's backfired on her, which is going to make her love me even more. Won't that be lovely?'

Laughing, he said, 'Where are you now? Have you eaten, because I'm starving?'

'No, I haven't, and so am I, so let's meet up at the pub. How soon can you get there?'

'I'm just pulling up outside the Vicarage, so I'll walk down . . . What the hell? Jesus Christ! What's happened to your car, Alex? How did you get all those scratches?'

'Oh, God, don't remind me,' Alex sighed, as the morning's ordeal came flooding back to her. 'I'll tell you about it when I see you, but it's OK, it didn't happen in Mulgrove.'

'I didn't think so, but do you know who did it?'

'Actually, I was in the car at the time, but please don't let's get into it now. It's been a long day, and I have a feeling tomorrow's going to be even longer, so I'd like to just chill out for a while and forget about everything except you, me and a lovely big plate of fish and chips.'

Chapter Eight

'So, Ottilie, you understand what's happening later, don't you?' Brian Wade was saying as he dabbed his face with an already damp handkerchief. It was humid outside and grey, a prowling beast of a day.

Ottilie's big eyes were regarding him carefully. She was standing in the middle of her bedroom, hands hanging limply at her sides, her wispy hair uncombed and stuck in places to her head.

'Don't you?' he prompted.

She nodded.

Raindrops began pattering on the window, and somewhere far in the distance the sound of a siren wailed through the gathering storm. The world was going about its business, fast, furious, totally apart from what was going on in here.

It was the way he wanted it to stay.

He went over it again.

'A lady is coming to see us. She'll tell you not to be afraid, that she won't hurt you, but she will if you tell her certain things. Do you understand?'

Ottilie nodded, an urgency to please making her narrow shoulders shake. Her cardigan was inside out; her Velcro-top trainers were on the wrong feet. Noticing, he quickly sat her on the bed and pulled the shoes off. Ottilie turned her face into the pillow as giant sobs engulfed her.

'I know it hurts,' he soothed softly, 'but the bruises will go soon.' They were all over her, big purple clouds staining her baby-soft skin from her fall down the stairs. 'We don't want anyone to see them, do we?' he whispered as he eased off her cardigan to put it on the right way round. 'We have to keep bruises all covered up until they heal.'

Ottilie was sobbing uncontrollably.

'Ssh, ssh,' he murmured, kissing her gently on the head. The bumps didn't show, they were concealed by her hair. It was lucky nothing had been broken. So lucky, it could stop his heart to think of what might have happened if it had. 'I'll go gently now,' he promised. 'We just have to put your clothes on the right way, that's all.'

Ottilie shielded her face with Boots, giving her father one arm at a time and hiding her eyes as he lifted one leg, then the other to refasten her shoes.

When she was straight, Brian sat her up and put a hand to her cheek. No cuts, thank God, just a small bruise beneath her left eye. 'The lady will ask you questions,' he told her, 'and she'll try very hard to make you say things about me and Mummy, but it'll be a trick, because if you tell her about our secret games terrible things will happen after and we don't want that, do we?'

Fear shone in Ottilie's eyes.

He leaned forward so that his face was very close to hers. 'No, of course we don't,' he said softly. 'We need to keep you safe and secure so that no one can ever hurt you.'

Ottilie's body shuddered as she tried to stop crying.

'She might want to see your room,' he cautioned, 'but that's all right. You can show her your toys and do some writing or drawing for her if you like, but you mustn't tell her anything about me or the next thing we know she'll steal your tongue.'

Ottile's tender pink lips disappeared between her teeth.

'Now, before I go back to school for the afternoon,' he went on, 'I'm going to tell you the story of William, a little boy who didn't do as he was told. Would you like to hear it?'

Though Ottilie nodded, her eyes were showing uncertainty.

'Come along then,' he said, holding out his arms. 'You can sit on my lap while I tell you all about how the wicked witch, disguised as a good fairy, put William's hands and feet in the fire and taped up his mouth so he wouldn't be able to scream. That was a terrible thing to do to a little boy, wasn't it? But we're not going to let that happen to you, are we, my angel?'

Ottilie's limbs were rigid with fear as she stared down at the floor.

'No, of course we won't let it happen to you,' he murmured, running a hand over her hair. 'My Ottilie's a good girl, she always does as Daddy says and that's why the wicked witch will never be able to get her.'

Erica didn't hear the front door closing behind Brian; she only knew he'd left when she sensed Ottilie behind her, staring into her back. The power of the child's eyes was unnatural.

They were in the kitchen. The radio was filling the room with Brahms's Piano Concerto No. 2. It was dreamy, playful, pumped with pomp and drama, decrescendo-ing to shy, skittish melodies, rising to bold stanzas and wildly important arpeggios. There was joy in the piece; exultation; adventure; danger. A great story was being conjured from a world of sound and imagination. She didn't want to leave it; it was where she belonged, in a place that had no rain streaking the windows, or wind howling at the door; a place where the telephone never rang, and children didn't fall down the stairs, or get themselves murdered.

Today, this morning, she'd finally stopped feeling like a person. She was a nothing now, a no one, an entity that had no more substance or form than the voices in her head. They were silent now, but for how long?

She'd heard what he'd said to Ottilie, so she knew that their daughter would remain silent throughout the ordeal at four thirty, and so would she. Silent and meek, eyes lowered, hands folded; a craven, tormented soul trapped in a body that still felt pain.

Focusing on the knife she was holding, she turned it over and over in her hands, watching the light catch in liquid-like spikes, while seeing it plunge and lift, arc and slice in a frenzied sort of ballet, a steel bird of prey going in for the kill.

She looked down as Ottilie moved in beside her. The child's head was bowed as she opened a cupboard to take out the plastic beaker she drank from. Her skinny neck, the tiny bumps at the top of her spinal cord were exposed. When she walked away Erica's eyes drifted to the studio shed at the end of the garden. His studio, his refuge, his private den of iniquity.

Turning around, she watched Ottilie put the

171

beaker on a chair and take a carton of juice from the fridge. 'Come here,' she said.

Ottilie looked up, startled and already afraid.

'I said, come here,' Erica repeated.

Leaving the fridge door open, and still clutching the juice, Ottilie came to look up at her mother.

Erica met the gaze and saw her daughter's unease. She knew exactly what she was going to do now, and thinking of Brian, it made her want to laugh. 'The woman who's coming later isn't the wicked witch,' she told her joyously, 'she's the good fairy, an angel even, and if you speak to her in whispers, telling her everything, she'll make all your wishes come true.'

Ottilie regarded her in confusion.

'She's the good fairy,' Erica growled angrily. 'Just remember that, all right?' and grabbing the juice she splashed some into Ottilie's beaker and thrust it at her.

It was just after four thirty when Alex turned into the Wades' stony drive and overgrown garden. The blustery day with its sudden downpours and random bursts of sunshine was darkening again, heralding the arrival of another storm. She'd already got drenched to the skin twice today, running to and from the police station with one of her teenagers who'd been giving further evidence against his sadistic uncle.

'I don't care what the police do to him in the end,' he'd stated as she'd driven him back to the residential unit, 'because I'm going to fucking kill him anyway.'

Now, as Alex parked behind a dark blue Citroën, she was trying to clear her mind of the past few hours, along with all the prejudice she'd sensed building up against Ottilie Wade's parents, the father in particular. Just because people didn't want to cooperate with social services didn't mean they were guilty of something. In many cases it meant they resented outside interference in their family's affairs, and she couldn't blame them for that – provided they were innocent of any crime, naturally. Establishing that could sometimes be one of the most testing parts of her job, for not every case of abuse or neglect was immediately evident. There were far too many harrowing situations she'd come across where the abuser was so clever at covering it up that the crime had gone undetected for years. Maybe if she and her colleagues weren't so hidebound by red tape and political correctness these cases would be exposed more quickly, but as Tommy often remarked to her, theirs had always been a world in which they were damned if they did and damned if they didn't, and he couldn't see it changing any time soon.

However, she wasn't approaching this visit to the Wades with the negative feeling of being unable to act if she needed to, because there were always steps she could take in any situation, and knowing that Tommy was back today, so at the end of the line ready to give his support if needed, was lending much confidence to her step.

Moments after she rang the bell a slight, balding man in his mid- to late thirties opened the door, all smiles as if she were a dear friend, and though she couldn't think where from, she felt sure she recognised him.

'Ms Lake,' he said cheerfully, holding out his hand. 'Brian Wade. Do come in.'

Feeling the clamminess of his palm pressing against hers, and pudginess of his fingers, she stepped into the hall to be greeted by the welcoming aroma of a home-bake. A ruse to throw her off the real scent? Or a genuine, everyday custom in the Wade household? 'Have we met?' she asked him as he closed the door. 'I feel as though I've seen you before.'

He gave a self-conscious laugh. 'Maybe you know me from the school?' he suggested.

Considering it unlikely, since Kesterly Rise wasn't in her area, she simply shrugged and shook her head as she followed him along the hall.

'Through here,' he directed chirpily. 'We're in the sitting room. My wife's made some tea and scones. I hope you like scones, they're one of Ottilie's favourites.'

Doing as she always did when going into a child's home for the first time, Alex began taking in details of the place in a way the owners – usually parents – would no doubt object to if they knew. However, she wasn't here to please them, but to gauge everything from Ottilie's point of view, or with Ottilie's best interests at heart. So far she wasn't seeing, hearing, or smelling anything to trouble her. What she was sensing, however, wasn't great, since Wade's ingratiating smile was already coming across as false, making her think that he was trying too hard. As she glanced around the large, high-ceilinged sitting room that overlooked the front garden, she was noting its warmth – a coal fire was glowing in the hearth, and its furniture and carpet appeared to be of fairly good quality and condition. No signs of dents in walls, suggesting uncontrolled violence, or stains on carpet or ceiling indicating many other possibilities.

There was a guard in front of the fire, a doll's house and pram in one corner, a TV tuned to CBeebies, and various toys scattered about the floor. The pictures on the walls were mostly old-fashioned landscapes and still lifes, and the books on the shelves seemed to be mainly reference and classics, apart from an untidy pile of children's books with the usual battered covers and crayoned-over pages. What she hadn't spotted yet was a photograph.

Or, more importantly, Ottilie.

'This is my wife, Erica,' Wade was saying as he ushered her towards the woman who'd just risen from a wing-back chair.

Mrs Wade turned out to be a good few inches taller than her husband, and was as lean as a ballerina with a posture to match. She was clad entirely in black, and so pale it was as though grief (this was what Alex imagined it to be) had sucked all the blood from her veins. Her sunken eyes, probably once beautiful, conveyed neither warmth nor animosity; they simply seemed to skim across Alex's as she mumbled a hello, and drifted on again.

Something definitely wasn't right there.

And what a mismatched pair, at least on the face of it.

'Please sit down,' Wade invited, pointing Alex towards the sofa. 'Will you have a cuppa? It's ordinary builders', I'm afraid, but I'm sure we can find something a little more exotic if you prefer.'

'What you have is fine,' Alex assured him, picking up a remote control and putting it on the table next to the tray.

Erica reached forward to take it, pointed it at the TV and plunged the room into silence.

'Ottilie was watching it before you came in,' Wade

175

explained. 'She's rather hooked, I'm afraid, but we do our best to make sure she doesn't overdo it. Milk and sugar?'

'Just milk,' Alex replied. 'Where is Ottilie?' she asked mildly.

Wade smiled, and Alex noticed the way one side of his upper lip rose higher than the other. *Where had she seen him before?* 'She's upstairs preparing a little surprise for you,' he said in a half-whisper. 'I'll go and get her in a moment. I thought it might be easier if we had a little chat first, just the three of us.'

Prepared to play along with the manipulation for the moment, she took the cup he was passing her and smiled a thank you. However, if either he, or his wife, thought she was leaving here without seeing the child, they were going to find out very soon that they were gravely mistaken.

'Scone?' Wade offered, thrusting a plateful Alex's way.

Since they looked delicious, she took one and set it down on the plate that came swiftly behind it.

'So,' Wade said brightly, as he settled into an armchair with his own afternoon treat. 'What can we tell you about Ottilie?'

Alex glanced at the mother who'd returned to the chair the other side of the hearth, and was now staring vacantly into the fire, apparently ignoring the tea her husband had put in front of her, and possibly everything else as well.

'Well, to begin with,' Alex replied, 'I'm wondering which nursery she attends. I haven't been able to find a record of her at any of the local schools.'

Wade's expression became fondly despairing. 'I'm afraid our little angel is terribly shy. We keep trying to encourage her to go, naturally, but she gets so upset when we leave her that neither of us has the heart to force her.'

Alex wouldn't have been impressed by the answer coming from any parent; from a deputy headmaster it wasn't acceptable at all. 'I'm sure, in your position,' she said, 'that you come across this sort of problem with small children all the time, so I'm surprised you're not taking a firmer stand, especially when you know very well how beneficial it is for a child to have social contact and stimulation . . .'

'Oh, indeed I do understand, and I can promise you, we haven't given up, and nor will we.' He glanced briefly at his wife before giving Alex a helpless sort of smile. From this Alex guessed he was trying to let her know that Erica, the bereaved mother, was clinging to their daughter out of fear of losing her too.

Though Alex sympathised, if it was true, it couldn't be allowed to continue.

'Meanwhile, we're making sure she's learning to read and write,' Wade ran on in his best jolly voice, 'and she's showing early signs of being rather good at sums.'

Alex's smile was faint. She really had to get over her dislike of this man, or it was going to colour her judgement before she had all the facts. On the other hand, there was a lot to be said for first impressions, so she wasn't going to start trying to like him just yet. 'Does she have any friends?' she asked.

Wade's jovial expression fell into hopeless collapse. 'As I said, she's very shy,' he reiterated mournfully.

Alex waited for him to enlarge on that, but he simply bit into a scone and used his fingers to push the extra cream and jam into his mouth. 'What about family?' she ventured. 'Does she have any cousins?'

Wade glanced at his wife. 'I'm afraid we're both only children, and all our parents have sadly passed on, so there's only the three of us now.'

'And you?' Alex said, putting her cup and saucer down. 'Have you made many friends since moving to Kesterly?' She was looking pointedly at Erica Wade now, hoping to get some sort of answer out of her.

'We have a few,' Wade replied, 'but we're not big dinner-party or dining-out sort of people.'

'Hobbies?' Alex prompted.

'Well, of course I'm involved in a number of after-school activities, and Erica is very fond of music.'

Alex waited for Erica Wade to enlarge on this, but she simply sat staring at her bony hands as they rotated the remote control she was still holding. 'And what sort of places do you take Ottilie to when you go out?' she enquired.

Wade's eyebrows rose. 'Oh let me see, we go down to the beach, of course, if the weather's fine. She's a little afraid of the donkeys, but I think she's starting to get over it now. And we take her to the pier, or to the park. She's not terribly keen on those outings though, not when there are so many other children around. What we really need to do, I keep saying, is to find someone of her own age, just one little girl or boy, that she can get to know gradually. I'm sure it would help her immensely.'

Though tempted to ask why they hadn't already done this, she didn't want to come across too aggressively on the first visit, so changing tack for the moment, she said, 'Can you tell me why you haven't registered Ottilie with the local health authority?'

He seemed amazed. 'Oh, but we have,' he protested. 'We're with Dr Aiden over on Abbottswood Way.'

'Yes, but at her age she should still be receiving checks from a health visitor, and I haven't been able to find any record of her having one.'

Wade's cheeks glowed pink. 'Oh my goodness, I'm embarrassed to say that I had totally forgotten about those checks. Of course, we must set them up immediately. I take full responsibility for the oversight, I should have registered her as soon as we moved here, but with the upheaval of it all, and trying to get settled . . .' He glanced anxiously at his wife. 'It was a very difficult time for us,' he said in a low voice. 'In many ways it still is.'

Understanding that he was referring to the death of their son, and deciding that there was nothing to be gained from going into it now, Alex made a mental note to check with the doctor as to why *he* hadn't organised the health visitor, and said, 'I'd really like to see Ottilie now. Could you go and get her, please?'

Wade looked at his wife. 'Why don't you go, dear, while I pour Ms Lake another cup of tea?'

Alex watched Erica Wade rise wordlessly from her chair, put the remote control back on the table and, without glancing at either Alex, or her husband, move like a shadow out of the room.

After closing the door behind her, Wade returned to his chair and said quietly, 'There are a couple of things I should probably tell you about Ottilie before you meet her.'

Intrigued as to what they might be, Alex watched him clasp his hands together on his knees in a womanish sort of gesture. 'Like any parents,' he began earnestly, 'we encourage her not to speak to strangers. I'm sure you'll agree that this is very good advice, but I'm afraid in Ottilie's case she has taken it very much to heart. So please don't be surprised if you find her . . . well, not as communicative as you'd like. She won't be difficult, I can assure you of that, because it isn't in her nature to be, but being as shy as she is means that it can take her some time to build up the confidence to speak.' He paused. 'Of course, she's quite chatty with us,' he gave a jolly little laugh, 'you know what children are like, it's often difficult to make them stop. It's just with people she doesn't know that she tends to clam up. I thought I should mention this so it doesn't come as a surprise, or cause you any offence if she doesn't answer your questions today. Would you care for some more tea?'

Alex put up a hand. 'One's plenty, thank you,' she said. Then, 'I couldn't help noticing that your wife isn't very communicative herself . . .'

'Which isn't a good influence on Ottilie, I know. I admit, I worry about it a lot, but grief is a strange beast, isn't it? There's no knowing how it's going to take a person, and poor Erica, she's still suffering terribly over our tragic loss. She hardly leaves the house, and as for letting Ottilie out of her sight, she almost never does. She's terrified, of course, of losing her too. Between us, I'm sure it's why Ottilie can't settle at nursery – in her own three-year-old way she's worried about her mother, and feels it's her responsibility to take care of her.'

Which is a situation that absolutely can't be allowed to continue, Alex was thinking. 'What about when it comes time for her to start school?' she asked. 'She'll have to be parted from her mother then.'

'Well, yes – and no. If it's still an issue, and obviously I hope it isn't, we'll probably go in for home schooling.'

Which was their right, but almost certainly not in Ottilie's best interests.

'Have you tried to get some help for your wife?' Alex asked bluntly.

'Oh indeed I have, but as you'll know very well, you can't force someone into counselling. They have to want the help or there's really no point, and I'm afraid my wife seems to feel that her grief is her final connection to Jonathan. If she lets that go, then there won't be anything left of him at all.'

Alex knew mothers who'd taken many years to start functioning again after the death of a child. While entirely sympathetic, her main concern was always for the effect the withdrawal, or instability, might be having on any siblings. 'What about Ottilie?' she asked. 'How well does your wife engage with her?'

Wade nodded, as though pondering the question. 'I'd say reasonably well,' he replied. 'Of course, I don't see them together when I'm at school, but there never appears to be any disharmony when I get home.'

As he picked up his tea and scone, apparently seeming to think he'd said enough for now, Alex made a quick assessment of what she'd learned so far. Mrs Wade was clearly not in a healthy state of mind, while Mr Wade, though insisting he was doing his best, wasn't taking the steps he must know he needed to take.

She wanted to know why.

'Oh, there is just one other minor thing,' he added, 'you'll probably notice that Ottilie has a small bruise under one eye. I'm afraid she tripped and fell in the garden the other day, you know how children do? I only mention it so you won't go getting the wrong idea.'

Alex nodded benignly, and reining in the wrong idea until she'd seen the bruise for herself, she turned at the sound of footsteps out in the hall. She was already bracing herself for an excuse as to why Ottilie couldn't come down to see her, but her misgivings faded as the door opened and Erica Wade came in first, saying, 'It's all right, there's nothing to be afraid of.'

Noting the lack of warmth in her tone, together with the fact that it was the first time she'd actually heard the woman speak, Alex rose to her feet – and as the dearest, sweetest little creature came in through the door she felt such a tender catch in her heart that she almost gasped a laugh.

And then it hit her. This was the little girl she'd seen in the park, the one she'd found alone on a swing, then watched walk away with her father. The one she'd worried about afterwards without quite knowing why.

Someone up there had brought them together again.

At first glance, Ottilie didn't appear to resemble either of her parents: her eyes were large and anxious in her pixie face, and her cloud of fluffy dark hair looked as soft and mussed as a baby's. She was wearing blue leggings, pink trainers and a white cardigan top that Alex couldn't quite see, thanks to the large sheet of paper she had clutched to her chest.

'Come along, there's a good girl,' Wade beckoned. 'This is Ms Lake who I told you about.'

Ottilie came forward, her eyes going cautiously to Alex. Alex wondered if she recognised her, but if she did she gave no sign of it.

Stooping to the child's height, she smiled a welcome. 'Hello,' she said softly. 'I'm very pleased to meet you. You can call me Alex if you like.'

Ottilie was still a few feet away and seemed afraid to come any further.

'Show Ms Lake – Alex – what you have for her,' Wade encouraged.

Ottilie glanced at the mother, but Erica Wade was behind Alex now, so Alex couldn't see how the woman responded. However, after a further quick look at her father, Ottilie held out her sheet of paper.

'It's for you,' Wade told Alex.

'For me?' Alex cried, feigning surprise and delight, and taking it she turned it around to get a better look. 'Is this your house?' she asked admiringly, though there wasn't much telling what it might be.

Ottilie didn't answer.

'Or is it a palace for a beautiful princess?'

Whatever it was, Ottilie's gaze was fixed on Alex as though she simply couldn't tear it away. The bruise, Alex noted, wasn't especially big and could easily have been acquired in a fall, but just as easily not.

'Can I take the picture home with me?' she asked.

At that, Ottilie turned to her father.

'Say yes,' he told her.

She looked at Alex again and nodded.

'That's lovely,' Alex murmured, wishing she could touch the little girl's cheek or smooth her hair, even sweep her up into her arms, she was so adorable. But she didn't want to frighten her, or startle the parents, so she simply admired the picture again, and placed it on top of her bag so as not to forget it.

As she settled more comfortably on her knees, she was surprised, and touched, when Ottilie did the same. 'You're a very pretty little girl,' she whispered with a smile.

Ottilie only blinked.

'Can you tell me how old you are?'

Ottilie's eyes went down and Alex recalled noticing the lavish curl of lashes before. Then she realised that Ottilie had three fingers splayed on her knee.

'You're three!' Alex exclaimed, sounding impressed.

Ottilie's eyes came up again.

'And what sort of things do you like to do?'

Ottilie only bit her lips.

'You're very good at drawing, so I expect you like that, don't you?'

Ottilie's eyes darted to the picture and back again.

'What about stories? Do you have any favourites?'

'Oh, she's very fond of Peppa Pig, aren't you?' Wade chipped in. 'And she likes the *Little Penguin Puppet Book*, and *The Hairy Fairy*.'

'*The Hairy Fairy*,' Alex cried with a laugh. 'I think I'd like that story too.'

Ottilie was watching her closely, seeming unsure what to make of her, though apparently not ready to run and hide yet.

'I bet you've got a lovely bedroom,' Alex said. 'Will you show it to me?'

Ottilie's mouth started to tremble as she looked anxiously at her father.

'Oh, I think we can do that, can't we?' Wade declared, getting to his feet.

'I hope it's tidy, Ottilie. You did tidy it, the way you were told to, didn't you?'

184

Ottilie nodded.

Alex turned to find out what Mrs Wade thought of the idea, but apparently Mrs Wade had nothing to say. However, she was watching Ottilie, and Alex could see that Ottilie was aware of it in the way she glanced back at her mother as Wade took her hand and started to walk her towards the door.

Getting to her feet, Alex said, 'Actually, this could be a good opportunity for me to have a little chat with Ottilie on her own.'

Wade stopped and turned around. He appeared both surprised and worried. 'Why would you want to do that?' he enquired.

'It's normal procedure,' she assured him with a smile, 'but you . . .'

'I've already explained that Ottilie isn't comfortable with strangers.'

'And I was about to say that you can be nearby, and anyway, I think Ottilie will be fine with me, won't you, Ottilie?'

Ottilie looked at her mother again, then up at her father.

Not having quite worked out what was going on, Alex dropped back down to Ottilie's height. 'It's OK,' she told her gently. 'I just want to have a look at your toys and books and see where you sleep. If you don't want to speak to me you don't have to, but it would be very nice if you did.'

For such a shy child, Alex was thinking, she didn't seem to have any trouble holding a gaze; however, this was the second or third time she'd noticed Ottilie pulling her lips between her teeth.

'Tell you what, why don't we all go upstairs?' Wade suggested. 'Then if Ottilie's feeling big and brave perhaps it'll be all right for her to be with Ms Lake – Alex – on her own.'

Not missing Ottilie's confusion, Alex followed father and child out into the hall, taking note of her surroundings again. The place appeared perfectly clean, and there was a gate at the top of the stairs obviously installed for Ottilie's safety.

'Does she sleepwalk?' she asked, watching Ottilie's tiny legs taking the stairs one at a time, while noting no sign of a nappy or a dummy.

'No, never,' Wade replied, glancing back over his shoulder.

'But you still need the gate?'

With an amused groan, he said, 'I'm afraid it's one of those things I keep meaning to get round to, you know how it is. It's never closed these days though, because you can manage the stairs very well on your own, can't you, Ottilie?'

Ottilie's head stayed down as she climbed.

Alex felt such a swell of affection for the child that it seemed to fill her up completely, and though she hadn't taken an instant shine to Wade it pleased her to see how proud he was of his daughter.

Ottilie's bedroom turned out to be as large as she'd expected, given the size of the house and small number of occupants, and was cluttered with the usual little-girl paraphernalia – indeed it was clear that in a material sense at least, Ottilie Wade didn't want for much.

'This is a very special room,' Alex told her, as Ottilie gazed up at her, apparently waiting for a response.

Letting go of her father's hand, Ottilie trotted over to a pile of jigsaws and turned one of the boxes upside down so the pieces fell out on to the floor.

'Ottilie, really,' Wade admonished.

Ottilie's eyes immediately showed how worried she was that she'd done something wrong.

Going to her, Alex said, 'Will you teach me how to do the puzzle?'

Ottilie was still watching her father.

Turning to Wade, Alex noticed that he'd started to sweat. She was curious to know why, unless it was the climb up the stairs. Since she was unable to ask, she said, 'I really would like to have a chat with Ottilie. Perhaps you wouldn't mind . . .'

Wade clearly did. 'But if she gets upset . . .'

'Don't worry. You can leave the door open.' Though she'd have preferred a few minutes' total privacy with the child, at this stage of proceedings Ottilie wasn't under protection, so being completely alone with her was neither allowed nor wise.

Wade was staring down at Ottilie, who seemed more confused than ever, with her lips sucked tightly between her teeth.

'Really, Mr Wade, it'll be fine,' Alex assured him.

Apparently realising he had no choice but to accept, he said, 'You'll be a good girl now, Ottilie, won't you? I'll be out on the landing – and don't forget the little chat we had, will you?'

Ottilie's face looked more pinched than ever.

'It's OK,' he said softly. 'There's nothing to worry about. You just have to do as you're told.'

Wondering what might have been said in this little chat, Alex waited for him to leave, then turning to Ottilie she said, 'Shall we sit on the floor to do the puzzle?'

Ottilie took a step back.

'It's OK,' Alex assured her, 'I promise there's nothing to be afraid of. I'd just like to see how good you are at doing puzzles. Is this one of your favourites?'

Ottilie looked down at the pieces and nodded her head.

'Come on then,' Alex said, sitting cross-legged in front of it, 'you can show me how it's done.'

Needing no more persuading Ottilie plonked herself down, crossed her own little legs, and began putting the large, colourful pieces together.

For a few minutes Alex simply watched, captivated by the way the inexpert fingers searched and pressed, while the sound of her almost babylike breathing as she concentrated was as softly rhythmic as the rain outside.

'You're very good at this,' she praised, as Ottilie completed the picture of a train with two children on board in surprisingly good time. 'I think that's the fastest I've ever seen it done.'

Though Ottilie didn't smile exactly, Alex felt sure she was pleased.

'Have you got many puzzles?' Alex asked.

Immediately getting up, Ottilie went to fetch two more and put them down on the floor between them.

'Can you do these on your own too?'

Ottilie nodded.

'You're clearly very good at puzzles. What else do you like to play with?'

Ottilie looked around uncertainly, then standing up she touched her nose and her toes, then gave an awkward little twirl as she clapped her hands.

Enchanted, Alex laughed and clapped too. 'You're a lovely dancer,' she told her. How had she not noticed before that neither parent had touched this child in her presence, apart from when her father had helped her up the stairs? For her part she could barely keep her hands to herself, she wanted to squeeze her so much.

Ottilie was off across the room again, this time coming back with a large pad of white paper and a box that turned out to be full of chalks and crayons. For such a shy child, she certainly seemed to love having someone to show off to.

'I can see you like drawing,' Alex remarked, noticing several colourful pictures pinned to a board next to the bed, also dangling from the shelves and pasted on to the walls. The bedding, she'd already noted, looked fresh and clean, as did the rest of the room. Whatever else might be happening to Ottilie, her basic needs appeared to be taken care of. 'Do you have lots of lovely pretty clothes?' she asked.

When Ottilie didn't answer, Alex turned to find her staring at her with an unreadable expression.

'I like clothes, do you?' Alex ventured.

Ottilie seemed unsure.

'I know, why don't we have a look in your wardrobe?'

Immediately Ottilie got up and went to stand in front of a cupboard door. Since the latch was too high for her to reach Alex opened it herself, and found everything inside exactly as it should be. There turned out to be nothing in the chest of drawers to concern her either.

Realising Ottilie was watching her, she started to twinkle. 'I expect you think I'm really nosy, don't you?' she said.

Ottilie didn't answer.

Alex clapped a hand over her face. 'Oh no, I think my nose is growing. It'll serve me right for poking it into places I shouldn't go.'

Ottilie's eyes widened with awe.

'Does it look big?' Alex asked, taking her hand away.

Ottilie looked and shook her head.

'Oh, thank goodness for that,' Alex gasped in relief. 'I wouldn't want to have a big nose, would you?'

Again Ottilie shook her head.

Alex knelt down in front of her and smiled.

Ottilie quickly sucked in her lips.

It was true to say that most children affected Alex deeply, no matter their age, background, colour or problems, but there was something about this little girl that was folding around her heart in a way that felt more tender, more potent than anything she generally experienced. It made her think of petals, soft and fragrant, or threads of silk weaving and spinning them together.

Leaning back to get a clearer look at her, she said, 'You're not afraid of me, are you?'

Ottilie looked as though she might be.

'I promise, you've no need to be. I'm here to be your friend.'

At that Ottilie went to fetch a teddy from the bed. Hugging it closely to her chest she turned back to Alex again.

Thinking she understood, Alex said, 'Is teddy your friend too?'

Ottilie nodded and rested her cheek on top of the bear's head.

'I expect he's a very good friend, isn't he? Does he have a name?'

Ottilie tightened her hug and began twisting from side to side.

'I'm sure he has a name. Is it Paddington?'

Ottilie shook her head.

'Dumbo?'

Again no.

'Eddie?'

Still no.

They went through several more options until to Alex's amazement Ottilie whispered something.

'What did you say?' Alex prompted gently.

'Boots,' Ottilie repeated, and buried her face in his fur.

Having to force back another urge to scoop her into an enveloping embrace, Alex sat quietly waiting to see what Ottilie would do next.

What was really going on here? she asked herself, as Ottilie set her bear down between them and held a crayon to his paw. Why didn't she speak when she almost certainly could, and even wanted to, and what had her father chatted to her about before Alex had come here? Picturing him outside on the landing, listening, hovering, she felt a sinking sensation inside, as though he was some sort of intruder in his own home. She really had to get past her antipathy for the man, or it was going to make it even more impossible to remain objective, particularly in view of her instant fondness for Ottilie.

'Does Boots always join in your games?' she asked, as Ottilie gripped the teddy's paw and crayon to make it look as though he was doing the drawing.

Ottilie shook her head.

'No? So what sort of games do you play without him?' Potentially one of the most leading questions she'd asked so far, and as Ottilie got up from the floor her father broke his silence to pop his head round the door.

'Everything all right in here?' he asked, trying to make it seem as though he was just passing by.

Finding it annoying – and interesting – that he'd chosen that moment to reappear, Alex stood up, saying, 'Ottilie was about to show me some of the games she plays.'

His eyes lit up. 'Oh, there are plenty of those, aren't there?' he encouraged Ottilie. 'Dress-up, and schools and cooking and tiddlywinks. We play lots of games together, don't we, dear?'

'Not tiger,' Ottilie said worriedly.

'Ssh, no, not tiger,' he promised.

Confused, Alex said, 'Tyre?'

Wade's face seemed flushed. 'It's nothing . . . It's . . .' He gave a little laugh. 'We had a tyre as a swing once and she fell off, I'm afraid.'

Alex looked down at Ottilie again who was now fumbling with the waistband of her leggings.

'Now, now, if you want to go to the toilet,' Wade said sharply, 'you know where it is,' and holding the door wide he watched her walk under his arm to go and do as she was told. 'Well,' he said when he and Alex were alone, 'you certainly seem to have a way with children. I haven't seen Ottilie quite so forthcoming before with someone she doesn't know.'

Putting the bear back on the bed, Alex asked, 'How often does she actually see people she doesn't know?'

Reddening, he shifted his gaze as he said, 'Well, not regularly, it's true, because we haven't wanted to foist it on her when she finds it so hard.'

'But surely, the more frequently you try the more she'll get used to it.'

'Yes, yes, I'm sure you're right. I expect I have been a bit . . . overprotective in that respect, but I

192

hope you'll agree she's a perfectly healthy and happy little girl who wants for nothing.'

Apart from friends, a brother, or sister, a functioning mother, and a father who's not so controlling he's practically smothering her, Alex thought, but didn't say. And then there was the enormous issue of Ottilie not speaking; Alex would have very much liked to know what lay behind that.

The next few minutes were spent back downstairs in the sitting room going over what would happen in the days to come, which she noticed seemed to fluster Wade. Quite what effect it might have had on Mrs Wade was anyone's guess, since she'd disappeared from the sitting room now, and from the sound of it was in the kitchen.

Suspecting that Wade had assumed – or at least hoped – that today would be her first and last visit, she said, 'I'll come again next week to bring you a copy of my initial assessment, which . . .'

'Initial? But you can see she's fine.'

Alex's expression remained neutral. 'Here's a leaflet explaining what the assessment will cover,' she said, taking one from her bag and handing it over. 'It also outlines your rights and tells you how to submit your own comments, should you wish to.'

Taking it without looking at it, he said, 'I really don't think all this is necessary . . .'

'Mr Wade, Ottilie doesn't speak,' she broke in firmly. 'She doesn't go to nursery school, and she doesn't have a health visitor. These are all causes for concern. Perhaps you'll have addressed them by the time I come back. I certainly hope so. Now, I'd like to see a copy of Ottilie's little red book.' This was the Personal Child Health Record given to every infant at birth. 'Do you have it to hand?'

'Um, I'm not entirely sure where it is,' he replied, hunting around with his eyes, 'but we do have one, naturally. It probably hasn't been updated since we left Northumbria though.'

It wouldn't have been, if they didn't have a health visitor – an oversight that Alex was finding increasingly incredible, given his position. 'It would be helpful if you could locate it by my next visit,' she said evenly.

'Of course, I-I'll certainly do that.'

As they walked out to the hall she said, 'I'd like your permission to seek background information from Ottilie's doctor and Northumbria Healthcare to help with my assessment.'

His neck turned crimson. 'I really don't think you need to go to all that trouble,' he protested.

Forcing herself not to snap, she said, 'Once again, Mr Wade, Ottilie isn't speaking, nor is she being properly socialised . . .'

'I understand that, but I'd rather we tackled this our way.'

'With respect, your way clearly isn't working. She's either too shy to speak, or too afraid . . .'

'To strangers, yes, but not to us. I told you, she's very chatty with us.'

Not pointing out that she'd seen no evidence of it, Alex said, 'Do I have your permission to make the contacts?'

'Well, no, I'm afraid I can't give it, not without knowing exactly who you're going to contact.'

'As I said, it'll be your doctor, Northumbria Health Authority, the police . . .'

'The police! Why on earth . . . ?'

'It's a formality.' She threw out her hands. 'Surely you know that running background checks is normal practice when we receive a referral?'

'And who did this referral come from? Someone who wouldn't give her name. I've already told you about the woman who was harassing me. She's obviously found out where I am and is up to her old tricks again.'

'Whether that's true or not, it doesn't change what I've observed here today. Now I'd like your permission to carry out the checks.'

Apparently too rattled to think clearly, he said, 'It doesn't seem as though you're giving me much choice. If I say no I'll be damning myself in your eyes for heaven only knows what – and if I say yes I'll be allowing you to bother people who are far too busy with much more important matters to want to waste their time . . .'

'Do I have your permission?' Alex cut in.

He was stiff with frustration. 'As I said, I don't seem to have much choice.'

'Thank you,' Alex responded. 'I appreciate your time today. I'm sure it goes without saying that we all have Ottilie's best interests at heart . . .'

'And you think I don't?'

'I did say we. I can see that you're very attached to your daughter. Now, I'm afraid I really must be going,' and slipping past him before he could say any more she ran through the rain to her car.

It was as she opened the door to get into the driver's seat that she glanced up at a front bedroom window and spotted Ottilie's little face looking down at her. Melting into a smile, she hoped Ottilie might smile back, but she didn't. She merely carried on watching until Alex had turned the car around and disappeared from view.

* * *

Cooling his hot cheeks with his trembling hands, Brian Wade stormed into the kitchen to find his wife. 'Did you talk to Ottilie this afternoon?' he demanded roughly.

Erica simply went on washing up the teacups.

'I said, did you talk to Ottilie this afternoon?' he growled.

When she continued to ignore him he grabbed her arm and turned her to face him. Clocking her smirk, he purpled with anger and leaned in towards her. 'Be very careful, Erica,' he warned. 'Be very, very careful,' and turning on his heel he went upstairs to find Ottilie.

She was in her room, lying on the bed with Boots her bear, her back turned to the door, her thumb jammed comfortingly in her mouth. She'd obviously left her trainers and leggings in the bathroom, but she was still wearing her top and a pair of daisy-covered pants. Her legs were black and blue. Thank God the social worker hadn't seen them.

'Stand up,' he said quietly.

Obediently she rolled over and slid down on to her feet.

'You were a good girl and a naughty girl today, weren't you?' he said, wiping his neck with a handkerchief.

Ottilie's eyes filled with fear.

'You behaved very well,' he told her, 'until you spoke to the wicked witch.'

Ottilie gave a little flinch and held on tighter to her bear.

'Your mother told you it was safe to do so, didn't she?' he demanded. 'But she's wrong, Ottilie. It isn't safe. You were lucky this time, the wicked witch didn't steal your tongue, but now she's going to make you see lots of other people and I won't always be there to make sure nothing bad happens. So you must promise me now that you won't speak to any of them. Do I have your promise?'

Ottilie quickly nodded.

'Good girl. And what happens when you're good? You get a reward, don't you? But first you have to be punished for disobeying me today,' and going to the door he closed and locked it. 'Are you ready?' he asked as he turned back.

Tears were pearling in Ottilie's eyes as a trickle of urine started to run down one leg.

Chapter Nine

It was gone six by the time Alex returned to the office, feeling oddly drained by the time she'd spent at the Wades', and as worried about Ottilie as she'd been that day at the park. The difference now was that she knew she had something to worry about.

'On the face of it,' she told Tommy, who was still at his desk, 'she seems perfectly healthy and well taken care of, but the fact that she doesn't speak, has no health visitor and isn't being socialised in any way . . .' She shook her head in mounting concern. 'Something's definitely not right in that house. I'm not sure what it is yet, or whether it's connected to the mother or father – it could be both – but what I do know is that Ottilie Wade isn't living the life of a normal three-going-on-four-year-old child.'

Being a champion of gut instincts, Tommy said, 'Do you know if she *can* speak and just doesn't, or if she's never learned?'

'I'm pretty sure she's capable, though to what extent I've no idea. The only word I got out of her was the name of her teddy, Boots. Isn't that sweet? He has little black felt wellies.'

Tommy's eyebrows rose in amusement.

Shrugging, she said, 'The father claims she can

be very chatty. I can't say I noticed it, but then he did say she's shy with strangers.'

'But you managed to carry out all the normal checks and the parents were cooperative?'

'Yes, in so far as they let me in and allowed me to speak to her. She was wearing leggings and a long-sleeved top, so I didn't get a proper look at her, she didn't seem to be in any pain or discomfort though. I'm concerned about her teeth, because apart from the couple of words she spoke to me she kept her mouth very firmly shut – I mean sucking-in-between-the-teeth shut.' She lifted her eyes to Tommy and as a knowing look passed between them, she went on, 'It's either a dental problem, or more likely someone's told her that the nasty lady will steal her tongue if she speaks to her – or something along those lines.'

'A common form of manipulation in cases of mental or sexual abuse,' Tommy said gravely. 'Did you get the impression there might be any going on?'

Alex inhaled deeply. The mere thought of Brian Wade with his pudgy fingers and sweaty skin touching that dear little soul in any kind of an inappropriate way could make her nauseous with disgust. 'I've tried to tell myself that the father is simply being ultra-protective after the death of their son,' she said. 'I only wish I believed it ended there.'

'OK, but sometimes it's our job to think the worst,' Tommy reminded her softly, 'even when the victim is a little girl who's getting to our hearts.'

Alex flicked him a glance. Tommy always read her too easily. 'Sexual abuse is definitely possible,' she conceded, 'of course it is, but I came across no evidence of it today, apart from a moment when she started to pull down her leggings.'

Tommy's eyes widened.

Alex shrugged. 'The father told her to go and use the toilet if she needed to, and off she went, so it could be that she starts stripping off before she gets to the bathroom. Plenty of kids do.'

'And you're prepared to give this bloke the benefit of the doubt?'

'No, not really, but we have to take into consideration the fact that he's a deputy headmaster so he'll have undergone all the necessary checks.'

'True, but that doesn't buy him a free pass.'

'Of course not, far from it, but if there is anything untoward going on it could be the mother, who, I have to say, is distinctly weird.'

'In what way?'

'Well, to begin with she hardly speaks either, and there was zero interaction between her and the child, or the husband. She just sat there most of the time, in a world of her own.'

'A drinker?'

'I don't think so, but who knows? She could be on drugs of some kind, possibly even prescription to help deal with the loss of her son.'

'How long has he been dead?'

'Just over three years.'

'Mm, long enough for her to be functioning normally again. On the other hand, there's never any knowing how anyone's going to react in grief, especially when it comes to the loss of a child.'

'If you saw her,' Alex continued, 'you'd think she'd just risen up from the grave. Honest to God, she's so pale and thin she must hardly ever eat, or go out.'

'Anorexic? Agoraphobic?'

'Possibly both. Ottilie might be small for her age,

but at least she looks as though she's fed, and she has a reasonable colour, so she presumably goes out sometimes. In fact I saw her once, a couple of months ago, at Dillersby Park.' She took a deep breath and let it go slowly. The way Ottilie had haunted her after that seemed to be stirring inside her again. It was as though something was drawing them together, and she could no more resist it than she could explain it. 'I definitely need to speak to the mother alone,' she decided. 'He wouldn't let her get a word in, not that she tried, mind you.'

Tommy glanced at his watch. 'It's a bit late now to start writing it up,' he said, 'so if I were you I'd take yourself off home, and try to switch off for a while. It'll all still be here in the morning.'

Knowing very well that it would, Alex pushed her hands through her hair and tried to stop seeing Ottilie's face watching her from an upstairs window – those soulful dark eyes, those sweet little tufty curls. Was she still there, gazing out into a world she was hardly a part of? No, of course not, it was ludicrous to think it. But what was she doing now? Playing alone in her room with Boots her bear? Having her tea? She didn't want to let her mind go to where her instincts were taking her, not now when there was still a chance, please God, that she was wrong.

Looking up as Tommy put a comforting hand on her shoulder, she found herself having to swallow a rise of emotion. This was what she loved most about Tommy, he never lectured or launched off into warnings when he sensed one of his team becoming more attached than usual to a child. He understood that it happened, and took the view that if they didn't care then they were in the wrong job.

'It'll be all right, pet,' he said gently. 'You're on her case now, which makes her a lucky girl indeed, because if anyone can do right by her, we know it's you.'

Alex smiled. 'No pressure there then.' She sighed wearily. 'The really awful part of this,' she said, 'is how much more abuse she might have to suffer before we can prove it, and act. You know how long it can take to gather evidence when we're dealing with people like this . . .'

'First things first,' he cautioned. 'Get your initial assessment written up and a health worker on the case and we'll take it from there. Now, I mean it this time, take yourself off home.'

'I will, I will, just tell me, is it true there are going to be redundancies when the hubs merge?'

His expression turned grave. 'Possibly. I don't know yet, I'm still trying to find out. Now off you go, and don't think about this place again until you come in tomorrow.'

With his sensible advice ringing in her ears, Alex picked up her bag and bundles of paperwork and started back down to her car. Normally she didn't find it too hard to switch off, especially when she had a show to be thinking about, but there was no rehearsal tonight, and even more than the threat of losing her job, she simply couldn't get Ottilie Wade out of her mind.

However, she had to try at least for a while, because dear old Millie deserved her full attention when she got to the care home, which was where she was now headed. It wouldn't be a long visit, it was too late in the day for that, but knowing how much pleasure Millie got from seeing her made her want to drop in, even if it was only for a few minutes.

She'd love to ask about her mother again, but knew already that the chances of Millie pulling anything coherent together were about as remote as her being able to dance the fandango at the Christmas ball.

Finding Millie fast asleep, she sat with her for a while in case she woke up, but she didn't, so she spent a few minutes chatting with a couple of the other residents, thanking one for the banana he insisted on giving her, and guiding another back to her room to put on some clothes. After a brief word with one of the nurses, who told her that Millie's niece was planning to visit sometime the following week, she returned to the car to find a message on her personal mobile from Gabby.

'Hi you, hope everything's great. Just ringing to say we're all feeling much better now, and I thought, if it works for you, I'd come up to have some lunch with you on Sunday. Wish I could make the show on Saturday – great stuff on Facebook, by the way, really puts that nasty piece of work Heather Hancock in her place – but we've got this wedding, remember? Obviously I can't get out of that, but maybe I can get there the week after. Anyway, Sunday would be lovely if you're free, just the two of us so we can have a nice little chat. Let me know when you can.'

A nice little chat, Alex was thinking as she clicked off, usually meant there was something Gabby needed to get off her chest, or to seek advice about, or to plot, such as some new crazy idea for how to celebrate the twins' birthday. Whatever, it would be lovely to see her, and since Jason would almost certainly be spending the day with his kids there shouldn't be any problem making it just the two of them.

By the time she'd called Gabby back and got the

ins and outs of everything that was happening in her sister's world – presumably apart from what Gabby really wanted to talk about – she was pulling up next to Jason's car, and loving the fact that he was already home. Just as wonderful was knowing that there was nothing on the agenda for either of them tonight, so for once they could rustle up something simple to eat and chill out in front of the TV to watch whatever they'd recorded. Unless she decided to write up her notes on Ottilie. Maybe she should do that while it was all still fresh in her mind.

'Hi honey, I'm home,' she called out as she let herself in the front door.

'In here,' Jason called back from the kitchen.

'I hope there's a nice big drink waiting for me,' she teased, as she let her bags fall to the floor and shrugged off her jacket.

Receiving no response, she went through to the kitchen expecting to find him with his head in a recipe book, or filling a glass, but to her surprise he was sitting at the table with nothing at all in front of him and a look on his face that was so serious that her heart immediately tripped with alarm.

'What is it?' she cried, hoping to God nothing had happened to one of his kids, but he wouldn't be here if it had. And it couldn't be Gabby, because she'd just been speaking to her, or Millie, who'd been fine when she'd left the home. One of his mates had lost a limb on the job, or been killed . . .

'You need to listen to the message on the machine,' he told her, in a voice that did nothing to put her mind at rest.

Baffled, she glanced at the answerphone. 'Why? Who's it from?' she demanded, not sure she wanted to hear whatever it was.

'Actually, I'm expecting you to tell me.'

Going to push the button, she listened to some muffled noises that went on for a while until finally someone spoke. The instant she heard the voice she knew exactly who it was, even though he didn't give his name.

'I know it was you what came round here harassing my family,' Shane Prince growled. 'You just keep your fucking self to yourself, do you hear me? We don't want you coming back here, messing with us. If you do, you're finished, right? We know your boyfriend's got kids, so watch out for them, lady, and keep your distance, or it's them what's going to be needing care. Tiffany, Heidi, Tom.' He disconnected abruptly.

Her face was as ashen as Jason's as she turned to look at him. She felt sick, disoriented, afraid of what might happen next.

'Who the hell is that?' Jason demanded. 'No, don't answer. He's obviously one of the scumbags you deal with over on the Temple Fields estate. This is what your job's bringing home to us, Alex. Threats to you, my *kids*, for God's sake . . .'

'Jason, stop, please. He won't mean that. He's just saying it to try and scare me off . . .'

'Well he's bloody well managed it for me. He knows their names, for Christ's sake. How can he know their names?'

'I don't know, but it doesn't mean anything . . .'

'Are you crazy? Of course it means something. It means he's gone to the trouble of finding out how to get to you and now he's using it to get what he wants. So what is it that he wants? Why are you harassing his family?'

'We're not harassing them, we're trying to see his

205

sister. She's fourteen and has an STD that . . .' She stumbled as she remembered what had happened to the doctor who'd reported it.

'Well, if I were you I'd leave the sister alone,' he growled, 'because that guy sounds pretty dangerous to me. How am I supposed to protect my kids from someone like that?' He gave a bitter laugh. 'What an irony this is, there's you, all about helping strangers, the down-and-outs, the bleeding hearts, but when it comes to the kids who matter to me you've got them right in the firing line.'

'Jase, please, I had no idea this would happen, but I promise you as soon as I tell Tommy about it he'll take me off the case, then there'll be no reason for us to worry about it again.'

He looked far from convinced as he pushed a hand through his hair, trying to make himself calm down.

'Honest to God, I never wanted to get involved with that family in the first place,' she told him, going to sit down with him. 'Everyone knows what they're like, but if it's any consolation no social workers, or their families, have ever actually been harmed.' She couldn't mention the doctor, she just couldn't. 'Threatened, yes,' she admitted, 'but you know that goes with the job.'

'It's not something my kids should be dragged into.'

'I know that, and I'm really sorry. I'll try to make sure it never happens again.'

'By doing what, exactly? Asking him nicely not to call you at home?'

'By making sure I'm taken off the case and don't have to go near them again. I only got it because Wendy didn't give me a choice, but now Tommy's back I can do something about it.'

'If it's not already too late.'

'It isn't, we haven't taken his sister into care, and I'm not even sure that we will.' There was nothing to be gained from telling him she'd wanted an EPO, especially when it had been turned down. Nor was it going to help if she told him that Shane Prince had been targeting her for no reason for a while now. She'd discuss it all with Tommy in the morning, but meanwhile she had to do whatever it took to put Jason's mind at rest.

As he got to his feet she could see just how strained he was, and when he walked to the window to stare out at the twilight a bolt of unease moved slowly through her. There was something else, she could tell, either that or he wasn't ready yet to let this go away.

When he turned to face her he looked so pale, so tense, that she felt she could see the bones, the veins beneath his skin. She swallowed hard and bunched her hands together, suddenly afraid of what might be coming next.

He turned his head aside as he said, 'Look, I didn't want to tell you like this, God knows I didn't want to tell you at all, but now, with that call and the way everything's going . . .' He pressed a hand to his head as he forced himself to continue. 'Alex, I'm really sorry, I'm already hating myself for this, especially after that fuckwit threatened you and all, but I . . . I just can't live with you any more.'

Alex started to reel.

'It's not that I don't care about you,' he pressed on quickly, 'because you know I do, I mean I *really* do. It's just that Gina and I . . . Well, with the kids and everything . . . It's not fair on anyone to go on the way we are.'

When he stopped Alex almost felt as though she was floating. She couldn't quite get a grip on this. It couldn't be real, surely. 'What – what do you mean, it's not fair going on the way we are?' she stammered.

'Not you and me, me and Gina.' He threw back his head with his eyes tightly closed, as though trying to force himself to go on. 'It's crazy,' he spluttered. 'It's like I'm having an affair with my own wife, when really I should be with her, taking care of her and the kids, being a proper husband and dad, and this . . . this tonight only proves it. I just didn't want to hurt you, or let you down in any way.'

Alex could only stare at him. 'What do you mean, an affair?' she finally blurted.

His eyes darted to her and away again. 'You know what I mean,' he replied.

He'd been deceiving her, cheating on her, and she'd had no idea. She was trying to think what to say, or do, but she was finding it too hard to connect with the words. Suddenly they all seemed to be coming at once. 'I don't believe this!' she yelled. 'You told me your marriage was over! When we got together you said there would never be any going back . . .'

'I didn't think then that there would be . . .'

'I'd never have let you move in here if I'd known you were going to do something like this. I trusted you, Jason! I thought you were a decent, honest person . . .'

'I am! I mean, I try to be. I swear I had no idea things were going to turn out like this. The last thing I ever wanted was to hurt you . . .'

'Well, you're making a pretty damned good job

of it now! I thought you . . .' She broke off as a sob wrenched away her words. This couldn't be happening, please God, it just couldn't.

'I'm sorry,' he murmured, making to put a hand on her, then drawing it back. 'But you don't need to worry. I'll still do all the technical stuff for the show, and obviously I'll pay my share of the bills up to the end of the month.'

She was shaking her head. 'I should have seen this coming,' she muttered angrily. 'I can't believe I didn't see it coming.'

Sitting down at the table, he took her hands and waited for her eyes to come to his. When she saw how tormented and guilty he looked, she pulled sharply away. 'How long?' she demanded, her temper rising again.

He shook his head. 'It doesn't matter.'

'It does to me.'

'OK, a few weeks, maybe months.'

Alex wanted to take a breath, but was afraid to.

'If you think about it,' he went on gently, 'we were both in a really bad place when we met. Your dad hadn't long died and my marriage was in pieces . . . I guess we kind of needed each other then, but now time's gone on and things have changed . . .'

'For you, maybe, but not for me. I still love you, Jason, and I really, really don't want you to go.' Tears were swamping her eyes as panic started to climb into her heart. She couldn't bear to think of him going, walking out of the door and leaving her here all alone. He was such a big part of her life, the very centre of it, how was she going to cope without him?

When he was gone there'd be no one.

'Alex, I'm sorry,' he groaned. 'I swear to God if

I could make this any easier I would, but I have to be true to myself as well as to everyone else, and if I stayed here, well, it just wouldn't be the right thing to do.'

'Maybe not for you, but what about me?' she cried, hating how desperate she sounded, but it was how she felt. And afraid, terrified even of letting him go. 'You can't do this, I won't let you. You said you were going to fix this place up so we could sell it for more, so what was that all about if you knew we didn't have a future? Oh God, don't tell me, you offered out of guilt, didn't you? You thought that if you did something nice for me you wouldn't have to feel so bad when you left. It was never about us and what kind of house it would help us to buy together, because you never had any intention of buying anything with me.'

'Listen to me,' he said, grabbing her hands as she tried to get up. 'I'm not going to deny that was part of the reason I offered, but I still want to do it. For *you*, so you'll have something . . .'

'Stop it, just stop,' she shouted. 'I don't want your pity, for God's sake. I want you, the man I trust and need and . . .'

'No, you only think you need me, but when it comes right down to it you don't, not really. It's your job that really matters to you, and all those kids whose lives would be even worse than they already are if it weren't for you. Don't get me wrong, I think it's great what you do, and I understand why you do it after what's happened to you, but it's not what my life is about.'

'I'm not saying it has to be. I'm not about building houses or extensions or any of the things you do either, but that doesn't mean we're not right for each other. We've been really happy here, or that's what I thought, so are you telling me now that you weren't, that what we had never meant anything to you?'

'You know I'm not saying that. I've loved being with you, and if it weren't for Gina and the kids this is exactly where I'd want to be, but I have to put them first, surely you understand that, especially now that fuckwit's started threatening them. I can't leave them to fend for themselves. They haven't got a clue how to deal with people like that.'

'And I have, so it's OK to leave me on my own?' Her eyes were flashing the challenge as behind her anger, misery and despair were trying to choke her.

She wanted to beg him, plead with him, barricade him in, anything to make him stay, but for the moment at least her pride wouldn't allow it.

'Are you leaving tonight?' she managed to make herself ask.

He looked up at her, and seeing the answer in his eyes she felt herself starting to break down. 'It's OK,' she told him, trying desperately to hold it together. 'It's probably for the best if you go straight away.'

'You understand, don't you,' he said, 'that it's because I feel the way I do about you that this is so hard. I'm going to miss you like crazy . . .'

'Don't patronise me,' she spat, moving away from him. 'You'll get over it. We both will.'

He got up too and seemed at a loss for what to do next.

'You should go and pack a bag,' she told him sharply. 'We can arrange for you to collect the rest of your things another time.'

As he went upstairs it took every ounce of will-power she possessed not to go after him and beg him to change his mind. Instead, she turned to the sink and clung to the edge as denial tore through her with a terrible might, trying to stop her from believing it, or fool her into thinking he'd only be gone a few days and then he'd come back. He wouldn't, though, she knew it, because he'd always told her that his children came first, and now he was proving it. They mattered far more than she did, and always would. She didn't blame him for that, he was their father so it was the way it should be; she simply couldn't stand the wrenching loneliness that was already trying to engulf her, the terrible chill of isolation as she realised it was why he'd never really tried to make her feel a part of his family.

When he finally came down again he stood at the front door and watched her come into the hall. 'You realise, don't you,' she said, masking her pain with anger, 'that you're making me feel as though I've been having an affair with a married man all this time.'

'But it's not true . . .'

'I wish it weren't, but actually, you are still married, legally, it's just that you told me it was over.' Her eyes were flashing the challenge as her heart shrank from the hurt.

'I thought it was,' he said miserably.

'I trusted you,' she cried. 'I've told you things I've never told anyone else in my life.'

'And I swear they'll always stay with me.'

'And I'm supposed to believe that?'

His eyes gazed deeply into hers. 'I hope you do,' he said softly.

She turned abruptly aside, unable to bear the way he was looking at her.

It was too tender, too regretful – and final.

'I'm sorry,' he whispered.

Suddenly she wanted to strike him, shake him, barricade the door so he couldn't get out, but somehow she managed to stay where she was.

'Are you going to be all right?' he asked.

'What do you think?' she retorted.

He flinched and put his head down. 'I'll see you on Saturday then,' he mumbled.

She'd have preferred him not to come, but it wasn't possible to stage the play without him, and it would have been selfish to ruin it for the others.

'If that idiot calls again you ring me, OK?'

She almost wanted to laugh. Exactly what did he think he was going to do with the likes of Shane Prince? Or was the concern mainly for his children? 'He won't,' she said, not really caring for herself in that moment whether he did or didn't.

He returned his eyes to hers and her heart gave a painful twist to see how anguished he was inside, but as he made to reach for her she took a swift step back. 'You should go,' she told him. She was so close to breaking now that she didn't think she could hold on another moment.

He nodded silently, then turning around he opened the door.

As it closed behind him she could feel the breath starting to shudder and catch inside her. She clasped a hand to her mouth in an effort to keep control, but she couldn't. Her knees buckled and as she slumped helplessly to her knees she buried her face in her hands, sobbing with wretched, tormented despair. *This wasn't happening. It just couldn't be. He hadn't left.* It was a nightmare and any minute now she was going to wake up to find him coming down the stairs to take her back to bed. Yet even through her sobs she could hear him getting into his car, starting the engine and driving away. She pressed her hands to her mouth, trying to stifle the desperate cries for him to come back. *Jason, please, please, I don't want to be without you. I thought you loved me.*

She had to go after him, do something, anything to make him understand that she couldn't go on without him. He was all she had and she felt so afraid now, so lost and rejected. What was the matter with her? What was she doing wrong? Why was it that no one ever loved her enough?

Chapter Ten

The following morning Alex woke early, having barely slept, but at least, when she looked in the mirror, her eyes weren't too puffy or red to be seen, and mercifully no one would be able to tell what wrenching emotions were churning about inside her. Nor would they have any way of knowing how vividly she'd dreamt in the night, though it was hard to be sure whether they'd been dreams when she hadn't even been sure she was sleeping. Maybe they were memories, coming from a past so distant it was virtually impossible to reach. There had been a man throwing a ball on a beach, and a woman running down a staircase with a child in her arms. She had no idea who the man was, but perhaps the woman was her, and the child who she used to be? Or maybe it had no significance at all.

She wondered with a horrible ache in her heart if Jason had been awake too, missing her, or worrying about her. Maybe he was sleeping peacefully, relieved that he'd finally told her so he could get on with his life. Picturing him with Gina was a crazy, masochistic thing to do, but it was hard to make herself stop. She imagined the children leaping on him in delight as he came through the door, thrilled to have him back with them, and to be rid of her. They'd never have to sleep in, or even visit her creepy house again. Hurrah!

It was no good now wishing she'd tried harder to win them over. She should have done it while she'd had the chance, instead of always putting it off, or making excuses. Realising that Jason had never really encouraged it brought in fresh waves of hurt and rejection, but nevertheless there was so much she could have done to make them feel special and a part of her life. Instead, she'd viewed them almost as rivals, certainly obstacles to their father's affections. Why had she done that when they were just children, and had so much more of a right to him than she could ever claim? She'd hardly spared a thought for their broken home and the angst, self-blame, confusion it must have caused them. She could see it all now, even feel it and wanted desperately to help heal it, but during the time she and Jason were together she'd barely allowed herself to recognise it.

And she was supposed to be all about protecting children.

She *was* all about that, because he'd been right when he'd said it was what really mattered to her, and his children had him and Gina to take care of them. Those who came into her world depended on her. It was why, after he'd gone last night, she'd picked herself up from the floor and forced herself to open her laptop so she could write up her visit to Ottilie. Ottilie's needs were far greater than hers, though there had been moments, she had to admit, when she'd seemed to get herself confused with Ottilie. It must have been the latch on Ottilie's cupboard door that had got her thinking of how she'd been locked in a room as a child, crying for her mother and her mother never coming to find her. Every now and again, when the terrible truth of Jason leaving had come over her, she'd had to break off for a while and remind herself that she had no right to long for a man who belonged to somebody else. He was with his children now, where he wanted to be, so it was wrong to will him to come back. It was almost impossible to stop trying, however, and nothing, but nothing was making the longing or despair go away. As the hours passed it was only getting worse.

It surprised her when she read through her report before leaving for work to find that none of her own issues had ended up clouding the details. Somehow she'd managed to pull together a succinct and accurate account of what she'd witnessed at the Wades', and a summary of what her next steps would be. However, before she could get started on them she needed to deal with the call from Shane Prince to make sure she was removed from the case.

'It's not a problem, pet,' Tommy assured her when she'd finished telling him about the threats in Shane's message. 'I was never keen on you being sent there in the first place. How did Jason take it? I don't suppose he was too happy having his kids brought into it.'

'No, he wasn't,' Alex confirmed, feeling a void opening up inside her simply to hear his name. 'It was – he was quite shaken up by it.'

'Did Prince give any indication of knowing where to find Jason's kids?'

Thank God the answer to that was no. 'But he knew their names,' she reminded him.

'Mm, definitely not good. I think we need to have a chat with the police to make them aware of what's happened. Meantime, you can consider yourself officially free of that family. I'll take it on from here.' He regarded her closely. 'Now, what else is troubling you, pet? I can see you're not yourself this morning. Is it something you want to talk about?'

Alex shook her head, unable to speak for fear of the words being pushed out by a sob. 'I'm OK,' she finally managed.

'Well, that's not true, so maybe you ought to give me a heads-up here so I can see if there's anything I can do.'

Alex was still trying to choke back the tears as she said, 'OK, but please don't make a big deal of it. Jason's gone back to his wife and . . . He's . . . I'll be fine, honestly. I just need to get on with some work.'

Looking deeply concerned, Tommy said, 'Did it have something to with this call?'

'No, not really. I mean, I think it triggered it, but he says he's been thinking about it for a while.'

Tommy nodded gravely. 'Well, I'm very sorry to hear that, pet. These things are never easy, so you know where I am if you need a shoulder, and they're both pretty big so if you get fed up with one you can always try the other.'

With a splutter of laughter, Alex grabbed a tissue from the box he was offering and not trusting herself to say any more she quickly returned to her desk.

Minutes later she was making her first call of the day to children's services in Northumbria, where a very helpful woman, Dee, carried out an immediate search of their records. It transpired that the Wades were on file; they'd been visited several times after the loss of their son, Jonathan, who'd died following an asthma attack. She could find no mention of either Erica or Brian Wade being harassed by anyone during the time they were receiving family support.

After thanking her, Alex spoke to a health visitor from the same authority who had taken over from the midwife after Ottilie's birth, and continued to visit her regularly up until the time the Wades had left the area. She'd never had any concerns about the child, she told Alex, but the mother had certainly been suffering with depression.

'Do you know if she was receiving any treatment for it?' Alex asked.

'She told me she was, but I can't say I ever saw any signs of improvement. If anything, by the time they moved she seemed more withdrawn than ever, and was hardly relating to the baby at all. It was the father who was bonding with the child, bathing her, feeding her, taking her out for walks. I discussed the situation with a social worker, but by the time she got round to visiting the family they were already packing up for the move.'

After thanking the health visitor and entering everything she'd learned into Ottilie's file, Alex carried out a quick search on Google just in case there was a newspaper report on Jonathan Wade's death, or something interesting about the school where Wade had taught that might not have made the official files, but she found nothing she didn't already know. So, looking up the number of Northumbria police she connected to the central station. It took an eternity to get through to someone who sounded willing to help, but even she ended up taking Alex's details and assuring her that someone would get back to her by the end of the day.

And if Alex believed that she'd believe Father Christmas landed on rooftops and squashed himself down chimneys.

Next on her list was Ottilie's GP, Timothy Aiden, who this time turned out to be free to take her call and sounded appalled when he learned that Ottilie didn't have a health visitor. An oversight, he told her, that would be corrected immediately.

'Before you go,' Alex said hastily, 'are you also Mrs Wade's GP?'

'I am,' he confirmed. 'But you understand that I'm not at liberty to discuss . . .'

'Yes, of course, but it would be helpful to know if she's receiving any sort of treatment, or medication for her . . . Depression? Agoraphobia? What I'm saying is, something's clearly wrong with her, and if it's impacting on Ottilie, which it's bound to be, I'll need to have some idea of what's going on.'

'I see. Well, I can tell you that Mrs Wade is on tranquillisers, but they're only mild and so shouldn't be having any adverse effect on her daughter. Indeed, if they were, I've no doubt in my mind that Mr Wade would have informed me by now.'

'Is he a patient too?'

In a clipped voice he said, 'It's not unusual, you know, for the whole family to be with the same GP.'

'Of course not.' Why was he being so defensive? 'So you've known the Wades for, what, about a year?'

'That's right.'

'But you presumably have records from the previous GP . . .'

'Indeed I do, but I can assure you they don't contain anything that would be of any interest or help to you.'

'And you know this because?'

220

'Because I'm familiar with the records, and I know what you're looking for.'

'Really? And what would that be?'

'You're a social worker attached to child protection. I think the answer speaks for itself.'

'Excuse me for saying, but you sound as though you don't really approve of my concern for Ottilie.'

'Well, that's just nonsense because of course I approve. You do a marvellous job, all of you, most of the time. But you have to admit there are occasions when you get it wrong, and I'm telling you Brian and Erica Wade are very good parents and Ottilie is in excellent health.'

'Except she doesn't have a health visitor and nor does she speak and her mother's a . . .' she wanted to say basket case, but settled for, 'very withdrawn. Thank you for your help, Dr Aiden, I'm sure I'll be in touch again.'

'Wow,' Saffy commented from the next desk, 'someone just got short shrift.'

Alex sighed irritably. 'Remind me if I ever need a doctor, never to go to him. Timothy Aiden. Ring any bells?'

Saffy shook her head. 'Kesterly South?'

'That's right. I'll have a chat with someone over there to find out what they think of him. By the way, any news from their end about the merger?'

'Not that I know of, but it wouldn't hurt to ask while you're speaking to them. Are you OK, Alex? You look a bit peaky this morning.'

Feeling a wave of misery closing around her, Alex quickly pushed past it, saying, 'Oh I'm fine, just a bit of a headache that's all. Anyway, the good news is, I'm off the Prince case. Tommy's taking it on from here.'

'Brilliant. That old dragon should never have forced you to take it in the first place.'

In total agreement with that, Alex picked up the phone again, and now the office was filling up she had to use a finger to block out the noise of so many people talking at once.

To her surprise there was no reply from Brian Wade's old school in Northumbria.

'Ben! Ben!' she cried, spotting him coming in through the door. 'I need to talk to you about the Wade family on North Hill. You took . . .'

'Sorry, not now,' he interrupted. 'I'm already late for a meeting with legal.'

'Just tell me if you spoke to anyone in Northumbria,' she called after him.

'If I did, it'll be in the file,' he called back, and he was gone, the swing doors to the far corridor flapping like rubber wings after him.

Catching Saffy's eye Alex pulled a face, and dialled the school in Northumbria again. This time someone picked up, but she was forced to leave a message for Derek Tolland, the headmaster, to call her back. Though she was used to finding herself at the bottom of most priority lists it could still be irksome at times, particularly when she wasn't seeming to make much headway with Ottilie's case. Still, she had no choice but to wait, so pulling up the case notes for Tawny Hopkins, a fifteen-year-old drug addict and habitual absconder from care, she started updating them until her mobile rang to interrupt her. It was Winston Tucker, the probation officer for the parents of at least two youngsters in her caseload, so she had to take the call even though it was likely to go on for some time. If anyone from

Northumbria rang meanwhile, they'd just have to leave a message and she'd get back as soon as she could.

Back and forth, back and forth. She knew already that it could go on for days.

However, just after five that evening Derek Tolland rang with a brusque apology for not calling sooner.

'Well, I must say,' he declared snappishly when she'd finished explaining why she was calling, 'I really didn't expect this to come up again. I'm sorry to say that the woman you're referring to, the one who made the accusations against poor Brian Wade, is extremely unstable. The last I heard of her she was undergoing specialist treatment, but from what you're saying she's apparently managed to track Brian down and start up her old tricks again. If you like, I'll make some enquiries this end to find out where she is and how she can be stopped.'

'Thank you,' Alex said evenly, 'that would be very helpful. Before you go, can I ask how well you knew Mrs Wade?'

'As a matter of fact I don't recall ever meeting her, so I'm afraid I'm not in a position to assist you with that. I imagine she's still very upset by the loss of her son.'

'Indeed, she is. Did you ever meet Ottilie, by any chance?'

'No, I don't believe I did. Now, if that's all, I'm rather busy so I'll get back to you when I have something more concrete to tell you. Meantime, if you speak to Brian, please send him my best. He's a very good teacher, he was a great loss to this school.'

After ringing off she was about to go and talk to

Tommy when she noticed that Wendy was in with him, so decided to open up her emails instead. To her amazement there was a message from a PC Scott Danes of Northumbria Police with an attachment that, intriguingly since she hadn't asked for it, turned out to be the autopsy report on Jonathan Wade's death.

However, before she could start reading it Wendy was sweeping her way towards her, all dowdy midi skirt, frilly-front blouse and old-fashioned pageboy haircut.

'Alex, Tommy's just told me about the call you received from Shane Prince last night,' she announced. 'I want you to know that I'm fully supportive of taking you off the case, and I'll be speaking to the police myself about what kind of backup they can provide when we go to visit that family in the future.'

We? Where was the 'we' in this?

Without waiting for a response Wendy swept away, and exchanging impressed glances with Saffy, Alex returned to the autopsy report.

'It's definitely saying he died of an asthma attack,' she told Tommy later as he glanced through it himself, 'which is what we already know, so I'm not sure why Scott Danes sent it. I tried calling him, but he's finished his shift for today and isn't back in again till next Wednesday, so I'll have to wait to catch up with him then.'

Handing the report back, Tommy said, 'Have you been in touch with the Wade family themselves today?'

She shook her head. 'I thought about it, but I don't actually have a good reason to call at this point, much as I'd like to. I'll ring tomorrow though, to make sure some steps have been taken to get Ottilie into a nursery, and to find out if anything's happened yet about a health visitor.'

'Good,' Tommy said, glancing at his watch. 'Crikey, is that the time already? I promised her indoors I wouldn't be late again tonight, so I'd better get my skates on.'

'Give her my love,' Alex said, turning to the door and trying desperately hard not to wish that she was rushing home to Jason.

'Hang on, what are you doing tonight?' Tommy demanded. 'Why don't you come and have a bite with us? Jackie's always happy to see you, you know that.'

Alex smiled past the ache in her heart. 'Thanks,' she said, 'but we've got a rehearsal tonight, so I'm not going to be on my own.'

His eyes remained on hers. 'We'll be there at the weekend, to see the show,' he told her. 'I'm just sorry we missed the opening night. I hear your old friend Heather Hancock gave you a bit of a savaging after.'

Alex laughed. 'Apparently she's big on grudges,' she said wryly. 'However, I'd far rather spend my time worrying about Ottilie Wade than I would Heather Hancock.'

'Far more useful,' he agreed. 'So, you have yourself a good rehearsal and barring lottery wins, alien invasions or better offers, I'll see you in the morning.'

'Actually, you won't,' she replied. 'I'm out on visits for most of the day so I probably won't be back here till late, which means the next time I see you could be at the show on Saturday. If it is, I'll make sure to look out for you and if you're very lucky I'll let you buy me a drink.'

'You can count on it,' he assured her. 'Go safely now, and any more nonsense from the Princes you let me know.'

Though North Hill wasn't exactly on her way home, as Alex drove along the seafront she couldn't help responding to the instinct that seemed to be pulling her there. There was no explaining it, she wasn't even going to try, she simply turned the car up the hill and crawled with the traffic until she reached the open gate of number forty-two. It wasn't until she turned in that she realised she'd been half expecting to find Ottilie at the window, as though she might have been there all this time, but there was no sign of her, or of anyone else.

With a jolt of unease she wondered if the Wades had upped and left, but then to her relief, and alarm, the front door suddenly opened and Brian Wade came out.

'Can I help you?' he asked, walking up to her car. 'Oh, it's you,' he stated when he realised who she was. 'Did you forget something, or have you brought your assessment for me to look over?'

'Neither, actually,' she said pleasantly. 'I was just passing and I thought . . . I was hoping it might be convenient to say hello to Ottilie.'

He didn't appear pleased. 'Well I'm afraid it isn't,' he retorted. 'She's in the bath and about to get ready for bed.'

Since she was hardly in a position to argue, she simply said, 'OK, sorry to bother you. I'll be in touch as soon as my assessment's ready.' As she put the car in reverse she added, almost as an afterthought, 'Have you heard from a health visitor yet, by the way?'

Frowning, though actually sounding less hostile, he said, 'Someone contacted me this afternoon. She'll be coming to meet Ottilie next Thursday.'

So the doctor had got on to it. Excellent. 'And any luck with a nursery school?' she wondered.

'We're looking into it. It has to be the right one and I'm afraid I don't have much time to carry out the necessary vetting process.'

'I'd be happy to make some recommendations.'

'Thank you. If I have any problems I'll let you know.'

She smiled in her most friendly way. She didn't want to alienate him, at least not yet, or he might contact Wendy and ask for her to be replaced. Being who he was, chances were Wendy would cooperate and though it might sound like nonsense to anyone else, she couldn't help feeling as though Ottilie was meant to be hers.

'Incidentally,' he said as she started to reverse back down the drive, 'I believe you've been making enquiries about my wife.'

Intrigued to know who'd told him – the doctor, his old headmaster, someone at social services in Northumbria, possibly even the police, though she strongly doubted that – she said, 'I admit she is causing me some concern. It might not be unheard of for a mother not to interact with her child, but it is unusual.'

'I wouldn't argue with that,' he conceded, 'I just ask you to keep in mind what she's been through, and try not to add any further anxieties to those she's already struggling with.'

Less moved than she appeared, Alex said, 'Of course. I understand your concern, and please be assured I shall treat her as sensitively as possible.'

Unless I find out she's doing anything to hurt that little girl. If she is I'm afraid I won't be very sensitive at all.

Ottilie was sleeping. Brian had bathed her, put her to bed and read her a story. Now he was in his studio engrossed in his computer.

Erica was in front of the TV, her eyes fixed on the screen, filling her mind with someone else's reality.

Switch on to switch off.

Grand Designs, *A Place in the Sun*, *Escape to the Country*. She enjoyed the property programmes; they conjured other worlds, unknown people, faraway places. Sometimes she climbed inside the set and felt the rain, the sun, the snow on her skin. It was always a great pity when she had to come back. If she could find a way to stay she'd never have to see Brian or Ottilie again.

She knew the social worker had wanted to come in earlier, because Brian had told her.

'She's going to carry on nosing around unless you do something to pull yourself together,' he'd snapped at her angrily.

She hadn't answered, because she'd had nothing to say.

'Is that what you want, that she carries on coming here?' he'd challenged.

'I know it's not what you want,' she'd replied acidly.

He'd looked as though he wanted to hit her, but then his face had softened with pity as he'd said, 'I know this is difficult for you, but I'm doing my best to help. You understand that, don't you?'

She'd nodded, because she did understand – he brought her the medication she needed to keep her calm, to make her sleep, to quieten the voices in her head, the ones that told her she'd killed Jonathan and that she must do the same to Ottilie. He didn't know about the orders she put in herself, the extra remedies for fear, paranoia, and the serotonin syndrome an online doctor had told her she had.

She wasn't always afraid of the voices, only when they started screaming at her to walk up walls, or sail away in the sitting room, or squeeze herself down the plughole with all the bubbles and grime.

They were silent now; so was she.

On the table in front of her was the new tea set Brian had brought home for Ottilie. Before going to bed Ottilie had made pretend tea with the water she'd got from the outside tap, because unless she used a chair it was the only one she could reach. She'd put buttons on the plates as if they were biscuits, and tiny bits of screwed-up newspaper that Erica had presumed were cakes. She'd set four places: one for Boots, one for herself and one each for her mother and father. When Erica hadn't picked up her cup Ottilie had brought it to her and set it down on an arm of the sofa.

It was still there, untouched.

Her mother had always hated it when Erica had behaved like a slave; yet she'd done her utmost to turn her into one.

Brian had played along with Ottilie's game, but then Brian would. He played along with everything Ottilie did. She was his special girl, his princess, his second and last child.

He'd taken a very long time putting Ottilie to bed.

He'd looked flustered and hot when he'd come down again, as though he needed a shower, but

229

he'd simply taken himself off to his shed – studio – and Erica didn't expect to hear him come in again. She'd be in bed herself by then, in the room at the end of the landing, glad she'd never have to sleep with him again.

Hearing a noise behind her, she looked round to find Ottilie standing in the doorway hugging Boots to her narrow chest. She was wearing a thin nightie that had got hooked up at the front, exposing her baby-smooth legs. The bruises from her fall down the stairs were still there, but fading fast. 'What's the matter?' Erica said sharply.

'I couldn't sleep,' Ottilie answered in her whispery little voice.

Erica returned her eyes to the TV, saying nothing, so Ottilie climbed into an armchair and snuggled into a ball. Her big eyes stayed on her mother, but it was a long time before Erica looked back.

For several seconds they simply stared at one another.

In the end Erica said, 'Stop it. *Just stop.*'

Immediately Ottilie lowered her eyes.

Erica got to her feet, walked to the window and back again. 'You shouldn't be here,' she told Ottilie. 'Go away.'

A single tear dropped on to one of Boots's ears.

'I don't know what to do with you,' Erica cried. 'Stop sitting there like that. Go back to bed where I can't see you.'

Obediently Ottilie got to her feet, and still clutching Boots padded out to the hall. Suddenly Erica swept up behind her, grabbing her arm and dragging her up the stairs. When they reached Ottilie's room Erica shoved her on to the bed.

Ottilie stared up at her with frightened eyes.

'Stop looking at me,' Erica raged.

Ottilie quickly hid her face in Boots.

'I can't do anything,' Erica shouted. 'I can't make them stop, all right,' and clasping her hands to her head as the voices began shrilling again she stormed out of the room, unable to bear another moment alone with the monster on the bed.

Chapter Eleven

Alex still hadn't told anyone – apart from Tommy – about her break-up with Jason. It was easier to cope with that way, she'd decided, though it was a painful reminder of the fact that she wasn't really close to anyone, didn't even have a best friend. *What was wrong with her, why couldn't she seem to make any lasting relationships?*

She might have talked to Gabby if Gabby weren't so busy with the kids, but at least she was coming tomorrow. They could probably chat then, unless she ended up bringing the twins, which was highly likely because she usually did even when she said she was coming alone. There was always Aunt Sheila, of course, except the dear old soul was mortified by intense emotion unless it concerned horses, and lovely Mattie didn't do much along the lines of intimacy at all. And confiding in any of the cast or crew of *Gender Swap* was completely out of the question. They'd only end up feeling sorry for her, or torn in their loyalties, at least while Jason was around, and she didn't want that at all. It was important that everyone stayed focused on their performance, and went on being as friendly and natural with him as they'd always been. After all, it wasn't as if he'd done anything wrong. Quite the reverse, in fact, because it was absolutely right that he should be with his family rather than with her.

She just wished it didn't hurt so much, and that she wasn't finding it so hard to stop wishing he'd come back. Harder still was watching now, as laughing and joking with the others he swung himself up on to the gantry to sort out the lights.

He'd texted first thing to remind her that he wasn't going to let her down today, he'd just be a bit later arriving for the set-up than he'd expected, but Clive Woodley was going to stand in until he got there. She had no idea what had held him up, she only knew that his life was a closed book to her now and she had no business trying to open it.

As she busied herself about the hall, helping to set out the chairs, carry in the costumes or sort out the props, she felt sure no one would guess how she was feeling. She was as quick and lively about giving instructions as ever, managing to laugh in all the right places and even make the odd joke or two herself. It simply couldn't be possible for anyone to tell that she was both loving and hating being near him, especially when she was forced to engage with him. Meeting his eyes was even more difficult than she'd feared, because seeing the concern and guilt reflected in his made the longing so intense it was almost impossible to bear.

Just thank goodness he wasn't a cruel person – or maybe it might be easier if he was, at least then she could hate him and tell herself she was better off without him.

Seeing him coming towards her now, she performed a rapid and stupid about turn to where she'd just left the WI women setting up the bar. She had to avoid speaking to him unless it was about the play, and even then it was much safer to do so while others were in earshot in case he was tempted to try and make it personal.

'Alex,' he said, coming up behind her, 'can we have a word outside a minute?'

Feeling her heart wrench as she realised there was no escaping him without at least raising a few eyebrows, she kept her tone as light as his as she said, 'OK, be right with you.'

Moments later she followed him out of the door, hugging her cardigan around her to keep out the cold, and making a big show of greeting Sarah Grant who'd warned them last week that she was going to be late joining them today.

'I'll leave you two lovebirds to it,' Sarah teased, as she pushed her back against the door to go inside. 'I hope you're both coming to the pub after, it's Johnny's birthday, don't forget.'

'We haven't,' Alex assured her, 'he won't let us.'

Laughing, Sarah disappeared inside, and as Jason's eyes came to hers Alex felt the heaviness in her heart pulling down her smile. She didn't want to be alone with him like this, and yet what she really wanted was for him to sweep her into his arms and say he'd made a terrible mistake.

'Are you OK?' they both asked at the same time, though in quite different tones. Hers was much more inquisitive and light-hearted, while his was loaded with concern.

'Yeah, I'm great,' she assured him, trying to quash his guilt with the implication of *why shouldn't I be?* 'Everything seems to be going to plan. The audience should start arriving any minute.'

It was impossible to know what he was thinking as he gazed searchingly into her eyes, but whatever it was she realised he'd decided to take his cue from her as he said, 'I guess it's still a sell-out?'

Not wanting to be skimming the surface like this, but knowing it would be disastrous to go any deeper, she replied, 'As far as I know. Mattie hasn't said any different. By the way, thanks for coming. I don't suppose it was easy getting away.'

His eyes wouldn't let go of hers. 'It was OK,' he said, as though it was something he was hardly thinking about. Then he added, 'I'm afraid I won't be able to make it to the pub after, though.'

Even though she'd expected it the disappointment crushed her, and to her dismay she felt tears burning her eyes. 'That's fine,' she told him crisply. 'In fact you can go now, if you like. I don't want you to feel beholden . . .'

'I don't . . .'

'I'm just saying. I know you want out . . .'

'Alex, don't do this . . .'

'You're the one who's doing it,' she almost shouted.

He turned his head aside, almost as though she'd slapped him.

She wished she had. At the same time, she wanted to run and run and never stop until she knew he was coming after her – or at least until she'd escaped the misery inside her. 'I guess everyone will want to know where you are if you don't come to the pub,' she said, trying not to sound terse, 'so our secret'll be out. Well, I don't suppose you particularly want it to be a secret anyway.'

Turning back to her, he said, 'I want whatever you want.'

Her eyes flashed. 'Well, that's blatantly not true,' she declared, 'and if you're standing there feeling sorry for me then please don't. I'm fine, better than fine in fact, because you were right when you said that we just fitted the bill for each other when we met. We both needed someone to help get us past all the stuff that was happening to us then. Now it's all behind us, it definitely makes sense for us to move on.'

Though he seemed surprised, even hurt by her words, she could tell that he wasn't quite believing her either, but what did it matter? She'd had enough now. If she stood here with him any longer she knew she'd end up saying or doing something she'd bitterly regret later.

'Oh, just one thing before we go back in,' she suddenly blurted, having no idea why she was bringing this up when she didn't even really want to know the answer. 'Last Sunday, when you took the children to stay at your mother's, I guess you were at home really, with Gina?'

Though he didn't answer, the guilt in his eyes was enough to confirm it, and furious with herself for even going there, she started back into the hall.

'Wait,' he said, catching her arm. 'This isn't easy for me either, you know. The way I feel about you . . .'

'Has nothing to do with anything,' she interrupted fiercely. 'So please let me go. We've got a show to put on and after that, I've got the rest of my life waiting for me.'

As she went inside she was cringing at her last comment, wanting to take it back, or at least make it sound less ridiculous. But what the hell? She had other things to think about now, and too bad if he wasn't finding this easy either. He'd get over it, and no doubt a lot quicker than she would. So what?

She'd survive. She only had to look at what had happened to her as a child to know that she'd already survived a lot worse.

So just watch me do it again, she was thinking as he came in behind her, and immediately she felt glad that she hadn't blurted that out too.

'Oh Alex, I don't know how you stand it,' Gabby wailed the following day as she came into the house. 'I still miss them so much, don't you, and when I look around the place it's like any minute one of them's going to walk in the door.'

Passing her a box of Kleenex as she went to pour the tea, Alex smiled tenderly as Gabby blew her nose in an effort to pull herself together.

'I'm sorry,' she gulped. 'I guess you're used to it, being here all the time, but for me . . . I don't know if I'll ever be. All our memories are here, aren't they? Everywhere I look reminds me of something to do with Mum or Dad, or both of them, and us, obviously. And coming past the church just now . . . To think of them in the graveyard instead of inside at the service –' her breath caught on another sob '– it seems so wrong, doesn't it? Neither of them was even that old. I suppose I should just feel thankful they were around long enough to know their grandchildren, at least for a while.'

'The twins meant the world to them,' Alex assured her softly. And it was true, their parents had adored Phoebe and Jackson, and she was sure they'd have loved her children too, if she'd had any, though maybe not quite so much. Her father would never have let it show, of course, he'd always been too kind and too canny for that, but for their mother any child of Alex's would have been just like Alex, at one remove from the actual family, and possibly even tainted by the killer's genes.

Was that really what her adoptive mother had thought about her? She'd never actually said so, but it was the impression Alex had got, time after time, particularly in her turbulent teenage years.

'I suppose it's a bit easier for you,' Gabby sniffed, 'being adopted and everything, but I know you loved them, especially Dad. He was really special, wasn't he?'

'Definitely,' Alex agreed, because he had been, in so many ways, especially with his flock who, she'd often suspected, mattered the most to him. However, she'd never be anything but thankful that she'd grown up with him as a father, rather than the monster whose blood ran in her veins. Chances were she'd never have grown up at all, left to him.

'I guess all their stuff is still upstairs,' Gabby said, starting to well up again. 'I know I have to bring myself to go through it one of these days, but I'm absolutely dreading it.'

'There's no rush,' Alex assured her. 'It's not as if it's going anywhere.'

Gabby sat staring at her hands for a moment, and almost leapt with what seemed like relief as her mobile rang. 'It's Martin, I'd better take it,' she said, and getting up from the table she took the phone into the sitting room and closed the door.

Surprised by her desire for privacy, since she normally talked into her mobile for the world to hear, Alex set about washing the few dishes that had accumulated since last night. No doubt Gabby wanted to share this upsurge of grief with her husband so he could comfort her and remind her that she was still very much loved by him and their children. It would mean a lot to Gabby to hear it, Alex knew that, because Gabby had never been as secure in herself as she tried to make out.

'You always cope with things so much better than I do,' she frequently told Alex, more admiringly than grudgingly. 'I know you never used to, when you were young and always going off on one, but now you're like really together, at least most of the time, and when you consider where you came from and everything and all you've had to deal with . . . I don't think I could have stood it if I'd found out that Mum and Dad weren't my real parents. It would have totally killed me.'

Alex knew that Gabby had never really understood what it had been like for her back then, and still didn't, but it hardly mattered, because there was no need for her to understand at any deeper a level than she already did. Besides, there had never been any doubt in her mind that Gabby truly cared about her, and actually thought of her as a sister in spite of how difficult Alex had been with Myra for a while. There had been times when Gabby had even sided with her in arguments, as though borrowing the nerve to backchat, rant and rebel that hadn't come to her naturally.

They were close, there was no doubt about that, but they were also very different and Alex couldn't deny that sometimes she wished Gabby would make things a little less about herself. She'd always want to be supportive to her, that went without saying, and she was definitely interested in everything Gabby did, but there were times, like today, when she wouldn't have minded Gabby taking a bit more of an interest in her. So far she hadn't even asked how the show had gone last night (another triumph, everyone had declared as they'd repaired to the pub); nor had she stopped to wonder where Jason was today. She'd apparently taken it for granted that everything was totally chilled in Alex's world, and that Alex had done whatever was necessary to make sure it was just the two of them for lunch.

Still, to be fair, she hadn't been here that long, so there was plenty of time for her to surprise Alex with a sudden flurry of interest in Alex's world. Alex knew all the signs, though. Gabby was gearing up for a long and sentimental stroll down memory lane before finally coming to the real reason she was here. And once that was dealt with she'd probably have to go rushing back to see to Martin and the kids without even realising that she'd totally forgotten to ask Alex how she was, or what news she might have.

'Everyone's fine,' Gabby declared, dabbing her eyes as she came back into the kitchen. As she looked at Alex she sighed heavily and broke into a watery smile. 'I know I shouldn't still be getting so upset about Mum and Dad,' she said, coming to give Alex a hug. 'I just can't seem to help it, and you're always so easy to talk to.'

Hugging her back, Alex said, 'It's what sisters are for. So,' she went on as Gabby went to pick up her tea, 'I thought we'd go to the pub for lunch, if it's OK with you. I've been so busy this week that I haven't had time to do a shop.'

'That's fine,' Gabby assured her. 'It'll be lovely to see everyone – we'll just have to hope they don't set me off again, saying how much they miss Mum and Dad. You know what they're like. I suppose they don't do it so much with you any more, given that they see you all the time. Any chance of a top-up? This one's gone a bit cold.'

Taking the mug of tea, Alex flipped the switch on the kettle and kept her head down for a moment, waiting for a sudden wave of longing for Jason to pass. There was never any knowing when it would take her, or how painful it would be, she simply had to ride it out and hope that she didn't become submerged while anyone was around.

Maybe now was the time to tell Gabby.

'Just now,' Gabby said, sitting at the table again, 'you know we were saying that there's no rush about sorting through Mum and Dad's things?'

Turning around, Alex forced a smile as she replied, 'There honestly isn't. It's all packed up in our old bedrooms, so it's not in the way.'

Gabby looked awkwardly down at her hands as she nodded. 'It's just that Martin and I . . . Well, we've been talking, and with the twins at school now and things being the way they are . . . Oh God, I feel terrible saying this, but I know you'll understand . . . We thought we ought to put this house on the market so we'd be able to send the children to a private school.' Still not quite able to look at Alex, she went on, 'We've been trying to find a way of affording it without having to sell, but the fees are so high, and well, I think it's what Mum and Dad would have wanted, don't you, that it should go towards helping Phoebs and Jackson get a good start in life?'

Alex was reeling, almost buckling. She wanted to protest, to make Gabby understand that she couldn't lose her home too, not after everything else, she'd go to pieces if she did. Except it wasn't her home, it was Gabby's, so she had every right to sell.

'I'm sorry,' Gabby said woefully. 'I can see you're upset . . .'

'No, honestly, I'm fine,' Alex assured her, the lie spinning in her head. 'It's just a bit of a shock, that's all, but you're right, it's definitely what Mum and Dad would want.' *Myra certainly, though perhaps not Douglas.* 'It's – it's a wonderful idea,' she heard herself adding.

Gabby's relief broke into a smile. 'I was hoping you'd think so,' she gushed. 'I told Martin, "She knows our arrangement for her to be there has always been temporary," and we've never charged you any rent, so I expect you've managed to save up a really good deposit for a place of your own by now, haven't you?' She looked a little hesitant, as though not sure whether she believed that or not, although clearly she wanted to.

Alex didn't bother crushing her hopes with the truth – that the fifteen hundred or so pounds she'd managed to put aside since their mother had died and she'd no longer had to pay rent would never get her started with a mortgage. It was barely enough for a down payment on a bedsit in the seamier areas of Kesterly. The more desirable town centre, or anywhere in Mulgrove, would be completely out of the question.

'Of course with Jason doing his bit as well I expect you'll be able to afford somewhere really nice,' Gabby rattled on. 'I mean, I realise he's still got to pay maintenance for his kids and everything, but he earns quite well, doesn't he? I'm sure he does, because he's really good at his job, and it'll be great for you two to have a place of your own. Obviously, it's been lovely for you here, but it's all a bit shabby now, and run-down, isn't it? It needs so much attention . . . Actually we were thinking about asking Jason to fix it up before we sold it, but with the way the market is, whatever we put into it now we might not end up getting back later, so what's the point?'

Because she couldn't think of anything else to say, Alex gave a shrug as she replied, 'He'd have been happy to do it. In fact, he talked about it himself only recently. I was going to mention it to you, but well, it doesn't matter now I suppose.'

Guilt clouded Gabby's eyes again. 'Of course, nothing's going to happen straight away,' she announced reassuringly. 'We haven't even spoken to an estate agent yet. Martin thinks we should put it on with one of the nationals, as well as with Elaine in the village, that way we'll get maximum exposure.' She pulled an anxious face. 'Obviously, it won't be very pleasant having strangers traipsing through all the time, poking and prying into cupboards and drawers, but I thought if we gave Elaine a key she could do it while you're at work. That way, you won't even have to know that they've been.'

Wondering if she'd ever felt the need for Jason more, if only to fill in the spaces she was finding so hard, Alex said, 'That sounds like a good idea. I probably ought to know when someone's coming, though, so I can make sure everything's spick and span.'

Gabby waved a dismissive hand. 'I wouldn't worry too much about that, I'm sure whoever buys it will gut the place anyway.' Apparently connecting with the harshness of her own words, tears filled her eyes again. 'Oh God, it's awful, isn't it, to think of them ripping out everything of Mum and Dad. It's going to be like losing them all over again.'

Unable to think of a suitable response to that, Alex turned away to carry on with the tea. She felt faintly dizzy and as though this was happening at a slight remove, or to someone else and she was simply listening in. If only.

This was her home; *she was about to lose her home*.

'So when do you think you might start looking for somewhere else?' Gabby asked, appearing excited. 'I'll be more than happy to come with you when I can. I love viewing houses, don't you? I remember when we were looking for ours, God I've lost count now of how many we saw, but it took an age for us to settle on the one we have. And then we almost lost it. What a nightmare that was. I don't think we'll be putting ourselves through it again in a hurry, that's for sure.' Apparently again making a late connection with her words, she quickly added, 'It'll be different for you, of course. You're much better at making up your mind than I am, and you're not anywhere near as fussy.'

If she'd had a smile in her then, Alex might have found it, but all she managed was the ghost of one. 'There you are,' she said, putting a fresh mug of tea down in front of Gabby. 'Nice and hot, the way you like it.'

'Lovely,' Gabby enthused. 'You make the best cup of tea, you know. Martin always says that too.'

Somehow affecting a playful tone, Alex said, 'My ultimate ambition achieved.'

Gabby laughed, and started slightly as she scalded her lip. 'So did you book us in at the pub for lunch?' she asked.

Alex nodded. 'One o'clock.'

'That's perfect. I thought maybe we could stop at the church on the way down the hill and go to the graves. I brought some flowers, they're in the car.'

'Good idea,' Alex replied, feeling bad for not going more often than the few times she'd managed since Myra's death.

'I'm so pleased everything's all settled and you're OK about me wanting to sell,' Gabby declared later as she linked Alex's arm on their way down to the church. 'I hoped you would be, but at the same time, I know it won't be easy for you letting go of the home where we grew up. I'm going to find it incredibly difficult myself, I can tell you that, but at least I don't live there any more.'

'It'll be OK,' Alex said quietly. 'It'll be fine.' It would have to be, because there was nothing she could do to change it. All she could do was deal with the blows as they came and hope to God that the next one wasn't going to be losing her job.

It was the middle of the afternoon now, and after waving Gabby off Alex had got into her car to drive through the countryside and across town to Temple Fields. Not the notorious estate, but the once grander adjacent area that rose in colourful terraces and leafy cul-de-sacs up over the slopes of Kesterly Mount, where the properties at the top and down the westerly face revelled in spectacular views out to sea. There used once to be a modest detached house sitting in amongst an assortment of fishermen's cottages and fifties eyesores, but both the house and cottages had long since been torn down. The detached place had been the idyll her grandparents had bought for their retirement. It was also where the terrible events of that long-ago summer night had unfolded.

A small complex of luxury executive homes now

sprawled over the brink of the hill with a private thoroughfare leading up from the main coast road below, each house having its own high redbrick wall and set of electric gates. Alex had no idea who lived in them, nor was she especially interested. She was only here to visit St Mark's, the stoic, unassuming Norman church whose rambling cemetery gardens had, for centuries, claimed several acres of the hillside, allowing its resting occupants an enduring view of the sea.

She guessed it was the time spent with Gabby at Myra and Douglas's graveside earlier that had prompted her to come here today. That, and a feeling of being slowly, irrevocably cut adrift from everything and everyone she loved. Not that visiting the graves of her real family was likely to provide an anchor to some sense of normalcy or constancy, but maybe it would remind her that she had once belonged to people who'd loved and wanted her, even if her mother had changed her mind later.

As she picked her way amongst rows of crumbling and shiny headstones, noticing how many young men had lost their lives at sea, and the tragic number of children who'd died long before their time, the salty tang of the sea blew around her on the breeze while the sun made an occasional break through the clouds. In spite of the five or more years that had passed since she'd last been here she recognised the old memorial bench with a broken arm that sat crouched into a hedgerow. It was only feet from the four marble steps and single headstone that marked the grave her grandparents shared with their daughter and grandson – Alex's aunt and brother.

She knew that her Great-Aunt Helen had arranged it all, from the rosy hue of the stone, to the simple inscription of names, dates of birth and year of death, to the yearly donation to the church to help keep down the weeds and grass. Alex had no idea if her great-aunt ever visited the grave, but apparently someone had, and quite recently, if the fragrant bunch of sweet peas on the highest step was anything to go by.

Though she could easily have felt intrigued by the flowers and allowed herself to speculate about how they might have got there, having grown up with a rector for a father she knew that the most likely benefactor was either a friend of the church, or a relative of someone who took pleasure in brightening neglected graves. So, reining in her imagination before it could conjure all sorts of fantasies, she stood for a moment, as still as the monuments around her, gazing out at the breathtaking view below. In the far distance hazy bands of sunlight were fanning over the steel-grey sea, and a massive cargo ship was slipping soundlessly across the horizon. A dozen or more sailboats were skimming about the bay, while seagulls soared and plunged and hardy surfers rode the waves. Everything around her was so peaceful and still. Hardly anyone was about, just an elderly couple making their way towards the newer graves further down the hill, while any number of songbirds chirruped in the trees.

She was never sure if she felt any real sense of connection to her family while she was here, she only knew that the first time she'd come she'd found it strangely calming, and it had never felt wrong to be there. Fanciful though it was, she wondered if her grandparents were watching her, or her aunt, or her brother. It was thinking of her brother, Hugo, that she usually found the hardest: the brave, frightened little five-year-old who'd left her shut up in a cupboard while he went to try and save his mother. How dearly she'd love to know him, to be a part of his life. *A brother. She should have a brother.* He'd have been thirty-one in a few weeks if he'd lived, he might even be married with children of his own and have an important career. Unlike her, he'd borne a strong resemblance to their father, with his dark complexion and thin face. She wondered what kind of relationship they'd had before it had come to such an appalling end.

All it said on the gravestone was Hugo, aged 5. There was no mention of their father's name, Albescu, and she had always felt thankful for that, since it rarely failed to send chills down her spine. It did now as she recalled the images she'd found of him in old newspaper stories online. Darkly handsome with close-set, penetrating eyes and a small, unsmiling mouth that should have looked cruel, but somehow didn't. She'd never delved deeply into his side of the family, she was afraid to, in case her interest acted like some kind of magnet that might bring him back to her.

I'm part Romanian, she told herself, and just like all the other times she'd said it she waited for something to resonate in a way that might connect with her roots. It never did. She knew from her Internet searches that her father had been born in a remote mountain village whose name she could never pronounce, the youngest of four children – three boys and a girl.

In her searches she'd found mention of him working as a janitor at the University of Bucharest, also as a tour guide in Hamburg, and as a long-distance lorry driver based out of Prague. (A good cover, she supposed, for what had turned out to be his actual career.) She'd never been able to find any mention of him living in England, though she imagined he must have for a while at least, even if illegally, since she'd never turned up anything about her mother living abroad. She wondered how they'd met. She knew her mother had won a place at UCL to read English (so she was bright, but apparently not bright enough to avoid getting involved with the wrong man – though Alex doubted many women were capable of that). For her mother it had presumably happened during her gap year, while she'd been travelling around Europe with a friend whose name Alex had never been able to find.

Because she'd always wanted her mother to be different (to Myra, she supposed) and glamorous (which Myra wasn't, very), she remembered how one of her favourite fantasies, aged fifteen or sixteen, had cast her parents as the glittering stars of an exotic European circus – her mother fearless and exultant as she flew from the trapeze into her lover's manly arms. Or pinned to a revolving board in sequins and feathers, laughing playfully as he demonstrated his breathtaking marksmanship skills. Or draped deliciously over a table as he flipped back his Zorro cloak and sawed her in half.

Maybe they'd been clowns. Ha, ha, ha.

Turning to the gravestone where her grandparents' names were engraved above the other two, Andy and Peggy Nicholls, she began tracing the lettering with one finger. It was as though the shaping of their names was somehow creating them in person, or perhaps securing them in her heart. Her grandfather had worked for most of his life as a crane driver at Mersey docks. According to his friends he'd been a larger-than-life character who'd boosted his wages by singing in working men's clubs and pubs. Apparently it was how he'd managed to save for their retirement in Kesterly, the south-westerly seaside town that they'd brought their girls to most years for a holiday. Her grandmother, Peggy, had been a midwife who'd delivered many of the local community into the world. She was lively, and always laughing, one newspaper had said, with a kind word for everyone. Apparently she'd been a bit of a dab hand with a sewing machine, because a few of her friends had remarked on the 'loveliest curtains and cushions' always being found at Peggy's house.

The photographs of her aunt, Yvonne – her mother's younger sister by two years – had shown a tousle-haired blonde with large blue eyes and such a clear, happy face it was almost impossible to believe in the fate she had met. She'd been a flighty little miss, someone had said about her, but in the sweetest way. 'She could never stay still for a minute, not even to finish a meal.' During the months leading up to her untimely death she'd been staying with her parents at their new home in Kesterly, and working at a local Co-op on the checkout. This was apparently, someone had presumed, where she'd met her boyfriend, Nigel Carrington. According to one friend, Yvonne and Nigel had been talking about getting married during the weeks before the attack, but Alex guessed she'd never know now if that were true.

Of course Nigel wasn't in this grave, but she'd read about him during her searches too, so she knew that he'd been a gifted carpenter with a workshop in a converted barn on Exmoor, and a client list that had boasted some celebrities of the day. Several of the celebrities had spoken of him fondly, saying how well liked he had been, lively and humorous, and what a tragic loss he was for his family and friends. Had they secretly commented amongst themselves that he'd still be alive if he'd kept to his own sort, Alex occasionally wondered. Certainly he seemed to have come from a more landed kind of background than Yvonne could boast. Perhaps this was why she, Alex, had never tried to track any of Nigel's relatives down. Why on earth would they want to be reminded of his murderer, much less have anything to do with the child who'd got away – blameless though that child might be?

Sitting on the bottom step of the grave, she picked up the sweet peas and inhaled the pleasure of their heady perfume. It was starting to get cold now and the sky was darkening overhead, but she didn't feel quite ready to leave yet. She knew that once she did she'd have to start coping with the awfulness of missing Jason again, and the dread of having to find somewhere else to live. She wasn't going to allow herself to think about the insecurity surrounding her job, she just had to trust to the fact that if redundancies were in the offing she wouldn't be amongst them. If she was, there would be nothing left to hold her to Kesterly or Mulgrove, apart from memories and the many friends she'd made over the years. Of course there were the children too, the precious little souls whose welfare and happiness meant so much to her: how could she possibly leave them?

It won't come to that, she told herself firmly as she got to her feet. And even if it did there would always be someone to take care of them; after all, Myra had been there for her when her mother had gone. It was small comfort, in fact almost no comfort at all, because she knew very well that the chances of her little charges finding as good a home as she had were so slim as to be almost non-existent. However, she must be careful not to make them even more important to her now that she was in such a vulnerable state herself, because her job was to take care of their needs, not the other way around.

Chapter Twelve

'I couldn't care less, I never wanted to stay here anyway. They're just fucking stupid and weird and into all that God stuff. It makes me gag being around them.'

Alex could see the heartbreak in twelve-year-old Sophie Leonard's eyes, in spite of all the bluster and aggression. She felt heartbroken herself, and frustrated, having to restrain herself from lashing out at Sophie's foster-mother in a way that would get her fired and possibly even sued. For months now Linda Jarrow had been leading Sophie – and social services – to believe that she and her husband were ready to adopt Sophie into their family.

Now, apparently, they'd changed their minds.

At the age of eight, when Alex had first met her, Sophie had been like a little savage, ready to claw the eyes out of anyone who approached her. She had no friends, no life outside her abusive home, apart from the days she took herself off to school, more for something to do than because she wanted to acquire an education. It had taken time, and a saintly amount of patience, but eventually the Jarrows had shown her another way of living that hadn't included violence, or booze or any amount of neglect. Lately when Alex had visited her she'd seemed so transformed from the feral little urchin she used to know that it was a welcome reminder of how well the system could work at times. Now, out of the blue, the Jarrows had decided that it would be in Sophie's best interests if another family was found to continue the work they'd begun.

'But why?' Alex had protested when Linda Jarrow had rung to break the news.

'As I said, we think it would be best for Sophie.'

'Just tell me what she's done. There must be something. You wouldn't be doing this otherwise.'

In a clipped, guilty tone, Linda Jarrow said, 'Every child deserves to be loved and I'm afraid, though we've tried, heaven knows we've tried, we just don't feel that we care for Sophie as deeply as we expected to. However, we care enough to want her to be with someone who is fully able to bond with her.'

'She's been with you all this time and you're deciding this now?' Alex had retorted scathingly.

'I'm sorry,' was all Linda Jarrow would say.

Tugging open Alex's passenger door now, Sophie snarled, 'I'm not going back to that bitch Tina and her fucking slob of . . .'

'You're not going to your aunt's,' Alex assured her. She hadn't yet told her that her aunt had long since moved out of the area – perhaps even to Spain to join her sister, Sophie's mother – it would have only added to the sense of rejection. 'I've got my boss to pull some strings,' she went on, 'and it's worked out for you to go to a really lovely family over in Westleigh.'

Sophie's taut young face, that had been so sunny and happy over the last few months, remained closed and hostile as Alex left her buckling up while she went to put the last of her luggage into the boot.

Linda Jarrow and her husband were nowhere to be seen, but since the front door of the house was still open Alex walked into the hall and called out that they were leaving.

She was half expecting to be ignored, but after a moment Linda Jarrow appeared from the kitchen, wiping her hands on a tea towel. 'Does she have everything?' she asked, not meeting Alex's eyes.

'I think so.' Alex's tone was as cold as she could make it. 'I know what you told me on the phone,' she continued, 'but if Sophie's done something we need to know about . . .'

'She hasn't. It's simply that it would be wrong of us to continue any further along the adoption path when we've decided that we wouldn't be the best parents for her.'

Unable to stop herself, Alex said, 'And never mind how much damage your decision is causing her?'

Linda Jarrow's colour rose. 'In the long run I think we'll all find . . .'

'In the long run she'll have even more scars to be coping with than she had when she came here, but let's not worry about that now. Let's make sure we get her off your property and out of your world . . .'

'Alex, I understand that you're angry,' Linda Jarrow cut in sharply, 'but I don't find this conversation to be in any way helpful.'

'No, I don't suppose you do. Much easier just to throw her out, not worry about where she goes next or even if she has anywhere to go.'

'I know she's in good hands with you . . .'

'I'm her social worker, not her mother, or her carer. She needs much more than I can give her, and I thought – *she* thought – she had it with you. Apparently we were wrong, but I hope you realise

255

this can't be an end to it. There's a mountain of paperwork to fill in, which is on its way to you, and people a lot higher up than me are going to want the questions properly answered. You see, you can't mess about with children like they were toys . . .'

'I think you should go now,' Linda Jarrow interrupted, easing Alex to the door. 'I'm sorry you're so upset, it hasn't been easy for us either, but I wish Sophie well and I can assure you that when the paperwork arrives we will do our best to complete it as accurately as possible.'

'Aren't you at least going to say cheerio?' Alex demanded incredulously.

Linda Jarrow glanced at the car. 'I don't think she wants that, so please tell her that if we find she's left anything behind we'll be sure to send it on to her.'

'And just how do you get hopes, dreams, happiness into an envelope?' Alex snarled, and not bothering to wait for a response she marched back to the car, so angry that she didn't care one bit that she'd let rip the way she had. She might get into trouble for it later, but as far as she was concerned someone had to speak up for Sophie, and she was certainly not going to allow the Jarrows to think that what they'd just done to an innocent child was in any way acceptable.

As she drove away she had no idea if Linda Jarrow was waving, or even watching, and she guessed Sophie hadn't either, because neither of them turned to look. They simply kept their eyes straight ahead and stayed that way until they were well clear of the Jarrows' street.

'Fancy stopping for a coffee and piece of cake?' Alex suggested as they approached the seafront. She didn't have time, in fact she wasn't supposed to be here at all, but there was no way she could have left it to someone else to come and pick Sophie up. She'd known the child too long not to be there for her today, and she wanted to do something now to try and make her feel better, even if it was just a simple drink and bite to eat. *What kind of person let a child think they were going to be adopted, then said, oh sorry, got it wrong, it's not going to happen after all?*

Better not get into what she'd like to do to them.

When she got no reply from Sophie she glanced over at her, and seeing the tears running down her cheeks her heart immediately flooded with pity and love. Quickly pulling over she gathered the child tightly into her arms. 'It's all right,' she soothed fiercely. 'Everything's going to be fine, I promise.'

'Why – why didn't they want me?' Sophie sobbed. 'What did I do wrong?'

Feeling her pain so deeply that it was making her cry too, Alex said, 'I don't think you did anything, sweetheart. They just changed their minds, that's all.'

'I don't get why they're allowed to do that. It's just mean. I really liked being with them, even though they made me do all that church stuff and sing and play the guitar which I'm totally rubbish at. I thought they were going to be my mum and dad, and now no one's going to be, are they?'

Clasping Sophie's tear-stained face in her hands so she could look into her eyes, Alex said, 'Maybe not for the moment, but I promise you we're going to work something out, and you definitely won't be on your own. You're going to love your new foster carers, you wait and see.'

Sophie's eyes went down. 'What about my real

mum?' she whispered brokenly. 'Do you reckon she might want me again by now?'

Almost unable to bear it, Alex pulled her into another embrace. 'I'll do my best to find out,' she told her, 'but try not to get your hopes too high, OK? We're not too sure of where she is any more, but hey, for all we know she could be back from Spain.'

Still sounding wretchedly hopeless, Sophie said, 'If she is she obviously doesn't want me or she'd have come to find me, wouldn't she? And anyway I couldn't be adopted without her permission and she said yes, so it just goes to show how much she cares. She was OK about giving me away.'

Feeling the resonance with her own life, Alex said gently, 'You know she has a problem with drink, so until she gets that sorted out it's . . .'

'She'll never get it sorted out. She's like that bitch Tina, it's all she ever thinks about, booze and blokes. Well, I couldn't give a fuck about them either. I hope they fucking die, both of them.'

Dismayed by the aggression and language that she hadn't heard from Sophie in a long time, Alex watched her turn away and wished she knew what more to say. Just thank God the Fenns were able to take her in. As soon as Alex had realised there were no local authority places for Sophie in their area, she'd gone straight to Tommy to ask him to fix it for the child to go to a family she felt instinctively would want to help.

Half an hour later Maggie Fenn was waiting on the doorstep to greet them, and to Alex's relief as Sophie got out of the car she appeared more cautiously impressed by the smart house and garden than hostile towards the unknown.

'How lovely.' Maggie smiled warmly as she came to shake Sophie's hand. 'You're as pretty as Alex told me.'

Though Alex had said nothing of the sort she certainly wasn't about to admit it, especially not when it was true.

'I'm Maggie and you must be Sophie,' Maggie was saying.

Sophie mumbled something that Alex didn't quite catch, but fortunately Maggie wasn't looking offended, so Alex breathed easily and came round the car to greet Sophie's saviour herself.

'We've got a bedroom all ready for you,' Maggie was informing Sophie as she ushered her inside. 'And there's some soup on for lunch. Maybe Alex can stay and join us?'

Feeling her stomach rumble, Alex replied, 'I'd love to, but I'm afraid I have to run. I'll come back again later, if it's OK, to make sure she's settled in all right.'

'That's fine, and of course she will be. Ah, here's Britney come to meet you. I wondered where she'd got to. Britney's the same age as you, Sophie. She's been here for a little while now, so I'm hoping she'll give us a good rating.'

Turning her wary scowl into a long-suffering smile, a yellow-haired, freckle-faced Britney said, 'Yeah, you're cool.'

'Oh, such praise,' Maggie gasped in joy. 'So now why don't you take Sophie inside and show her where everything is, while I have a quick chat with Alex.'

After throwing Alex a look that Alex couldn't quite read, Sophie obediently followed Britney into the house while Alex tugged open the boot to start unloading. 'I can't thank you enough for this,' she told Maggie. 'It's all happened so fast – one minute they wanted her, the next they were telling us to come and get her. You can probably imagine how traumatised she is by it, so you might find her a bit difficult at first, unable to trust, scared of forming any sort of attachment, but she's terribly sweet at heart and I don't think it'll take long to win her over, because all she really wants is to be loved.'

'Of course it is,' Maggie agreed sympathetically, 'and you don't need to worry, we shall do our best to make her feel just that. Here, let me take those,' and seizing a couple of bags she led the way inside. 'It's a pity you can't stay for lunch, but maybe another time. Now, tell me quickly before you rush off, how did the play go on Saturday? Another dazzling success I hope.'

Loving her for asking, and pushing aside the sudden painful thought of Jason, Alex replied, 'It was great, thank you. And please pass on my thanks to your brother for the lovely things he said on our Facebook page. Everyone was dead impressed, getting praise from a big-time lawyer.'

Twinkling with delight, Maggie said, 'I'm not sure he'd describe himself that way, but as I keep telling him, he's far too modest. Anyway, I shall be happy to pass along your message, and I have your number should any problems crop up with Sophie, but I'm sure they won't. Just let me know when you're on your way back and I'll let them out of the attic. Joke! Sorry, not in good taste.'

Laughing, Alex shouted up the stairs, 'Sophes, I'm off. See you later, OK?'

'OK,' Sophie called back.

Turning to Maggie with raised eyebrows, showing

how impressed she was that Sophie hadn't kicked up a fuss (so far), Alex thanked her again and ran back to the car.

She'd had to reschedule her morning appointments when the call came in about Sophie, and now, before rushing over to see the Wades, she must try to get hold of the police officer, Scott Danes, who'd sent her a copy of an autopsy report she hadn't requested.

'I don't suppose you found anything to concern you when you read it,' he remarked, in an accent very like Tommy's when she finally got through to him.

'Not really,' she replied, 'but I'm guessing you sent it for a reason, so I'm hoping you'll tell me what the reason is.'

With a sigh, he said, 'I was called to the scene when it happened. Little boy, suffocated to death by an asthma attack. Terrible, tragic, I'm sure you can imagine. Three years old he was – it makes you wonder what it's all about, taking a kiddie that young. The parents were in shock; the father was the worst, he just couldn't seem to take it in. We found him hunched up in a garden shed, and had the devil of a time trying to get him out. He didn't want to go near the mother, he was blaming her, saying she should have saved him, that she hadn't done what she was supposed to when the boy had an attack.'

'And had she?'

'It would seem so. The trouble was it didn't work and she panicked. She tried giving him the kiss of life, CPR, anything she could think of, which is what caused the bruising you'll have read about around the boy's nose and mouth, and to his chest.'

He broke off for a moment, leaving Alex to wonder what this was leading to. 'I don't really know what I'm trying to tell you here,' he said, 'I only know that something wasn't right in that house and I've never really been able to get it out of my mind. So when I heard you were making enquiries about them . . . You must get this in your job all the time, where your gut tells you one thing while the facts, or what looks like the facts, are telling you another.'

'They're always the most difficult cases,' she agreed.

'I don't know that the autopsy's going to be of any use to you, I just felt it was important for you to have everything to hand, should you need it. I hope you don't, obviously, because I hope the little girl is safe and properly cared for and that I was wrong about the parents. I never got to know them, so the chances are I was, and I can't even tell you what I thought was wrong. It just sits there in me, never making itself clear, but never going away either. Do you know what I'm saying?'

'Yes, I do,' Alex replied, 'because it's the way I feel about them too. Did you know that Mr Wade received some anonymous calls after his son's death, accusing him of killing him?'

'Are you serious? No, I didn't know that.'

'Apparently it was a woman by the name of Jill McCarthy. Mr Wade says she was a paranoid schizophrenic who'd bothered others before him, and Derek Tolland, the headmaster at Wade's old school, confirmed this when I spoke to him, though he couldn't remember the name. Does it ring any bells for you?'

'I can't say it does, but I'll happily look into it and let you know what I come up with.'

'Thanks, that would be great. You have my mobile number.'

'Indeed. Let me give you mine.'

After ringing off Alex started the engine again and turned the car in the direction of North Hill. She'd been worried about Ottilie before this call, and now, finding out that a police officer was uncomfortable about the family too had seriously added to her concerns, not least because she knew she wasn't dealing with just anyone in Brian Wade. He was going to be a heck of a lot smarter than most of the parents or guardians she came across, and chances were his very peculiar wife was too. So whatever else she did over the next couple of hours at their home, she must be sure to keep all her wits about her and never forget for a single moment that Jonathan Wade had been three years old when he died, the very same age that Ottilie was now.

There might not be any significance to this, but there again there just might.

'"At risk?"' Brian Wade demanded, quoting from Alex's initial assessment of Ottilie's family situation. 'What on earth do you imagine Ottilie is at risk of, may I ask?'

Keeping her tone light, while throwing a playful look Ottilie's way, Alex said, 'If you read on it will explain why I consider this to be the case.'

He was already doing so, and from the look of his wife she was engrossed in the report too.

They were in the sitting room of the North Hill house – no fire, or tea and scones this time. Ottilie was sitting cross-legged on the floor next to her mother's chair, her solemn brown eyes fixed watchfully on Alex. She was wearing a purple corduroy dress with red tights and black buckled shoes. Her hair was bunched into two curly topknots, making her look so cute that Alex wanted to eat her all up. Who did her hair, she wondered, her mother, or her father? What had been the thinking behind presenting her this way, and who had made the decision?

'You're looking very pretty today,' Alex told her softly.

Without taking her eyes from Alex, Ottilie hugged her bear more tightly and rested her cheek on his head.

Alex wondered what she had been told about her since the last visit. What crafty little messages, or threats, or lies had been drummed into her to prepare her for today? Perhaps none, since she didn't look frightened, or even anxious, more curious if anything. However, she still wasn't communicating, so who knew what was going around in her impressionable child's mind?

'Has Boots been behaving himself?' Alex asked chattily.

Erica shifted in her chair, knocking Ottilie with her foot.

Alex wondered if it was deliberate, a reminder not to speak – or perhaps a prompt to answer, because Ottilie gave a little nod.

Whether Brian Wade noticed any of this seemed doubtful; his eyes were still riveted to the page.

Smiling at Ottilie, Alex said, 'I expect you're pleased, because we like good teddies, don't we?'

Again Ottilie nodded, this time unprompted, or at least Erica Wade didn't move.

An uneasy silence ticked on as the Wades

continued to read, so Alex put a hand over her eyes to start a game of peekaboo. From Ottilie's reaction it was doubtful she'd ever played it before, since she appeared to have no idea what Alex was doing. However, after several more goes, to Alex's amusement she put a hand over her own eyes and peered out through her fingers.

'Boo,' Alex whispered.

Ottilie stayed as she was.

'Boo,' Alex said again.

Ottilie took in a large, noisy breath and, to Alex's amazement, she broke into a smile.

Just about melting, Alex quickly noted that there was nothing wrong with her teeth; they were as perfect as pearls. She was an absolute picture, in fact; so sweet and huggable that it was hard to resist gathering her up off the floor and squeezing her.

Her hand was over her eyes again, but before Alex could return to the game, Brian Wade said, 'Well, I suppose it's good to know that you people are so thorough when it comes to protecting the nation's children.'

Letting the patronising tone sweep past her, Alex replied, 'We do our best.'

He appeared slightly affronted. 'I'm sure you do, but your diligence where my family is concerned can only be viewed as a waste of valuable resources. You see, my daughter is not at risk of anything, and certainly not neglect, so I can't help taking offence at your suggestion here that she is.'

Alex's tone remained friendly as she said, 'You'll also see written there that she doesn't speak . . .'

'And I explained at our first meeting that she's very shy with strangers. With us she's as talkative as any child her age.'

'That may be so, but the fact that she is so nervous with strangers strongly suggests that she is not being properly socialised. And we know she isn't because by your own admission she doesn't have any friends, or cousins, nor does she go to nursery. She also hasn't had a visit from a health worker since moving here – I'm sure you'll agree that all of the above can be classified as neglect . . .'

'Not at all, the health visitor was nothing more than an oversight on my part which most would consider understandable, given the stressful circumstances surrounding our move.'

'I'm not going to argue that point, but I will say . . .'

'. . . and I told you last week that a health visitor is coming tomorrow.'

'Which is noted in that report. I've already got her details from your doctor, so I'll have a chat with her after she's been to get her initial assessment of Ottilie's physical health.'

'Well, I think you can see for yourself that there's absolutely nothing wrong with my daughter, but I accept that the system requires all children to be under the care of a health worker until the age of five.'

Alex nodded, feeling far less impressed than she looked. 'May I ask if you've had any luck finding a nursery?' she said pleasantly.

At that he gave a weary sigh. 'Well, we've certainly been looking,' he assured her, 'but I'm afraid we haven't been able to find anywhere that has a vacancy yet. At least not one that we could afford.'

Unsurprised by that, since it was famously

difficult to get children into the most sought-after pre-schools, Alex said, 'Not to worry. I thought you might have a problem, applying this late in the day, so I took the liberty of making a few calls myself. I hope you don't mind – well, I'm sure you won't because the Pumpkin playgroup, next to the station, has a fantastic reputation and the really good news is their rates are very reasonable. What's more, they can take Ottilie from next Monday. I'm not sure if you're aware of this group,' she ran on, as Wade's frown deepened – he clearly didn't take well to being railroaded, even if it was in his daughter's best interests, 'but it's highly sought after, so we're very lucky to get her in there. I'd say, given how new it'll all be to her, that just a couple of hours three times a week will be plenty enough to get her socialising under way.'

Wade glanced at his wife, who was still staring at the report, and folded his hands together in a patient, headmasterly sort of way. 'I'm sorry, but we'll need to know more about this place before we can agree to anything.'

Reaching into her bag, Alex pulled out a smart colour brochure for the Pumpkin playgroup. 'They also have an excellent website,' she informed him as he took the brochure. 'They're Ofsted registered, and have passed all the required health and safety checks.' She looked at Ottilie. 'Would you like to go to school and play with other children?' she asked excitedly. 'It'll be fun, won't it?'

Ottilie didn't look sure, on the other hand she didn't appear too worried either.

'Mrs Wade,' Alex said, 'I imagine you'll be the one taking her, so can I . . .'

'Actually, my wife doesn't like to go out,' Wade

interrupted. 'And as I've just said, we'll need to carry out our own background checks before . . .'

'Oh, you won't find anything to object to with the Pumpkin,' Alex assured him. 'It's received some glowing recommendations from parents who've sent their children over the years. You can always contact them directly, should you wish, to discuss any particular concerns you might have.' It wasn't unusual for her to pressurise parents like this and most complied, particularly if they thought there was a risk of their child being taken from them. However, she could tell that Mr Wade was far too used to being in the driving seat himself to enjoy being pushed around.

Too bad, his daughter should be mixing with other children her age, and he knew it.

'Is there anything you'd like to ask, Mrs Wade?' Alex invited, turning to her again.

Though Erica Wade took a while to register the fact that she'd been spoken to, Alex felt certain she hadn't missed a word of what had been said. However, she simply shook her head while mumbling, 'I don't think so,' and since her husband had returned to the assessment, Alex said to Ottilie, 'Shall we teach Boots to play peekaboo?'

Ottilie looked down at her bear, but before she could make any kind of response her father was saying, 'Would you mind explaining to me why you felt it necessary to delve into our time in Northumbria? You already know what happened while we were there, so . . .'

'We talked about this during my last visit,' Alex reminded him. 'I've simply put it there, in writing, in order to make our agreement official.'

'Agreement?' he echoed with a frown.

'You gave me your permission to contact the authorities you dealt with before, so I could . . .'

'Yes, yes, I remember that, and I'm aware that you've spoken to Derek Tolland . . .'

'Your old headmaster . . .'

'And he told you what I've already told you myself. Did you have any reason to think I was lying to you?'

'Not at all, but I'm sure you're aware that not everyone is as forthcoming as we'd like, and all too often people who sound perfectly plausible turn out to be anything but.'

'I doubt I fall into the same category as most people you deal with.'

'We don't make exceptions for status of any kind.'

'Mm, well, I suppose that's a good thing,' he grunted grudgingly. 'It's simply that Derek Tolland is a very busy man, as am I, so I'd hoped you might factor in a useful amount of common sense when deciding on how best to spend the taxpayers' money.'

Well used to that one, Alex said, 'I think the taxpayer would be outraged to think that we excluded anyone of any standing from the process of investigation where a child's welfare is concerned.'

Colouring, Wade put the assessment down on the coffee table. 'Let me assure you my wife and I are willing to comply with the recommendations you have outlined, but only up to a point,' he informed her. 'After that I would like you to bear in mind that *I* am ultimately responsible for Ottilie's welfare, not you. She's my daughter and as such she will only do what I feel is in her best interests.'

Oh really, Alex was thinking. *Well, we'll see about*

that. What she said – because in her position it was all she could say – was, 'Of course, I respect that. I'm simply trying to help you . . .'

'But I don't need your help. However, I'm fully aware of the kind of conclusions you people jump to if things don't happen your way. So it's with this in mind that I shall not withdraw my consent to you continuing your background checks, but I would like it on the record that I feel them to be a complete waste of time and resources. There are plenty of children out there in need of your care, which is where your efforts should be focused, not into the home of a child who is loved, extremely well cared for and who happens to be a little shyer than most.'

'You'll find the section for your comments at the back of the report,' Alex told him helpfully. And moving on, 'Do you think Ottilie will be ready to attend the Pumpkin next Monday?' She glanced at Ottilie and gave her a hopeful shrug, as if it was exactly what Ottilie herself wanted.

Wade was regarding her in astonishment. 'Did you not hear what I said just now?' he enquired.

'That you'd like to carry out some checks? Yes, I heard, but that isn't going to take more than an hour, and I'd like to let the playgroup know whether or not to expect her.'

'I'm sure you would, but there are a number of other things to sort out before I can answer that.'

'Such as?'

'Such as how she's going to get there, for one thing. I can't keep taking time off to suit you, Ms Lake . . .'

'Not me, Ottilie. This is about her, remember?'

He flushed. 'Indeed. Nevertheless, I have my own

position to consider, and unless you've forgotten I have more than two hundred other children in my care.'

'I'll take her,' Erica suddenly stated.

The words were so unexpected that both Alex and Wade gaped at her.

'Well,' Alex finally managed, 'that's that sorted. Good.' *Excellent, so the mother was going to step up to the plate, meaning that agoraphobia might not be the problem after all.*

One step at a time.

To Ottilie, she said, 'Isn't it exciting, you're going to school? You'll be able to make lots of friends and . . .'

'Please don't discuss this with her until I've had a chance to do so myself,' Wade broke in crossly.

Alex flushed. 'I was simply . . .'

'Ottilie, go to your room.'

Ottilie immediately got to her feet and kept her head down as she went, her face buried in her bear. Alex wanted to ask why he'd done that, but he was already standing up, making it clear that it was time for her to leave.

To Erica Wade she said, 'I think it would be useful if we had a chat, just the two of us, Mrs Wade. Maybe I could come back tomorrow?'

'My wife wouldn't be comfortable with that,' Wade informed her shortly.

Alex waited for Erica to contradict him, but she didn't even focus her gaze.

Following Wade into the hall, Alex said, 'You'll have seen my recommendation that your wife should undergo a mental health check . . .'

'Indeed I have, but I thought this was about Ottilie, not me, or my wife.'

Alex wondered if he had any idea how badly he was coming out of this, and suspected not. On the other hand, he wasn't giving her any good reason to remove Ottilie from the home either, which actually she felt glad of (provided nothing untoward was happening to her, of course), because putting a child into care, especially in this area, was often no more than the best of the worst options. And if it happened, she couldn't see a tender little soul like Ottilie faring well at all. 'Your wife's state of mind will be highly influential on Ottilie,' she was saying as he opened the door, 'so we'd like an independent psychiatric check as soon as possible. I can arrange this for you . . .'

'Please don't do anything until I've had a chance to discuss this with my wife. She's extremely fragile, as you can see, and being pushed into having the kind of tests you're talking about could have a most detrimental effect on her. However, if you wish to discuss her situation with our family GP you have his details, so please feel free to do so.'

'Thank you. Perhaps you'd be kind enough to let him know that I have your permission for this, because he wasn't terribly forthcoming when we spoke last week.'

'I'll be sure to call by the end of the day.'

Impressed by the sudden compliance, Alex said, 'I'll be in touch at some point tomorrow regarding the time your wife should take Ottilie next Monday – provided you feel the Pumpkin is of the right standard, naturally.'

He didn't appear amused.

'And once I've had a chat with the health visitor,' she continued, 'I expect a speech therapist will be brought on board fairly swiftly. Either the health visitor, or I, will keep you informed about that. I must say, I'm quite looking forward to hearing Ottilie speak. Hopefully it won't be any time at all before she's as chatty with us as she is with you.'

Though the gauntlet lay between them, smouldering and unmissable, he simply ignored it as he swept a hand forward, an indication for her to pass. 'I'll be sending my comments on your assessment direct to your superior,' he advised her.

'His name is Tommy Burgess,' Alex replied. 'You'll find it written on the front of the information pack I gave you.' Feeling suddenly certain that Ottilie was watching her, she turned to look up and broke into a smile when she saw the child sitting on the top stair.

'Bye Ottilie,' she said with a wave. 'Bye Boots.'

Instead of encouraging her to respond, as most parents would, Wade simply stood waiting for Alex to leave. Then following her out into the porch, he pulled the door behind him. 'I apologise if I have appeared less than thrilled by what is happening,' he said, 'but after everything we've been through – all the enquiries following Jonathan's death, the endless prying into our affairs, the awful suspicions and then the accusations from an unfortunately deranged person, perhaps you can understand why we have become such a private family.'

Not unmoved by his little speech, Alex met his eyes, and wished she had a way to read what was really going on behind them. They had indeed been through a difficult time, and she mustn't allow herself to forget it – or to be thrown off by it. 'Of course I understand,' she told him kindly, 'and I'm very sorry for what you've been through.'

He nodded briefly, and as Alex turned to walk to her car she heard the front door click closed behind her.

Hearing the creak of the floorboards as her husband came back into the room, Erica got up from her chair and went to select an opera from her personal collection of CDs.

'Why did you say that?' he demanded, quietly closing the door.

Ignoring him, she ran a finger along the narrow spines of the discs, hearing her nail click on the perspex, taking her time to decide which one she felt like listening to now that Alex Lake had gone.

'Why did you say you'd take her to the nursery school?' he repeated with the kind of calm she knew was supposed to unnerve her.

Choosing Angela Gheorghiu performing Mimi in *La Bohème*, she slotted it into the player and tilted her head in a kind of whimsy as she pressed play. A moment later the sound of violins, flutes, harps swelled into the room, making her heart sing in anticipation of the most beautiful voice in the world.

The sudden silence as Brian ripped out the plug was like a physical blow.

He was her stepfather again.

'You know,' he said, as she turned round, trembling, 'that you can't go to the playgroup, so why did you say that you would?'

'Leave me alone,' she retorted huskily.

He continued to glare at her, his crescent-shaped eyes covering her with contempt. 'Don't forget what they do to people like you in prison,' he said thickly.

Though she flinched, she kept her thoughts – and her fear – to herself. *What are you going to do*, she wanted to ask, *when they find out about you?* It made her want to laugh.

'I'm leaving now,' he told her. 'I'll be home at my usual time.'

After he'd gone, she stood at the window, staring at the empty driveway, not moving until she felt sure he wasn't coming back. Then putting on her coat she went out to the back garden. Finding his shed-cum-studio as it always was, padlocked top, bottom and middle, she fetched a spade from the lean-to next to the house, and smashed it straight through the shed's double window. Taking care not to cut herself, she eased the most lethal daggers of glass from the frame, then stepped on to an upturned dustbin and hoisted herself up on to the sill. A moment later, she was swinging her legs into the darkened interior and slipping soundlessly to the floor. The smell to her was sickening, because it was of him, mingled with candlewax and turps. She looked at the tissue box on the long desk, the packs of disposable gloves, the various toys, and felt sicker than ever.

She touched none of it: the contamination might kill her and she wasn't ready to die yet.

To her surprise there were only two computers, though she couldn't be sure why she'd expected more. A lot of his photographic equipment was around too, not as neatly stored as she'd imagined it to be, but most of it was in cases or wrapped in soft cloths. There were no examples of his work decorating the walls, nor any further signs of the hobbies he pursued in here.

Quickly turning on both computers she waited, her head swimming with voices and images, as they whirred and bleeped into life. It was as though they were preparing to take her on a journey into a bizarre other world – the kind of world where memories would rise up like hands to grasp her throat and choke her into oblivion.

She needed her pills.

Both computers required passwords for entry. She should have thought of that. She typed in Ottilie, Jonathan, Brian, even her own name, but none allowed access. She combined them, added figures, tried putting in their surname, address, previous house in Northumbria, but each attempt was rejected.

In the end she shut the computers down, climbed back through the window, righted the bin, replaced the spade and returned to the house. She was going to enjoy telling him about the vandals who'd sneaked into the garden in broad daylight and wilfully smashed his shed window. Of course he'd guess it was her, but he wouldn't be able to prove it, nor could he report it to the police. He'd simply have to call in a glazier to repair it and when it was finished she'd smash it again.

Why had she never thought of doing this before?

In the kitchen, snatching her pills from a drawer, she swallowed four in one go. Sleep would come soon, blessed sleep, her only friend, her only escape from the voices, the pain, the memories that sprang from her body with monstrous bodies of their own.

Who had sent Alex Lake?

Remembering she'd put on a CD before Brian had left, she returned to the sitting room, but instead of pressing play she decided to switch on the TV instead. A rerun of *A Place in the Sun: Home or Away* should be on by now. She liked Jasmine and Jonnie, the presenters, even though Jasmine's grammar was annoying. Why did she always have to say at the end of a programme, '. . . join Johnnie and I next time around . . .' Wasn't there a producer or someone to explain to her why that was wrong?

Ottilie would stay upstairs for the rest of the afternoon watching her favourite CBeebies, or drawing pictures for Alex Lake. Had she remembered to tell her to do that? It didn't matter, there was plenty of time before Alex Lake came again.

She didn't want to think about Ottilie now.

She never wanted to think about Ottilie.

Later, when Brian came home, she'd tell him about the shed window and then she'd try not to laugh as she watched his eyes glaze with fear.

Chapter Thirteen

Alex woke with a start. For a moment she couldn't quite grasp a sense of where, or even who she was. The dream felt so real, so urgent that her heart was still thudding and the woman's fear continued pounding through her. She still couldn't be sure if the woman was her; she only knew that she'd been running from something that had no form, or sound, or even a presence.

Forcing herself to focus on the darkness around her, she realised that she was at home, in the sitting room, amongst the books and chests and cosy old furniture she'd grown up with. Evidently she'd fallen asleep on the sofa, though not for long it would seem, because the clock was only showing eight thirty, yet it felt as though she'd been out for hours.

She wondered if Jason was home yet, then remembered with a painful pang that he wouldn't be coming. She closed her eyes and wished she could go back to sleep.

There had been a child in the dream, she realised, a small girl. She was slipping away now, vanishing like a ghost into thin air. Her mind went to Ottilie. She'd been rereading her notes from yesterday's meeting with the Wades when she'd fallen asleep.

They were still on the floor beside her, rough print-outs of a report she was finding hard to sum up. She wasn't sure her judgement could be trusted when her own life was in such turmoil. Jason had gone, she had to leave her home, her job wasn't secure, and earlier she'd received an email from Millie's niece telling her that Millie was going to be moved to a care home closer to York.

It felt as though everything, everyone was slipping away.

It was only when the phone started to ring that she realised it was what had woken her just now. Obviously whoever it was had rung off, unless there was a message on the machine.

'Hi, it's me,' Gabby said when she went through to the kitchen to pick up. 'Are you dashing out? Have you got a minute?'

'I'm not going anywhere,' Alex told her, taking the phone back to the sofa and curling into one corner. 'Did you ring a moment ago?'

'No, wasn't me. You're not rehearsing tonight?'

'We've put it off to tomorrow. It's our last show on Saturday. Do you think you'll be able to make it?'

'I'm trying, and actually it's looking good, provided Martin's mum can babysit. He's off on one of his golfing days, otherwise he'd do it. Anyway, the reason I'm calling is to find out where you're going to be tomorrow during the day.'

Stifling a yawn, Alex said, 'At work, where I always am. Why?'

'Well, would you believe, Elaine, the estate agent in the village, has this property developer who's interested in the Vicarage *and* Millie's cottage. Apparently he might want to knock them into one and create a much bigger house for him and his family to live in. I was hoping you might be there at some point to let them in so he can have a look around. If it's not convenient, don't worry. You can always drop a key in to Elaine in the morning and let her get on with it.'

Feeling as though she was being dragged back into a nightmare, Alex said, 'I – I wasn't expecting it to happen this fast.'

Gabby's laugh was awkward. 'No, me neither,' she confessed. 'I only contacted Elaine on Monday, so it was a bit of a shock when she rang earlier. I thought it was going to be about taking photos and measurements and stuff, but apparently this guy's been looking for somewhere in the area for ages, and he reckons the Vicarage and cottage are going to suit him perfectly. Once he's fixed them up, obviously.'

Was Gabby really not getting what this was going to mean for her, or was she just trying to avoid the guilt? It had to be the latter, because self-absorbed as Gabby was, she was neither stupid nor completely insensitive. 'What sort of price are you looking for?' Alex asked, and immediately wished she hadn't. It was only going to make her feel worse to know how much she'd have been entitled to, if their mother had decided to leave the house to both of them.

'Well, Elaine reckons we could probably get somewhere around four hundred thousand, but that sounds a bit over the top to me.'

Not missing the catch of excitement in her voice, Alex said, 'I should think it's worth about that. It's got lovely views, remember, and great access to the village. Have you spoken to Millie's niece about it? She'll be glad to know there might be a buyer for the cottage at last – though obviously whatever it makes will have to go towards Millie's care.'

'Actually I was on the phone to her for about an hour earlier,' Gabby admitted. 'She's dead keen to go ahead with the sale if this guy does come through, so at least that won't be a problem. She said she'd emailed you earlier about moving Millie. I think it'll be so much better for the old duck to be close to her family, don't you?'

You mean the family that hardly ever comes to see her, and who've no doubt found a far less expensive home in the north to try and make sure there's some money left for them when Millie finally croaks? She didn't voice her thoughts because they were horribly cynical, in spite of probably being true. What she said instead was, 'Actually, I think it'll be quite disruptive for Millie, because she's used to where she is now. She knows the staff and she always knows me when I go to see her. I wouldn't tell her niece this, but she never asks about any of her family. I think she's forgotten them.'

'You're probably right on both counts,' Gabby sighed, 'but I could hardly tell her I thought it was a bad decision, could I? After all, Millie's her aunt, not ours, so it's up to her what she does with her. I did think it was a bit bad not even consulting you, though, when you've always been quite close to the old dear in your way. I expect you'll miss her when she's gone, won't you?'

More than you can imagine, Alex was thinking as tears blurred her eyes. Right now she simply couldn't bear the idea of Millie going anywhere, but maybe she was being selfish, trying to hold on to something, someone, from her past who'd always seemed to care when Alex had felt that no one else did. 'So what shall we do about Elaine?' she asked, pushing past her emotions. 'Will you call to let her know I'll post a key through in the morning, or shall I?'

'I'll send her a text,' Gabby replied. 'I think she's quite excited about this, because the market's been a bit slow lately, she said. Actually, why don't you ask her if she's got anything on the books that might work for you and Jason? I'll bet she has.'

Realising that to tell her about Jason now was going to end up making them both feel terrible, Alex simply said, 'I'm not sure about being able to afford anywhere around here.'

'Well, you never know, it could still be worth asking. Maybe one of the houses on the new estate over by the ice cream factory is up for sale. They always look so cute, I think.'

With a smile, Alex replied, 'I'm not sure you're really clued in to what properties cost these days, but I'll bear it in mind. How are the twins? I guess they're already in bed.'

'Finally. It took me ages to get them down tonight and Martin doesn't help, with pillow fights and tugs of war just when they're supposed to be going to sleep. You'd think, as a doctor, he'd know better, wouldn't you?'

'It seems ages since I saw them,' Alex said sadly. 'Maybe I could come down on Sunday. I'll be happy to babysit if you and Martin feel like going out for lunch somewhere.'

'You are such an angel, and we'll definitely take you up on it another weekend. Unfortunately this Sunday we're going to one of his partners for lunch. Otherwise I know the kids would be mad keen to see you. I'll send them your love though.'

'Yes, please do.' Her breath caught on a rising sob. 'Actually, I should go now, someone's trying to get through. Call as soon as you know if you can come on Saturday and I'll make sure your room is ready.'

'Oh God, that's what makes me so worried about coming, I don't know if I could bear it. Anyway, you'd best find out who's ringing. Love to Jason, and to you, obviously.'

As the line went dead Alex braced herself and clicked on again. *Please let it be Jason, please, please.*

'Hi, you're there,' Jason said brightly. 'Who've you been chatting to?'

Alex's heart contracted. *So natural and airy. Had he forgotten he'd left her?*

'Sorry, none of my business,' he said. 'Habit, I guess. Anyway, how are you?'

'I'm fine thanks,' she replied, somehow managing to sound it when it was hard to imagine feeling any worse. 'How about you?'

'Yeah, I'm good. Got a couple of new jobs this week, although one of them's for my parents, so I guess that doesn't count too much, because I'll have to do it at cost. Still, it's better than giving quotes that no one ever gets back to me on.'

'Of course,' she mumbled.

'So, what's new in your world?'

Oh now let me think about that – Gabby's selling the house and might already have found a buyer; Millie's being transported off to a care home in the north where she knows no one and will be too far away for me to visit; a little girl who thought she was being adopted now isn't and because I spoke my mind to her foster carer I've been hauled over the coals by Wendy. Then there's another little girl who breaks my heart just to look at her and has the world's weirdest mother and I swear an abusive father, but how am I going to prove it? Oh yes, and you left me, so I'm actually in pieces but pretending really hard not to be. Is that enough to be going on with? What she said was, 'Oh, nothing much. I was talking to Gabby when you rang, she asked me to send her love.'

With an uneasy laugh he said, 'That's good of her when I don't suppose I'm her favourite person right now.'

'She doesn't know we've broken up, but I'll probably tell her this weekend. If you prefer I'll leave it until after the show, so you don't have to feel awkward when you see her.' *Why should she care? As far as she was concerned he could feel as awkward as a pork chop in a synagogue and it still wouldn't be awkward enough.* 'Anyway, I can't imagine you just called up for a chat,' she went on breezily, 'so what can I do for you?'

He took a breath. 'Actually, I just kind of wanted to know how you are.'

Bristling, she said, 'Please don't feel sorry for me, Jason, there's no need, because I'm absolutely fine. I hope everything's working out for you too.'

'Yeah, yeah, it's cool,' he replied a little too quickly. 'The kids are behaving themselves a bit better now. I think they like me being here.'

He was evidently calling from home, so where was Gina? Out with her mates, or off on a date with another bloke already?

'Actually, I ought to come and pick up the rest of my stuff at some point,' he said, trying to make it sound like a pop in for a drink.

At last the real reason he was calling, and wishing she could make herself just hang up, she said, 'Yeah, you probably should. Would you like me to pack for you?' *Why the hell had she offered to do that, what was wrong with her? Since when had she decided to remodel herself as a doormat?*

'It's OK, I can do it,' he assured her, 'but thanks. I was hoping Sunday might work if it's convenient for you.'

'Actually, I'm sorry but it's not,' she lied. 'I'm going out on Sunday.' *She'd find somewhere to go. Another visit to her dead family's grave?* Hopefully Millie would still be around. Of course she would, nothing with the NHS moved that fast.

'Maybe it'll be easier if you're not there,' he suggested. 'I'll just take my clothes and computer and stuff and leave the key when I go. Would that be OK?'

'That's fine,' she retorted. *Had she sounded bitter? Did it matter if she had?* 'It would be best if you didn't come after twelve, or before five,' she ran on. 'I've got some friends coming over for lunch.' *Eat your heart out that you won't be here too – and wonder who they are, because one of them might be another man.* Then she remembered she'd just told him she was going out.

'Oh right, that's cool,' he said hesitantly. 'I don't want to interrupt anything. Whatever suits you.'

And now, Alex, you have to get to the end of this call without making an even bigger fool of yourself than you've already managed. 'I'll see you on Saturday then, for the show,' she said.

'Ah, yes, there's a bit of a problem with that, I'm afraid. Don't worry, I'm not letting you down, it's just that I can't make it myself, but Cliff is definitely going to be there. And he's way more experienced at it all than I am, so everything'll probably turn out to be ten times better than when I'm there.'

Is that what you think? Is that what you really think?

Why was she still holding the phone? Why didn't she just say what she actually thought and hang up? Did she even know what she thought? 'Before you go,' she said, 'did you ring me earlier? It's just that someone did but I didn't get to the phone in time.'

'No, this is the first time I've rung tonight. Why? Oh God, please don't tell me that scumbag from the estate is still bothering you?'

Shane Prince hadn't even crossed her mind – until now. 'His sister's not in my caseload any more,' she told him, as if it were an answer when actually it wasn't. Maybe it had been Shane. Maybe he was also responsible for the two or three calls she'd found on the answering machine when she'd got home, where whoever it was had rung off without leaving a message. It was too late now to dial 1471, because all she'd get was Jason's number since he'd been the last one to call.

'I should go,' she said. 'If you could text to let me know when you're coming on Sunday that would be great,' and before he could say goodbye, or anything else, she quickly cut the call and pressed her hands to her face.

She didn't want to cry, she really, really didn't, but she was suddenly so overwhelmed by a childish, primal sort of need to let go that there was no way she could make herself stop.

It's just loneliness, Alex, she told herself sharply, as if that was going to help in some way. Loneliness and never feeling she was doing enough for the pathetic, vulnerable kids with whom she spent so much of her time.

There was such a cacophony going on in the office that Alex could barely hear herself think, never mind make out what Scott Danes, the Northumbrian police officer, was trying to tell her down the phone. In the end, asking him to hang on, she grabbed her notebook and pen and dived into Tommy's office, closing the door behind her.

'Sorry, but it's a madhouse out there,' she explained to a startled Tommy, and going back to her call, 'OK, I'm here. So let me get this straight, you haven't been able to find a record of anyone called Jill McCarthy – either with a J or a G, or the various spellings of the surname?'

'Nothing in our records,' Scott Danes confirmed, 'but as I was saying just now, you should try your own people up here, or the local health authority. They're more likely to have records of paranoid schizophrenics than we are, unless a crime's been committed, of course.'

'Actually, I've already spoken to them,' she assured him. 'I just wanted to know if she was showing up for you in any way, and obviously she isn't, but thanks for checking.'

'Any time. Is that all for now?'

'I think so, unless you can help me with Erica Wade's medical records, but I'm already on to her old GP about that, Andy Miller. Do you know him? Hang on, I've got his address somewhere.'

'It's OK, I know him and he's a pretty regular sort of chap, but if you have any problem accessing what you need give me a call and I'll go round and have a chat.'

'You're brilliant, thanks so much. I'll be in touch.' As she rang off, she said to Tommy, 'Are you following any of this?'

'Better refresh me,' he told her.

'Well, it seems that the woman who hassled, or

harassed Brian Wade after his son's death, you know, calling him a child-killer and all that, isn't showing up on anyone's records. Even the head-master up there – Derek Tolland – admits he never actually spoke to her himself, or clapped eyes on her.'

Tommy nodded his interest. 'So what are we deducing from this?' he enquired.

'That it's a lie?' she suggested. 'I mean, someone who's been diagnosed a paranoid schizophrenic has to be registered somewhere, and apparently this woman isn't.'

'Maybe it's not her real name – or the diagnosis was more layman observation than a specialist's findings.'

Alex deflated. 'Actually, I'd thought of that, but it was so unhelpful I decided to overlook it.'

'Sorry,' Tommy murmured. 'So how's the rest of it going?'

Alex pushed her hands through her hair. 'Let me see. OK, there's now a health visitor on the case, Vicky Barnes, which is great. She went round yesterday, and when we spoke later she said that on the face of it Ottilie's in good physical shape. A few old bruises apparently, but she wasn't particularly concerned about them, thought they'd come from a fall or walking into furniture, the way kids do. But there was a nasty burn on her hand which definitely wasn't there when I visited on Wednesday.'

Tommy was frowning. 'And how did she come by this burn?'

'Apparently she'd tried to heat up some milk for her teddy bear.'

Tommy looked as dubious as Alex felt; however,

having no way of knowing exactly how Ottilie had come by the injury, they had no choice but to accept the explanation – for now.

'The health visitor's gone ahead and set up an appointment with the community paediatrician for the twenty-ninth of this month,' Alex continued. 'Apparently the father's going to take her, but he was quite shirty about having to arrange for more time off work.'

'What's the matter with the mother taking her?'

'I don't think she ever goes out, though she told me she'd take Ottilie to nursery on Monday. I guess we'll have to wait and see if she means it when Monday comes.'

'Mm. This mother really is a bit of a problem, isn't she? What kind of background have you got on her?'

Alex pulled a face. 'I'm still working on it,' she confessed. 'But so far, until their son died she was a part-time private music teacher – piano, I'm told, but there's no piano in the house now. Unless it's upstairs in a bedroom. I've only seen Ottilie's room – if I'd tried looking in any of the others Brian Wade would have had a blue fit. He's a very private man, you understand.'

Tommy's expression was wry. 'I often wonder what private people have to be so private about, don't you?'

'I do indeed, and in his case I've got absolutely no doubt that there's something. Question is, how do we unearth it?' She shook her head in frustration. 'This is turning into one of those situations when I feel more like a detective than a flaming social worker.'

'If we had anything like the same powers as a

detective we'd probably get somewhere a lot faster, and save a lot more kids from harm, but don't get me started on that or I'll go on all day. So, we still don't know enough about Mrs Wade, apart from the fact that she used to teach music and is a bit of a . . . How would you describe it?'

'Weirdo, space cadet, call it what you like. I keep trying to work out what's going on with her. Obviously I've recommended a mental health check, but it's looking as though I might have to force that through, because Mr Wade's not coming across as very keen.'

Tommy raised an eyebrow. 'So what's your next move?'

'I carry on making phone calls trying to piece together what happened when the son died – I'm waiting for more calls back on that, and the family's old GP said he'd ring between four and five today.'

Tommy nodded his approval. 'OK, sounds good. Incidentally, I haven't heard anything from Mr Wade about your assessment yet, but I guess it's still early days. Now, tell me what's really going on with you, because I can see from the way you look . . .'

'Actually,' she cut in quickly before he could get into anything personal, 'I wanted to talk to you about Shane Prince. I think he might be calling me and not leaving messages. You know, a kind of intimidation thing. I haven't been able to check with 1471 yet, but we know he's got my home number so I thought I should mention it.'

'You did right, and don't you worry, pet, if it is him I'll make sure he understands it'll be better for him if he forgets your number.'

Alex gave him a mocking look. 'Just like that?'

she teased. 'Shane, you stop pestering Alex Lake or you're going to find yourself in big trouble. He'll be so scared.'

Tommy cocked an eyebrow. 'He's got no reason to be coming after you now, remember that, not that he had in the first place . . .'

'But don't you know, he's cast me as the ugly face of social services?'

'Which just goes to show what a dickhead he is. And if it's an ugly face he wants, wait till he sees mine.'

'But you're gorgeous,' Alex protested with a laugh. 'So when are you planning to go over there?'

'Actually, I went yesterday but there was no one at home, so I'll try again Monday. If I don't clap eyes on the girl then I'll be going in on Tuesday with an EPO and we can imagine how much they'll enjoy that, especially if the police have to bash the door down.'

Alex shuddered. 'Just as long as he doesn't hold me responsible, because I so don't need him on my case right now.'

Tommy's eyes immediately narrowed with concern.

'Don't,' she warned softly. 'The last thing I need is someone being nice to me.'

'Oh, right, then get the hell out of here . . .'

'Alex!' Saffy shouted. 'Call for you. Sounds urgent.'

'On my way,' Alex called back, and going to take the phone she sank into her chair and listened in dismay to what the manager of a residential unit was telling her. Apparently one of her teenagers had absconded from the unit, taking an eleven-year-old girl with him. The police had been called, but the manager was insisting that Alex should come over to help sort things out.

After assuring him she was on her way, she was about to ring to cancel her visit to a family in Camberside when a peevish voice said, 'I know what your game is, so don't think I don't. We can all see straight through you, you know.'

Stunned, as much by the tone as the words, Alex looked up and didn't even bother to hide her dislike when she found Ben's long, bony face quivering over her. 'Exactly what's your problem?' she demanded, starting to pack up her bag.

Ben's hands were on his snaky little hips. 'Oh, let's make out like we don't know,' he retorted, playing to the gallery. 'I mean, we're not blowing this whole Ottilie Wade thing up into a drama to try to make someone else look bad, are we?'

Aware of the others watching, Alex decided to ignore him and grabbed her coat.

'I spoke to her father – the deputy headmaster of Kesterly Rise – after both *anonymous* calls,' Ben told her waspishly. 'Someone's obviously trying to make mischief for him – probably the same someone who started harassing him after his son died . . .'

'Ben, I really don't have time for this,' she interrupted, trying to push past him.

'There's nothing wrong with that girl,' he hissed. 'You're only doing this to try to paint me in a bad light for not following up . . .'

Alex swung round, eyes blazing. 'This is not about you,' she spat furiously. 'It's about a child who doesn't speak and a mother who's clearly a basket case, which you would know if you'd bothered . . .'

'Alex, I need to speak to you.' It was Wendy, standing at the door with a stack of files in her arms.

'Sorry, I can't right now,' Alex told her, hefting her bag on to her shoulder.

'She's too busy being a saint,' Ben snorted nastily.

'Oh grow up,' Alex shot back.

'Alex,' Wendy said firmly, 'before you go anywhere I need these forms completed.'

Alex was in no mood for Wendy's pettiness. Grabbing a black marker she scribbled where she was going on the board, then turning to Wendy she said, 'As you can see I have a bit of a crisis on my hands, so your forms will have to wait. And, Ben, just fuck off!'

As the door banged shut behind her she heard Lizzy shout, 'Go girl!'

Though it afforded her a fleeting smile she was still shaking with anger as she ran down the stairs. It was rare for her to lose her temper in the office, rarer still for her to swear like that, but for God's sake! What was the matter with everyone? Ben was in serious danger of getting lost in his own ego, the way he was carrying on. How could he possibly think she'd only followed up on Ottilie's case to try and get the better of him? As if! She hadn't even thought about him since taking it on – and anyway, the hell was she going to get into defending herself when there was absolutely no doubt in her mind that something was very wrong in that family.

And she sure as hell wasn't going to prioritise filling in some stupid bloody forms for Wendy either.

Chapter Fourteen

The past weekend had turned into one that Alex would rather forget than ever have to live through again. She'd tried hard not to be hurt that Gabby hadn't made it to the show, and done her level best to keep her true feelings hidden when it had come out, as it had to, just before the dress run on Saturday, that she and Jason were no longer together. Much as she'd expected, everyone had been shocked and sympathetic and ready to side with her, which had perversely made it worse, but at least she hadn't broken down in front of them all.

'It's OK, honestly,' she'd assured them. 'I'd been expecting it anyway.'

'But you're so good together,' Sarah had protested. 'I reckon he's mad going back to her. She'll only mess him around again, the way she did last time.'

'She's always been a bit of a slapper,' Johnny announced. 'And she can be a right cow if you get on the wrong side of her.'

'That'll be why he's not here today,' Sarah decided, 'because she won't let him come.'

'He should be a man and stand up to her more,' Steve chipped in.

'He's going to regret it,' Mattie insisted. 'He's

bound to, because everyone knows he's mad about you.'

Finding that almost too hard to take, Alex had said, 'Whatever, he's made up his mind and I'm not about to try and change it, not when he's always said that his children have to come first. So let's forget it now and focus on making Cliff's life as easy as possible, shall we, given that he's on his own doing the lights tonight.'

In the end the show hadn't gone badly considering, and everyone had given their all in spite of the audience being much thinner on the ground than for the previous two performances. Just thank goodness Elaine, the estate agent, who'd brought her sister and brother-in-law along, hadn't mentioned anything about the Vicarage being up for sale. There was only so much sympathy and curiosity she could take in one day: the news that she was soon to become homeless on top of being dumped would have increased her friends' reactions to a level that would have been out-and-out unbearable.

She'd spent part of yesterday, Sunday, at the care home with Millie, who'd been delighted to see her when she'd finally woken up and found her there.

'Is it Christmas?' she'd asked. 'I likes Christmas, don't you? You always did when you was a lickle girl.'

'It's not Christmas yet,' Alex had told her, 'but when it comes this year you'll be with your family up north. Won't that be lovely?'

Millie had seemed confused. 'Can I have me breakfast now?' she asked, pulling at the sheets in an effort to sit up. 'I asked for porridge, but they don't always bring it. I shan't stay in this hotel again.'

With a smile Alex said, 'I thought you liked it here.'

'Oh, I do, they'm lovely people. Ever so kind and they gives you anything you asks for. How's your dad? I saw him yesterday, coming out of the church. He said he'd mow my lawn for me today.'

Reaching for her hand, Alex held it between both of hers as she struggled with a silly rise of tears. 'I'm going to miss you,' she told Millie in a whisper she'd felt sure Millie couldn't hear.

'Oh now, I'm not going nowhere yet,' Millie assured her. 'There's plenty of life left in these old bones, you wait and see.'

Alex wasn't sure now whether she felt sorry for that, or glad – after all, what kind of life was it stuck in bed all day, unable to do anything for yourself or stop anyone else doing things to you either? Like moving you to a strange place full of people you didn't know, with a family nearby who might never come to see you. Still, she had to remember that at least Millie wasn't one of the tragically traumatised souls who never stopped screaming, or swearing, or cowering in fear of something or someone who wasn't even there.

And she herself, for now at any rate, wasn't one of the pathetic people who might have rushed home yesterday afternoon to try and catch Jason, hoping to make it look as though she'd totally forgotten he was going to be there. Consequently she hadn't seen him at all, when she'd really wanted to. But how great would that have made her feel, watching him packing his bags and leaving for good? She might have ended up begging him to stay and making everything ten times worse for them both, if that was possible, and she was hardly able to imagine that it was. So what she'd actually arrived home to, after a long, solitary walk along the sands trying not to feel sorry for herself and failing miserably, were gaping holes in the wardrobe where his clothes used to be, a toothbrush missing from the holder that had made hers look wretchedly lonely, and a general air of emptiness that had seemed to swallow her up in an awful despair.

It didn't matter though, she'd get through it, somehow, mainly because she only had to look at the way other people – like the little boy sitting opposite her now – managed to cope with what life threw at them, to realise that what was happening to her had virtually no significance.

Fortunately, in six-year-old Peter Leach's case there was no parental or guardian abuse involved, as such. It was all coming from his eight- and nine-year-old peers, because Peter was different. His problems had now been diagnosed as Asperger's which his stepfather, in particular, was finding very hard to deal with. However, at least Mr Leach was here at a core meeting today, taking part in deciding on the best way forward for his stepson, who appeared not to be taking any interest at all in what either the paediatrician or the psychiatrist was saying.

At that precise moment Alex wasn't totally focused either, because she'd just received a two-word text from Janet Bookman, the owner of the Pumpkin playgroup: *No Show*.

Knowing it was about Ottilie, Alex's heart sank, but as she looked across the conference table at Peter she knew that whatever was happening with Ottilie, her priority right now had to be this little boy. Thanks to his obsessiveness and poor communication skills it was highly probable that no one was ever going to care as much about him as his mother did, though his stepfather was obviously trying. However, being long-term unemployed, and undereducated in almost every way, neither parent seemed to have any idea what to do with the child – except try their hardest to blame social services for the unwelcome and baffling diagnosis.

As Peter's health visitor began explaining what came next in Peter's care plan, Alex took the opportunity to send a quick text back to Janet. *On it. Please don't let place go.* Then, taking a bathroom break, she rang Kesterly Primary and asked to be put through to Brian Wade.

'I'm sorry,' came the reply, 'he's in a meeting this morning and can't be disturbed unless it's an emergency.'

Tempted to tell the woman it was exactly that, Alex ended the call and returned to the meeting, determined to stay focused on Peter in spite of how strongly she wanted to drive over to North Hill right now to find out what the heck Erica Wade was up to. She'd said she'd take Ottilie to the playgroup, but clearly it had been a ruse to get Alex off their backs, or that was how it was seeming right now.

As she listened to Gail from Family Support outlining the proposed procedure that she and Alex had drawn up for the month ahead, Alex could feel herself becoming angrier and angrier with Erica Wade for not sticking to her word. OK, Alex hadn't exactly expected her to, but that wasn't making the woman's failure to do what was right for Ottilie any easier to stomach. Didn't she realise, or care, that she might end up losing her daughter if she carried on like this?

At least Peter's mother wanted him, but the way she was shouting at them now, accusing them of neglect, false allegations and prejudice wasn't helping to sort anything out here. The paediatrician tried speaking over her, so did Gail, then Alex endeavoured, as diplomatically as possible, to point out to the woman that she was going into denial about Peter's problems.

That was it: the mother erupted in a blaze of fury, the boy started screaming and Tommy's roar to calm things down only succeeded in making matters worse. In the end, the stepfather and Tommy had to prise Peter's mother off the health worker, while the psychiatrist and Alex did their best to placate the child.

All in all it turned into one of the most disastrous core meetings Alex had had in a long time, and by the time she was finally able to run down to her car she was still so upset, even outraged, by the way Peter's mother had suddenly turned on them with all her wild accusations, that she wasn't entirely clear about where she was going to take this next. Just thank God notes were meticulously filed after every visit, so everything was on record, nevertheless it continued to incense Alex that Mrs Leach had spewed all the slanders and obscenities she could come up with over the very people who were trying to help her.

Swinging the car out on to the main road, she began heading towards North Hill.

Lies, lies and more lies.

Why couldn't anyone ever tell the truth, for God's sake? Her mind flashed back to the union meeting she'd attended on Saturday morning, which inflamed her all over again. What the hell was the point in taking strike action? Who exactly was that going to help? Certainly not the kids who needed them, and not them either, because in case no one had noticed the government wasn't listening. It was too busy making cuts, cuts and more cuts while pretending to have all the answers, when really all they were doing was *lying*. They were so far out of touch with the families in need that they couldn't hear those at the bottom mocking and ridiculing their frankly absurd new policies to beat crime, or the wretchedly impoverished crying with hunger as their benefits were slashed, mainly because the policy-makers were too damned busy listening to themselves. And what lies they told, saying they understood how difficult it was to live on a sink estate without the prospect of a job, government assistance being ripped out from under them and tax credits cancelled. They didn't have the first idea, stuck up there in their smart London mansions with millions under the mattress, and quantitive easing coming out of every orifice.

It made her so mad, *so damned mad*, that she was ready to storm Downing Street right now. If it weren't so far away she would. However, she had to make herself calm down, because she was coming very close to North Hill and if she carried on like this she might just find herself tearing into Erica Wade in a way that would frighten poor little Ottilie out of her wits.

And get her taken off Ottilie's case, which she didn't want at all.

Mercifully, by the time she drove in through the bramble-snarled gates she had herself in better control, though she certainly wasn't happy with Brian Wade whom she'd tried – unsuccessfully – to contact again. Knowing from experience how unlikely it was she'd get a response from inside the house unless he was there, she was already holding him responsible for her failure.

However, to her surprise, when she went to ring the bell she found the front door slightly ajar. Not quite sure what to make of this, she pushed the door open and called out hello.

Receiving no reply she stepped into the hall and called out again.

Still no response.

Starting to feel uneasy, she wondered if the wisest course now might be to ring Brian Wade and get him out of his meeting.

'Mrs Wade,' she called again. 'Ottilie? Are you in here?'

Still nothing.

It was always possible, she reminded herself, that Erica Wade had taken Ottilie to the nursery after all, and not realised she'd left the front door open. With this little bolster to her nerves she pushed open the sitting-room door and gave a gasp of surprise when she saw Erica Wade and Ottilie standing side by side in front of the empty hearth – looking for all the world as though they were waiting for her.

This woman is definitely off her trolley, Alex was thinking as she forced a smile. 'Here you are,' she said, trying to sound cheery as she looked at Ottilie. 'And there was me thinking no one was at home.'

Ottilie pressed Boots against her chin and looked up at her with big, velvety eyes. She was wearing denim dungarees and trainers under a pale pink anorak. *Who bought her clothes? They were very cute and good quality*. And unless Alex was greatly mistaken, she was dressed to go out. However, her mother didn't appear to be, so it was difficult to tell what was going on.

'I'd hoped,' Alex said to Erica, 'that you'd keep your word, and take Ottilie to the Pumpkin today.'

Erica Wade looked down at Ottilie. 'Go on,' she said. 'It's time to go.'

Alex watched Ottilie walk forward and come to stand next to her.

'You can take her,' Erica Wade said, making it sound like she was doing Alex a favour.

Having been in this situation before, Alex didn't find it hard to reply, 'The point is, Mrs Wade, for you to take her, not . . .'

'If you want her to go, then there she is.'

Alex looked down at Ottilie and found her gazing worriedly up at her. What else could she do but smile? 'You look very smart,' she told her. 'Is that a new jacket?'

Ottilie didn't answer, but her free hand grabbed the collar of the anorak so it seemed she'd understood.

Since she didn't have much time to argue with Mrs Wade, Alex went down to Ottilie's height and said, 'Would you like me to take you to nursery today?'

'Yes, she would,' Erica answered for her.

Apparently taking her cue, Ottilie nodded.

Knowing better than to get into a scene with a parent in front of a child, much as she'd have liked to, Alex took Ottilie's hand and stood up again. 'Do you have a car seat?' she asked Erica, making her tone as disapproving as she could without alarming Ottilie.

'There's one in the garage,' Erica told her, appearing unmoved. 'The door's not locked.'

Alex glanced down at Ottilie again and smiled at her sweet little face. This child needed friends and an education, and if Alex couldn't help to give her that then she was very definitely in the wrong job. So, tightening her grip on Ottilie's hand, she said, 'I'll take you today. Is that all right?'

Ottilie nodded.

To Erica, Alex said, 'Before we go, I want to ask if you know someone by the name of Jill McCarthy.'

As Erica visibly flinched Alex felt herself tense.

'You do, don't you?' she prompted.

Though Erica didn't answer, Alex could see she'd started to shake. 'Who is Jill McCarthy?' she pressed.

In a waspish tone Erica replied, 'I don't know who you're talking about. Now either take the child with you, or leave her here. It's all the same to me.'

The child?

Feeling Ottilie's eyes watching her, Alex said, 'We need to talk, Mrs Wade, you understand that, don't you?'

Erica made no response, and not wanting to go any further in front of Ottilie, Alex smiled down at her again as she said, 'Are you ready?'

Ottilie's eyes returned to her mother, and this time Alex caught Erica's nod before she saw Ottilie's.

Something highly manipulative – and odd – was going on here.

She wasn't sure if Erica Wade was following them as they left the room, but when she and Ottilie were on the drive she heard the front door close behind them.

Not wasting any more time, Alex opened the garage door, found a child's seat and minutes later she was strapping Ottilie into the back of her car. Moved by how compliant, and even trusting she was, while concerned by how unperturbed she seemed at leaving her mother, Alex put a finger under her chin and smiled at her. 'Do you really want to go to nursery?' she asked softly, having no idea what she'd do if Ottilie said no.

Ottilie's eyes remained round.

She might not even know what nursery is, Alex thought sadly.

'I think you'll like it,' Alex told her, injecting her voice with cheer while hoping it turned out to be true. 'The teachers are very kind and there are lots of children and toys to play with. Does that sound nice?'

Ottilie still said nothing. However, she drew Boots up against her face, which might have been a response of some kind, Alex wasn't sure. She guessed she'd get to know the more time she spent with her.

It wasn't far to the Pumpkin, simply up and over the hill, down to the coast road then across Victoria Square towards the station. Throughout the journey Alex kept an eye on Ottilie in the back seat, watching her staring out of the window, seeming to take in everything they were passing, but not exuding much of a response. She wished she knew what was going through her mind, but at least she didn't seem scared, which had been Alex's biggest concern, and she didn't appear particularly fazed either, which suggested that she did indeed get taken out of that house from time to time. At least more than the once Alex had seen her with her father in the park. Presumably her mother never took her anywhere, because after today Alex couldn't imagine Erica Wade even putting on a coat, never mind setting foot into the great outdoors.

What was Erica Wade doing now? Curiously, worryingly, she hadn't appeared at all bothered by letting Ottilie go. Was there no bond between them at all?

Still, at least Ottilie's welfare was in hand now, and after driving round to the car park at the back of the Pumpkin, Alex went to unbuckle her from her seat and lifted her up and out of the car. She was such a tiny scrap of a thing that it was almost impossible not to hug her; however, Alex had no idea at this stage if Ottilie was used to such displays of affection – certainly she hadn't seen any – and might be frightened by one.

'Are you all right?' she asked, putting Ottilie down on the ground and taking her hand. Why did she feel so drawn to this child? What was it about her that seemed to be setting her apart in a way she'd never felt with one of her charges before? It was crazy to think that some greater force had brought them together, but she couldn't deny that it was how it felt, and had long before she'd broken up with Jason, so it couldn't be a strange sort of reaction to that. It was just there, a strong and quiet force at the core of her that seemed, oddly, to belong more to Ottilie than it did to her.

Ottilie was looking around. At her height she wouldn't be able to see much more than a mass of car tyres and shiny bodywork, while from Alex's viewpoint there were large, red-brick walls that formed the back of the station, and the old ruin of an arch that led through to the narrowing end of the coast road. She wondered what Ottilie was hearing, the sound of traffic mingling with the cry of gulls? An optimistic ice cream van somewhere in the distance? The jingle of a merry-go-round not too far away? Maybe she was smelling or feeling the salty air on her skin, but she wouldn't be able to see the way it was creating tiny crystal beads in her wispy hair.

As they started towards the arch Alex wondered how well Ottilie had been prepared for what was about to happen, and worried that she hadn't been at all, or in a way that was going to cause some problems, she said, 'The boys and girls at the Pumpkin are all very friendly, you know, and Janet, who's in charge, is really looking forward to meeting you. I've told her what a lovely girl you are, and I think you'll really like her too.'

As she glanced down at Ottilie, Ottilie looked up and Alex's heart flooded with feeling. 'Oh look,' she said, pointing as they walked out on to the coast road, 'do you see the donkeys over on the beach? They seem a bit sad, don't they? I'm sure that's because no one's riding them today. It's not the right weather for it though, is it? Too cold and windy. I expect they'll be taken home to their winter stables soon, don't you?'

As Ottilie came to a stop, staring at the donkeys, Alex waited with her and found herself caught up in delight as Ottilie suddenly broke into a smile.

'Do you like donkeys?' Alex asked, remembering how Brian Wade had told her she was afraid of them.

Ottilie pointed at them.

'Has Daddy taken you for a ride on them?'

Ottilie was still pointing, but then she turned to look out along the headland to where the tide was flying off the cliffs in flurries of spray and a few hardy hikers were like stick men in the distance. She turned back suddenly as the music of a carousel started up across the road, and her eyes rounded with awe as it began going round.

'Have you ever been on one of those?' Alex asked.

Ottilie didn't answer.

'Would you like to have a ride on it?'

Ottilie couldn't stop staring, apparently entranced by the vision of open-top cars and large pink rabbits, ships with seats and funnels and a tiny gold carriage for a princess. There was only one little boy riding, sitting at the back of a ship and waving each time he passed what looked like his granny.

'I know,' Alex said in a conspiratorial whisper, 'we'll go and have a look at it after nursery, shall we?'

Ottilie barely blinked; it wasn't even clear if she'd heard.

'Come on,' Alex said, gently tugging her along the road to where the Pumpkin's colourful sign was displayed over a wide, lavender-blue door. 'There are going to be lots of things to play with inside.'

Though Ottilie followed, she kept glancing over her shoulder until a cheery voice caught her attention, and she looked up to find Janet already at the door to meet them.

'I'm guessing this is Ottilie,' Janet declared happily. Her rosy cheeks and sky-blue eyes were as warm as her smile, while her chalk-stained clothes and paint-spattered arms showed just how hands-on she was with her little brood. 'You've come at just the right time,' she told Ottilie, 'because we're about to have a story. Do you like stories?'

Ottilie pulled back slightly, so Alex stooped to her height and put an arm around her. 'I think you do, don't you?' she whispered.

'I wonder if you have a favourite,' Janet said,

tilting her head to one side as though trying to guess. 'Or maybe this little one does,' she ventured, looking at Boots. 'Are you going to tell me his name?'

Ottilie didn't answer.

'I'm sure he's got one, and I'll bet it's Paddington.'

Ottilie's throaty little voice was barely audible as she said, 'Boots.'

Alex's heart contracted with surprise and pleasure as Janet beamed. 'Of course,' Janet cried. 'Because he has some very smart boots. He's a lucky bear is all I can say, because I'd love some boots like that, wouldn't you?'

Ottilie managed the hint of a nod.

Filling up with pride, Alex said, 'Shall we go into the warm now and take off your coat before you join the others?'

As Ottilie lifted Boots to her face, Alex guessed that might be a no.

'OK, we'll leave your coat on for now,' she said, choosing to ignore the possibility that Ottilie might not want to go in.

'Come along then,' Janet encouraged, holding out a hand to take Ottilie's. 'Let's see if we can find everyone else.'

Ottilie stayed where she was, gripping tightly to Alex's hand, so Alex led her through to the large, brightly lit playroom where twenty or more children were building, shouting, crayoning, elbowing, throwing sponge balls, or in one dear little soul's case singing at the top of his voice into a toy microphone. Like any nursery, the walls were covered in abstract drawings and vividly coloured posters, while the floor was all mapped out for a myriad of different games. There were a dozen or more bright red tables with matching chairs currently pushed up against one wall, a rainbow of vast bouncy cushions, toys galore and boxes upon boxes of children's games.

'What do you think of this?' Alex whispered to Ottilie. 'Doesn't it look like fun?'

Ottilie only stared, her hand still rigidly clamped to Alex's.

'I'm not going to make a big fuss of introducing her,' Janet said quietly. 'We'll let her find her own way in.' And turning, she clapped her hands for everyone to get ready for story time.

'Hello. What's your name?' a little blonde girl came to ask Ottilie.

When Ottilie didn't answer Alex said it for her. 'And what's yours?' she asked the girl.

'I'm Chloe,' she replied. 'And I'm nearly four.'

'Are you? Well, you look very grown up for four.'

'How old are you?' Chloe asked Ottilie.

'Ottilie's three,' Alex answered. 'And she's a little bit shy, but I think she'd really like to make a friend.'

'I'll be your friend,' Chloe said earnestly.

Loving Chloe on sight, Alex said, 'Isn't that lovely, Ottilie?'

Ottilie only looked at the girl.

'I'm not shy,' Chloe declared.

'No, I can see that,' Alex smiled.

Chloe's wide blue eyes remained earnest until she turned them back to Ottilie. 'Shall I get you some squash and a piece of cake?' she offered. 'That's what we have at story time.'

Realising Ottilie was all at sea, Alex said, 'That's very kind of you, Chloe, because I'm sure Ottilie would love some squash and cake.'

As she skipped off, Alex caught Janet's eye and smiled.

'Put her here,' Janet mouthed, pointing to a chair at the back of the group. 'I'll stay by her.'

Taking Ottilie to the chair, Alex sat her down, still holding her hand, and dropped to her knees. 'I have to go now,' she told her softly, 'but I'll be back in a couple of hours to pick you up, OK?'

Ottilie immediately looked panicked and started to stand up.

Reminding herself that she had no idea what nonsense Ottilie might have been fed about the Pumpkin, Alex gently smoothed back her hair as she said, 'You'll be fine, honestly. Janet and Chloe will take care of you, and Boots is here looking after you too. I expect he'll like hearing a story and making some new friends, won't he?'

Ottilie shook her head and looked so desperate that Alex wasn't sure what to do. 'Oh, sweetheart, I know it's hard,' she said tenderly, 'but truly you're going to fit in just fine here, and you needn't be afraid to speak, because you can hear everyone else chatting, can't you? Chat, chat, chat, chat. They never stop. You can do that too, can't you?'

Ottilie buried her face in Boots.

It was when Alex realised she was crying that she accepted she really didn't have the heart to leave her yet even if it was the right thing to do, and she wasn't convinced that it was. She didn't come from a secure background, like other children, so making her feel confident was going to take extra effort and time. 'I think, just for today, I ought to stay,' she explained to Janet when she came to check on them. She could always reschedule her afternoon visits and work on into the evening to make up for the couple of hours she was going to spend here.

'No problem,' Janet assured her. 'Everyone's welcome, aren't they?' she said to Ottilie.

'I just need to make some calls,' Alex said. 'Will you wait here while I do that?' she asked Ottilie.

As Ottilie kept hold of her hand Alex looked down at her face and felt such a wrench in her heart that she almost picked Ottilie up to take her with her. 'I won't be long,' she promised. 'You just sit there like a good girl and before you know it I'll be right back.'

To her relief Janet knelt down beside Ottilie, and spotting Chloe coming carefully towards them balancing some squash and cake on a book-sized tray, Janet said, 'Oh now look, isn't that kind of Chloe to fetch you a snack? You're a little angel, Chloe, you really are, but don't forget to get some for yourself.'

'Don't worry, I won't,' Chloe assured her, and stooping towards Ottilie she offered her the beaker and plate.

Slipping her hand out of Alex's, Ottilie kept hold of Boots as she took the plate.

'Can you say thank you?' Alex prompted.

'Thank you,' Ottilie whispered.

'Good girl,' Janet praised, 'and we'll put your drink on the table over here so you can fetch it when you're ready.'

'Can I come back and sit next to her?' Chloe asked Alex.

'Of course you can,' Alex smiled, thinking how lovely it was to be amongst children who weren't disturbed in any way – a rarity for her. 'She'd like that very much, wouldn't you, Ottilie?'

Seeming to take Ottilie's failure to answer as a yes, Chloe zoomed off to get her own snack, while Alex, leaving Janet kneeling beside Ottilie, slipped quietly into the office to rearrange her day.

No more than ten minutes had passed by the time she returned to the playroom, and when she saw Ottilie sitting where she'd left her, her cake plate perched on one knee with the cake half eaten as she listened to the story, she felt her heart swell with relief. She was even tempted for a moment to leave her there, and come back at the end of the session, but it would have been wrong to break a promise, and besides she no longer had to rush off.

So, pulling up a chair to sit behind her, she busied herself with texts and emails on her BlackBerry while the story continued, until finally it was over and it was time to play games.

Ottilie was still too shy to join in; however, she appeared totally fascinated, and when it came time to play music she accepted a little hammer from Janet and tapped out a few notes on a xylophone.

This child has been so starved of social contact, Alex was remarking to herself later as she sat squashed up next to Ottilie on the carousel, *that she's practically bursting with the need for it*. What she'd have really loved to know was how many words Ottilie could actually say, since she'd only heard 'Boots' and 'thank you' so far; however, she certainly didn't appear to have any problem understanding what was being said. She could clearly read a little too, which had been established simply by Janet asking her to point to certain words on a page. So apparently her father was taking time to educate her, even if he wasn't encouraging her to speak, or mix with other children.

All that was coming to an end now though, thank goodness. Come hell or high water this little girl was going to start living as normal a life as it was possible for her to live, given the problem parents she had – and therein was a truth she came across all the time, that it was never the children who were the problem, it was the people who were supposed to be taking care of them.

'Would you like to have a little walk on the beach now?' she asked, after the fourth go round on the carousel. 'The donkeys have gone, but maybe we can collect some shells.' Then noticing how tired Ottilie was looking, she decided simply to gather her up in her arms and carry her back to the car.

'You did very well today,' she murmured softly as she put her into her seat. 'I'm very proud of you, and so was Janet. Do you think you and Boots would like to go again on Wednesday?'

'Yes please,' Ottilie answered in her whispery little voice, and once again Alex was overcome by a sense of pride that could almost have been maternal.

'She can go,' Erica Wade stated, when they got back to the house and Alex had laid Ottilie down on the sofa, 'provided you take her.'

Reminding herself that there was no point in arguing the case with an agoraphobic, Alex said, 'It's not my responsibility to . . .'

'I know that, but she's used to you now.'

Used to me, Alex was thinking incredulously as she gazed down at Ottilie's sleeping face. She was still in her coat and trainers and Boots was snuggled up under her chin. How on earth could Erica Wade think Ottilie was used to her when they'd only spent three hours together? And yet Alex couldn't deny that the bond they already seemed to share had strengthened in that time, at least it had for her, and she felt sure it had for Ottilie too.

'I'd like to ask you again about Jill McCarthy,' she said, turning back to Erica. 'Who is she?'

Erica's face was ashen, but as it was always that way it wasn't telling Alex much.

'I'm sure you know, but I don't understand why you won't tell me,' Alex pressed.

'I thought you were here to see about Ottilie,' Erica retorted, avoiding her eyes.

'I am, but as her parent you're also my concern. Your husband knows who Jill McCarthy is, because he's the one who told me her name in the first place.'

'Then you should speak to him.'

'I shall, but I can't help wondering . . .'

'Please go now,' Erica interrupted. 'I have things to do and I'd like to get on with them.'

Unmoved, Alex said, 'In my assessment I recommended that you undergo certain tests . . .'

'For my mental health, yes I know. They won't be necessary.'

'Why do you say that?'

'Because they won't.'

'When I spoke to your old GP on Monday morning she told me that you'd suffered a nervous collapse after the death of your son . . .'

'I don't want to talk about that. I'm fine now. It's all in the past.'

'But your current GP tells me that you're still on medication.'

'For depression, and to help me sleep. I don't think that makes me very different to half the women in this country.'

'But you are different in the way you treat Ottilie.'

Erica turned abruptly away. 'I'll have her ready for you on Wednesday at eleven,' she said, starting from the room. 'Is there anything she needs to take with her? Food, a drink?'

'It's all provided,' Alex replied, following her into

the hall. 'Does your husband know that you didn't take her this morning?'

Opening the front door, Erica said, 'Thank you for coming. You can keep the seat in your car if you like, or return it to the garage, it's up to you.'

'Won't your husband need it if he takes her out?'

'He has one.' Sweat was breaking out on her sallow skin, and her bony hands were trembling.

Had there been more time Alex might have tried harder to keep her talking, but she was already late for her next appointment, and besides, Erica Wade appeared on the verge of physically pushing her out of the door.

'I don't know what to make of her really,' she said to Tommy at the end of the day. 'She definitely doesn't seem in any fit state to have charge of a child, at least not to me, but she's not alone in that, and convincing the courts will be a whole other story. Especially once Mr Wade starts weighing in with his exemplary credentials.'

'And we've got a lot more hoops to jump before we can take it to legal,' Tommy reminded her, 'but it's good that you're forming a relationship with the child. Once you get her talking it'll be interesting to hear what she has to say.'

'Mm, won't it just,' Alex agreed. Then, noticing the time, 'Oh God, I have to be somewhere by seven.'

Luckily he didn't ask where, because she definitely didn't want to tell him about the fifth-floor bedsit she was going to view, tucked away at the back of an old town house in the less than desirable area of Camberside.

'I thought you might like to know that I had a chat with Shane Prince today,' he said, escorting her to the door.

Surprised and impressed, she said, 'I didn't know it was possible to have a *chat* with him. And?'

'He's insistent that he hasn't been ringing you, but whether or not we believe him . . . I'm not sure what he would gain by it though, if it is him, are you?'

'Apart from intimidation? How are you getting on with the sister?'

'Well, I've seen her now, and what an enriching little experience that was. So full of grace and charm, just like her mother.'

Alex gave a splutter of laughter. 'So what's going to happen?'

'For the time being young Polly stays where she is, because they've agreed to seek treatment for the STD and to daily visits, which is going to be a boundless joy for us all. Apart from you, I'm afraid, because given the cheery little message we know he left for you, I think it's best you keep out of his way.'

'Oh dear, there I go missing out on all the fun again. Anyway, I'll look forward to the updates, and as soon as I've got hold of Brian Wade to get his take on what happened today I'll let you know.'

Ottilie was watching her father coming into the kitchen, but he failed to give her as much as a glance. 'Alex Lake was trying to get hold of me today,' he said to Erica. 'Why?'

Keeping her attention focused on the lamb stew that had arrived in tins and she'd poured into a cooking pot, Erica replied, 'Didn't you speak to her?'

'If I had I wouldn't be asking you what she wanted.'

'I expect it was to do with Ottilie.'

His face tightened with impatience. 'Did you take her to nursery?'

'No.'

Unsurprised, he said, 'You understand why she has to go?'

Replacing the pot's lid, Erica picked up a tea towel and folded it. 'Alex Lake took her,' she said, going to the sink.

His eyes hardened as he watched her. 'What are you up to?' he demanded roughly.

She didn't bother to answer.

Realising Ottilie was gazing up at him, he said, 'You shouldn't be listening to this. Go to your room.'

As Ottilie ran across the kitchen Erica said, 'You're scared, and so you should be.'

Grabbing her arm, he pulled her to him. 'You're the one who needs to be scared,' he growled.

Her eyes blazed into his.

'You think you were clever, breaking into my studio, don't you?' he snarled.

'Are you sure it was me?' she sneered.

He was, but the shock of finding the window smashed, of thinking, even for a moment, that someone had broken into his computers, was still keeping him awake at night. He now knew the meaning of true terror.

Shoving her away, he turned around and walked back out again.

She watched him go. He was probably off to inspect the new window of his shed. Studio, she corrected herself.

Chances were they'd seen the last of him until she sent Ottilie to bang on the door – time for dinner. He might even ask for his to be served on a tray, in the shed, which was where he belonged, like a dog.

317

Leaving the lamb stew to go on sticking to the pot, she took herself into the sitting room. A repeat series of *Fantasy Homes by the Sea* was due to start at six. She hated to miss any of the property programmes.

A few minutes into the episode Ottilie came into the room, clutching her bear in one hand and a half-eaten biscuit in the other. There were crumbs on her cheek and a strap of her dungarees was tumbling off one shoulder.

Erica's attention returned to the screen.

Sitting down on the floor, Ottilie took a while to remove her shoes. Then she climbed on to the sofa next to her mother, bringing the bear with her. Her legs were sticking out in front of her, not quite reaching the end of the seat. She sat very still as though she too was absorbed in the programme, then she shifted in closer to her mother so she was up against her all down one side.

Neither of them moved for several minutes, until Ottilie's sleepy head drooped against Erica's arm and Erica shot to her feet.

'What are you doing?' she demanded, her heart thudding an unnatural beat. 'I've told you before . . .' She caught the words back, stuffed them deep down inside her, locked them away.

Ottilie buried her face in the seat of the sofa.

Realising she was crying, Erica walked out of the room and into the kitchen, almost colliding with Brian as he came in the back door.

'What's the matter?' he demanded, as Erica switched on the radio.

Ignoring him, she went to start dishing up the stew.

Going into the sitting room and finding Ottilie sobbing on the sofa he scooped her up and held her in his arms. 'It's all right,' he told her softly. 'I'm sorry I shouted just now. Everything's going to be all right.'

Her arms and legs hung limply against him as her head fell on to his shoulder.

'That's a good girl,' he whispered gently. 'Now you're going to come out to the studio with me and tell me all about your time at nursery today. Would you like that?'

Ottilie shook her head.

'Yes you would,' and setting her on the floor he took her by the hand.

'No,' Ottilie whimpered, trying to pull back.

'Don't be silly now,' he said crossly.

Wrenching her hand free she ran to pick up Boots.

'OK, you can bring him,' her father sighed. 'He's very good at keeping secrets, and you know how important it is that you do too. If you don't I'll have to take him away and you wouldn't want that, would you?'

Ottilie's eyes filled with tears as she shook her head.

'Of course you wouldn't, which is why you're going to keep our secret and never tell anyone about the games we play, aren't you?'

She nodded.

'Don't cry now, Ottilie. I said *don't cry*!'

Ottilie was trying hard to do as she was told, but the sobbing in her chest wouldn't go away.

Getting down on his knees he gripped her shoulders in his hands. 'Guess what I brought home today?' he whispered, his face very close to hers. 'Some film of the boys and girls who play in my schoolyard. Would you like to come and watch it with me?'

Though Ottilie looked frightened, she nodded her head again.

Sighing pleasurably, he said, 'Oh, Ottilie, you're such a good girl that I think you might deserve your very first ride on the tiger tonight.'

Her head was jerking as the sobs began choking her. 'No,' she begged in her feathery little voice.

'Oh, now I know you don't mean that, because you love the tiger really and he loves you very much indeed. So come on, let's go and cheer him up, shall we, because he's been a bit lonely today.'

As he took her hand and led her from the room her head was bowed and fat tears were soaking into the top of Boots's head.

Erica didn't look round as they passed her in the kitchen. She was gazing out at the night as though her mind was floating far off into the darkness.

'Isn't it time you took your pills?' he snapped.

'I just have,' she replied.

He smiled at Ottilie. 'You see, Mummy's a good girl too, sometimes.'

Reaching for the bowls of stew she'd served up, Erica tipped them back into the pot and replaced the lid.

'When is Alex Lake coming again?' he asked, seeing her shiver as he opened the back door and a cold wind blew in.

She looked down at Ottilie, but her eyes weren't focused. 'I've no idea,' she replied, and turning away she went back to the sitting room.

Chapter Fifteen

Alex was working from home today, making calls and writing up her notes from the day before. It was as she went back over the time she'd spent with Ottilie at the Pumpkin and afterwards that she realised how calming she'd found it, or distracting anyway. She'd been so wound up before going there, mainly thanks to the awful scene with the Leaches, but with everything else going on in her life too, that those few unscheduled hours were feeling a bit like an oasis now – or perhaps more like the eye of a storm.

There was no doubt it was all going to start whipping up again later when she went into the office, because on her way out last night she'd spotted a snippy little note from Wendy on the board for all to see, saying she'd like to see Alex Lake 'as soon as Ms Lake can find the time'.

Though Wendy might be the least of her problems right now, she could still feel a band tightening around her head merely to think of her. So abruptly banishing her from her mind she clicked through to her inbox to check for any urgent emails. There turned out to be none from Jason, which hurt far more than she wanted to deal with, and none that couldn't wait. However, before clicking off again she took a moment to read a message from a fellow social worker over at the South Kesterly hub. She was writing to let everyone know that one of their colleagues, Penny Gunter, had been signed off by the doctor for the next three months due to stress. Not at all surprised by this, since everyone knew how hard Penny had been struggling with the horrific injuries inflicted on one of her charges by his stepmother and grandfather, Alex immediately set about sending Penny a message of moral support.

By the time she'd finished her head was spinning, and her stomach was rumbling so noisily that her hunger could no longer be ignored. However, she only had to look at food at the moment for her mouth to turn dry and her appetite to go running for cover. She wasn't sleeping particularly well either; last night she'd been unable to get the awful bedsit she'd viewed out of her mind. She had no idea when it might last have been properly cleaned or decorated, and as for imagining herself living there . . . With its one grimy window looking out on to the backs of other desolate houses, it had been so soulless and gloomy that she'd probably end up topping herself if she had to move in. It wasn't that she minded downsizing, in many ways she'd be happy to, but please God not to somewhere like that.

And if the prospect of becoming homeless, or at best thoroughly depressed, hadn't been enough to make sleep elusive, then worrying about Ottilie had been more than ready to step into the breach. Had those peculiar parents of hers bothered to ask how she'd got on at school? She couldn't imagine her father wouldn't. Surely, being who he was, it would be the first thing he'd ask when coming in the door.

Had Ottilie told them about Chloe and riding on the carousel? Had she spoken to them at all? Was she looking forward to going to the Pumpkin again tomorrow? She, Alex, would pick her up at eleven, as arranged, and she was even now trying to organise the day so she could spend some time with her after nursery before taking her home again. She probably could manage to squeeze in another ride on the carousel, or maybe a little jog along the beach on a donkey if the sorry-looking beasts were still there. Or maybe she could take her to Stanson's, the kids' emporium, and watch which toys she was drawn to. It might tell her something important about her.

Jumping as the phone rang she quickly snatched it up, hoping it might be Tommy – or Jason – but it turned out to be a wrong number, so she put the receiver down again and tried not to feel oppressed by the silence closing in around her. The house seemed so empty, so forlorn even, or perhaps it was her mood making it seem that way.

Dropping her head in her hands, she waited a moment for the wave of longing to pass. She missed Jason so much, and fearing the loss of her home and Millie, not to mention her job, she kept finding her thoughts being pulled towards the family she'd been born into. She knew it was pointless trying to imagine how different her life might have been if she'd been able to stay with them, but sometimes it was hard to make herself stop.

Her mother and father might not have wanted her, but what about her grandparents, and her brother?

She'd had a brother.

A brother. How wonderful was that?

As she thought of the brother Ottilie had never known she tried warning herself that she was becoming far too involved with the child, but how could she possibly draw back? It was as though dear little Ottilie had curled up around her heart, like a kitten making itself perfectly at home.

Suddenly she was sobbing. She hated self-pity more than anything, but she was feeling so desolate and miserable today that thinking of Ottilie was breaking her apart inside. If Ottilie was as lonely and confused as she feared, then she, Alex, absolutely had to do something to help her. She was already trying, and she wasn't going to give up until she was sure Ottilie was safe and receiving all the love she deserved. But what if that meant taking her away from her parents and putting her into care? Would she get that love from a foster family, or would she, God forbid, become another victim of the system that so often turned innocent young children into deeply troubled and even violent individuals?

Whenever she asked herself those questions, she couldn't help wondering what her job was really about. It was the cruellest of all ironies that protecting children could sometimes mean putting them into another kind of danger altogether. If she were able she'd become a foster carer herself, she might even consider adopting, but without a supportive, and permanent partner she wouldn't even be considered, because she had to work in order to live. If only Jason had stayed . . .

She really had to stop this. She needed to pull herself together now and forget all about how things might have been, or what she would do if only . . . The property developer had apparently loved the house and was bringing his wife for a viewing the day after tomorrow. This didn't mean she had to move out this week, or even next. These things often took months to go through, so there was plenty of time to find herself somewhere that didn't feel as though it was going to crush her very soul every time she walked in the door.

Reaching for her mobile as it started to ring, she was so eager to speak to someone that she didn't even bother to check who it was before clicking on.

'Hi, is that Alex Lake?' a voice rather like Tommy's asked.

Realising who it must be, her heart gave a peculiar sort of lurch. 'Scott?' she said.

'Yep, it's me, your friendly PC from up north. I hope I haven't caught you at a bad time.'

'No, not at all,' she assured him. 'What can I do for you?'

'Well, this could be more a case of what I've done for you. After we spoke the other day I decided to have a bit more of a dig around about this Jill McCarthy character, and I've come up with something that's got me pretty baffled, I must admit.'

Curious to know more, Alex said, 'Go on.'

'Well, whether this is mere coincidence or not I can't tell you, but it turns out that Erica Wade's maiden name was McCarthy and her mother was called Jill.'

Startled, Alex said, 'So are you saying Brian Wade's mother-in-law was making the calls accusing him of killing his son?'

'You might think so from that,' he replied, 'but Jill McCarthy – at least this Jill McCarthy – died over ten years ago, so she couldn't have made the calls.'

Alex was trying to assimilate, but coming up as baffled as Scott Danes clearly was.

'If it is a coincidence,' he went on, 'then I'll be in goal for Man U next match, but how else to explain it . . .'

'Could you find anything to say Erica Wade's mother was mentally disturbed?'

'Not yet, but I can always go on looking. I just thought I should give you a heads-up on what I've found so far.'

'Thank you,' Alex said, her mind already racing ahead. 'I really appreciate this, and anything else you find, no matter what it is, please give me a call, any time day or night.'

Brian Wade's tone was long-suffering, bordering on the irritable, as he said, 'Well, of course it's a co-incidence, Ms Lake. What else could it be when my mother-in-law died even before my wife and I were married?'

Wishing she'd done this face to face so she could at least see his eyes as he lied, Alex said, 'I'm interested to know why you never mentioned it when we first spoke about Jill McCarthy. Surely the fact that she has the same name as your wife's mother must have struck you as, well, curious at the very least.'

'Indeed it did when I first heard it, but please remember that it was almost three years ago that the wretched woman began making the calls, so any curiosity I might have had back then has long since faded.'

'Did you report any of the calls to the police?' She knew he hadn't, or Scott Danes would have a record of it, so she was keen to hear his reply.

'Not formally,' he responded, 'but I did mention it to an officer I knew at the time. He shared my opinion that unless the woman made any physical threats it was best to ignore her and hope she went away.'

'Did you discuss any of it with your wife?'

'As a matter of fact I didn't. She was already suffering deeply enough over the loss of our son, so I certainly wasn't going to make matters worse by telling her about a deranged woman's telephone calls, especially when the woman was either using, or had, the same name as her mother.'

'Using, as in she could have been someone who actually knew you?'

'I don't think there's much doubt that she knew something *about* me, but she's certainly not someone I knew.'

Alex remained silent for a moment.

'Are you still there?' he asked.

'I'm just wondering,' she said, 'how, if you didn't know her, that you knew she was "deranged?"'

There was an awkward moment during which she got the sense of a trap shutting – then opening again as he said, 'I believe I mentioned during our early conversations that this woman had contacted other people at the school, before setting her sights on me. Someone must have told me what they knew about her, and, given her behaviour, I had no reason to doubt them.'

'I see,' Alex said thoughtfully. 'So can you give me any suggestions as to why there's no record in that area of a Jill McCarthy with severe mental problems?'

Another awkward moment before he said, 'I don't actually recall ever having said she was local. In fact, I have no idea where she was calling from, either then or more recently.'

It was true, he hadn't ever said that, she'd just assumed the woman was from somewhere in Northumbria, and now she was left with the thrilling prospect of a nationwide search for a nutjob she wasn't entirely sure existed. Except she'd taken one of the anonymous calls herself, and Ben had recorded two, so someone was making them, just not Mr Wade's mother-in-law.

Having no choice but to thank him for his time, she rang off and sat staring at her computer screen as she tried to assemble her thoughts. She was at the office now and would have gone to talk it all over with Tommy had he been there, but according to the board he was on one of the new daily visits to the Princes.

Lucky him.

'Alex, there you are. Didn't you get my message?'

Flinching at Wendy's schoolmarmish tone, Alex forced her head up.

'I'd like to have a word with you please,' Wendy snapped.

Pushing back from her desk, Alex got to her feet.

'Here, take this,' Tamsin called out, throwing a child's skipping rope her way. 'Give her enough of it and you'll be doing us all a favour.'

Stifling a laugh, Alex followed Wendy into her office and would have left the door open had Wendy not told her to close it.

'Please sit down,' Wendy invited, waving Alex to the visitor's chair in front of the desk.

Making sure not to roll her eyes – a reflex action where Wendy was concerned – Alex did as she was told and clasped her hands meekly in her lap. Wendy

328

liked meekness almost as much as she liked power.

'I have to begin by saying,' Wendy sighed, 'that I'm very sorry to be having this conversation with you, but your attitude lately, Alex, has been raising more than a few eyebrows around the department, as well as causing some personal offence.'

Feeling that very attitude boiling up ready for a fight, Alex said, as smoothly as possible, 'Do you mean offence to you, or to Ben? Just so we've got it clear.'

Wendy's jaw tightened. 'Actually to both of us, and we're not the only ones who are feeling it. You don't run this place, Alex, though I realise you like to think you do, so perhaps now would be a good time to remind you that you're not indispensable either.'

Alex felt the warning like a burn. Surely to God Wendy wasn't about to sack her? For what, exactly? She hadn't done anything wrong, apart from get right up Wendy's back just about every time their paths crossed, which actually wasn't always unintentional.

'I know you find all the paperwork irritating,' Wendy bleated on, 'you probably even consider it a waste of your precious time, but it's as important a part of what we do here as anything else.'

'Have I ever not done it?' Alex challenged, and immediately wished she'd used a less hostile tone. Even if Wendy wasn't going to fire her today, having been so crudely reminded of redundancies amassing like marauders on the horizon, now would not be a good time to alienate her any further.

'On the whole you do,' Wendy conceded, 'but only when it suits you and not always in the time frame allotted. I know you're going to say that's because you're out there dealing with the really important stuff, like protecting children, but it's that sort of response that has earned you a reputation amongst your colleagues for considering yourself a cut above everyone else.'

Alex blinked. She definitely hadn't seen that one coming, but nor had she ever felt it.

Wendy glanced at the time. 'I think I've made myself clear . . .'

'I'm sorry,' Alex interrupted, 'but what you just said, about the way everyone thinks of me, is that true?'

Wendy seemed surprised to be asked. 'Obviously I'm not saying it counts for everyone,' she replied. 'I know you have some good friends out there, but some of your colleagues . . . Well, I don't think it will do you any harm to realise, if you don't know it already, that you have a habit of creating resentment amongst your peers. I dare say it's not intentional, but together with your imperious atti- tude . . . Well, you can't deny that you're an extremely fortunate young lady in almost every way. You've had a very privileged upbringing compared to most – and life isn't much of a struggle for you now either, is it, not when you think of how hard some of your colleagues have to work to keep on top of their jobs, their families and to make ends meet.'

She was smiling so pleasantly that Alex was in no doubt she was enjoying this, and even believed it.

'I'm sure most of them would love to live in a large house in a beautiful village with no mortgage weighing them down,' Wendy continued. 'And your car is a lot newer than most, isn't it, and is presumably all bought and paid for.'

'Actually, it's seven years old and was only paid off at the end of last year,' Alex informed her – as if it was of the slightest importance.

'Well, that's as maybe. What the others see when they look at you is the daughter of a man who was widely respected in this area, so most people are drawn to you just for that. I'm talking about your adoptive father, of course, the rector.'

Alex was speechless. She couldn't get her head round which parts of that were insulting, and which were just plain mean. Not that the picture Wendy had painted was inaccurate, because obviously it wasn't, but clearly she was only seeing it from her own myopic viewpoint. 'Well,' she finally managed, 'I can only apologise if I'm causing offence to anyone by being myself. I certainly don't mean to, but from now on I'll do my best to be less fortunate,' and tugging open the door she stormed out of the room.

As Alex turned into the Wades' drive on Wednesday morning she immediately had to reverse out again to allow a Sainsbury's delivery van to leave. As the driver waved a thank you and Alex smiled, she realised this could very well have been the woman who'd raised the alarm about Ottilie. Certainly the anonymous caller's voice had sounded local, and as far as Alex was aware the only visits the Wades ever seemed to have were when they received a delivery. It was possible that Brian Wade took Ottilie shopping for her clothes and toys, but it seemed much more likely that most of their purchases were made via the Internet, and though she'd never seen a computer in the house, that didn't mean there wasn't one somewhere.

As she pulled up in front of the garage she turned off the blathering on the radio about yet more cuts, and hauling her bag from the back seat she started for the house. She'd arrived early deliberately, in the hope of having a word with Erica Wade before taking Ottilie to nursery. How successful her efforts were going to prove, given how resistant the woman was to any normal kind of communication, never mind questioning, she guessed she was about to find out. First, though, she was going to say hello to Ottilie, who was already making her heart light up with the way she was standing in the open doorway, apparently waiting for her, in her cute pink anorak with fur-trimmed hood and trainers on the wrong feet.

'Look at you,' she said softly, going down to her. 'Are you all ready to go?'

Ottilie nodded and held up Boots, presumably to show that he was too.

Laughing at her shy pleasure, Alex said, 'So are you looking forward to nursery today?'

Again Ottilie nodded, and Alex felt so thrilled by the two tiny gestures of a response that she couldn't hold on to a single shred of the bad feelings Wendy had aroused in her.

'I'll just have a quick chat with Mummy before we leave, is that OK?'

Ottilie didn't answer, only turned to watch her walk into the hall.

'Where is she? In the kitchen?' Alex asked, guessing she'd be unpacking the groceries that had just been delivered.

Going on through, she reached the door in time

332

to see Erica Wade pushing a handful of pills into her mouth and washing them down with a large glass of what was presumably water. Guessing they were the antidepressants Dr Aiden the family GP had admitted to prescribing, Trazodone, he'd said, she could only wonder at what appeared such a huge dosage, or maybe Erica was taking something else besides.

'Mrs Wade?' she said.

Erica spun round. Her eyes were unnaturally bright and her cheeks stained with a colour Alex had never seen in them before.

'Can I have a word?' Alex asked.

'Ottilie's ready . . .'

'I know, but . . .'

'I'm not taking her, I can't. You do it.'

'I'm going to, but we'll have to address the reasons why you can't . . .'

'Not now. I'm too busy. It'll have to wait.'

'For the moment maybe, but I hope you understand that you really will have to go for a mental health assessment, because if you aren't capable of taking care of Ottilie . . .'

'Does she look uncared for? She's fed, clothed, has plenty of toys, a roof over her head. I don't suppose most of the children you come across have anything like as much as she does.'

'Maybe not in a material sense, but a lot of them have love and . . .'

'Oh don't worry, she's not deprived of that.' The bitterness was so scathing that Alex almost felt it cut through her.

'What do you mean?' she asked quietly.

Erica tossed her head. 'What I said. Now, if you don't mind . . .'

'Actually, I do mind. I need to ask you about something else.'

Erica sucked in a sharp breath and hung her head.

'Are you OK?' Alex asked.

'I will be when I'm left alone.'

Alex was no longer sure about continuing. If there was something wrong with her physically, maybe she needed help . . .

'What is it?' Erica snapped. 'Just come out with it, please, then we can both get on with our day.'

Deciding simply to go for it, Alex braced herself as she said, 'I'd like to ask you about your mother.'

Erica stiffened and drew back. 'What about her?' she demanded.

Before Alex could answer Erica was saying, 'She's dead. She died ten years ago. Why are you asking about her now?'

Sensing the need to tread carefully, Alex said, 'Are you aware of the anonymous calls your husband received while you were still in Northumbria? Calls accusing him of killing your son?'

Erica flinched and started to turn away.

'Did you make those calls, Mrs Wade?' Alex asked quickly. Her heart was thudding, her palms prickling. It was a long shot, but so far it was the only logical explanation she'd been able to come up with – if it could even be termed that way, and she didn't really think it could.

'I don't know what you're talking about,' Erica muttered. Her back was fully turned now, her thin hands gripping the edge of the sink.

'I think you do,' Alex insisted. 'I just don't understand why you'd have made them, when according to everything I've read your husband was at work when it happened.'

'I said I don't know what you're talking about,' Erica seethed. 'Now please, take Ottilie and go.'

Accepting that she might have gone far enough for the time being, Alex said, 'We'll be back around two. Maybe you'll feel more up to having a chat then.'

When Erica didn't answer or turn around she decided not to press any further, and returned to where Ottilie was still standing by the front door.

'Tell you what,' Alex said cheerily, 'shall we swap your lovely trainers around or your feet might start going off in opposite directions, and we don't want that, do we, or you might end up splitting in two.'

Ottilie's eyes rounded, and as Alex sat her on the bottom stair to right her shoes she seemed transfixed by every move Alex made.

'There, I expect that feels better, doesn't it?' Alex encouraged her, when it was all done. 'Shall we go now?'

Getting to her feet, Ottilie reached for her hand.

Oh God, she really does want to go. Alex could hardly believe how good that made her feel, and loving the tiny, trusting fingers tucked into hers she led the way out to the garage to collect the car seat. Moments later Ottilie and Boots were buckled safely into the back of her Punto.

'Are you looking forward to seeing Chloe?' Alex asked, glancing at her in the rear-view mirror as she pulled out into the traffic. 'And Janet, and the others? I know they're looking forward to seeing you.'

Ottilie was gazing out of the window, her solemn eyes seeming to take in everything they were passing.

'Did you tell Mummy and Daddy about Chloe?' Alex went on, making it sound chatty rather than inquisitive.

Ottilie didn't reply.

'She was very kind to you, wasn't she? I think she'd really like to be your friend. Would you like that?'

Though Ottilie's eyes didn't move she gave a tiny nod of her head.

'That's lovely,' Alex smiled. 'She'll be very pleased, you wait and see. Can you say Chloe?'

Ottilie pressed Boots up against the window, apparently letting him have a look out too.

'What about Boots, do you think he can say Chloe?'

Ottilie nodded.

'But only you can hear him?'

Again she nodded.

'Perhaps you can say it for him.'

'Chloe,' Ottilie said in such a fragile whisper that Alex barely heard it.

'That's fantastic,' Alex told her warmly. 'He's a very clever bear being able to say that, isn't he?'

Ottilie planted a kiss on Boots's face and Alex thought she was going to burst with affection.

Fifteen minutes later they were at the Pumpkin and darling, wonderful little Chloe was at Ottilie's side, trying to find out what Ottilie would like to do.

'We've got lots of things here,' Chloe was telling her earnestly, her hands planted on her knees like an adult as she gazed into Ottilie's face. 'Puzzles and plasticine and playdough and crayons. You can have a go on any of it, can't she, Janet?'

'Of course she can,' Janet agreed.

Ottilie's eyes went up to Janet, then still holding on to Alex's hand she moved in a little closer to her.

'Ottilie's very good at puzzles,' Alex said, realising

at this early stage it might be wise, if only to get things moving, to take a decision for her. 'Shall we go and find one?'

'I'll get it,' Chloe offered.

'I know, why don't you go with Chloe and choose one?' Alex suggested to Ottilie.

'I'll hold your hand,' Chloe told her, seeming to realise that Ottilie might feel a bit vulnerable toddling over there without holding on to someone, and to Alex's delight, though Ottilie's grip visibly tightened on Boots, she slipped her hand from Alex's and put it into Chloe's.

As the two of them wound their way amongst the others, one so dark, the other so angelically blonde, Alex felt herself smiling like a fool.

'Who is Chloe?' she asked Janet. 'She's adorable.'

'Isn't she?' Janet agreed. 'She's the youngest of four – two boys, two girls – which is probably why she's so confident. The kindness she definitely gets from her mother.'

Though naturally glad for Chloe that she had a wonderful mother, it suddenly made Alex feel even more protective towards Ottilie. Not that Erica Wade was incapable of being a wonderful mother, or Alex assumed she wasn't, but so far she was showing precious few signs of it.

'Do you mind if I use your office to make a few calls?' she asked.

'No, go right ahead,' Janet replied, waving her on. 'Unless you fancy some nappy-changing? Someone needs it, can't you tell? Time to find out who.'

Laughing, Alex started for the door. Then hearing footsteps running up behind her she turned to find

Ottilie coming worriedly after her. 'Hey, it's all right,' she said, stooping to her height. 'I'm just going to use the phone, I'll be back in a few minutes.'

Ottilie reached for her hand and clung on to it tightly.

'OK,' Alex said, lifting her up, 'I'll stay here with you while Chloe sets out the jigsaw, shall I? Then I'll go and use the phone, just like I did last time – and I came back then, didn't I? So you don't have to worry. I'm not going to leave you.'

Chloe had joined them by now and was looking up at them with a jigsaw box in both hands. 'You can go first if you like,' she said to Ottilie. 'We can do a piece each. That's how I do it with my sister.'

'Come on, there's a free table over there,' Alex said, carrying Ottilie to it. 'And by the time you've finished the puzzle I'll be back to see how well you've done.'

Fortunately, Ottilie didn't object, so Alex set her down, and stood watching as Chloe spread out the colourful pieces of an animal picture. 'That's a lion,' Chloe said, using the lid of the box to demonstrate. 'And that's an elephant, and that's a giraffe.'

'Well done,' Alex said, clapping. 'Can you name some of the animals too, Ottilie?'

Ottilie's arms tightened round Boots.

'OK, so why don't you show me the snake?' Alex suggested, going down to their level.

Seeming more comfortable now, Ottilie leaned forward and prodded her finger on the merry-faced cobra.

'Very good,' Alex cried, clapping again. 'And now the bear.'

Ottilie didn't even hesitate as she plonked her hand down on the grizzly.

'He's a bit like Boots, isn't he?' Alex laughed.

Ottilie's eyes were shining.

'And now what about the tiger?' Alex challenged.

To her amazement Ottilie drew back, shaking her head.

'What's the matter? Don't you like tigers?' Alex asked curiously.

Ottilie hid her face.

'I do,' Chloe told her. 'They're one of my favourites.'

Ottilie peeped up at her, then hid her face again.

Chloe seemed at a loss. 'I know, shall we choose another puzzle?' she suggested.

Alex wasn't sure what to say, but since the question was for Ottilie she waited to see what happened. To her surprise Ottilie shook her head and pointed to the one on the table.

'Don't worry, I'll do the bit with the tiger,' Chloe decided, and putting the lid down she pulled up a chair ready to start the puzzle. 'All right, which piece do you want to choose first?' she asked Ottilie.

Ottilie glanced up at Alex, then after a moment she sat forward and selected a corner piece covered in grass.

'That's really good,' Chloe told her. 'My dad says you should always start with the corners, that way it's easier.'

Ottilie looked at her, seeming slightly mystified, but after Chloe made her selection Ottilie went happily ahead with hers, and so it went on for another few pieces, until Alex said to Ottilie, 'Are you OK, sweetheart? Do you mind if I go and make some calls now?'

Ottilie was engrossed in the puzzle.

'I'll keep an eye on them,' Janet, who had seen Ottilie's reaction to the tiger, said quietly.

'I don't know what that was about,' Alex commented 'but she seems all right now.'

'Mm, strange,' Janet agreed, 'and she's just picked up the tiger's head so now I'm really confused, but I'm sure she'll be fine, so go do what you have to.'

Alex's first call was to Maggie Fenn to check on Sophie, and because Maggie was so chatty and full of news they were on the line for at least twenty minutes before Alex could ring the office. After leaving a long message on Tommy's voicemail and picking up her own messages, almost half an hour had passed by the time she went back into the playroom. Ottilie was so intent on building a Lego house with Chloe now that she almost seemed not to notice her coming back. So, taking heart, Alex slipped out quietly, and went to make a call over on Leonard's Way where she learned that young Gemma Knight was, mercifully, settling in well with her carers.

'She still cries for her mother, naturally,' Frances Simms the foster-mother admitted, 'but we have nice long chats about her, which I think she likes. Poor little thing.'

'Are you still involved with Winston's Wish?' Alex wanted to know.

'Oh yes, and they're being marvellous. I'm not sure we'd have coped anywhere near as well as we have without them.'

Knowing what a godsend the charity was for bereaved children, Alex wrote a note for Gemma to say that she'd called round and to assure her that she'd be back again soon to spend some time with her, then thanking Frances for her time she quickly drove back to the nursery.

To her relief Ottilie was sitting with Chloe apparently absorbed in the story Janet was reading, but as soon as she spotted Alex coming into the room she toddled over to climb up on a chair beside her.

'Tired?' Alex asked with a smile.

Ottilie's only answer was to settle herself more comfortably on the chair.

'Can I sit with you too?' Chloe asked.

'Of course,' Alex replied.

A few minutes later Alex noticed that the two little girls were holding hands, and if she'd ever witnessed a simpler, yet more touching scene she couldn't remember what it was.

'I honestly don't know what's going on with the parents,' Alex was saying to Tommy later on the phone. She was at home now, having had to dash back to change after getting caught in a violent downpour. 'They're playing out something between them, but God knows what it is. I take it you got my message about Erica Wade using her mother's name to make anonymous calls?'

'I did, but you don't know for certain that's the case yet?'

'No, but having seen the way she reacted I'm definitely not ready to throw it out.'

'Did you manage to speak to her again when you dropped Ottilie home?'

'No, not really, because after nursery I took Ottilie for a walk along the pier and wouldn't you just know it, the heavens opened up when we were on our way back to the car, so we got soaked to the skin. This meant that as soon as I got her home she needed to go straight in the bath. And that's something else. Her mother only asked me to do it. It's like she doesn't want to do anything for the child that calls for some kind of intimacy.'

'Mm, definitely not good. So did you bath her?'

'No, but Ottilie was trying to drag me up the stairs as if I'd already said I would, and when I told her I couldn't she started to cry. I felt terrible, awful, but I was drenched myself, so I needed to get home. Besides, it's not my place to bath her.'

'It certainly isn't. So what's happening next?'

With a sigh, Alex said, 'I'm taking her to nursery again on Friday. If I don't she'll end up not going and we don't want that, especially when she seems to be settling in already. It's funny, but you'd expect a child who's been deprived of normal contact and affection to be much more withdrawn – though I guess the non-speaking qualifies as that. But she's not completely switched off, far from it in fact. She understands everything you're saying, and she seems fascinated by what's going on around her.'

'When's she due to see the psychologist?'

'I'm waiting for Vicky Barnes, the health visitor, to get back to me about that, but soon I hope. And the mother definitely has to see a shrink, so I need to talk to Mr Wade about that again, because I think he's the only one who can persuade her. I'd also like Ottilie to see the community paediatrician at some point. I know her GP's given her a clean bill of health and Vicky didn't find anything to worry about, but I'd feel easier in my mind if she had a thorough exam.'

'OK, I'll trust your instincts on that, but you know Wendy's going to start asking questions about how much time you're putting into this case.'

Feeling herself tensing with resentment, Alex said, 'Can you help me out with that? I just need to get through these first few weeks, find out what's really going on there, and the closer I get to the family the easier it's going to be.'

'And if you end up having to take her out of there?'

Alex felt a catch in her heart. 'I'll deal with it when, if the time comes, but better that than leave her with parents who are damaging her.'

'Mentally if not physically?'

'Exactly. It could be that they're just cold people unable to show normal levels of affection. Or maybe they're afraid of allowing her too close in case they lose her, the way they did their son. The trouble is, I can't shake the feeling that there's more to it, and if there is I have to find out what.'

'Of course, and you know you always have my support. I'm just pointing out that you're not Wendy's favourite person at the moment, so best not to give her any more ammunition to use against you.'

'Only she would see helping a child as ammunition,' Alex retorted tightly. She was tempted to ask Tommy if he knew that some of her colleagues were saying negative things about her, but hurtful though it was, it seemed too petty to get into. So after assuring him she'd keep him up to speed with everything that was happening with the Wades, she rang off and went to turn on the shower. She needed to get herself warm and dry before zooming back into town to make her last calls of the day.

Twenty minutes later, as she was rushing out of the door, she almost bumped into Elaine, the estate agent.

'Oh gosh, sorry,' Alex gasped, stepping back from Elaine's expensively shod toe.

'That's fine,' Elaine assured her, trying not to wince. She was as immaculately turned out as ever, with her platinum-blonde hair cut in a razor-sharp bob and the black kohl round her eyes, artfully flicked up at the corners, making her look faintly exotic. 'I saw your car, and was just about to knock. Do you mind if I go in and take some measurements for Mr Quigley? He called just now and he's quite keen to know the square footage of the kitchen and dining room. I think he's planning to knock them into one.'

Wishing she could close the door and tell everyone to keep out, Alex said, 'Of course, go ahead, but I thought he was coming with his wife, tomorrow.'

'He is, but for some reason he wants this information now. I don't think it's going to turn into any kind of deal-breaker, he's probably just trying to get a rough idea of how much the renovation's likely to cost in order to work out his offer.'

Hearing the phone ringing inside, Alex said, 'Come in, I'll just go and get that.'

As she turned back Elaine suddenly dropped her clipboard, spilling paperwork all over the front step.

'Don't worry, go and get the phone,' she insisted as Alex started to help her.

'Are you sure?'

'Of course, go on.'

Running to the kitchen Alex could already hear the machine kicking in as she grabbed the receiver, and by the time she said hello whoever it was had already rung off. Quickly dialling 1471, she waited for the number to be announced, and after writing it down she sighed irritably as she hung up,

'It's not local,' she stated as Elaine came in. Why on earth had she thought it might be Jason when he'd never call her at home in the middle of the day? Maybe because she kept hoping that every call was from him. 'I'll bet it was some flaming telemarketer,' she growled in frustration.

'They're such a nuisance,' Elaine agreed, peering down at the number. Then, 'Oh gosh, I forgot I gave Mr Quigley this number so he could call while I was here. I can't get a reception on my mobile once I'm past the church. I definitely have to change my server.'

Feeling like a small bird being turfed from its nest by magpies and cuckoos, Alex said, 'I'll leave you to it then,' and scooping up her keys she ran out to her car.

The disappointment that it hadn't been Jason on the phone was crushing her. *He's not coming back, so stop trying to convince yourself he will,* she seethed angrily at herself as she pulled away. *Just focus on what you're meant to be doing and put him out of your mind.*

It wasn't easy though, because it never was, and having just left Elaine measuring up the house for Mr Quigley was making her think sadly how much more bearable all this would have been if she and Jason were trying to find somewhere else together. But they weren't, so she had to stop that too and remember where she was going, because the last thing she needed was Wendy on her case accusing her of neglecting her other families in favour of Ottilie Wade. She felt sure this wasn't so, but at the same time she couldn't help wishing that she was able to drop in on Ottilie now just to check that she'd had her bath safely and was all tucked up in bed having an afternoon nap.

* * *

After Alex had left the house on North Hill, Erica Wade had closed the front door and gone upstairs to find Ottilie standing in the bathroom hunched over her bear. 'Get those wet clothes off,' she barked, turning on the taps and pulling a warm towel from the rail.

Obediently Ottilie put Boots down and started to undress.

'Are you still crying?' Erica asked sharply.

Ottilie shook her head, but she was.

'You like her, don't you?'

Ottilie didn't answer.

'I told you she was the good fairy. Don't listen to what your father says. He doesn't know.'

Ottilie sniffed and tried not to sob.

Erica gripped her shoulders and wrenched her upright. 'She's going to take care of you,' she told her fiercely. 'Do you understand that? She'll make it stop.'

More tears fell on to Ottilie's cheeks.

Erica pushed her away and dipped a hand in the water. After running in more cold she dumped Ottilie into it and left her to bath herself.

In her bedroom she opened up her laptop and typed in the date followed by: *Alex Lake has guessed I made the calls accusing him of killing our son. I know he didn't, but I wanted to make him suffer. I was foolish to use my mother's name – may she rot in hell.*

She reached for her pills, swallowed them and carried on typing. *I don't know who made the most recent calls, maybe it was me. I have no memory of it. The voices are so loud these days I can't hear anything else. I have to do as they say or they'll never stop. I hate myself . . .*

Suddenly hitting the save button, she switched

off and went to find Ottilie trying to climb out of the bath and in danger of slipping. Grabbing her arm, Erica hauled her up and dumped her on the floor.

'Dry yourself and go to bed,' she snapped, turning to hike out the plug. 'You can put the TV on, but quietly, I don't want it waking me up.' As she started to straighten up a wave of dizziness caught her. She clutched the edge of the bath and tried to make herself breathe. In, out, in out. The floor began buckling under her, the walls undulating, towering, closing in like tidal waves. She sank to her knees, sweating and panting. The ceiling was falling; chunks were landing on her head. Someone was screaming. Ottilie was watching her . . .

Suddenly she grabbed Ottilie's hair with both hands and began shaking her. She forced her to the ground and banged her head up and down on the tiles. Up and down, up and down. She was gagging and gasping. The voices in her head were screaming.

Kill her, kill her.

Ottilie was screaming.

Erica choked, and clutched her hands to her gut. 'Get out,' she spluttered. '*Get out of here.*'

Ottilie clambered to her feet, grabbed Boots and ran. Reaching her room she shut the door behind her, her damp, naked little body quivering with terror.

Chapter Sixteen

Over the following week Alex's feet barely touched the ground as she dashed from one visit to the next, and tried to squeeze in as many meetings as possible, while making sure she was always on time to take Ottilie to the Pumpkin. Though she loved all her charges, there was no doubt that the hours she spent with Ottilie were fast becoming the highlight of her day, providing so many moments to be treasured that when she finally got home at night exhausted, even drained, she didn't even want to imagine how lonely she might have felt without them.

As it was, she was waking most mornings with such an awful sense of dread of her life falling apart that if it weren't for the children she cared for, she knew that a fear of the future would be blighting her entire day. Luckily no one seemed to notice her flagging spirits, apart from Tommy who always saw too much, but in spite of knowing she could trust him she didn't want to discuss her situation. It would only make her feel worse, she was sure of it, so better to press on and do her best not to think about missing Jason, or the offer Gabby was about to accept on the house, or the growing horror of becoming homeless, and possibly jobless, or the dread of Millie going. That horrible wrench was due to happen this weekend, and already simply to think of it was pushing her to the edge.

'I'm sorry, I know I'm being foolish,' she said to Maggie Fenn on Friday morning, dabbing her eyes and trying to laugh away the tears. 'It's just that I've known Millie for most of my life, so she feels a bit like a grandparent in a way. Anyway, I shouldn't be burdening you with my troubles, especially when I'm supposed to be here checking on Sophie.'

'Sophie's absolutely fine,' Maggie assured her, while placing some delicious-looking slabs of buttery shortbread on a plate to go with the hot chocolate she'd just made. 'She goes to school as sweet as anything, and she and Britney have bonded like a dream. So let's forget about them for now and talk about what's happening to you.'

'Honestly, nothing's wrong really,' Alex insisted, trying not to get too settled in this wonderfully cosy kitchen or she might never want to leave.

'But you're going to miss the old lady? I can quite understand that if you've known her for so long.'

'She has Alzheimer's,' Alex told her, 'but she always seems to know me when I go in, and there are times when we still manage a few laughs, or a little stroll down memory lane. She's not going to understand what's happening to her, and I can hardly bear to think of her being all confused and upset.' She bit her lips as her throat tightened again. Dear God, she really was in a hopeless state today.

'Have you tried explaining it to her?' Maggie asked gently.

'I did last night, and the carers have been doing their best to prepare her too, but she just forgets, or seems not to hear us anyway. Maybe that's a blessing, who knows? I'll go to see her again tomorrow, before the ambulance comes to take her.'

'She's very lucky to have you,' Maggie smiled. 'So many in her position don't seem to have anyone at all.'

'I know, I see them in there every time I go. The daft thing is, I'll miss them too. Maybe I'll carry on going to see them. I just hope Millie's niece and nephew will visit her, because it's too far for me to go very often.' *Unless I lose my job and end up finding another close to York.* Not in a million years would she ever dream of saying that to Maggie, she'd already made a big enough fool of herself with the stupid surge of tears that had erupted just because Maggie had asked if she was all right. She was certainly not going to start abusing Maggie's kindness by weighing in with everything else.

'Oh dear, oh dear,' Maggie clucked as Alex's eyes overflowed again. 'This is a very difficult thing you're facing. I wish there was something I could do to help.'

'You're already doing it,' Alex assured her, taking another tissue from the box Maggie was passing, 'but you have to stop being so nice to me or I'm going to end up feeling even sorrier for myself than I already do.'

Maggie chuckled, and pushed the biscuits Alex's way.

'I'd love one,' Alex said, glancing at the time, 'but I really ought to be going. I have to pick up a little girl over on North Hill at a quarter to eleven and I don't want to be late.'

'Of course not,' Maggie agreed, 'but I want you to know that if you do ever need to chat, I'm always here.'

'There you go, being nice again,' Alex warned through more tears.

Maggie rolled her eyes. 'I really must stop that, it's a terrible habit of mine.'

Alex turned at the sound of the front door opening and closing.

'That'll be Anthony,' Maggie told her. 'In here,' she called out. 'Now, I think I shall wrap up a few of these biscuits for you to take to the little girl you're picking up. Do you think she likes biscuits? How old is she?'

'Three.'

'Then she's sure to.'

'Oh, she does. I took her to the Seafront Café the other day and she wolfed down an entire brownie all to herself. You should have seen her face after, crumbs all over it, and all over her, but she was so pleased with herself I think she'd have eaten another if I'd let her.' She was spending too much time with Ottilie, becoming far, far too attached to her, but she simply didn't have what it took to make herself stop.

'Three years old and in need of protection?' Maggie sighed sadly. 'Poor little soul.'

Before Alex could respond Anthony Goodman was coming into the kitchen, and she was instantly reminded of how intimidating he'd appeared the first time she'd seen him. In this smaller, more homely environment his presence still felt unsettling, and his scowl seemed to be bordering on scary. Then he broke into a smile as he saw her, and the transformation caused a small catch in her heart. 'Hello,' she said, hoping she didn't look as much of a wreck as she felt. 'You probably don't remember me, but we met after the play . . .'

351

'Of course I remember you,' he corrected, enclosing her hand in a grip that made her own feel rather small, 'but I confess your name is escaping me.'

'Alex,' she reminded him, 'and thank you so much for the lovely comment you put on Facebook. It gave the cast such a boost, coming from someone like you.'

He seemed amazed. 'Someone like me?' He looked at his sister. 'Is that good?'

'Don't listen to him,' Maggie chided, going to kiss him, 'he's fishing for compliments.'

'Rather than trout?' Alex quipped.

He appeared confused and she felt herself colouring.

'Sorry, it was a joke,' she explained. 'You were out fishing the last time I was here.'

'Which is indeed where I'm off to this weekend, and sorry I was a bit slow on the uptake. Got a lot on my mind, or that's my excuse anyway. So, any coffee going, Mags?'

'Help yourself, I'll just see Alex out.'

'I hope you're not leaving on my account?'

'No, I have another appointment to get to. It was lovely seeing you.'

'Likewise. Don't forget to let us know if you have any more village romps in the offing. I meant what I said about the last one, it's been a long time since anything made me laugh out loud like that.'

'Two promises: I'll definitely let you know, and I won't write the jokes.'

Laughing, he said, 'I won't hold you to that,' and taking out his mobile as it rang he turned to pour himself a coffee.

'It's good to see him in spirits after everything he's been through,' Maggie said quietly as she walked Alex to the front door. 'His fiancée was killed in a light-aircraft accident just over a year ago, and he hasn't found it easy. Not that he'd ever tell you that, or let it show, but I know him too well for him to hide it from me.'

Moved by his tragedy, Alex echoed the words Maggie had spoken to her a few minutes ago. 'He's lucky to have you.'

Maggie smiled. 'We've always been close in spite of the gap in our ages. He doesn't look forty, does he, and I'm sure I don't look fifty.'

Wishing she could hug her, Alex said, 'More like thirty,' and she was still smiling warmly to herself as she got into her car.

If only Ottilie could have someone like that in her life, she was thinking as she drove away, in fact she wouldn't mind someone like it too. And what a shock it would be for Jason if she were to become involved with a top lawyer like Anthony Goodman. Come to think of it, it would be a pretty big shock for her too.

Time to rein in the wild fantasies and focus on the day ahead, she reminded herself. Already her spirits were lifting to think of Ottilie and the impressive progress she was making at the Pumpkin. This wasn't to say she'd come out of her shell completely, she still only played with Chloe, and if any of the other children joined in she'd immediately withdraw. However, Alex was able to leave her for an hour or so without any problems now, and the greatest joy of all had happened on Wednesday when she'd made a choice of where to go for a little treat after nursery. OK, she'd only uttered three words, 'On the car'sel,' but the fact that she'd said them, rather than waiting for Alex to run through suggestions with her nodding or shaking her head, had felt like a major breakthrough.

'It certainly is,' Vicky the health worker had agreed when Alex had rung her later – not for that specifically, but she'd been so thrilled she'd had to tell someone. 'And you'll be happy to hear we've got her an appointment with the paediatrician. It can't be for another two weeks, I'm afraid, the poor woman's always run off her feet as you know, but at least we're in. I'll email you the exact date when I'm back at my desk.'

Already feeling anxious about what the doctors might find, Alex said, 'And what did you make of the bruises on her head when you saw her?'

'Well, they're obviously quite tender, poor little mite, but she could easily have got them falling off the bed.'

Which was what both parents had claimed when Alex had challenged them on Monday morning – Erica face to face at the house; Brian over the phone, Alex having forced him out of class.

'Yes, it is an emergency,' she'd informed the secretary furiously. OK, children were always falling over and injuring themselves, but her suspicions of the Wades weren't going to allow her to accept the explanation of tumbling off the bed without calling them on it first.

In the end she'd had no choice but to accept it, especially when Ottilie herself hadn't denied her parents' story. In fact, she'd pointed at her bed and touched the bruises when Alex had asked her how she'd got them. 'I fell,' she'd whispered. Of course, that didn't mean much, because the Wades could easily have told her it was the answer she had to give; they might even have brainwashed her into thinking it was how it had happened.

Or they were telling the truth.

Though Alex was still finding that option difficult to swallow, the alternative, that one of them had deliberately hurt her, was even harder to take. So, for the time being there wasn't much she could do, apart from continue to monitor things as closely as the restrictions of her job would allow, which she was doing during every available minute. At least when Ottilie was with her she knew she was safe and in an environment that was far healthier than the one she seemed to be in at home. She had to tread so carefully with this, not only for Ottilie's sake, but for the whole community, because she didn't even want to think about the ructions it would cause if she got it wrong about Brian Wade.

Far worse though, would be if she turned out to be right.

As had become the custom when she arrived at the Wades she found the door on the latch, and as she pushed it open her heart swelled at the sound of running feet. As soon as Ottilie arrived at her side she came to a stop with her head down and Boots hugged to her chest.

'And how are you today?' Alex asked, stooping to her height. The bruises on her forehead were turning an earthy yellow and green now, and the swelling had all but vanished.

How had it happened?

'I'm fine,' Ottilie whispered.

Having spent some time on Wednesday, while they were at the café, encouraging her to say the words, Alex's eyes widened with approval as she said, 'That's very good to hear. And what about Boots?'

'He's fine too.'

Alex nodded. 'I thought he would be, because he has you to take care of him.'

Ottilie reached for her hand, and started to pull Alex to the door.

Loving how eager she was, Alex gently released her hand as she said, 'Well, I'll just go and let Mummy know . . .'

'I'm here.'

Starting, Alex looked up to find Erica Wade staring down at them from the top of the stairs. Dressed in black with her hair loose and her feet as bare as her bloodless face, she looked unnervingly as though she'd arrived through a séance.

'Are you all right?' Alex asked, aware of how often she asked this woman that question.

'Yes, I'm fine. Ottilie, have you got your bag?'

Ottilie held up the new pink backpack Alex had bought her in the 99p shop on Wednesday. 'She has a drink and an apple,' Erica informed Alex. 'I don't know what else she might have put in.'

Alex glanced down at Ottilie and smiled. Then to Erica she said, 'Why have you cancelled your appointment with the psychiatrist? We went to a lot of trouble to get you in as early as next week . . .'

'It was on Tuesday,' Erica interrupted. 'Ottilie's health visitor comes on Tuesdays so I have to be here.'

Annoyed with herself for not having foreseen this, Alex said, 'You should have rung me first. I'd have come to take care of Ottilie.'

Erica had no answer for that.

'Have you made another appointment?' Alex demanded.

'My husband's doing it. It's not easy for him to take time off.'

Alex couldn't help wondering if they were working together to make sure the appointment never happened. 'I can always take you myself and the health visitor can stay here with Ottilie . . . Mrs Wade, don't walk away.'

Erica didn't stop.

'You can't keep doing this,' Alex cried in frustration. 'Don't you realise what the consequences could be if you don't cooperate?'

At the sound of a door closing Alex almost banged a fist on the banister, and might have if Ottilie hadn't been watching her. She felt sorely tempted to go up there and shake the woman, but even if she did, what then? There was clearly no reasoning with her, or not in the normal sense, so once again resigning herself to trying to get hold of Brian Wade by phone, she took Ottilie out to the car and buckled her into the child's seat which was constantly there now.

Dropping a kiss lightly on her head, she got into the front and decided the call to Brian Wade would have to wait until she was at the Pumpkin, since she didn't want to get into any sort of scene with Ottilie in the car.

As usual Chloe was waiting when they arrived, ready to share the sweets she'd brought from home, and looked surprised, then delighted when Ottilie gave her an apple. While they toddled off across the room in search of Lego, or playdough, or whatever they'd decided on today, Alex looked down at Boots who Ottilie had left in her safe keeping, and felt ridiculously honoured to be invested with so much trust.

Tucking the bear under one arm, she took out her

mobile and gave Janet a wave as she went to the back of the room to make the call to Brian Wade.

'I'm afraid he's not here this morning,' she was told. 'Can I take a message?'

'Do you happen to know where he is? It's about his daughter.'

'I believe he has a doctor's appointment. If it's urgent I can try to find out which surgery . . .'

'It's OK, I know which surgery he's with, and it can wait until later.'

Wondering what Brian Wade might need to see a doctor for, she rang off and went to offer Janet some help, since for once she had no urgent calls to rush off to. Unsurprisingly her offer was leapt on, and the next two hours passed so swiftly and enjoyably that it made her wonder, as she and Ottilie were leaving, if this might be a job for her in the future, if, God forbid, she ended up losing the one she had.

'OK, so what would you like to do now?' she asked as she zipped up Ottilie's pink anorak and dutifully returned Boots to her waiting arms. 'Where's your backpack?'

Ottilie gasped and clapped a hand to her mouth, and Alex had a struggle not to laugh, since it was exactly what Chloe would have done if she'd forgotten her bag.

Racing back into the playroom Ottilie returned in seconds, the bag over one arm and Boots still safely snuggled under the other.

'It's pouring with rain out there,' Alex told her, 'so I don't think the carousel will be working, but if you like, we could go to the pool and watch the swimmers. Or what about the aquarium? I think you'd like that, do you?'

Ottilie nodded, though she probably had no idea what an aquarium was. 'And the café?' she asked shyly.

Thrilled, Alex said, 'Of course the café.' Then, remembering, she rolled her eyes playfully. 'You want to eat another brownie all to yourself, don't you?'

Ottilie's solemn face broke into a smile.

'You little piggy, you,' Alex teased, giving her a tickle.

Ottilie started to laugh and wriggle, and in a surge of exuberance Alex swept her up in her arms to blow a giant raspberry kiss on her cheek.

Ottilie's smile fled.

'Oh dear, what is it?' Alex cried worriedly. 'Did I scare you?'

Ottilie only looked at her.

'I was just playing, but if you didn't like it, I won't do it again.'

Ottilie said nothing, and it was impossible to tell what she might be thinking. It wasn't until their visit to the aquarium was over and Alex was carrying a tray of drinks and brownies to the table in the café that she spotted Ottilie blowing on Boots's cheek. Realising what she was doing, her heart folded with pity – if she was reading this correctly then Ottilie might never have had a raspberry kiss before, so Alex hadn't scared her, she'd simply startled and confused her.

'I almost forgot,' she said, putting the brownie and a beaker of milk in front of Ottilie, 'a very kind lady gave me some biscuits for you earlier, so I'll pop them in your bag for you and Boots to share later, OK?'

Ottilie turned to look up at her, then taking a breath she burst into a sunny smile.

Laughing as she put an arm around her, Alex said, 'You are utterly adorable, I hope you know that.'

Nodding, Ottilie reached for her milk with both hands and carefully brought it to her mouth. Then after touching the beaker to Boots's face, she put it down and picked up the brownie.

After she'd taken a couple of bites Alex said, 'Aren't you going to share it with Boots?'

Ottilie's cheek was bulging as she looked up at her and shook her head. 'Biscuits,' she said, blowing out a little storm of crumbs.

'I see, he has the biscuits for later? That's OK then, and we have to learn not to speak with our mouths full, don't we?'

Ottilie's eyes and mouth turned into three small circles.

'Finish what you're eating before you speak,' Alex explained, 'and then you can say anything you like.'

Apparently understanding, Ottilie waited until she'd swallowed her mouthful and said, 'Boots can have the biscuits.'

'That's lovely,' Alex praised, hugely impressed by the amount of words all in one go. 'I suppose he's not hungry now?'

Ottilie shook her head.

'What time does he normally have his tea?'

'Same as me.'

'And do you know what time that is? Can you tell the time?'

She looked up at the clock on the wall. 'Big hand and small hand,' she announced earnestly.

Realising she was perhaps a bit young to do any better than that, Alex said, 'That's very good indeed. Do you help Mummy to make the tea?'

Ottilie picked up her brownie and took another bite.

Waiting until she'd finished, Alex said, 'What sorts of things do you do in the evenings with Mummy and Daddy?'

At that Ottilie put her biscuit down and began shaking her head. She kept on shaking it until Alex tilted up her chin to make her stop. 'It's all right, you don't have to tell me if you don't want to, but if it's anything that hurts you, or makes you upset . . .'

'Drink now.' Ottilie reached for the milk.

Picking it up for her, Alex said, 'You will tell me if anything bad happens to you, won't you?'

'Not bad,' Ottilie said. 'I'm a good girl.'

'Yes you are, a very good girl and we don't want anyone to hurt you, do we?'

Ottilie was staring at her milk.

'Does anyone hurt you, Ottilie?' Alex asked carefully.

Bringing the beaker to her mouth Ottilie drank, spilling some down her chin.

Wiping it away, Alex let her put the milk down herself, and repeated her question.

Ottilie clearly didn't want to answer as she picked up Boots and cuddled him to her face.

Knowing she couldn't let this go, Alex said, 'Do Mummy or Daddy ever hurt you, Ottilie?'

Ottilie shook her head and rested it against Alex's arm.

'Do you play games with them?'

Ottilie nodded.

'What sorts of games?'

No answer.

'Ottilie?'

'Sleepy,' she mumbled. 'We play sleepy and watch lots of children.'

Confused, Alex asked, 'Do you mean on the TV?'

Ottilie nodded.

Alex was about to ask which programmes when she happened to look out of the window, and the words dried on her lips. Gina, Jason's wife, was across the road, standing next to a car with a man. They were so engrossed in whatever they were saying that neither of them seemed to notice the rain, though it was much lighter now, might even have stopped.

Alex tried to tear her eyes away, but couldn't. Was Gina seeing someone else already?

She was getting ahead of herself here; she had no idea who the man was, and creating an affair where there probably wasn't one was really grasping at straws.

Feeling Ottilie slump against her, fast asleep, she lifted her on to her lap and after cuddling her in cosily she looked up again and was in time to see Gina and the man parting from an embrace. Of course it might simply have been a friendly one, but there again it might not. Then they were laughing and greeting someone else whose flaming red hair Alex recognised immediately. It was Heather Hancock – and as the three of them crossed the road, coming towards the café, Alex was suddenly desperate to find a way to disappear.

To her relief, they walked past the window without even glancing in and then they were gone.

For several minutes she sat holding Ottilie, grateful for the bulk of her in her arms, or the emptiness she was feeling might have been swallowing her into a pit of despair. It was pointless, she knew, being jealous of Gina, it was hardly going to make Jason come back, or suddenly conjure her a best friend – or indeed a lover – but it was how she was feeling and she was finding it hard to suppress it. How had she managed to come to this point in her life and be so alone? Besides Jason and the children, Gina had a mother and a father, a brother and a sister, cousins, aunts, uncles – her life was full of people who loved her. It wasn't that she, Alex, had no one, she must keep reminding herself of that, because she knew that Gabby and Aunt Sheila cared for her in their ways, and so did many of her friends in the village. She just didn't have anyone to call her own.

Realising her old stalker, self-pity, was back, she tightened her hold on Ottilie and buried her face in her hair. If she wanted to feel sorry for herself there would be plenty of time for it later; now she had to get Ottilie home, and remember to call Brian Wade again – and Tommy to find out if he was staying late at the office.

By the time they returned to the house Ottilie had woken up, but when Alex went to lift her out of her seat she drew back.

'Stay with you?' she said, looking pleadingly into Alex's eyes.

Feeling her heart fill up, Alex wanted, more than anything, to tell her she could, but putting a hand to her flushed cheek she said, 'It's not possible, sweetheart. You have to go inside with Mummy. She'll be waiting for you.'

Ottilie shook her head.

'Yes, she will, and you'll be able to tell her all about the games you played with Chloe, and the fishes we saw at the aquarium. Can you remember what they were?'

Again Ottilie shook her head, and Alex realised how difficult she was finding it to imagine Erica Wade showing an interest in Ottilie's day. She had to do something about it, she really did, but the question was what, when she still had no evidence to satisfy a court that Ottilie should be removed from the home. And until Erica Wade had undergone a psychiatric assessment Alex wasn't even in a position to claim that the woman was mentally unfit to have a child in her care, even though, in her opinion, it seemed blindingly obvious.

'You've been such a good girl today,' she said to Ottilie, gently smoothing her hair, 'so I'll tell you what. On Monday, as a very special treat after nursery, if it's not raining like it's been today, I'll take you to the zoo. How does that sound? It'll be lovely, won't it, to see all the animals? We'll probably even be able to feed the monkeys. Would you like that?'

Ottilie nodded warily.

Smiling, Alex unfastened the seat belt. Since most of her other charges were of school age she couldn't see them until much later in the day anyway, and her paperwork could always be done at home. 'Come along then,' she said, lifting her out. 'Let's get you inside now, and over the weekend perhaps you can draw me pictures of as many animals as you can think of. Will you do that for me?'

Ottilie nodded. 'Lions and bears,' she replied.

'Nice friendly ones, yes?'

'Yes.'

'And snakes and pandas and tortoises. They've got all sorts of animals at Dean Valley zoo. They've even got a baby elephant. I expect you'd like to see him, wouldn't you?'

'Yes, and Boots?'

'Of course Boots can come too. We'd never go anywhere without him, would we?'

Ottilie was shaking her head as Alex pushed open the front door and set her down in the hall. 'We're back,' she called out.

Erica Wade appeared from the kitchen still dressed in black, but her hair was clipped neatly behind her head now, and her eyes seemed calmer, even if they were ringed in dark shadows.

'She's had a nap,' Alex told her, 'and a snack. We went to the aquarium, which she'll tell you about.'

'Thank you,' Erica responded. 'Run upstairs and take off your coat,' she said to Ottilie. 'And go to the bathroom if you need to.'

No warm embrace to welcome her home, no physical or emotional contact at all. Was it any wonder Ottilie wanted to stay with someone who showed her affection? If it were allowed Alex knew she'd take her home right now and keep her for the whole weekend, but alas it wasn't.

'Has your husband managed to make another appointment with the psychiatrist yet?' she asked bluntly.

'I don't know. He hasn't rung.'

And I wonder, would you answer the phone if he did? 'I'm going to try reaching him when I get back to the car,' Alex said. 'If I don't manage it perhaps you could ask him to call me. I'll have my phone on over the weekend.'

'I'll tell him.'

'The same goes for you,' Alex told her. 'If you need me for any reason, please feel free to call.'

'Thank you.'

'I'm here to help you,' Alex reminded her. 'I know it might not seem like that sometimes, but it's the

365

truth, and I'm a good listener if you ever feel the need to open up to someone.'

Erica's expression was unreadable, but Alex could tell she was listening. 'Thank you,' she said in the end. 'I'll have Ottilie ready at the same time on Monday.'

Not bothering to remind her, yet again, that she should be doing the nursery run herself, Alex simply said, 'OK. And do ask her about the fishes. She was fascinated by them.'

When Erica didn't respond Alex glanced up the stairs, and spotting Ottilie peering between the banister rails she gave her a wave.

Ottilie's little fist clenched and unclenched a couple of times and Alex had to fight back the urge to go up and get her. What was her weekend going to be like in this morbid house? Lonely, isolated, shut up in her room for most of the time with no other children to play with? If only she could take her to Gabby's to meet the twins, or shopping in Kesterly, or for more rides on the carousel. There were a hundred things they could do together, but none of them could happen without her parents' permission, and besides, it wouldn't be good for either of them to become even more attached than they already were. 'See you Monday,' she said with a smile, and forcing herself to turn away she cast Erica a despairing look, and left.

Erica was watching her own hand as it drew a small package from Ottilie's bag, except it wasn't her hand. To her it seemed vast and rough, with black hairs on the skin and wounded, crooked joints at the knuckles.

It was her stepfather's hand, growing out of her wrist.

She tried to shake it off, but it wouldn't go.

Panicking, she grabbed a knife, ready to chop it off, but before she struck it transformed into her hand again.

Sweat was beading on her face; her breath was ragged and short. She couldn't think where she was. Nothing seemed familiar. She looked around, her eyes glittering with confusion, her heart thudding hard in her chest. Then she saw the silver-foil package she'd dropped on the floor and everything slipped into focus again.

'Ottilie! Ottilie, come here, *now*,' she shouted, almost screamed.

Ottilie came down the stairs as fast as she could, and ran into the kitchen.

'What's this?' Erica cried, her face twitching, spittle foaming at the corners of her mouth. 'Where did you get it? You stole it, didn't you?'

Ottilie's eyes were wide with fear as she shook her head.

'Yes you did, you stole it, you wicked child.'

'No, no, Lex gave them . . .'

'Don't lie. I hate liars.'

Ottilie was starting to shake.

Erica pushed the package in her face.

'What's going on?' Brian demanded, coming in the door. 'What are you shouting about?'

'She's a thief,' Erica shrieked at him. 'I found this in her bag – well *that's* what we'll do with it,' she snarled, and opening the bin she dumped the package inside.

Without asking what had been in it, Brian looked at Ottilie so sternly that she cowered away. 'Did you steal something?' he asked gravely.

Ottilie shook her head. 'No, Lex gave me them.'

'Are you lying?'

'No,' she sobbed.

He sighed in a despairing way. 'Oh dear, Ottilie,' he said, 'you know what happens to little girls who lie and steal, don't you?'

'No, didn't lie or steal.'

'And little girls who answer back.'

Ottilie immediately hung her head.

'They have to be spanked, don't they?' he said, making it sound like an awful chore. 'So come along with me.'

As he took her by the hand, Erica stood watching them, her eyes glittering with a wild malice. 'You're going to get what you deserve,' she shouted, as he led Ottilie outside. *You're going to get what you deserve . . . get what you deserve . . . get what you deserve.* The words were like zombies rising from graves. *You're going to get what you deserve because you're a lying, thieving little bitch.*

It was almost seven o'clock in the evening and being in no hurry to go into the empty Vicarage, Alex was still outside in the car, checking the texts she'd heard pinging into both her mobiles while driving home. For someone who felt as though she had no one in the world, she seemed to be getting a lot of messages, she was thinking wryly as she opened the first. Seeing it was confirmation of the appointment she'd made for the following day to view a room in a shared house, about a mile from the seafront, she felt the black hole of her future yawning even wider. Not since she'd been a student had she lived like that, but she had to be realistic, it was probably all she could afford, and the ad had described the other residents as young professionals so maybe it would help to broaden her horizons.

It didn't surprise her to find that the next message was from Tommy, reminding her that she was welcome to drop in on him and Jackie any time over the weekend. *And don't worry too much about Ottilie Wade*, he'd added. *You're doing a great job and you wouldn't be human if you didn't get involved.*

'If I thought you wanted off the case it might be different,' he'd said an hour or so ago, when she'd gone to the office to discuss how concerned she was about her attachment to Ottilie, 'but I know you don't and I'm glad for it, because it sounds as though she's built up a confidence in you that she doesn't seem to have in anyone else. It would do her more harm than good to jeopardise it at this stage.'

Thankful to hear this, Alex had said, 'I finally managed to get hold of Brian Wade on the way here. He apologised profusely – most unlike him – for cancelling the appointment with the psychiatrist, but apparently he's made another for the week after next. It's a Thursday, so I'm going to try to swap one of Ottilie's nursery days so I don't have to take any more time out of my schedule to look after her.'

'OK. Have you broached the subject of a nanny with either of them yet?'

'No, I don't think I'll get anywhere with it until we know what the psychiatrist has to say about the mother, so the sooner we get his report, the better.'

Tommy nodded agreement. 'Any more news from your friendly policeman up north?'

'No, but I'm pretty confident he'll be in touch the minute he finds anything he thinks we should know.'

'And the paediatrician's all lined up, you say. I take it she's going to carry out a virginity test?'

Feeling the horror of it hitting her, Alex said, 'I'm hoping for a positive result, in that everything's still intact.' She didn't have to point out to Tommy that if a child that age had been subjected to penetration often enough there would no longer be any bruising, because Tommy already knew that. He also knew that a little girl's vagina was elastic enough to allow penetration more easily than most people realised. However, it would still be a brutally agonising experience in the early stages that, in her opinion, any perpetrator ought to be castrated for.

'Is she showing any signs of masturbation?' Tommy asked bluntly.

Alex shook her head. In spite of having done the job as long as she had, it still sickened her to think of a young child being sexually awoken to a point that he or she began behaving like an adult. 'All I can tell you,' she said, 'is that her drawings aren't suggesting anything unusual, and apart from holding herself when she wants to go to the toilet, I've never seen her touching herself down there.'

Thank God, she was thinking now as she scrolled on to her next message, because at least it afforded her some hope that nothing sexual was going on at Ottilie's home. However, it wasn't nearly enough to sweep away her suspicions – only the paediatrician could do that when she gave her report.

Seeing a text from Mattie, she almost groaned aloud. She'd totally forgotten to call her back after picking up a voicemail from her earlier, saying, 'Amazing news, you're a genius. Call me as soon as you can.'

Guessing it must be about the idea they'd put to

the local council several months ago of doing a *Mulgrove's Got Talent* contest, she decided the call back could wait until she was in the house with a drink in her hand. So she clicked on to the last message, and as soon as she saw who it was from her heart turned inside out.

Hi, just to say thinking of you. Hope you're OK. Love Jx

As her head fell back against the seat she tried to think why he'd have done that, unless he was genuinely thinking of her, and maybe even missing her too. He'd used the word love, but did he really mean that, or was it just habit, something he'd added without thinking? And now what was she supposed to do? Text back to say yes, I'm fine, btw did you know your wife's having another affair? Maybe he did know and that was why he was texting her. Suddenly convinced that was the case, she felt a burn of outrage and immediately sent a sharp message back saying *Please don't text again. You made your decision, now we both have to live with it.*

No sooner had it gone than she wanted to take it back, but it was too late now, it had probably already reached his phone.

That is so like you, Alexandra, she could hear Myra saying. *Act in haste, regret at leisure. If only you could learn to think first you might save yourself, and others, a lot of trouble.*

Not particularly enjoying the ghostly echo of the frequent reprimand, she got out of the car and went into the house. After pouring herself a glass of beer she decided she might as well get the rest of her messages over with, and hit the playback button on the answerphone.

The first, as she'd expected, was from Gabby,

letting her know that she had accepted Mr Quigley's offer subject to a couple of conditions, one of them being vacant possession on completion. 'He's not saying he wants you to leave straight away,' Gabby assured her, 'but obviously he won't want you there once he's signed and ready to send in the builders. That probably won't happen for another couple of months, so no panic. We need to talk about Mum and Dad's stuff, though. I thought maybe you could give all the clothes to a charity shop and I'll arrange to come up and get the papers and jewellery and stuff. Anyway, call me when you get home and we can have a chat about it then.'

Abruptly erasing the message, as though in some way it might make the whole horrible, unthinkable situation go away, she took another sip of her beer as the machine skipped on to the next call. Since it was a voice she didn't recognise, she assumed it was a telemarketer and was about to erase that one too when her heartbeat started to slow as she realised who it was.

Quickly going back to the top she pressed play again, and had to put her glass down as she listened carefully to what was being said.

'I'm afraid I don't like leaving messages,' the croaky voice told her, 'but it seems I must, so here goes. I've been trying to get hold of you for the last couple of weeks to tell you . . . It's Helen Drake here, by the way . . .' *Helen Drake, her great-aunt, her grandfather's sister.* 'You told me once that I was to let you know if I had any news of your mother. Well, I have, so if you'd like to call me back on this number . . .' Alex was so unprepared for this that she couldn't even fumble for a pen, much less register the number. It didn't matter, she could always play the message again. 'I'm at home most of the time these days,' her great-aunt continued, 'unlike you, it would seem. I shall wait to hear from you.'

Without giving herself a moment to think, Alex replayed the message, wrote down the number and started to dial. It was only as the call was about to connect that she heard Myra's warning, *Act in haste, regret at leisure,* and realising she had to give herself some time to think, deal with the shock even, she quickly hung up again.

Turning to the window, she gazed at the ghostly reflection of herself that seemed to hover over the garden, and had an eerie sensation of her mother looking at her from the past. She was shaking, she realised, feeling as though she wanted to run, though to where, or even to whom, she had no idea. It had been so long since she'd allowed herself to wish, yearn for her mother to be in touch, that trying to face it now was almost surreal. And shocking, even frightening, though she wasn't sure what she needed to fear.

Apart from her father, of course.

Her great-aunt hadn't mentioned him, but that didn't mean she wasn't going to speak of him when Alex rang back.

Her heart was pounding, her mind reeling so chaotically that she was finding it impossible to think straight.

Who was her mother, where was she, what news did her aunt have? If it was good . . . Alex almost took a step back as though to avoid the hope. What would good news be? That her mother wanted to meet? She could hardly begin to imagine where, how, when that might happen, or what might come of it. What did her mother look like now, what sort of person was she? The only pictures Alex had seen she'd found online, taken before the tragedy when Angela Nicholls was still in her twenties. She would be fifty now. *Her mother, the young girl in the pictures with shiny blonde hair and bright, laughing eyes – eyes that had had no way of seeing the future – was fifty.* Was she still Angela Nicholls? Almost certainly not, or the rector would have been able to find her.

She must have another family, a husband, children, grandchildren even.

Did they know about the child who'd been given up for adoption? The little girl who'd grown up apart from her mother, deprived of the family that should have been hers?

Her great-aunt's news might be bad. Perhaps she had somehow learned that her mother was in trouble, sick, even dead. Millie had planted the idea, and now it was seeming to take root again. What was she going to do if her mother had died? She couldn't grieve for someone she didn't know, and yet if it was what her aunt wanted to tell her, she knew already she was going to be devastated. Her mother had never been real, but the dream of her, the hope of something bringing them together one day, had never gone away, in spite of how hard she'd tried to banish it.

And now it was back and coming at her so forcefully, so hungrily that it might engulf her.

She turned to look at the phone. Would she be able to handle her mother's death on top of everything else she seemed to be losing? The answer was, she wouldn't know until she faced it, and it might not be that, *so just call, Alex, just pick up the phone and find out.*

After dialling the number again she allowed it to connect, and started to feel a little queasy as the same slightly stern, but thready voice that she'd heard on the machine said, 'Hello?'

'Hello, it's Alex Lake here,' Alex told her, hoping she sounded friendly and not defensive. 'I've just picked up your message.'

'Aha. I was beginning to wonder if something had happened to you,' came the reply.

'No, I'm fine, just . . . I'm out quite a lot. You said you had news . . .'

'Yes, and I hope it's going to be welcome. I know it would have been once, but times change, so do people.'

Please just tell me, Alex was silently urging, while at the same time dreading going any further.

'Your mother's been in touch with me . . .'

Alex lost her breath, to a sob. So she wasn't dead, and until this moment she'd had no idea how much those words might mean to her. Their impact was so huge, so shattering that she barely heard what her great-aunt said next.

'She would have rung you herself,' Helen Drake was saying, 'but she thought . . . She felt it would be easier for you if you had some time to think about whether or not you wanted to hear from her. So she's asked me to act as the go-between.'

'Where . . . Where is she?' Alex heard herself asking.

'I'm afraid she didn't tell me and I didn't think . . . Silly of me, but this is the first I've heard of her myself in almost thirty years, so I was quite taken aback.'

Easily able to believe that, Alex said, 'Is she . . . Is she all right?'

Sounding surprised, Helen Drake replied, 'I imagine so. She sounded it. I'm afraid I can't remember if I asked.'

Alex was trying to think what to say next. There was so much going round in her mind, questions, images, fears, hopes, that she couldn't seem to pluck any words from the chaos. 'When will you speak to her again?' she finally managed.

'Well, I expect it'll be soon, because she sounded quite keen to know if you'll see her.'

Her mother wanted to make contact, to see her, even. Not only that, she was giving her the option to say no if she wanted to. Alex wasn't going to do that, no matter what the consequences might be. 'Maybe I could call her,' she said. 'Do you have a number?'

Helen Drake made a tutting sound. 'I know I've written it down somewhere, but I can't seem to find it. I'm sure she'll ring again though. If she does, am I to tell her that you'd like to hear from her?'

'Yes, yes please,' Alex replied, hoping, praying that Helen Drake's loss of the number wouldn't lead her mother to think she didn't want to see her. 'If you find it before she rings will you call me back?'

'Of course. I'm sure it's here somewhere – unless I wrote it on an envelope that found its way into the bin.'

Imagining the old lady's house full of clutter and randomly jotted numbers with no names attached, Alex felt her heart sinking. 'Thanks for ringing,' she said bleakly, 'and if you do speak to her again will you tell her . . .' Tell her what? She didn't know what she wanted to say, so she simply added, 'I guess . . . I hope I'll get the chance to tell her myself.'

Chapter Seventeen

The following morning, unable to let Millie leave without saying goodbye to her, Alex changed the message on her answering machine to include her mobile number, just in case her great-aunt or her mother rang, and drove off to the care home. She was so preoccupied by the possibility of receiving a call and how wonderful it might be if she did connect with her mother, that she hadn't yet allowed the dread of not hearing anything to exert its grip.

During the night she'd been riddled with vivid, nonsensical dreams about people she didn't know and places she'd never been. Some of them were alarming, waking her with a start, but whatever her subconscious had conjured managed to dart away before she could grasp it. At one point she'd seen the woman with a child under her arm dashing down a staircase in panic, but if it was a hidden memory rising to the surface she couldn't connect it to reality or to anything she'd been told. Her mother hadn't returned for her after the killings, she knew that, so maybe it was a flashback to something that had happened before that time. Perhaps it had nothing to do with her mother at all.

She could hardly believe that she might soon find out.

Her mother wanted to be in touch.

Please, Helen Drake, find that number.

The worst of her dreams had been of Ottilie screaming and sobbing as she was violated in the worst imaginable way. She'd had similar nightmares about other children in her care and woken up in a state, wanting to run to them right away. Last night the dreams had felt so disturbingly, horrifyingly real that she'd been too afraid to try and go back to sleep in case they returned, so she'd lain awake, tossing and turning, until it was time to get up.

Now, having finally managed to push those dreadful images from her mind, she was so full of questions for herself, and her mother, that one had barely formed before another was taking its place. She'd get to ask them all, she felt sure of it, because God, fate, the Universe, wouldn't be so cruel as to let nothing come of this, it just wouldn't. She was going to see her mother, talk to her, find out who she was now, and maybe even become a part of her life. *She might actually have a family of her own.* Though she knew she could be setting herself up for the most crushing of falls, what else was she to do? Think the worst? No, she wasn't going to allow herself to do that. Something had to go right for her at last, and she had to believe it would be this if only because right now there seemed little else to hope for.

On arriving at Millie's care home, she was just pulling into a parking space when her mobile rang, and almost gasping at the giant leap in her heart she clicked on her Bluetooth with a tentative 'Hello?'

'Hey, it's me,' Gabby cried. 'Are you OK? I thought you'd have rung me back by now. Did you get my message last night, about the house?'

Swallowing a mix of guilt, disappointment and relief, Alex said, 'Yes, I did, but something happened . . . I had a call . . . Oh God, Gabby, you're not going to believe this, but you remember my Great-aunt Helen who lives in Wales?'

Sounding baffled, Gabby said, 'Sort of. I mean, we never met her, did we? Why? Is she dead, or something? Is that why you didn't ring?'

'No, she's not dead, she's very much alive and apparently – wait for this – she's only heard from my mother and *my mother wants to be in touch with me.* Isn't that fantastic? I can hardly get my head around it, coming out of the blue like this. Remember how we used to make up stories about who and where she might be? Well, it seems I could be about to find out.'

Gabby didn't respond.

'Are you still there?' Alex asked, unprepared for Gabby to be anything but thrilled for her.

'Yeah, I'm here, and I'm a bit . . . Well, I guess a bit shocked and kind of . . . sad, I suppose.'

Alex was even more taken aback. 'What do you mean, sad?' she demanded, hardly able to cope with her own misgivings without trying to deal with Gabby's too.

'Well, I've always thought of us as having the same mother really . . . I mean, obviously I knew you were adopted, but all those stories we made up about your other mother, I never imagined any of them ever coming true.'

'I don't know if they will,' Alex told her, 'because I've still got no idea who or where she is, and I won't have until I've spoken to her. Helen Drake has lost the number, so I'm counting on my mother ringing her again.'

'And you're going to see her if she does?'

Trying to swallow her irritation while hardly able to believe the question, Alex said, 'Of course. Why on earth would you think I wouldn't?'

'I don't know, out of loyalty to Mum and Dad, I suppose.'

Alex's head spun. 'But she's my *mother*, Gabby.'

'I know, I know, or at least you're presuming she is, but what if it's all a hoax? Have you thought about how you are going to feel then?'

'Why would it be a hoax? My aunt seems convinced it's her, and what the heck would anyone gain from pretending to be my mother?'

'There are some really strange people out there, you know, and even if this woman does turn out to be for real, you've got no idea what she might be like.'

'Which is why I want to meet her, to find out. Gabby, you're being really negative about this and I thought . . . Well, I thought you'd be pleased for me.'

'I will be if it turns out all right, but until we know more I have to admit I'm more worried than pleased. And I guess a bit jealous, if I'm being honest, because it could end up meaning that you have a mother and I don't, which'll be really weird.'

Used to Gabby making things about herself, Alex said, 'But you'll still be my sister. Nothing's ever going to change that, and you never know, you might get along with her so you'll feel . . . Well, not that she's your mother too, but that we can be like family anyway.' *She was getting way ahead of herself here.*

Unsurprisingly, Gabby fell silent again, and feeling sorry now that she'd even brought the subject up, Alex said, 'I'm afraid I have to go. I'm at the care home to say goodbye to Millie. We can talk later, if you like. Well, we'll have to, about the house and things . . .'

'Is it going to be all right for you and Jason to move out before completion?'

Stopping as she opened the car door, Alex tried to think what to say, but couldn't get her mind to move beyond the truth. 'Jason and I aren't together any more,' she announced, wondering how she could make it sound so matter-of fact when even the words hurt. 'He's gone back to his wife.'

Gabby gasped. 'You're kidding me,' she cried. 'When?'

'About three weeks ago. I didn't say anything before because I didn't want to talk about it, and I suppose I was, you know, kind of hoping he might come back.'

'Will he? Of course he will.'

Thinking of the text she'd received yesterday, Alex said, 'Even if he wants to, and I'm not sure he does, it's already too late.' It was a truth that was as painful to realise as it was already proving to live with.

'Oh no, really? Are you sure about that?'

'Yes, I'm sure.'

'Oh Alex, I'm sorry. Are you terribly upset?'

Seeing no reason to go into it, Alex said, 'I'll get over it. What matters to me now is hearing from my mother, and obviously finding somewhere to live. And please don't worry about me still being in the house when the sale completes, I promise I'll have found somewhere by then.'

Gabby sighed heavily. 'I'm feeling really mean about making you move,' she declared, 'especially now you've told me about Jason.'

'It had to happen at some point, I always knew that, and you're doing what you have to for the kids.'

'Yes, but I wish it wasn't happening quite so fast now. On the other hand, I suppose we're lucky to have a buyer who's willing to pay such a good price in this market. Tell me, what are you going to do if you find out your mother's been with your father all this time?'

Feeling the dread of it jarring her insides, Alex said, 'I'll have to cross that bridge when I come to it, but I don't think it's very likely, really, do you, considering what he did?'

'I don't know. You're the one who always said she might be with him, I just went along with it because you seemed so sure. Anyway, if she does ring . . .'

'Not if, when.' She had to stay positive.

'OK, when she rings, you'll let me know, won't you?'

'Of course.'

After a moment, Gabby said, 'I hope she turns out to be everything you want her to be. It would be too awful if she wasn't.'

With that small effort at moral support still echoing in her ears Alex rang off, and dropping her earpiece into a pocket she took herself into the care home. When she got to Millie's room it was to find her already dressed and drooping tiredly in her wheelchair, her sparse white hair neatly combed behind her ears and her knotted hands folded over the handbag on her lap. 'Is she OK?' she whispered to the nurse who was with her.

'She's half asleep,' the nurse answered, 'but have a little chat with her while I go and check if the ambulance is here.'

With Millie's personal possessions already on their way up north the room seemed forlorn, almost desolate, though Alex guessed it wouldn't be long before someone else's belongings were transforming it again. Probably as early as this afternoon, given the demand for places.

Sitting on the edge of the bare mattress, she turned the wheelchair so Millie could see her. 'Hello there,' she smiled, as Millie's eyes flickered open. 'You're looking very chic today.'

'Oh, Alex, there's lovely,' Millie sighed with a smile. 'I've got me coat on. I'm going to Mexico.'

'Mexico?' Alex repeated, wondering where that had come from, and guessing a travel programme must have been on in the background while she was dozing.

Millie nodded, and her eyes drifted off to where her doll's house used to be. A moment later they were closed and her head was lolling forward again.

Gently easing it back to rest it on the cushion behind her, Alex abandoned the small and selfish hope she'd had of asking about her mother, and simply held her fragile hand instead. Millie was too far into the wilderness now; it wouldn't be fair to test her with questions that would probably just end up confusing her even further.

'I'm going to miss you, Millie Case,' she said softly. 'You're very special to me, I hope you know that, and you've always made me feel special too, for as long as I can remember.'

She took a tissue from a box on the windowsill and dabbed away the drool that had started to run from the corner of Millie's mouth. She was remembering how Millie used to wipe her mouth when she was little after she'd eaten chocolate cake, and how Millie had taught her to bake one. It was also Millie who'd helped her to embroider the word *Pegs* on a bag they'd made together, and who'd shown her how to pack soil tightly round a plant to make sure all its roots were covered. Millie had always seemed thrilled when she'd done well at school, ready to hear all about it; and she'd never shouted at her for climbing too high in a tree, or for pedalling her bike across the lawn and leaving grooves.

She found herself wondering if Ottilie had a bike.

'I'll come to see you as often as I can when you're in your new place,' she said gently to Millie, 'and I'll send you letters that I expect a nurse, or your niece or nephew will read out to you. They're looking forward to seeing you, and I know everyone will take very good care of you.' She didn't know that, but she wanted to believe it, and it was important for Millie to believe it too, if she was taking anything in.

'Your things are already on their way, so I expect they'll all be set out nicely by the time you get there to make it like home from home. And you're not to worry about the journey, OK? The ambulance crew will look after you and stop every now and again so you can have a drink and go to the loo.' How was she going to do that when she was unable to manage it on her own? Presumably they'd thought of this, and suspecting Millie was already thickly wadded up with incontinence pads she said, 'I'm glad you don't really understand what's going on, because I don't think you'd like it very much, but knowing you as I do I guess you'd try to find a way of laughing about it.'

Millie shuddered a sigh and started to smack her gums. 'Lost me teeth,' she croaked after a while.

Checking her bag and finding them safely tucked away in their case, Alex was about to reassure her when the nurse came back.

'OK, Millie, your chauffeur's here,' she said, coming to stroke Millie's cobwebby hair.

Millie snuffled and tried to lift her head. 'There's lovely, a chauffeur,' she wheezed. 'Is he wearing a hat?'

Alex and the nurse smiled. 'I'm sure he'll put it on if you ask him,' the nurse replied. Then to Alex, 'Would you like to wheel her down?'

Getting up and taking the handles of the chair, Alex could feel the heaviness in her heart becoming more onerous with each step she took. She'd thought, after finding out her mother wanted to be in touch, and having something to look forward to, that it was going to be easier to say goodbye to Millie today, but it wasn't, at all.

'You be good now,' she said, pressing a kiss to Millie's papery forehead before one of the ambulancemen took over in order to push the chair up the ramp into the back of the vehicle. At the top he turned Millie round so Alex could see her, and Alex felt a hundred fractures running through her heart as Millie lifted a spindly old hand to wave.

'Have a lovely time in Mexico,' Alex said shakily. 'Don't forget to send me a postcard, will you?'

'God bless,' Millie whispered. 'You're a lovely girl.'

As Alex choked back a sob, the doors were closed, and moments later the ambulance was driving away.

Alex remained on the kerb watching until it disappeared from view, and somehow knew that she was never going to see the old lady again.

* * *

385

Though it seemed callous to carry on with her day as though Millie's departure had meant no more than something she'd had to fit into the morning, Alex knew that the only way to cope with the sadness was to keep busy. Besides, sitting at home, thinking about the past while waiting for her aunt or her mother to ring, would only make matters worse. So returning to her car she headed off to the supermarket, as planned, going out of her way to pass the Wades' house en route, just in case . . . Though just in case of what she couldn't actually say.

Since the traffic wouldn't allow her to slow up much on the hill, she was given no more than a few fleeting moments to catch a glimpse of the place, which told her nothing of what might be going on inside. She thought of the way Ottilie had wanted to stay with her yesterday, and how her little hand had waved through the stair rails. If only Alex could go into the house! Had she left Ottilie feeling as though she didn't care, had abandoned her even? Or maybe she was happier to be with her parents than seemed likely. Alex wanted more than anything to think that, and yet couldn't quite make herself believe it.

Minutes into her trip round the supermarket she found herself in a tangle of indecision about whether to buy wine that she couldn't afford, for a woman she didn't even know would ring, never mind whether she was even planning to come. In the end, deciding one bottle of red and one of white would be handy anyway, she carried on filling her basket, wondering if she should be buying in enough to cook something for her mother, or if that would just be tempting fate.

Maybe weeks would go by before she heard from her, so it would be crazy to buy anything now. Maybe she wouldn't hear from her at all.

Realising she was getting caught up in a spiral of doubt and self-torment that was going to lead her nowhere she wanted to be, she did her best to switch her mind to other things. However, as the minutes turned into hours the dread of not hearing gave way to hopelessness and then anger. She'd been so ready to paint a saintly picture of her mother in her mind, transform her into an impossible icon of sensitivity and kindness, that she was clearly becoming delusional, desperate even, and utterly pathetic. After all, her mother was a woman who'd been able to give up her only surviving child and had never, in twenty-five years, even tried to see her, much less find out how she was. What kind of person did that make her? OK, she'd been traumatised by a terrible massacre at the time she'd made her decision, but she wasn't in trauma now. For all Alex knew she was a fugitive, a pitiful, obsessed hanger-on who'd spent her life keeping the monster she loved from the hands of the law. The monster who'd slain her parents, her sister, an innocent man, *their son*.

And where was he now? Waiting in the shadows, hoping to meet his daughter at last? Sending his battered wife to fetch her?

If he wanted to see her, if the subject even came up, Alex knew she'd slam the phone straight down again. For her entire life she'd been trying to forget that she carried that man's genes, to keep hidden the fact that she was the child who'd escaped the Temple Fields murders. She shuddered at the very idea of people pitying her, or worse, wondering if she had it in her to do the same. God knew, she'd wondered it about herself often enough – to have the rest of the world shrinking from her in doubt, or avoiding her altogether, would be a living hell.

On arriving home at the end of the afternoon and finding no message on the machine, she braced herself and rang her great-aunt to ask if she'd at least found the number.

'I'm afraid not,' came the reply, 'but I'm sure she'll call again when she's ready.'

Fervently hoping her aunt was right, while wishing she knew when that might be, Alex rang off. She had to do a better job of distracting herself than she was managing, or she was going to drive herself crazy. For this evening at least, it shouldn't be too difficult, because thankfully she'd arranged to get together with Mattie to draw up a list of judges and potential acts for *Mulgrove's Got Talent*.

In the end it was just after noon the following day when the phone rang, and somehow Alex knew instinctively that it was going to be her mother. Quite how she knew she had no idea, it was simply there in her heart, and for one crazy moment she felt too afraid to answer. Then the receiver was in her hand and to cover her nerves she was saying a ludicrously strident 'Hello?'

The woman at the other end sounded hesitant and throaty, with the trace of an accent, as she said, 'Is that Alex?' *Liverpool?* It was where her mother was from, but it didn't sound like that.

'Yes, it is,' she replied, starting to feel oddly light-headed.

'It's Anna Reeves here,' the voice told her. 'Maybe you know me better as Angela Nicholls.'

Experiencing a rush of emotion that was both

forceful and unexpected, Alex tried to answer and found she couldn't. She was speaking to her real mother!

'Helen said it was OK for me to call.'

Somehow managing to get the words out, Alex said, 'Yes, yes, it's fine.'

There was a slight turbulence in a laugh before Anna Reeves said, 'I can hardly believe I'm speaking to you, hearing your voice, knowing you're there, at the end of the line . . . Oh dear, I'm sorry, I promised myself I wouldn't get emotional . . .'

'It's OK,' Alex told her, not realising there were tears on her own cheeks. She was feeling a preposterous, irrepressible urge to turn back time and become three-year-old Charlotte again, to start over and know this woman all her life.

But you have no idea who she is.

'Can I see you?' Anna asked. 'It would mean so much to me, but I understand if you're not willing . . .'

'No, no it's OK. I'd like that,' Alex assured her. *How could she not want it, in spite of how disruptive, even devastating it might prove?*

'I'm at Heathrow now,' Anna said. 'I've just got off a flight, but I can come right away. It'll take me about three hours to get to you if I rent a car.'

Alex tried to assimilate, to make sense of Heathrow, flights, an accent she still couldn't make out.

'Helen told me you're still at the Vicarage,' Anna continued, 'but I believe your pare— Douglas and Myra are no longer with us.'

'That's right.' She was barely listening, was trying to imagine how she might be feeling were she talking to her child for the first time in over twenty-five years. The emotions would be so deep and overwhelming she might not be able to hold it together. Was that how Anna Reeves was feeling?

'I'm sorry to hear it,' Anna was saying. 'I expect it was hard, losing them both in such a short space of time.'

She seemed to know more than Alex might have imagined, but it wouldn't have been difficult to find out about Douglas from the Internet. 'It's been especially hard for Gabby,' she replied. 'She still misses them terribly.'

'Of course. And you?'

Wanting to be truthful, Alex said, 'Yes, I guess I do, in more ways than I expected.'

'Perhaps you'll tell me about them when I come?'

'Of course.' She didn't want to talk about Myra and Douglas, she wanted to hear about her real family, to find out what her mother had been doing all these years. 'Do you know where the Vicarage is?' she asked.

'I think I can remember the way. If I get lost I'll call again.'

'OK. I – I'll look out for you.'

There was a note of wryness in Anna's voice as she remarked, 'You sound very . . . grown up.'

Distantly amused, Alex said, 'I'm twenty-eight, so I guess that qualifies.'

With a catch in her voice, Anna said, 'There aren't words to express how much I've longed for this day. To think I'm going to see you at last, look into your eyes, see your lovely smile . . . I know it's lovely because I've seen you on Facebook.'

Feeling oddly unsettled by that, Alex remained silent.

'I found your theatre page,' Anna explained. 'I hope you don't mind.'

'No, not all,' Alex replied, not sure if it was true. 'I hope I . . . I hope I didn't disappoint you.' *Why had she said that, what would it matter if she had?*

'Quite the reverse,' Anna assured her. 'I'm afraid it's me who's more likely to disappoint you, but I'm going to do my best not to.'

For several minutes after putting the phone down Alex could barely make herself think straight. Somewhere deep inside she was sensing some sort of panic trying to emerge, but she wasn't going to allow it. She had to keep control of herself and try not to spoil what was about to happen with the dread of her worst nightmares coming true. Her mother had said nothing about Gavril Albescu, and not for a single moment had she sounded like the kind of person who'd lived her life in the shadow of the maniac who'd killed almost everyone in her family, and had intended to kill her too, at least at the time. Except how did anyone who'd been to hell and back sound? Probably just as capable of conveying gentleness and warmth as anyone else.

It was crazy, anyway, to think that her mother had gone to be with her father. He'd wanted her dead, had injured her so badly it was a miracle she'd survived, so what would have stopped him trying to kill her again?

So you see, she told herself, *all this nonsense about them being together for the past twenty-five years can only be that, plain nonsense.*

Of course her mother could be about to tell her that everything she believed about her father was wrong, that it wasn't him who'd slain her family, but the gangsters who'd controlled him. Maybe they'd been running, hiding from them all these years, and had been too terrified to come near their daughter in case the killers realised who she was. That could be it. Her mother had loved her father, and he was a good man really, who'd fallen in with the wrong people and had never been able to escape them.

If that was so, what had happened to make her mother feel safe enough to contact her now? The obvious answer was that her father had died, but maybe it was more sinister than that. Maybe times had become so hard for them that they were desperate for help. Her mother had known that Myra and Douglas were dead, so maybe she'd also found out that the house was for sale. She could be presuming that she, Alex, was to receive half the money, so she was going to ask Alex to spare whatever she could.

If her suspicions proved right . . . She felt dizzied and sickened by the prospect, but in that case her birth parents were going to find her of no use at all. They might even end up despising her as much as she would them.

Feeling tears pricking her eyes, she went to tear off a square of kitchen roll and tried to shake herself free of her fears. For a few precious moments during the call she'd allowed herself to hear her mother as a kind and decent woman who meant her no harm at all. She must hold on to that and try not to judge her before she'd even met her.

At three o'clock she went to position herself at the sitting-room window, waiting for a stranger's car to come up the hill and stop outside the house. She could handle this, she was telling herself. Though she knew more than most just what kind of damage a parent could inflict on a child, she was going to find the courage to face whatever might be thrown at her today. And she was going to find it because if the children in her care who'd had all kinds of hell thrown at them, far worse than anything she was ever likely to experience – if they could cope, then so could she.

What she wouldn't allow herself to think about was how broken, how ruined and unreachable so many – too many – of them eventually became.

Chapter Eighteen

It was just after four o'clock when a black Renault Megane turned out of the village and came slowly up the hill. As Alex waited for it to stop her heart was in her throat, each second seeming to pound like a hammer in her chest, each fear struggling to quash each hope. Then, realising she should go to open the door she ran into the hall, pausing at the mirror for a brief moment to check the mascara and lip shimmer she'd applied half an hour ago. She wanted it to look as though she'd made an effort, but not so much of one as to appear needy or foolish.

Hearing the slam of a car door, followed by the squeal of the front gate, she inhaled deeply to try and press back her nerves. *She was about to meet her mother – her* mother *– for the first time since she was three. Please don't let me be a disappointment, or do anything to screw it up.*

Please don't let her be a disappointment either.

Anna Reeves was already halfway up the path by the time Alex opened the door, and as their eyes found each other's Alex felt a bolt of unsteadying recognition hit her heart. She looked exactly like the woman in the photos, only older. She was chic in a casual way, blonde and slim and a little taller than Alex, but they were very alike, even she, Alex, could see it. Anna's eyes were suddenly filling with tears, her lips trembling with emotion.

'Oh my goodness,' she whispered, putting a hand to her mouth. 'You're so lovely, so like . . . so like Yvonne.'

Yvonne, her aunt. How hard this must be for her mother. 'And like you?' Alex said, feeling strangely detached and slightly breathless.

'Yes, yes, like me,' Anna laughed through a sob, and started to raise her arms for an embrace before suddenly holding back. 'May I?' she asked tentatively.

Seeing no reason why not, and feeling perhaps she wanted it too, Alex nodded, and as her mother's arms went round her she felt awkward for a moment, stiff and embarrassed. Then something stirred deep inside her, a memory perhaps woken by what seemed like something familiar – perhaps it was the smell of her.

In the end Alex started to laugh. 'You have to let me breathe,' she told her mother.

Anna laughed too, and putting a hand to Alex's face she gazed it at wonderingly, incredulously, as though unable to make herself believe this was real. 'I have dreamt so many times about how this might happen,' she said in her faintly accented voice. 'I was so afraid the day might never come, but it's here at last and you . . . you're all grown up. My baby girl, my precious little angel . . .' Her lips trembled and as she tried to stop herself breaking down, Alex, the professional, drew her into a comforting hug, the way she had so many mothers over the years.

Where were her own emotions? Why didn't she seem fully in touch with them?

'I'm sorry,' Anna whispered, trying to swallow her tears. 'I shall pull myself together in a minute.'

'Let's go inside,' Alex said, turning her to the door. 'Would you like some tea? I expect you're tired after the drive.'

'I'm too happy to see you to be tired.' Her eyes shone with mirth. 'I'm afraid I want to keep hugging you just to make sure you're real, or maybe it's to satisfy my arms, because they've felt so empty all these years. Sorry, does that embarrass you? I don't mean to. I should think before I speak.'

'It's fine,' Alex assured her, leading her into the kitchen. 'It's been the same for me, I guess, but now I have a mother, a *real* mother who gave birth to me . . .' She coloured deeply. 'How's that for embarrassing us both?' she said wryly.

'It's wonderful,' Anna laughed, 'because I am that person, and I remember it so well. You were such a precious gift that I was afraid, right from the start, that I loved you too much.' The laughter faded from her eyes. 'If I hadn't maybe things would have turned out differently, but I guess it's impossible to say that for sure. All I do know is that I've never given up hope of one day being with you again, and now here we are. That day has finally come.'

Though she wanted to launch straight into a hundred questions, Alex's inherent politeness made her put them aside, along with all the resentment and bitterness she could feel trying to assert themselves. They wouldn't be helpful now, and she would only end up hurting herself if she did or said something to spoil this reunion before it had even begun. 'I should make us that tea,' she said. 'Or would you prefer something stronger?'

Anna took a moment to think. 'Shall we have tea for now and save the stronger for later? I mean, if you don't have to rush off anywhere.'

'No, I don't,' Alex assured her, while liking the sense of there being a later. 'I have ordinary Tetley's, Earl Grey or peppermint.'

'What are you going to have?'

'Well, I quite like peppermint.'

'Then I shall have that too.' Anna looked around the kitchen, taking it all in.

Is she imagining me growing up here? Alex was wondering. *How is it comparing to the kind of life we might have had together?*

'Is Gabby out?' Anna asked, hanging her bag on the back of a chair.

Speaking over her, Alex said, 'I didn't realise you were following me on Facebook.'

Anna flushed. 'I was tempted to let you know, many times, but it just didn't seem the right way to introduce myself.'

Accepting that it probably wouldn't have been, Alex said, 'Gabby's married with two children and lives in Devon. It's only me here now, until the place is sold, which actually is about to happen.' *Please don't let her already know that. Please, please.*

Anna was looking concerned. 'Is that going to be difficult for you?' she asked sympathetically. 'I expect you're quite attached to it, having grown up here?'

'Yes, I am,' Alex admitted, feeling a small rush of relief – she had to stop being suspicious, nothing bad was going to happen, she could see already that this woman, *her mother*, wasn't here to harm her.

But where was her father?

'It has to go, though,' she added. Then, 'Sorry,

I'm forgetting my manners, would you like to use the bathroom?'

Anna brightened in a mischievous sort of way. 'That would be lovely, thank you.'

'It's at the top of the stairs, first door you come to.'

Watching her leave, Alex couldn't help admiring the way her silvery-blonde hair was folded into an elegant pleat at the back of her head, and how young she appeared from behind in black jeans and a cream-coloured sweater. They had such similar builds, she realised, that at a distance they could probably be mistaken for one another.

Taking two mugs from a cupboard she glanced at the phone as it rang, and decided to let it go through to messages.

'Hey, it's me,' Gabby said from the machine, and Alex felt instinctively glad that Anna was no longer in the room. 'Have you heard anything yet? Don't worry too much if you haven't. Martin and I have been talking it over, and we really think you should tread very carefully with this. I know your great-aunt seemed satisfied that the woman who rang her is your mother, but she's an old lady now so it could be dead easy to trick her. I mean, obviously, it might all be on the level, but we reckon, before you agree to see anyone or do anything, you should let one of us check her out first, or maybe be there with you. OK, that's more or less what I rang to say, and I hope you understand that we're only thinking of you and trying to make sure no one does anything to hurt you. You know where I am if you want to chat. Lots of love to you – the twins send theirs too.'

As the line went dead Alex walked over to the

machine and erased the message. She didn't feel angry with Gabby, but she wasn't especially thrilled to be treated as though she had no common sense where something so important was concerned. Besides, what did Gabby imagine anyone could possibly stand to gain from Alex Lake – apart from a share in the proceeds of the house that Gabby already knew were entirely hers? Anyway, once Gabby met Anna for herself she'd have no problem believing that she was exactly who she was claiming to be.

As Anna came back into the room she was smiling and looking at Alex so fondly that Alex almost felt herself starting to thaw.

'Are you OK?' Anna asked curiously. 'You're looking a little . . . worried?'

Alex shrugged. 'Not really. I suppose I'm just trying to get used to the fact that you're here. This time yesterday I had no idea where in the world you might be, and now . . .' She threw out a hand. 'Life is so strange, isn't it?'

With a captivating irony Anna said, 'Well, that would be one way of putting it.'

Though Alex smiled, she was thinking of what her mother had gone through all those years ago, and felt herself flush. Life had been a great deal more than merely strange for her. 'You said earlier, on the phone, that you'd just flown in,' she reminded her. 'I was wondering where from?'

Anna raised an eyebrow. 'Well, this morning I arrived from Dubai, but my journey actually started two days ago, in Auckland.'

Alex's eyes widened with astonishment. 'Auckland, New Zealand?' she asked, realising now where the accent was from – and thinking that it had never even occurred to her that her mother could be somewhere so far away.

And her father?

Anna was pulling out a chair. 'May I?'

'Of course,' Alex quickly replied. 'Sorry, I should have . . .'

'It's OK.' Sitting down, Anna rested her hands on the table as she said, 'There's such a lot to tell you . . . Of course, I had it all worked out, exactly how I was going to go about it, but now I seem hardly to know where to begin. However, in answer to your question, yes, Auckland, New Zealand. It's been my home for the past twenty-four years.'

Ever since she'd left the hospital.

Her head spinning, Alex reached into a cupboard for the tea bags and dropped one into each mug. Thinking of her mother being so far away all these years was throwing her quite badly. It meant that she'd never been close, not even in the moments Alex had felt sure that she was – unless perhaps they'd been thinking about each other at the same moment.

How were they ever to have a relationship from now on, being on opposite sides of the globe?

Why had she bothered to come?

'Thank you,' Anna smiled, as Alex handed her the tea. 'You know, I'm longing to hear all about you, what it was like growing up here. It's a lovely old house. I can imagine you running around, having a wild old time with Gabby, who's how much older than you?'

'Four years,' Alex replied shortly. She could feel herself starting to shake. She didn't want to talk about Gabby, or this house, or herself growing up; she wanted answers, truths, apologies . . . 'I'm sorry,' she suddenly blurted, 'I can understand that you have questions, but you've just turned up here, out of the blue, telling me you're living in New Zealand, not giving me the first idea of what you want from me, or why you've decided to come now . . .' A sob mangled her voice. 'I don't need to be messed around,' she choked angrily. 'I've been doing fine without you all these years, and if you're going to start disrupting my life . . .'

Anna was reaching for her hand, but Alex snatched it away.

'Please don't think like that,' Anna implored. 'I only want what's good and right for you, and I'm sorry I didn't give you more warning. I just didn't know how to go about it and I can see I'm not getting it right now . . .'

'But you've been stalking me on Facebook!'

Anna flinched. 'Not *stalking*,' she protested. 'Just needing to know about you, feeling proud of you and wishing we were a part of one another's lives.'

'We would have been if you hadn't *abandoned* me.'

Anna's face turned white and for several moments, as the word echoed horribly between them, there was a silence that neither of them could fill.

In the end, Anna said, 'I was always afraid you might see it like that, but that's not how it was, I swear it. What I did . . . The reasons I left you . . .' She took a gasp of air as she put a hand to her head.

As she watched her Alex found herself wanting to apologise, to go back and start again. She hated seeing how shaken she was, and knowing she'd caused it, but what did she expect?

'I'll tell you everything,' Anna said quietly. 'Of course I will, it's why I'm here, at least in part, but first I need you to tell me how much you already know. I'm sure you've read newspaper stories from back then, but do you actually remember anything of the . . . of the time before the rector took you into his family?'

Realising with a rush of guilt how difficult it was going to be for her mother to put the events of that terrible night into words, Alex shook her head. 'Not really. I have vague sorts of flashbacks sometimes about being by the sea with a man who keeps swinging me up and round and round. I've always thought it was my father, or grandfather . . .'

Anna smiled sadly and seemed to nod as she lowered her eyes for a moment. 'Anything else?' she prompted.

'I have dreams too,' Alex confessed, 'but they're memories really, of being shut in a cupboard and trying to reach the latch . . . The rector told me . . . My brother, Hugo, is with me . . .' She broke off as Anna seemed to flinch.

'Hugo,' Anna whispered, her eyes distant, as though seeing back across the years.

Alex waited, almost feeling the torment in her mother's heart. Whatever resentment she might have stored up towards her, she mustn't ever let herself forget how much worse the past had been for her.

'Go on,' Anna said finally.

Sorry she was putting her through this, but feeling she had to, Alex said, 'Hugo . . . told me to stay where I was, that he'd come back for me . . .'

Anna's head was down, and Alex noticed how tightly her hands were clenched. 'Do you . . . ? Do you remember me telling you to keep quiet?' she asked. 'I said you mustn't make a sound because evil men were coming . . . ?' She broke off and brought her eyes back to Alex's. They were so full of tragedy, a hopeless kind of despair, that Alex wanted to stop her going any further. 'I told you I'd come back for you,' she whispered hoarsely, 'but I didn't. I couldn't . . .'

'I know how badly you were injured,' Alex assured her.

Anna was shaking her head; there was no colour in her face now, her eyes were glazed with pain. 'He was insane, evil,' she said wretchedly. 'I knew he could be cruel, I'd seen it plenty of times by then, but I never imagined he could do anything like that.' She took a breath, as though to help her continue. 'If only I hadn't gone to Holland to start my gap year. If I'd listened to my friend Sarah and gone with her to Paris instead, I'd never have met him. But I didn't listen. I wanted to go to Amsterdam, so that's what I did, and he . . .' She swallowed hard and bunched her hands even more tightly together, as though trying to bolster herself. 'This might be even harder to believe than it is to say,' she whispered, 'but he was so charismatic, so handsome, and his foreign accent and air of confidence made him impossible to resist, at least for the highly impressionable, adventure-seeking teenager that I was then. He swept me off my feet . . . I'd never known anyone like him. Of course, I had no idea what he was involved in, the type of people he was mixing with, I only found out about that later. At the time I thought he was an ambitious, romantic young man who'd escaped the oppressive regime in his country and was now driving a lorry to make enough money to start his career. I don't think he ever told me what that career was to be. I didn't ask, I don't suppose I cared. I was so besotted, so ready to believe in him and whatever he wanted to be, that it didn't matter to me, as long as we were together.

'Then I got pregnant and he didn't even hesitate; he wanted to marry me, and it was what I wanted too, so after knowing each other for only four months we made the commitment. My parents were horrified. They hadn't even met him, and said they had no wish to either. They just wanted me home so they could sort out the mess I was in. They were furious, absolutely beside themselves, but at the time nothing, no one, seemed to matter to me but him. Afterwards, I realised he probably only married me to get easy access in and out of England, but I was so convinced by his euphoria on our wedding day that I truly believed he loved me.'

She swallowed, took a breath and started again. 'We moved to Liverpool quite soon after the wedding – at least I did. His work commitments meant that he had to spend most of his time in Europe, but he came to see me at least once a month, more often after Hugo was born.' She seemed to drift for a moment, caught in the memories of a time Alex suspected felt almost unreal to her now.

'It was wonderful being close to my parents again,' she continued. 'I'd missed them so much, more than I'd realised, and for Hugo's sake they tried harder with Gavril. I knew they still didn't trust him, and I'm sure he knew it too, but I don't think their opinion ever mattered to him. He was pleasant enough to them though, and even seemed grateful at times for the care they took of me and Hugo. I never told them, because I couldn't bear to, that I'd realised even before Hugo was born what a terrible mistake I'd made. I knew they'd try to make me divorce him and I was afraid of what he might do if I did. He'd never been violent with me, but by then I'd started to suspect what his business was, so I knew his morality, as well as his background, was very different from mine. Worse, far far worse, was the fear that he'd take Hugo away.

'So I stayed married to him, even pretended to love him and be pleased to entertain the friends he brought home. They were always men, hard drinkers, smokers, gamblers ... They spoke so many languages, Russian, Spanish, Chinese, that I could never understand what they were saying, but I didn't have to be fluent in anything to work out what they were talking about. It made me sick to my stomach to think of the young girls, kids most of them, that they were smuggling into the country to sell on for prostitution. Perhaps they were doing the pimping themselves, I never knew. I couldn't allow myself to know too much, it would be too dangerous and I had to think of Hugo.'

She lifted her tea, but didn't drink, and Alex could hardly begin to imagine the hell she was reliving.

'Hugo was about eighteen months old when my parents decided to buy a house overlooking the sea in Kesterly,' she went on. 'It was where we used to go for our holidays as children, and they'd always planned to retire there. For the first couple of years they had the place they were still working, so we only used it in the summer, and at Christmas, but then my dad had an accident at the docks and had to take early retirement. So they sold up in Liverpool and moved down south, and because my job at the local chemist's was easy enough to give up, I talked Gavril into letting me and Hugo go with them. The intention was for Gavril to sell our house in Liverpool so we could buy somewhere close to my parents, but it never happened. Gavril hung on to it – I guess it had become too handy a meeting place close to the docks for him to give up. I was glad of it though, more than glad, because by then I hated him almost as much as I feared him, so the last thing I wanted was him coming to Kesterly too. What we were all hoping for, more than anything, was that he'd get caught during one of his smuggling operations, or that he'd at least run out of interest in me and Hugo and leave us alone. But for almost two years he came every month to see us, taking over our lives, our home, practically everything we did, scaring us all half to death, even Hugo who he prized above everything, or so he said. Then you came along, and he was so besotted with you that he began insisting we move back to Liverpool where he'd be able to see more of us. The thought wasn't only horrifying because of having to be near him, but because of what he might do to us if he ever found out the truth about you.'

Alex's heart caught a beat as she frowned in confusion.

Anna's eyes came to hers and she smiled tenderly as she said, 'You don't know, do you?'

Alex was barely breathing. 'Know what?' she whispered.

'Gavril Albescu wasn't your father.'

Alex reeled, and almost gasped. She couldn't take this in; it was too much, too strange, too unexpected . . . *Gavril Albescu, the maniac, the murderer, wasn't her father.* All her life she'd been afraid of her genes, ashamed of her birthright, and now . . . She stared at Anna. 'So . . . ?' she faltered. 'So who . . . ?'

In a voice that was as prideful as it was gentle, Anna said, 'Your father was Nigel Carrington.'

Alex's mouth fell open. She didn't understand. Wasn't he her aunt's boyfriend? Quite suddenly dry, racking sobs began tearing from the depths of her. *The monster wasn't her father. She had a normal father like everyone else.* Someone she could feel proud of, talk about, even think about . . . As she struggled to catch her breath, Anna came to put her arms around her.

'Why . . . Why didn't anyone ever tell me?' Alex managed to choke, pushing her away. 'All my life I've lived with the horror, the terrible shame of being his . . .'

'I know, and I'm sorry, I truly am, but it was the only way of keeping you safe.'

Alex couldn't take it in; it wasn't making any sense.

'I loved your father, I wanted to be with him more than anything, but I was terrified of Gavril . . .' She inhaled raggedly. 'He found out, of course, I don't know how, but that wasn't the worst of it. It was when he realised you weren't his that he . . . He couldn't stand it. He adored you . . . He told me we'd all pay for what we'd done to him and . . .' She swallowed '. . . we did.'

As she turned away Alex watched her go to the window and put her hands over her face, as though blocking out the appalling memories of that night. She regretted pushing her mother back there, in spite of what she'd learned about herself. How terrible it must be, even after all these years, to revisit the horror of those she loved being massacred in front of her very eyes. Her parents, her sister, her son and the man she'd loved. *The man she'd loved.* The man who'd fathered three-year-old Charlotte; the man she, Alex, as Charlotte, should have grown up with.

Nigel Carrington was her father.

Her throat was tightening again. It was so hard to take in.

She knew so little about him. All these years she'd thought he was her aunt's boyfriend, an innocent victim who'd been in the wrong place at the wrong time. In fact, he'd probably been Gavril Albescu's main target that night – and so had she. The miracle of her survival was far greater than she had previously thought. Indeed, the only conceivable reason she and her mother had survived was because fate had decided that it wasn't their time.

Why them and not her grandparents, or her aunt, or her brother, who'd all been blameless in the deception that had driven Albescu over the edge?

'Are you all right?' she whispered, as her mother came back to the table.

Though she was horribly pale, Anna forced the ghost of a smile as she said, 'I try never to think about it, but I knew I'd have to today.'

'I'm sorry, I feel as though . . .'

'No, don't apologise. You have a right to know what happened back then, you've always had that right, but it simply wasn't possible to tell you before.'

Alex searched her eyes. 'So why is it possible now?' she asked.

Anna took a breath. 'Because Gavril Albescu is dead,' she replied.

Feeling an unsteadying rush of relief at the words, Alex struggled for something to say, but what was there to say about the death of a man who'd robbed her of most of her family?

'For as long as he was alive,' Anna continued, 'I never dared to come near you in case he was having me watched. He said he would, and made sure I knew it, because he sent someone to the hospital while I was still recovering to give me a message. He said that I would never escape him, that he would always be there, in the shadows, and one day he would make me take him to you. He said many other things that I feel it best not to repeat now; they were the threats, the *ravings* of a madman. The trouble was, he'd already shown me what he was capable of, so I never doubted that he meant you harm. He meant it for me too, which was why, when I left the hospital, the police arranged for me to go to a safe place while my name was changed and papers were drawn up for me to start a new life. I think they might have considered using me as bait to try and catch him, but someone must have decided that I'd already been through enough, because they never did.

'The only person from my past I was allowed to remain in contact with was Sarah, my best friend from school, the one I should have gone travelling with. She'd moved to New Zealand with her husband around the time you were born, and when she heard what had happened she flew over to visit me in hospital. She said that if I ever needed a home, I'd always have one with her, so when the time came, I got in touch with her. It wasn't only that I had nowhere else to go, and no one else I could trust, it was that New Zealand felt far enough away for Gavril never to find me.'

She looked at Alex, and Alex could almost feel the pain that showed in her eyes. 'The only problem was the biggest problem of all, leaving you. I couldn't bring myself to go without you, and yet I knew for your sake that I had to. I had no idea if Gavril or any of his people were watching me, but

I felt that they were so I couldn't take the risk of leading them to you.' She bit her lip and pushed herself past the emotion. 'Before I left the country the rector came to see me. He was such a sweet man. I knew you were with good people, and he assured me you'd settled in well with his family and that you and his daughter were already close. I asked him if you called his wife Mummy and he said that you did. It broke my heart all over again, but I realised that to take you away from the people you'd come to think of as your family would be an unforgivably selfish thing to do when I knew I'd be putting you in danger.'

She closed her eyes, as though trying to overcome the devastation of her world. 'If Nigel had lived,' she went on shakily, 'maybe we'd have found a way for us all to be together, but he . . . I wanted to contact his mother to let her know where you were, but she was old even then, and I knew she was terrified for her life. She only visited me once in hospital, and that was to tell me that someone had turned up at Nigel's funeral. They hadn't spoken to anyone, she said, they'd just hung around watching, and she'd felt sure they were looking for you. So she was very sorry, but she didn't feel able to be a part of your life. My Aunt Helen felt much the same way. No one had approached her directly, but she'd been followed often enough to be certain that someone was watching her, and who else would it be but Gavril or one of his people?'

Her eyes looked searchingly into Alex's as she said, 'I'm so sorry. I never wanted to leave you, I swear it, but do you understand now why I did?'

Alex nodded. 'Of course,' she replied. How could she not when it was only natural for a mother to do what she must to save her child? It just felt so awful to think of all they'd been cheated of.

'Is this too much all at once?' Anna asked, after a while. 'Maybe I should stop now.'

Alex shook her head, though in truth she was feeling overwhelmed . . . Nigel Carrington, not Gavril Albescu, was her father. It was cause for so much relief, celebration even, that were it not for the fact that she'd never know her real father now, she might be feeling far less heavy-hearted. 'I thought . . . I read that your sister, Yvonne, was seeing Nigel,' she said quietly. 'I had no idea that you and he . . .'

'It was what we wanted everyone to think, that he and Yvonne were together. It gave him the freedom to come and go from the house as he pleased, to be with you and me without raising Gavril's suspicions. I was making plans to divorce Gavril, of course, and Nigel was all for telling him straight, but I was so afraid of what Gavril might do that I wouldn't let him.

'I guess the biggest tragedy of all is that the day before it all happened, my father and Nigel had gone to the police to offer to work with them in whatever way they could to help them arrest him. It was the only way we'd ever be rid of him, we felt. The police took them up on the offer, but there was no time to set anything up. It all happened . . . We got a call about ten minutes before he arrived to say he was coming. I don't know who rang, it must have been one of his people . . . If we hadn't received that call we'd never have had time to hide you.'

She looked down at her tea as she said, 'You'll probably have read about the attack being revenge

411

killings for reporting the trafficking to the authorities. It was what the police wanted everyone to
think. They felt it was best no one knew you weren't
Gavril's, it would only increase the danger you were
already in. Thank God they took that decision – if
they hadn't . . .' She shook her head, neither needing
nor wanting to finish the sentence.

'A lot of arrests were made over the weeks that
followed,' she continued, 'but Gavril somehow
managed to slip the net and as we know, they never
did manage to find him.'

'Did you know where he was?' Alex asked.

Anna shook her head again. 'I expect he was
shipped straight out of the country before any
blocks were set up. Maybe he returned to Romania,
but I'm sure they looked for him there, so who
knows where he went. He had contacts all over
Europe and Asia, and any one of them could have
helped him to change his name, probably even his
appearance, to keep him out of jail. In truth, I have
no idea how he managed to escape the law for as
long as he did.'

'So how did you find out he was dead?'

Anna swallowed drily. 'His sister, Erina, contacted
me to let me know.'

Alex's eyes widened. 'How did she find you?'

'I've no idea, but it shook me up terribly when
she did, because it probably meant that he'd known
all along where I was and could have struck at any
time.'

'Do you think that is the case?'

Anna nodded. 'There were times when I felt as
though I was being watched, but then nothing
would happen so I'd end up putting it down to
paranoia. If it weren't for those feelings I'd have

tried to find you a long time ago, but I was terrified that it was all he was waiting for. I still don't know if it was all in my mind, but the fact that Erina got in touch to tell me he was dead . . . She must have known that he still had a hold over me, that it was important for me to know that I no longer had to fear him. In her message she said that it was a great relief to her that he was no longer in the world, and she felt sure it would be for me too.'

'Weren't you afraid it was a trick?'

'Yes, of course, but Bob – he's my husband who I'll tell you all about later.' Her expression had visibly softened. 'I know you'll love him if you meet him and I hope you will, because he's one of those people it's impossible not to love. For now, though, all you need to know about him is that he had everything thoroughly checked out before either of us was ready to believe that Gavril Albescu really had gone to meet his Maker.'

'So when . . .' Alex cleared her throat. 'When did he die?'

Anna nodded, as though she'd expected the question. 'About a year ago. It's taken most of that time for us to be fully convinced that it really was him who'd been killed in a shooting in Ghana, but once we were I was desperate to come and find you. The only problem was deciding on the best way to do it. Bob was all for inviting you to New Zealand, mainly because you're living so close to where everything went so terribly wrong . . . He's worried about how upsetting it might be for me to be back in the area, but I knew I could handle it as long as everything went well with you.'

Alex's heart skipped a beat. Were things going well between them? On the face of it they seemed

413

to be, more or less, but there were still so many emotions and fears churning around inside her that she couldn't be sure how she was really feeling about anything. Unwilling to explore it now, she said, 'How long have you been married?'

Anna smiled. 'We've recently celebrated our twentieth wedding anniversary, so quite a long time.'

Twenty years. Two whole decades of being happy and loved, living in a world with people Alex couldn't even begin to imagine, while she, Alex, had felt like an outsider in her own home. She'd spent so much time wondering where her mother was and why she didn't come. She had the answers now, but still wasn't sure they were enough. 'And do you . . . Do you have any children?' she asked.

'No,' Anna answered, her eyes coming to Alex's. 'I only have you.'

Though it was selfish, Alex realised it was what she'd hoped to hear.

'Bob has a son and a daughter from his first marriage,' Anna went on. 'He's ten years older than me, so they're both in their thirties. They live close by and Shelley, his daughter, is married to Philip. They have a little boy, Craig, who's just turned eight and is utterly adorable, and a ten-year-old, Danni, who's the bossiest yet sweetest little minx on the planet.' She was smiling so fondly that Alex found herself smiling too. 'Bob's son Rick,' Anna continued, 'is engaged to Kate who is the niece of my dear friend Sarah who I've already told you about. They're due to get married next summer.'

Not quite sure what to say to that, Alex simply let her continue.

'They're all very keen for me to pass on how much they're hoping to meet you,' Anna said. 'Bob's even posted a greeting online with an invitation to come whenever you like, *and* he's offering to pay for your ticket.'

Feeling herself withdrawing from that, Alex replied, 'That's very generous of him, but I don't think . . . I mean, I'm not sure . . .'

'Don't worry, you don't have to make a decision about anything until you feel ready to. It's just his way, and mine, of letting you know how welcome you'll be if you do decide to come.'

It was almost midnight by the time Alex turned out the light next to her bed, knowing that sleep was probably still a long way off, given how deeply conflicted she was feeling. On the one hand she could easily let elation take over, but on the other she was still horribly anxious and doubtful. It was the fact that her mother lived in New Zealand that was bothering her the most, she realised, since she could see no point to them being in each other's lives now, with so much distance between them. Wouldn't it have been better simply to have left things the way they were?

Her mother was just along the landing in Alex's old room, having been persuaded to stay rather than try to book herself into the pub. Alex suspected she'd all but passed out as soon as her head had hit the pillow, given how jet-lagged she must be, but her need to hear all about Alex's young life had kept her awake until long after she might normally have dropped.

As she lay in the darkness with the unsettling emotions of the day still coasting about inside her,

Alex could feel the demon of dread growing larger all the time. How long was her mother planning to stay? Surely she wouldn't have come all this way just to turn around and go back again, but maybe she had? Or there might be friends from the past she was hoping to catch up with, old haunts she wanted to visit. Presumably she'd want to see her family's grave, and perhaps the one belonging to Nigel Carrington. *My father*, Alex said softly to herself, and though it seemed strange, as if she might in some way be fooling herself, at the same time she was aware of a sense of calm surpassing the loss. She knew from what she'd read that he'd been a master carpenter and had lived somewhere on Exmoor. She needed to find out as much as she could about him, and felt sure her mother would be ready to tell, provided she was going to be around long enough. Perhaps there was family it would be safe for them to see now. They could go together if her mother was willing; they might even receive a warm welcome.

How special and yet strange it would seem to have a family of her own. One whose blood ran in her veins, whose history she shared.

Recalling Bob's invite to New Zealand, she lay thinking about it for a while. *New Zealand*! It seemed so exotic, so far away and impossible to imagine. What was his family like? Did they really want to meet her? Though she'd baulked at the idea of going earlier, she was finding herself becoming quite curious now, even intrigued. Perhaps when she spoke to Tommy tomorrow she'd explore the possibility of taking a fortnight at Christmas.

'Oh, Alex, that would be wonderful,' Anna smiled happily, when Alex suggested it to her at around four a.m. They were curled snugly at either end of the sofa now, having found each other awake several minutes ago when Alex had crept along the landing just to make sure her mother was OK.

'Obviously I can't make any promises,' Alex said, 'but I can give it a go.' She could feel herself starting to tense again as she struggled with the urge to say what was on her mind. In the end she just blurted it out. 'I was wondering how long you're planning to stay. Only I have to work, you see, and I expect you've got other people you want to visit . . . Well, I just wanted to get some idea of what your plans might be.'

Anna started to answer, but Alex hadn't finished.

'If you're going to fly off straight away,' she cut in, 'that's fine, I don't have a problem with it, I just need to know, that's all.'

Anna was smiling tenderly. 'Well, actually, I was hoping,' she said, 'I mean, if it's all right with you, to spend as much time with you as you can spare for the next two weeks.' She grimaced jokily. 'I thought you might feel that was long enough to begin with, but if you think it's too long you must say.'

Since she hadn't had any clear idea what to expect, all Alex knew was relief that her mother hadn't planned to go rushing off again. 'No, it's fine,' she replied.

'I'll be happy to entertain myself during the day while you work,' Anna continued, 'and maybe I can have a meal waiting for you when you get home at night. Or we could go out to eat, whichever you prefer.'

Finding herself entranced by the idea of her mother cooking for her, Alex said, 'I don't mind.'

She wouldn't mention how short she was of money which would make it difficult to eat out, nor was she going to ask her mother to join her in her search for somewhere to live. The kinds of places she was looking at were too dark and depressing; she really didn't want anyone to know where she might end up. 'I'll call my team leader in the morning,' she told Anna, 'to see if I can rearrange a few things this week. I'll still have to visit the children in my caseload, obviously, I couldn't let them down. In fact, there's one, Ottilie, who I have to see tomorrow because I told her on Friday that I'd take her to the zoo after nursery.'

Anna was twinkling. 'Ottilie. What a pretty name,' she declared. 'How old is she?'

Smiling too as she pictured Ottilie's sweet little face, Alex said, 'Three and a half, but she's quite small for her age. Intelligent though, she picks things up very quickly and has an amazing understanding of what's going on, but she's so shy it's not always easy to know what she's really thinking.'

'Dear thing,' Anna murmured. 'What's happened for you to be involved with her?'

Alex sighed and shook her head. 'It's what I'm trying to find out, but there are certainly problems with her mother. Very probably with her father too, but he's a tricky customer. I think he'd like nothing better than to be rid of me pretty damned fast, but I can't see that happening any time soon, not with the way things are.'

As Anna started to reply she lost it to a yawn.

'You must be tired again by now,' Alex said, getting to her feet.

'Mm, I guess I am,' Anna admitted, standing up too, 'but before we go back to bed I have a suggestion. How about I come to the zoo with you and Ottilie tomorrow? Would that be allowed?'

Alex's eyes widened with surprise. 'I don't see why not,' she replied. 'In fact, it might be good for Ottilie to get to know more people.'

Chapter Nineteen

'What do you mean?' Alex cried into the phone as she drove through the glistening country lanes towards Kesterly. 'Why can't Ottilie go to nursery today?'

'She has an extremely bad cold,' Brian Wade replied stiffly, 'which she almost certainly picked up when you got caught in the rain on Friday.'

Thinking of how long ago Friday seemed now, while having to concede that might well be true, Alex said, 'OK, I'll pop in to see her, and try to cheer her up.'

'Thank you, but as you've apparently escaped it yourself, I wouldn't want you to catch it.'

'I'm not worried about that. Has she seen a doctor if it's as serious as you say?'

'As a matter of fact, Dr Aiden was passing on Saturday so he dropped in to see us. He was of the opinion that she shouldn't go out until tomorrow at the earliest. Hopefully, by then the worst of it will have passed.'

Having no reasonable grounds to push her protest any further, Alex said, 'OK, well thanks for letting me know. I'll be on this number if there's anything I can do.'

After ringing off she was about to fork off towards

the office when she decided to keep going and drop in on the Wades anyway. From the number that had come up on her mobile, she knew that Mr Wade was at work, so there shouldn't be any risk of bumping into him. And since Mrs Wade might well not answer the door she needn't be too worried about upsetting her, either. On the other hand, if the highly unpredictable Mrs Wade did let her in, she'd be able to see Ottilie and satisfy herself that Brian Wade was telling the truth.

Funny how she never believed a word that man said.

In the event, she didn't even have to press the bell before Erica Wade was pulling open the door and asking her what she wanted. 'Didn't my husband tell you Ottilie's ill?' she demanded.

'Yes, he did, but I thought I'd call in and see how she is.'

Erica's face twitched. She seemed stymied, then suddenly, as the idea apparently came to her, she said, 'She's sleeping.'

Alex's eyebrows rose as her insides gave a flutter of unease. Not bothering to hide her disbelief, she replied, 'Then I'll go very quietly so's not to wake her.' She was determined now not to leave without at least laying eyes on Ottilie.

Unexpectedly, after a moment's ludicrous stand-off, Erica simply shrugged and moved aside.

Going past her, Alex ran up the stairs, and gently pushing open Ottilie's door she found, to her surprise, that Ottilie was sitting on the floor trying to fasten the Velcro on her trainers. She was wearing her coat and jeans and Boots's head was peeking out of the top of her bag.

'Hello,' Alex said softly.

Ottilie started and looked up.

'And where are you off to?' Alex asked.

Ottilie seemed confused, then worried. 'With you?' she replied uncertainly.

Realising Ottilie was afraid she was mistaken, Alex went to kneel in front of her, searching for signs of this terrible cold. There didn't appear to be any; she looked and sounded in perfect health. 'How are you feeling?' she asked, putting a hand on Ottilie's forehead to check for a temperature. 'Do you have a sore throat or a cough?'

Ottilie's eyes were wide as she shook her head.

'Does anything hurt?'

Ottilie dropped her eyes.

'What hurts?' Alex prompted.

Shaking her head, Ottilie pulled Boots out of her bag.

'Does Boots hurt?' Alex asked.

Again Ottilie shook her head. 'Go now?' she said softly.

Alex smiled past her concern. 'Yes, of course,' she said. If Brian Wade didn't like it, then Brian Wade could kindly explain why he'd said his daughter had a cold when she patently didn't.

Holding Ottilie's hand as they walked down the stairs, Alex swung her off the bottom step and after blowing a raspberry kiss on her cheek, she set her down on her feet and told her to wait for a moment.

'Why were you trying to make out she's sick?' she demanded of Erica Wade, who, bewilderingly, was on her knees in the middle of the kitchen.

'She's not sick?' Erica replied, making it a question.

Alex frowned. 'No, she isn't, so why did your husband call to tell me she was?'

'You'll have to ask him.'

'I shall, but maybe you can tell me if there's any reason why he wouldn't want her to go to school today?'

Erica hardly seemed to be listening.

'Mrs Wade, if there's something you need to tell me . . .'

'There's nothing,' and getting to her feet she pulled open the back door and went outside.

'I don't know what the heck it was all about,' Alex was remarking to Janet half an hour later, as they watched Ottilie tootling off with Chloe to have a go on the scooters. 'He even said the doctor had been to see her, but unless I'm missing something, there's nothing wrong with her.'

'She looks perfectly all right to me,' Janet agreed. 'And if you say she was already dressed when you got there, it seems no one had told her she wasn't coming today.'

Alex's eyes narrowed as the penny started to drop. 'I wonder if that was what it was about,' she said slowly. 'He wants to break the confidence she's building up in me by making it look as though I'm letting her down. So, he encourages her to think she's going to nursery, then I don't turn up and he can tell her that I'm too busy for her – or I have to put other children first, or whatever he's planning to tell her.'

Janet clearly wasn't liking the sound of that.

Alex's eyes went to hers. 'This is the trouble with people like him; they're too damned clever by half, at least they like to think they are, but if that man thinks he's dealing with a fool in me then he's about to find out that he's very much mistaken,' and taking out her phone she went into the office.

'I don't imagine Mr Wade's free,' she said to the secretary when she got through to the school, 'but perhaps you can give him a message. Please tell him that Alex Lake rang with the happy news that his daughter has staged a full recovery and is now at the nursery playing with her friend. If he'd like to ring me, he has my number,' and after making sure the secretary had all the details correct she ended the call and rang the doctor's surgery.

'I'll see if he's free,' the receptionist told her, after she'd explained what it was about. 'One moment.'

As Alex waited, her concern was fleetingly surpassed by a few flutters of excitement at the thought of her mother being at home, and possibly even coming to join her and Ottilie later. There was still so much for them to talk about, to find out about one another, that Alex was aware of conflicting swells of unease and elation at the mere thought of it. Maybe she'd ring after she'd spoken to the doctor, to find out if her mother was up yet, or still sleeping off the jet lag.

'Ms Lake, I have a few minutes,' Dr Aiden announced, coming on the line, 'how can I help you?'

'I'd like to know if you visited Ottilie Wade at home on Saturday,' Alex responded, coming straight to the point. 'Please don't plead patient confidentiality, because she's in my caseload and this is important.'

'Yes, as a matter of fact I did drop by the house,' he retorted stiffly. 'Why, is there a problem?'

'That's what I'm hoping you'll tell me. What exactly did you find to be wrong with her?'

There was a brief pause before he said, 'She has a touch of vulvovaginitis. Not uncommon in young girls, as I'm sure you're aware.'

Alex turned cold. Indeed she was aware, but when girls as small as Ottilie came into her world with any kind of soreness around their vaginas or bottoms, alarm bells immediately went off like sirens. 'How would she have contracted this condition?' she asked, trying to stay calm.

'It's not really possible to pin it to anything in particular,' he replied. 'It might be the bubble bath she's using, or a reaction to a laundry detergent. Or it's quite possible she still isn't able to wipe herself adequately after going to the toilet. That would cause things to flare up.'

It was true, it would, so now the only remaining question was, 'Did you see anything to cause you any other kind of concern?'

It took no time at all for him to register her meaning. 'I don't believe so,' he replied mildly. 'In every other way she seemed in good health.'

'Apart from her cold?'

Another short pause. 'I wasn't aware she had one. It must have come on since Saturday.'

'I guess it must have. Well, thanks for talking to me. I greatly appreciate it.'

As she rang off the door opened behind her and expecting it to be Janet she turned round saying, 'Well, that was interest—' She broke off as she saw Chloe with an arm round Ottilie, who was sobbing. 'Sweetheart, what is it?' she cried, going down to Ottilie. 'What's happened?'

'See, I told you she hadn't gone,' Chloe said to Ottilie. 'She got scared because she thought you'd left,' she explained to Alex.

'Oh, Ottilie,' Alex murmured, sweeping her up in her arms. She'd left her at nursery before without it causing any distress, so why was she upset today?

'Has something happened?' she asked gently. 'Did somebody say something mean?'

Ottilie's body was shuddering so violently that Alex tightened her arms around her.

'She looked round and you weren't there,' Chloe told her. 'I said you were probably only in the office, and Janet said you were, but she kept crying so I brought her to find you.'

Smoothing Ottilie's hair and pressing a kiss to her flushed forehead, Alex said, 'She's a little bit under the weather today, aren't you, sweetie?'

Chloe stood staring up at them, her dear angel face pale with concern. Suddenly she clapped a hand over her mouth. 'Where's Boots?' she gasped.

Ottilie's head came up, and as panic kicked in she all but leapt out of Alex's arms to race after Chloe into the playroom. Fortunately, they found him still hanging out with the couple of dolls and a fluffy duck they'd surrounded him with while they built him a Lego house.

Panic over.

Phew!

Troubled by how afraid Ottilie had seemed, Alex carried a chair to the corner of the room so she could continue making calls where Ottilie could see her. Though Ottilie's level of attachment to her wasn't exactly surprising, it was worrying nonetheless. However, now wasn't the time to start addressing it, it was time to try Brian Wade again to find out why he had lied about the cold.

'I gave him your last message,' the secretary informed her, 'but he's with some parents at the moment, so I can't interrupt him.'

'OK, well when you do get to speak to him will you please let him know that I've contacted Dr

Aiden about Ottilie and would very much appreciate it if he could ring me back before the end of the morning.'

'It's twelve o'clock,' the secretary pointed out, 'but I'm sure he'll get a chance over the lunch break.'

As she rang off, Janet was coming to sit beside her.

'What news?' Janet asked, shifting a sleeping baby into her other arm.

After relating what the doctor had told her, Alex said, 'I'm no expert, so there's no point in me examining Ottilie myself, but look at the way she's moving.'

Janet turned to watch Ottilie as she knelt, stretched and crawled to find the pieces to create Boots's house. 'She's definitely awkward,' she decided, 'and vulvovaginitis would do that.'

'Indeed, but it's what might have caused it that's really worrying me.'

Janet looked distinctly bleak. 'The doctor's seen her,' she said, 'so if anything like that had occurred . . .'

'Doctors have been known to miss the obvious,' Alex reminded her. 'An irritation that's common, bruising that can be explained in other ways . . . If they're not actually looking for what we're talking about . . .' She sighed. 'I wonder if we can bring her appointment with the paediatrician forward to this week instead of next.'

Janet's eyebrows rose. 'Good luck with that,' she responded, knowing as well as anyone how difficult it was to get any time with the community paediatrician without at least a three-week wait. Unless it was an emergency, of course, when it would happen the same day.

Alex gave a sigh of impatience. Though in her

mind Ottilie might require immediate attention, she knew already that without any actual evidence of abuse – and an otherwise explainable inflammation wouldn't do it – or a situation that could be termed life-threatening in some way, she was never going to get the appointment changed. However, there was no harm in putting Ottilie down for a cancellation just in case a slot came free. So scrolling through her numbers she spoke to the bookings clerk at the clinic, and managed to get Ottilie placed ninth on the waiting list. This meant that Ottilie was almost certainly not going to be able to see anyone until her scheduled appointment the Thursday after next.

Starting as her phone rang, she looked at the screen and for a heart-stopping moment she thought it was Jason calling. Then, remembering who was at the Vicarage, she felt an eddy of nerves going through her as she clicked on to answer. 'Hi, how are you?' she asked. 'You've managed to wake up at last?'

Anna laughed. 'Only just, I'm afraid. Is it convenient to talk?'

'Yes, it's fine. Did you have a good sleep?'

'In the end, but I have to admit I'm still feeling a bit woozy.'

'Then go back to bed. You don't have to come with us this afternoon . . .'

'But I want to. I never got to take you to the zoo when you were little, so this is my chance to make up for it.'

Alex laughed, and felt slightly ridiculous for liking the fact that her mother wanted to try and recapture some of what was lost. 'There'll be other opportunities when you're feeling more up to it,' she said. 'Maybe Wednesday. If Ottilie enjoys it today, I'm sure she'll want to go again.'

Trying to speak through a yawn, Anna said, 'OK, it's a deal, but I'm definitely cooking dinner for us tonight. No arguments. I'll find a supermarket and if I can get all the ingredients I need, I'll rustle you up one of my specials.'

Though Alex smiled, she couldn't help feeling the strangeness of her mother taking over Myra's kitchen. It didn't seem right, but she wasn't entirely sure it felt wrong either, and since there was nothing to be gained from mentioning it she said, 'I've got loads more questions for you, if you're up to it.'

'I will be,' Anna assured her, 'and I've got plenty for you too. Have you spoken to your team leader yet, to see if you can ease back a bit on your commitments this week?'

'I was just about to,' Alex replied, feeling her insides tightening with the dread of a no. 'Actually, if there's a problem with it, I've decided I'll take some unpaid leave anyway.'

'Oh Charlotte, I don't want you to get into trouble. As I said, I can easily entertain myself in the day and see you at night.'

Alex's expression had turned wry. 'Do you realise what you just called me?' she asked.

There was a moment before Anna said, 'Oh gosh, did I say Charlotte? I'm sorry, I really wasn't . . .'

'It doesn't matter,' Alex assured her – and it didn't, she realised. After all, it was just a name. *Her name.*

Anna was saying, 'It's how I've thought of you all these years, obviously, and the name was your dad's choice. Charlotte. Or Lottie Lollipop, as your grandfather used to call you.'

Touched by her grandfather having a special name for her, Alex said, 'Listen, I'm sure my boss will be his most understanding self once I tell him why I want to take a bit of time off, so let me ring the office now and see what I can do.'

In the end it took over half an hour to get through to Tommy, who sounded less than his usual jolly self when he came on the line. 'That bloody Prince family are doing my head in,' he grumbled. 'A fortnight ago we couldn't even get in the door, now the bloody mother never stops ringing me, and deciphering what she's saying in between all those cuss words is like trying to get my head round some Ikea instructions. So, now, whatever this is about, please make it good, because it's only Monday and I need the week to be off to a better start than this.'

Alex's voice was brimming with laughter as she replied, 'Then let me do my best. I have some news, some pretty amazing news actually, but for the time being I'd like it to be just between us.'

'You're going to tell me you've won the lottery – and that you're remembering who your friends are so *I* can help you pop all those corks.'

'If I had, then believe me, I'd be paying off your mortgage, buying you a great big fancy car and flying you round the world so many times it'd make your head spin. But that's for next week. For this week, are you ready for this?'

'Getting there.'

'You need to be sitting down.'

'Practically horizontal.'

'OK, here goes. I've heard from my mother – I mean my real mother. In fact, she's *here* in Mulgrove. She came to see me yesterday and . . .'

'Whoa, whoa,' he cried urgently. 'This is seriously

big news, pet, and I couldn't be happier for you. Just one thing though, you have checked her out, I hope . . . ?'

Alex's heart sank. 'Tommy, don't do this,' she groaned. 'I know you're only being protective, but wait till you meet her, then you'll see there's no way she's anyone but who she says she is. And let me ask you this, what would anyone gain from trying to pretend they were my mother – apart from a whole heap of trouble?'

'Actually, you've taken the words out of my mouth. There wouldn't be much more to gain than that, so as a devoted believer in your instincts I guess I'll go with them. So where is she now?'

'Still sleeping off her jet lag. She lives in New Zealand and only flew in yesterday.'

'Yikes, it's going to take her days to feel normal again. I know, I've done that flight. Anyway, down to the real reason you're calling, which has to be because you'd like to spend some time with her. Am I right?'

'You're a mind-reader. Do you think we can swing it? I'm not asking for my whole caseload to go to someone else or anything drastic like that. I'll carry on with my home visits, it's just the paperwork and meetings . . .'

'It's OK, I get the picture and I know you won't let the kids down, which is what really matters. So drop me an email outlining what cover you need and I'll sort something out.'

'Tommy, if I've never told you this before, I'm telling you now, I love you. Oh, and there's something else I'll put in the email; however, in a nutshell for now, it seems Ottilie Wade has developed vulvo-vaginitis and I'm worried it might have been brought on by something a bit more sinister than bubble bath.'

'Mm,' Tommy commented darkly. 'How many times have we heard that as an excuse before?'

'Too many. I've tried to bring the appointment with the paediatrician forward to this week, but the best I could manage was the waiting list.'

'OK, leave it with me, I'll see if I can pull some strings. Incidentally, now may or may not be the time to tell you that the merger of our two hubs is about to be made official. The head of social services is issuing a press release tomorrow.'

With a pang of unease, Alex asked, 'Anything about jobs?'

'Apparently fourteen are going across both bases, but don't you start worrying yourself about that now, you're far too good at what you do for anyone to want to lose you.'

It was almost three o'clock by the time Alex carried a very tired Ottilie back to the car, after spending an enchanting couple of hours with her exploring the Dean Valley zoo. It had been obvious from the way her eyes had rounded with amazement at just about every animal they saw that she'd never been to the place before, and it had made Alex's heart ache and sing to watch her gasping with excitement and laughing with glee as she gazed at them. The monkeys had scared her a little at first, but she'd soon started throwing nuts their way, and had almost flung Boots along with them at one point, she'd got so carried away.

One of her favourite stops had been at the bear pit.

'Like Boots,' she'd told Alex, peering down

through the railings to where a lazy-looking grizzly was slumped on a bed of straw.

'But a lot bigger,' Alex smiled.

Ottilie blinked up at her. 'Lot bigger,' she agreed. She held up Boots so he could see too, and gave a growl.

Below them, impervious to his audience, the Eurasian brown merely shifted his bulk, heaved a draughty sigh and closed his eyes.

'He's sleeping,' Ottilie told Alex.

'It looks like it.'

'Boots doesn't want to sleep.'

'No, he's got too many other animals to see. So where shall we go next? To the fruit bats? Or the pygmy hippos? I know, what about the lions?'

Ottilie gave another growl.

'That's right,' Alex laughed. 'Lions growl and so do bears.'

After the lions had come a panther with two cubs, and in the cage next to them was nothing at all.

'This is where the tiger lives,' Alex explained, reading from the plaque, 'but she must be asleep, like the bear.'

When Ottilie didn't respond she looked down to find her hanging her head.

'What's the matter?' she asked. 'Are you tired? Have you had enough?'

'Go now,' Ottilie whispered.

As she began tugging Alex's hand, the tiger came padding through from the darkness beyond. 'Here she is,' Alex said, lifting Ottilie up. 'Look at all her lovely stripes.'

Ottilie kept her face buried in Alex's neck. 'Go now,' she whimpered.

Baffled, Alex asked, 'Why don't you like the tiger?

She's just like the lion, but different colours.'

Ottilie gingerly turned her head, and Alex tried not to wince at the way her clenched hand had caught some of Alex's hair at the back of her collar.

'There, isn't she lovely?' Alex said soothingly.

Ottilie stared, transfixed. The beast was close to the front of the cage now, pacing up and down, her magnificent muscles rippling beneath the exotic hide.

'I think she could be Tigger's mummy, do you?' Alex suggested. 'You know Tigger, from *Winnie-the-Pooh*.'

'Tigger,' Ottilie repeated. 'Naughty Tigger.'

'He can be a bit naughty at times, can't he?'

Ottilie pointed a finger. 'Tigger's mummy,' she declared.

'That's right. So you see, there's nothing to be afraid of.'

'Not tiger, Tigger,' Ottilie said.

Alex laughed. 'All right, Tigger. So what next? I know, how about the café? Shall we see if they've got any brownies?'

Ottilie's eyes brightened.

It wasn't until they were turning into the Wades' drive a while later that Alex found herself remembering the tiger in the jigsaw on Ottilie's first day at nursery. She'd reacted oddly to that one too, wanting nothing to do with it one minute, then picking up that very puzzle piece to slot it into place the next.

Wondering what to make of it, she clicked on her earpiece as it rang and to her surprise it was Brian Wade's voice that said, 'Ms Lake. I'm told you went to the house this morning after I rang and asked you not to. Can you please tell me why you did that?'

Bristling, Alex replied, 'I went because I was

concerned about Ottilie, who I'm just about to take inside, so if you'll give me a minute . . .'

Grabbing the phone and dropping it in her pocket, she quickly got out of the car, lifted the sleeping Ottilie from the child's seat that seemed to live permanently in her car now, and carried her to the front door. As usual it was on the latch, but there was no sign of Erica Wade, so she went to lay Ottilie on the sofa and closed the sitting-room door quietly behind her.

'OK, I'm with you now,' she told Wade. 'I'm not sure where your wife is . . . Ah, I've found her,' she corrected, as she walked into the kitchen where Erica Wade was perched on a stool apparently listening to music. 'If you wouldn't mind turning that down,' she requested, pointing at the radio. 'Ottilie's asleep next door, and I'm speaking to your husband on the phone. I'd like you to hear what's being said,' and taking the mobile from her pocket she disconnected the Bluetooth and switched to speaker. 'Mr Wade, can you hear me?'

'Yes, I can hear you,' he replied irritably. 'Exactly what is going on . . . ?'

'You told me this morning,' Alex interrupted, 'that Ottilie had a cold, but that doesn't seem to be the case. In fact, Dr Aiden informs me that she has vulvovaginitis, which you didn't mention at all when we spoke.'

As Erica's eyes drifted to the dusk outside, Brian Wade said, 'We both know, Ms Lake, that if I'd told you what the problem really was, you'd do exactly what you are doing now and leap to conclusions that are as wrong as they are repugnant.'

Feeling the rug whipping out from under her, Alex found herself lost for a response.

'So, if you've quite finished playing the snooping policeman,' Wade continued sharply, 'I'll ask you to respect my wishes in the future and not force my daughter to go out when she is not in full health.'

As the line went dead Alex clicked off her end and looked at Erica, who might or might not have been listening, it wasn't possible to tell.

'I'll be here at the same time on Wednesday,' Alex told her.

Erica didn't look up, so leaving her to it Alex decided not to risk waking Ottilie by going into the sitting room, and returned to her car.

'He really put me in my place,' she was telling Tommy a few minutes later as she drove away from the house. 'I felt so foolish.'

'Well, you do need to be a bit more careful, pet,' he told her, 'nothing's been proved yet, so we have to try and keep an open mind. What did Mrs Wade have to say?'

'Her usual nothing. I'm not even sure she was on this planet, and I've just left Ottilie with her, which isn't filling me with confidence.'

'Well, the child spends most of her time with her mother, and no harm's come to her yet.'

'I don't like that word "yet",' Alex retorted, 'and I definitely don't like the way Mr Wade has just slithered out of his own lie. OK, he might be telling the truth about why he didn't come clean with the vulvovaginitis, because he's right, I did jump to the worst-case scenario – an occupational hazard, as we know – but the way that man goes about things . . . Incidentally, did you have any luck with the paediatrician appointment?'

'Not so far, but I'm still on it. When's her health visitor going in again? Remind me who it is.'

'Vicky Barnes, and she's due in tomorrow. I sent her an email earlier giving her the heads-up about today, and asking her to get back to me after she's been round there in the morning.'

'Good. Let me know what she says. So now you're on your way home I take it?'

Alex only wished she could have said yes, because the last thing she wanted right now was to go and view another flat fit only for depressives or drunks, but as soon as she'd finished her check on Gemma Knight it had to be done.

Fifteen minutes later, having had her appointment with Gemma Knight moved to the same time tomorrow, her heart was sinking to her boots as she pulled up outside a semi-derelict house with a pile of builder's debris in the front garden, and no curtains that she could see at any of the windows. Deciding she wasn't going to waste her time going inside, she made a quick call to the landlord's agent, who it turned out hadn't even left her office to meet her yet. Alex told her she couldn't make it anyway, and thankfully set off on the journey home.

'Hi, it's me,' she said, when her mother picked up the phone.

'Oh, what a relief,' Anna replied. 'I wasn't sure whether to answer or not. Do you mind that I did?'

'No, of course not,' Alex assured her, though actually she had found it a bit weird, but how else would she have got to speak to her if she hadn't picked up?

'How are you?' Anna asked. 'Did you have a good time at the zoo?'

'We did. I think Ottilie was a bit thrown by some of the animals, but in her typical way she rallied. Tiny as she is, she has the most incredible spirit.

Anyway, how's your day going? I'm on my way home now.'

'Lovely, but I don't think dinner will be ready for a while. I've only just got back from the supermarket. Boy, have they changed since I left. You can get almost anything these days, but I did come up a bit short with a couple of ingredients. No worries, though, I know how to work around it. What time shall I expect you?'

'In about half an hour, and the good news is, my team leader, Tommy, is OK about me scaling down my commitments. Luckily I don't have too many meetings scheduled for this week, and no court appearances, so it shouldn't cause too much of a problem at the office. There are just the home visits, and as things stand I only have half a dozen or so of them in the diary at the moment.'

'That's excellent . . . Now, before you go, are you able to get Skype here? Bob is really keen to chat to us on a video link, if you can bear it.'

Since she couldn't think of any reason why she couldn't bear it, apart from being apprehensive about confronting the life her mother was leading – and had long led – without her, Alex said, 'I'm sure it's possible, so we'll try to download it when I get home and give it a go.' And because she felt she should, she added, 'It'll be good to meet him, even if it is via a satellite.'

Since the traffic turned out to be lighter than usual, it was a mere twenty minutes later that she pulled up behind her mother's rental car. She was just turning off the engine when her mobile rang.

Seeing it was Brian Wade, she hardly knew whether to be worried or defensive as she clicked on her earpiece. 'Hello Mr Wade, I . . .'

'Where is she?' he demanded furiously. 'What have you done with my daughter?'

An icy fist snatched at Alex's heart as she replied, 'I haven't done anything with her. She was asleep on the sofa when I left . . .'

'Well, she's not there now, and I want to know why . . .'

'Oh my God,' Alex mumbled, trying not to panic. 'Doesn't your wife know where she is?' *She should never have left her there. The woman had been totally spaced out . . . If Ottilie had wandered into the road, anyone might have made off with her.*

She glanced up as Anna came down the path. 'I take it you've searched the house,' she said to Wade.

'Of course I have, and the garden and garage. I've looked everywhere and she's not damned well here. You were the last person to see her, so if . . .'

'She was with your wife when I left,' Alex cut in angrily. 'Have you called the police?'

'Of course not. I assumed you had her, and if I find out you have . . .'

'Please don't threaten me,' she seethed, getting out of the car. 'Now let's try to calm down and think of where she could be. Ottilie's gone missing,' she said to her mother, who was gazing curiously into the back of the car.

'Oh I don't think she has,' Anna replied, opening the rear door. 'In fact I think she's right here. Hello, lovely little girl. Would your name be Ottilie, by any chance?'

Choking with relief, Alex watched her mother lifting Ottilie and Boots from the footwell into her arms. 'It's OK,' she told Brian Wade. 'We've found her. It seems she smuggled herself into the back of my car and . . .'

'And I'm supposed to believe that?'

Furious, Alex retorted, 'Do I sound as though I'm lying?'

There was a beat before he said, 'No, I suppose not, but as she's never done anything like it before . . .'

Refraining from pointing out that she probably hadn't known anyone to run away to before, Alex said, 'Well, the important thing is she's perfectly safe, and once I've given her a drink and a little bite to eat I'll bring her home.'

'Or I can come and get her.'

'It's fine, I don't mind driving back.'

With a sigh he said, 'Are you sure you haven't done this on purpose? It's very out of character . . .'

'Mr Wade, before you start accusing me of kidnapping your daughter, maybe you should be asking yourself why she'd want to run away in the first place.'

Anna's eyes widened, showing how impressed she was by Alex's firmness.

Alex brushed a finger over Ottilie's cheek and signalled for her mother to take her inside.

'I'm sure, in your position,' Wade was saying acidly, 'that you're perfectly aware of the way children develop crushes on teachers or other adults they regularly come into contact with. If you can assure me that you didn't put Ottilie up to this, then I am prepared to believe that she has developed an attachment to you that should probably not be encouraged if it's going to lead to this sort of behaviour.'

Before she could stop herself, Alex snapped, 'She's three years old, Mr Wade, and from what I can make out she is starved of affection, particularly her mother's. That would be why she's developed an attachment to me, so I hope you're not thinking of changing your wife's appointment with the psychiatrist again, because this problem has to be sorted. Now, I think we've said enough for the moment, so I'll see you in about an hour – with Ottilie.'

Taking her bag from the car, she looked at the small space where Ottilie had stowed herself and felt her heart folding with so many emotions, as she pictured her there and the reasons why she'd hidden, that she barely knew what they all were.

She was becoming too involved with the child and she knew it, but there simply wasn't any way she could hand her over to someone else now. Besides, it would be even more unprofessional if she were to try and back out of the case before they had the medical assessments she'd insisted on. Once they were in and they had a clearer picture of what was – or wasn't – going on in the Wade household, the situation would very likely sort itself out.

'You're a little rascal,' she chided gently, as she entered the kitchen to find Ottilie seated at the table with a glass of milk in front of her and Boots in her lap. The smell wafting from the oven caused her stomach to rumble, and the way her mother was appearing so amused by the little episode she found both caring and endearing.

'Ottilie was just telling me that her bear is called Boots,' Anna informed her. 'And I thought that was a very clever name for him.'

Going to sit with Ottilie, Alex ran the backs of her fingers over her cheek as she gazed down at her fondly. 'Do you know who this is?' she asked, glancing at her mother.

Ottilie looked up at Anna.

'That's my mummy,' Alex told her.

Ottilie breathed in sharply, then lifting her bear she said, 'Boots.'

Alex had to laugh.

'You are utterly adorable, young lady. I hope you know that,' Anna said, coming to join them.

Ottilie showed her Boots.

'Yes, Boots is too. Does he like honey?'

Ottilie shook her head.

Anna's eyebrows rose. 'So what does he like?'

'M'lade.'

'Oh, of course,' Anna replied, rolling her eyes. 'I should have realised that. And do you like marmalade?'

Again Ottilie shook her head.

'What do you like then?'

Ottilie frowned as she thought. 'Brownies,' she said, 'and lickish.'

'Liquorice,' Alex explained. 'Her friend Chloe brought some to playgroup for her today.'

'Chloe,' Ottilie said to Anna.

'She has a pretty name too,' Anna chuckled, 'but I'm afraid I don't have any liquorice. What I do have, though, are some special little treats that I baked for Alex. Would you like to try one? I'm sure they're cool enough by now.'

Touched that her mother had done this, Alex said to Ottilie, 'I wonder what they can be?'

Ottilie was wide-eyed with intrigue as she watched Anna go to the stove and whip away a tea towel that was covering a tray. 'Dah dah!' she exclaimed, bringing the tray to the table. 'In Greece, which is the country they're from, they're called koulourakia, but that's a difficult word to say, so we'll just call them biscuits, shall we?'

442

Ottilie's mouth formed a little O as she stared at them.

'They look delicious, don't they?' Alex said, encouragingly. 'Shall I try one first?'

Ottilie's eyes followed Alex's hand from the tray to her mouth.

'Mmm,' Alex murmured, as the flavour enlivened all her taste buds.

'Now you,' Anna invited as Ottilie's gaze returned to the tray.

When she didn't pick a biscuit up, Alex chose one for her and broke off a morsel. 'There,' she said, handing it to her. 'And if you like it, we'll give one to Boots too.'

Ottilie shook her head.

Surprised, Alex asked, 'What's the matter? Aren't you hungry?'

Again Ottilie shook her head.

Alex glanced at her mother and shrugged, unable to explain the refusal. 'It doesn't matter,' she told Ottilie. 'We'll just do what we did the other day, shall we, and wrap some up for you to have later?'

'Not later,' Otttilie said in a tiny voice.

Baffled, Alex looked at her mother again. 'Are you sure, Ottilie? I think you'll like them. Maybe you can give one to Mummy and Daddy, then you'll all have one.'

Ottilie's lower lip started to tremble.

'Oh, it's OK,' Anna cried in alarm. 'You don't have to have one. I'll put them away, shall I?'

Ottilie nodded.

Bewildered and concerned by the oddness of the refusal, Alex watched her mother return the tray to a counter top and tried to think what might be behind it. Since she really didn't have any idea, and

443

because the time was ticking on, she turned back to Ottilie, hating herself as she said, 'It's lovely having you here, sweetheart, but I'll have to take you home soon.'

Ottilie's shoulders drooped as she hung her head.

Feeling utterly wretched now, and more concerned than ever, Alex told her, 'Your daddy is very worried about you. Mummy too, but it's OK . . .' She broke off as Ottilie started to shake her head.

'Stay here,' Ottilie whispered.

Alex looked at her mother, but Anna was as lost for a solution as Alex was.

Taking it very carefully, Alex said, 'Can you tell me, Ottilie, why you don't want to go home?'

Ottilie sucked in her lips as tears welled in her eyes.

'What is it?' Alex encouraged gently. 'Are you afraid of something?'

Still Ottilie didn't reply, and her lips stayed between her teeth.

'Is anyone unkind to you?' Alex pressed.

Ottilie drew Boots into her chest and hid her face.

'You can tell me if they are, and I'll make it stop.'

In the end it became clear that Ottilie wasn't going to answer, and it took all the powers of persuasion Alex possessed to get her back into the car. She was crying so hard as Anna fastened her seat belt that Alex very nearly called Brian Wade to tell him she'd keep her for the night. She would have if she'd thought he'd agree.

'Her father says she has a crush on me,' she whispered to her mother as she closed the rear door of the car. 'But there's more going on here than that. She seems genuinely scared.'

Anna was watching Ottilie in her car seat and

looking almost as worried as Alex. 'You're the expert,' she said quietly, 'but I have to agree. No child gets this distraught about going home to their parents. Isn't there anything you can do?'

'Believe me, if there was I would, but she's their daughter, and until I can prove anything against them, or get some kind of support from a psychiatrist or a paediatrician, I'm afraid she has to go back there.'

Anna looked so anguished in the moonlight that Alex almost felt she was letting her down too. How complicated her emotions were, erratic and even irrational. 'Would you like me to come with you?' Anna offered.

Though Alex was tempted to say yes, she shook her head. 'It's OK, I'll do it,' she said. 'Maybe you can have a go at downloading Skype while I'm gone,' and trying not to feel resentful of how easy her mother's world seemed in comparison to Ottilie's, she got into the driver's seat and started the engine.

Anna was still standing beside the car, seeming to sense she'd done something wrong, but wasn't quite sure what.

Wishing she hadn't been so abrupt, Alex wound down the window and softened her tone as she said, 'Thanks for being so lovely to her.'

Anna nodded and returned her gaze to Ottilie.

'I'll be back in about an hour,' Alex told her, and as their eyes met she managed a smile.

Minutes later she was driving towards town with Ottilie's sobs tearing through her heart. She had no words to comfort her, she could only continue the journey all the way to North Hill where she would have to leave her. However, as they reached the outskirts of Kesterly, she pulled into a layby and turned in her seat so she could see Ottilie's face in the lamplight.

Certain she'd never done anything this difficult in her life before, she said, 'I need you to help me with something, sweetheart. I need you to stop crying before we reach home, OK, because if your daddy thinks you get upset when you're with me he might stop me from coming, and we don't want that, do we?'

Ottilie's fragile frame jerked awkwardly as she shook her head.

Reaching for her hand, Alex whispered, 'It'll be all right, I promise. I'll come to pick you up on Wednesday, which is only the day after tomorrow, and my mummy will come too. You'll like that, won't you?'

Ottilie nodded.

Alex watched her and felt so wretched that it was the hardest thing in the world not to turn the car around and take her home again. 'Have you stopped crying now?' she asked.

Ottilie tried to nod again.

'Good girl,' and because there was nothing else she could do, she turned to drive on into town.

Brian Wade was standing at the front door with Ottilie, waving goodbye to Alex Lake. There was a smile on his face and tenderness in his eyes which remained until the car's tail lights disappeared from the end of the drive.

Keeping hold of Ottilie's hand he closed the door, turned her around and walked her upstairs to her room. 'You'll be going to bed with no supper tonight,' he told her as he took off her coat. 'That's what happens to little girls who run away from home. Do you understand that?'

Ottilie swallowed as she nodded.

Lifting her on to the bed, he started to remove her shoes. 'I hope you haven't told Alex Lake about any of our games,' he said severely.

Ottilie quickly shook her head.

He regarded her suspiciously. 'You understand that very bad things will happen to you if you do tell her, don't you?' he challenged.

Ottilie's eyes filled with tears as she nodded.

'And one of them will be that I'll have to take Boots away.'

With a sob of panic Ottilie hugged the bear tightly to her.

'Stop crying now,' he said coldly. 'You know it's not allowed.'

Ottilie was doing her best, but the sobs kept on coming.

'I really don't want to punish you,' he told her, 'but if you keep this up . . .'

'No – no more,' she choked.

'Good. Now you'll stay here until morning unless I decide to come and get you. If I do, I hope you'll have remembered by then the proper way for a little girl to behave.'

Downstairs in the kitchen Erica was staring across the garden at the shed. It was barely visible in the darkness, a black, shapeless mass lurking beneath the tree like a monster slumbering in the shadows. Earlier the lights had been on inside, turning the window into a huge, unblinking yellow eye staring back at her as if it knew all she was thinking.

He was on his way out there again now, she could hear his footsteps crossing the kitchen, the sound of the back door opening and closing, the crunch of his feet on the gravel before he stepped on to the grass. He moved through the hazy moonlight like a spectre, vanished into the hulk of the shed, appeared again in the glow of the eye.

Ottilie had tried to run away.

She herself had done that once, but it hadn't worked. It never did, it never could. There was only one way to escape, the way Jonathan had taken, and for that he'd needed her help.

Chapter Twenty

The following morning Anna was still in bed, trying to sleep off her jet lag, when Alex returned from a visit to Annie Ashe. Mercifully, Alex had found the struggling woman's weight still to be on the decrease, and she'd been greatly encouraged to hear that Annie's hours were to be increased at her part-time cleaning job.

'If you go on like this,' Alex told her, 'then the kids will be back with you in no time at all.'

Annie beamed as she became teary-eyed with relief. 'I'm doing me best,' she said gruffly.

Indeed she was, which was why Alex was so fond of her. 'Actually, I already have some good news,' she told her softly. 'I received notice yesterday that they're going to be allowed to stay with you for the entire weekend from now on, instead of just the day on Sundays.'

Now, as Alex dumped her bags on the kitchen table, her heart was still singing with the pleasure of watching Annie laugh and weep with joy. At least some things worked out well, in fact plenty did, it was just that they were constantly over-shadowed by the more difficult cases. Indeed, as her mobile rang and she saw who it was a cloud passed immediately over her spirits. 'I've been waiting for your call,' she told Vicky Barnes, Ottilie's health visitor, while closing the door so as not to wake her mother. 'Have you been to the Wades' yet this morning? Ottilie was horribly upset when I took her home last night, I've been really worried about her since. Please tell me she's all right.'

'Mm, well, it's hard to tell much when she doesn't speak,' Vicky answered, in a tone that sank Alex's heart even further. 'Which reminds me, I've made an appointment with the speech therapist for the twenty-fourth of next month. The psychologist can see her an hour later if you feel she's up to both visits on the same day.'

Fairly certain that Ottilie would be, Alex said, 'I'll take her myself. I don't want her father speaking for her or failing to mention something vital – or managing to get out of it altogether.'

'You think he'd do that?'

'You haven't met him, have you?'

'No, only the mother and I'm right with you about her. She definitely needs a shrink's assessment, and the sooner the better.'

'It's happening next Friday, at least it should be. If they cancel again there's going to be trouble. But tell me about the vulvovaginitis. Did you see any signs of it?'

'Yes, she's definitely inflamed in that area and even a little swollen, which might have been caused by rubbing herself.'

'So you're not thinking the worst?'

'No, but nor am I ruling it out, only the paediatrician can do that. You've got an appointment next week, you said in your email.'

'That's right. Sooner if I can get it. Otherwise, physically, she seems OK?'

450

'Still slightly underweight for her age, but she's gaining, which is good. Everything else seems to be functioning normally, apart from her readiness to speak, of course. She's clean, well dressed, lives in an environment with a good level of hygiene, which is more than we can say for a lot of our kids. It's going to be difficult to remove her, if that's what you're thinking, unless you can prove the mother's mentally incapable, and even then, if the father puts up a fight, or gets in a nanny . . .'

'He's quite opposed to a nanny at the moment, but he might well change his mind if the psych assessment shows that his wife shouldn't be left in sole charge of the child. We'll see. I'll keep you posted.'

As she rang off Alex turned to her mother who was coming into the kitchen, all bleary eyes and tousled hair, and felt an unexpected stirring of pleasure, even affection, before her defences quickly sprang up again. 'You're looking rather gorgeous today,' she quipped, impressing herself with how relaxed and familiar she could sound when inside she was a bundle of confusions.

With a splutter of surprised laughter, Anna said, 'I've got to get myself on to English time or I won't know whether I'm coming or going. Did I interrupt your call, I'm sorry.'

'No, don't be. It was Ottilie's health visitor. Apparently Ottilie seems fine this morning, in so far as Ottilie's ever fine.'

Anna sighed. 'Well, thank goodness for that,' she declared, going to take the milk from the fridge as Alex poured two coffees. 'I've been awake half the night worrying about her. She really didn't want to go home, did she?'

As Alex shook her head she was picturing Ottilie's

heartbreak, and feeling wretched about it all over again. 'I'm not proud of the way I got her to stop crying,' she said, 'but if I'd taken her back in that state, chances were her father would have tried to get me thrown off her case. As it stands I think he only tolerates me because he feels, better the devil you know – and because he thinks he can manipulate or intimidate me, which he's quickly finding out he can't.'

'He sounds absolutely dreadful,' Anna commented, taking her coffee to the table. 'It upsets me to think of any child being with someone who doesn't completely adore them, and having met her . . .' She shook her head in bewilderment.

Alex sighed. 'I guess we have to believe that he does care for her, and remember that there are plenty of kids a whole lot worse off than she is. At least she's fed, clothed, washed, has plenty of toys and a TV in her room – and is taken to nursery now . . . Actually, when I put it like that she hardly sounds deprived at all.'

Looking as unconvinced as Alex clearly felt, Anna took a sip of her coffee and said, 'So what's on the agenda today? Do you have to go out again?'

'Not until five when I'm due to see Gemma Knight. Her mother died quite recently, but after a bit of a tricky start with her carers she's starting to settle in. At least, I'm told she is, I'll know for certain when I've seen her for myself.'

Anna's expression was both tender and admiring. 'I keep thinking about you and all your children,' she said, 'and I know this might sound silly, or . . . Well, I was wondering if, in a way, you're lavishing all the love and attention on them that I . . . that you missed out on as a child. I mean, from me.'

452

Alex swallowed drily. Though she'd occasionally wondered the same thing, it made her uncomfortable to hear it put into words, especially from her mother.

'I'm sorry,' Anna said, apparently realising she'd gone too far.

'No, don't be,' Alex replied. 'It's just . . . Well, I expect you're right, but . . .' She shrugged, not knowing what else to say.

'Too deep for now?' Anna suggested.

Alex's eyes went briefly to hers. 'Maybe,' she admitted.

Anna took another sip of her coffee. Then injecting some brightness into a change of subject, she said, 'I was thinking that, if you did have some time to spare today, we could keep things nice and relaxed and perhaps just go down to the pub for lunch, have a walk around the village, carry on chatting . . . ?'

Alex smiled. 'Sounds good,' she replied, meaning it. 'And maybe we should have another go at downloading Skype, after the mess we made of it last night.'

Anna laughed as she pulled a face. 'We definitely didn't do well with it, did we, and I ought to be ready for Bob's call tonight, or I'll never hear the end of it.'

It was bang on seven that evening when the warbling ringtone coming from Alex's computer warned them that Bob was on the line.

'Are you ready?' Anna asked anxiously, her hand poised over the mouse. She and Alex were side by side at the kitchen table with Alex's laptop open in front of them.

'As I'll ever be,' Alex replied, feeling uncomfortably

like someone who'd received a late invitation to a party where she wasn't even sure she was going to be welcome.

'You'll love each other,' Anna assured her, as though she'd picked up on Alex's nerves, and with a quick click she made the connection. 'Hi darling,' she said as her husband's face appeared on the screen. 'Here we are, and we're feeling very clever for managing to set this up.'

In spite of the slightly distorted image in front of her, the first thing Alex noticed about Bob Reeves was how handsome he was, in a sixty-something sort of way. His hair was thick and silvery and as casual as the open neck of his navy shirt, and his smile seemed embedded in every line of his face. 'Hi Bob,' she said, sounding far more relaxed than she felt, 'it's lovely to meet you.'

He was shaking his head in what looked like amazement. 'I knew from Facebook that you were like your mother,' he declared, 'but seeing the two of you together . . . It's kind of strange, but lovely to see . . . You look just like she did when I first met her.'

'Only more gorgeous,' Anna piped up happily.

He raised an ironic eyebrow. 'Oh, now I'm not falling into that one,' he told her. Then to Alex, 'So how are you, Charlotte? And by the way, it's really good to meet you too.'

As Anna made to correct him, Alex put a hand on her arm. 'It's OK,' she whispered.

'What's going on?' he asked. 'Don't tell me I've put my foot in it already. What did I do?'

'You called me Charlotte,' Alex told him, 'but it's fine, honestly.'

He banged a hand against his head. 'Sorry about

that. I guess it's just how we've always thought of you . . .'

'Of course, and honestly I don't mind, after all I suppose it's who I am, really.'

Anna turned to look at her, but said nothing, and nor did Alex, though Alex was sure she felt some sort of current passing between them.

Bob was saying, 'I guess you girls have had a long chat by now, so sorry if I'm telling you things you already know, Char— Alex, but your mother has wanted this for so many years. We both have, and I'm hoping it won't be long now before I'll be seeing you in person. I'd have come this time, but I reckoned meeting you for the first time was something Anna needed to do on her own. I miss her, though. It's not the same here without you, my darling.'

'Oh, like you've had time to miss me,' Anna scoffed playfully. 'I know you, Bob Reeves, you'll have been out on that dive boat every morning, or whipping up some new property deal, or driving into town to drill a few teeth.'

Since Anna had already told her that he was a semi-retired dentist and full-time property developer with a typical Kiwi's passion for boats, wine and rugby, Alex commented, 'Sounds like you've got a very busy life.'

'I find it's the best way of staying out of trouble,' he quipped. 'But I've got to say, what you do for a living outshines us all.'

Before Alex could respond Anna was saying, 'We shouldn't really talk about it too much, it's very confidential . . .'

'It's OK,' Alex assured her.

Anna glanced at her, needing to be certain, before

she said to Bob, 'We had the dearest, sweetest little girl here last night. Her name's Ottilie, as in the jazz singer, Ottilie Patterson. She was so upset when she had to leave that we got upset too, and we've been worrying about her ever since. She's only three and there's a chance something bad is happening to her at home.'

Bob's face showed his concern. 'Do I need to ask what sort of something?' he asked darkly.

'We're not sure yet,' Alex replied. 'If we were, and it was what you're thinking, believe me she wouldn't be there any more.'

'Alex is seeing her again tomorrow,' Anna continued. 'Dear little mite is clearly very attached to her. I expect you get that a lot in your job, don't you?' she said to Alex.

'From time to time,' Alex admitted. 'But now, if you don't mind, I'd like to hear all about you,' she said to Bob. 'I know you and Anna have been married for twenty years . . .'

'We've just had an anniversary,' he came in chirpily, 'but it was a kind of low-key affair, because we're saving the big stuff for my sixtieth next month. Do you think there's a chance you might make it over for the party?'

Thrown by the suddenness of it, Alex found herself uttering the first words that came to mind. 'I'd love to,' she was saying, 'but I'm afraid I know already that I won't be able to take the time off at such short notice.' *Or be able to afford it*, she didn't add. 'It's lovely of you to invite me, though,' she said quickly.

'Of course you're invited,' he cried in surprise. 'I know you might not be used to the idea yet, but you're family, and we're all dying to meet you. In fact the whole clan wanted to be in on this call today, just to say hi and welcome and to let you know how thrilled we all are for Anna, but I thought it might be a bit overwhelming this first time out with us all coming at you at once. I'm not sure I'll be able to fight them off for the next one, though.'

Because she had to, Alex said, 'I'd love to see them and say hello.' And actually she would, she realised, especially with her mother sitting here, rather than there.

'I went online today to try and find the video you made,' Anna told him, 'but it doesn't seem to be there.'

'Ah, that's because I took it down,' he replied. 'I've shot some new stuff I want to edit in, and I've dug out some old footage too, so it should be up again by this time tomorrow.'

'And there was me thinking you'd already captured every last inch of where we live, how we live and who we all are,' Anna teased. 'If you shoot any more she won't need to come, she'll be able to go online for the whole Kiwi experience.'

'Oh, now I know I'm good,' he responded drily, 'but I don't think I'm that good, and showing her a lobster I just caught for breakfast isn't going to be the same as tasting it fresh off the barbie, is it? And watching me squeeze a fresh lime from one of our trees isn't going to be anywhere near as much fun as picking it and doing it herself.'

Anna seemed to tense. 'Sorry if he's being a bit over the top,' she whispered to Alex.

'It's fine,' Alex assured her.

'What have I done now?' he demanded, coming towards the camera in a comical way.

'Nothing,' Anna laughed. 'So what extra material have you put into the video?'

457

'You'll have to wait and see and then tell me if you spot it.'

Anna groaned. 'I'm bound to get it wrong,' she told Alex.

'She will,' Bob confirmed. 'So what time is it with you girls?'

Alex checked the clock. 'Quarter past seven in the evening,' she replied. 'Which makes it what time with you?'

'Quarter past eight in the morning.'

'Tomorrow,' Anna added.

'That's right. Now, am I allowed to ask what you've been up to today?'

Anna glanced at Alex. 'Actually, we've had a lovely lazy day, just the two of us,' she told him. 'We got off to a late start, mainly thanks to my jet lag, then we went to the local pub for lunch. It's so not like in my day when pubs were full of smokers and dartboards and beery old men – the food at the Mulgrove is fantastic and they serve some seriously decent wines.'

'Any from our neck of the woods?'

''Fraid not, the only New Zealand one they had was from the South Island, but it was pretty good.'

'Then we'll look forward to introducing you to our home brews,' he said to Alex, 'and I guess you realise I'm not talking about beer. So what did you do after getting tipsy over lunch?'

Alex and Anna laughed at the same time and in a very similar way. 'We just strolled around the village,' Anna replied. 'Charlotte – Alex – showed me where she fell over when she was six and cut open her head. All pretty grisly with lots of blood, she assures me. Then we went to the village hall where she danced in a German folk festival aged

458

nine, and organised a Santa's grotto aged fourteen. It's also where she now puts on her plays, the ones we've seen on Facebook.'

'I don't write them,' Alex was quick to point out. 'I just help produce and direct them.'

'I reckon you could give us some advice on our own efforts when you're down this way,' Bob told her. 'I guess we've kind of got the Santa's parades coined, though . . . Have you told her about them?' he asked Anna.

'No, but I will.'

'They're something special,' Bob asserted. 'Well, you'll see for yourself if we can persuade you to come for Christmas. I hope Anna told you that when you do come the ticket's on me . . .'

'Yes, but honestly, I couldn't . . .'

'Oh yes you can, and no arguing, as Anna knows it'll be a waste of time because I always win.'

'Actually, he never does,' Anna told her, 'but over this I probably won't put up too much resistance.'

Unable not to be moved by how wanted and welcome they were making her feel, Alex said, 'I think I should leave you two to catch up in private now. It's been great talking to you, Bob.'

'It's been an absolute pleasure for me,' he told her warmly. 'Seeing your mother this happy . . . Well, it does my heart good, I can tell you. She's always had us, of course, and we love her very much, but it's not like having someone of her own. You belong together now, you guys. Too many years have already gone by with you being apart.'

Swallowing the emotion tightening her throat, Alex replied, 'After everything she went through, it's wonderful to know that she ended up finding someone like you.'

'I only wish you could have been with us all this time,' he said frankly. 'You should have been, but I guess that's for another day. You take care of yourself now, and maybe we can talk again soon.'

As she started to say goodbye Alex felt the words faltering, so quickly covering her failure with a smile, she left her mother in front of the computer and ran upstairs to her room.

She knew she was being stupid, that she had so much to be thankful for, and even to look forward to now, but she was suddenly feeling so horribly lonely that the misery of it was coming over her in wave after wave of debilitating sadness. In no time at all her mother would be gone again, returned to a world that seemed so full of colour and happiness, love and togetherness, that her own small, drab existence was almost shaming by comparison. Worst of all, and she really hated admitting it, was the fact that her mother didn't actually feel like her mother, though she had no clear idea of how that was supposed to feel.

It's going to take time, she reminded herself as she tore a handful of tissues from a box on the chest. *It can't just happen overnight, much as you might like it to. And she's lovely. Really kind and friendly, so interested in everything you do, and you only have to recall how welcoming Bob was with you just now to be sure that they really do want you in their lives.*

It wasn't that she thought they didn't, the problem was . . . What was the problem? Fear that it might all suddenly disappear, or turn into some kind of nightmare? She guessed that was it, but why would it? There was no logical reason for her to be feeling this way, so she must try to let it go and remind herself that sometimes things did work out. And

460

she'd love to visit New Zealand, it sounded so idyllic – catching lobsters for breakfast, sailing round the islands, taking part in the Santa parade . . . and inspiring in ways she hadn't even known existed. But then how was it going to feel returning to a shabby bedsit in a part of Kesterly she detested, in the middle of winter and with few friends to speak of? No family either, apart from Gabby and Aunt Sheila whom she loved, but they were hardly around the corner, and weren't really any more involved in her life than she was in theirs.

It seemed different with her mother's family. They sounded so close, so much a part of each other's day-to-day existence. Her mother might not be a blood relative of theirs, but they'd clearly taken her into their hearts just as her mother had taken them. It was where Anna belonged, far, far more than she belonged here. She hardly sounded English any more, and though she seemed thrilled to have found her daughter, she must be longing to get home to Bob, who'd already said he was missing her – and her step-grandchildren, who made her eyes shine every time she mentioned them.

Quickly blowing her nose as her mother knocked on the door, Alex fought back her pathetic insecurities and called for her to come in. 'He's so lovely,' she said, smiling as the door opened. 'And very handsome.'

Her mother stood looking at her, taking in the teary eyes, crumpled tissues and nasal voice. Then, opening her arms, she said, 'Come on, come to me, my love, and tell me all about it.'

Alex and Anna were still sitting on the bed with their backs up against the head rail, neither of them crying now, though both had shed plenty of tears during the past couple of hours. They'd been talking mainly about how overwhelmed Alex was feeling, and Anna too in her way. They'd agreed that they were probably expecting too much of each other at such an early stage, and that they were both so afraid of what the future might hold that they could scarcely even bring themselves to mention it.

'I don't suppose it's any secret,' Anna had said, 'that Bob and I are hoping you'll consider coming to join us in New Zealand one of these days, I mean for good, but I understand that you have your life here, and why should you give it up just because it's what I want?'

Feeling forced to admit that in truth she didn't actually have much of a life to give up, Alex had suddenly found everything spilling forth, first about Jason, and how upset she still was by their break-up, then how big a failure she felt for not having a best friend. Next had come the confession about needing to find somewhere else to live, and because rents were so high and she had such a small amount of savings she was dreading where she'd end up. 'And I'm not even sure my job is safe,' she'd woefully concluded. 'So actually, the prospect of starting again in New Zealand is more appealing than you might think.'

Anna smiled tenderly. 'Well, obviously I wish you weren't going through such a difficult time,' she said gently, 'but maybe we could think of it this way, that life is gradually closing doors for you here in order to make you ready for a new beginning?'

Though the thought was tempting, even pleasing, Alex felt oddly panicked by it too.

'Obviously I'm not saying you should come

straight away,' Anna assured her, 'but why don't you take Bob up on his offer and fly over for Christmas? That way you can start to get a feel for the place and decide whether or not you think it'll suit you.'

Alex swallowed drily. 'I'd have to pay for myself . . .'

'No, my darling, you wouldn't have to pay for yourself. Bob can more than afford it and he wants to give you this gift. Please don't deprive him of it, especially when you're going to need every penny of your own money for your new flat.'

Alex's eyes went down.

'Actually, I can help there,' Anna went on, tilting Alex's chin up again. 'For a long time now I've been putting money aside for you, mainly in case something happened to me. I wanted to be able to leave you something, even if we never met. But what's the point in making you wait when you clearly need some assistance now . . .'

'No, no, I can't . . .'

'Yes you can. If it turns out that you want to stay living here in England then there should be enough to get you started without having to take out too big a mortgage – depending on the type of place you're looking for, obviously. For the time being though, we can use some of it to put down a deposit on a nice flat for you to rent. In fact, if Gabby's already done a deal on this house, I think it might be a good idea for us to start looking tomorrow.'

Feeling ashamed of how suspicious she and Gabby had been of Anna's motives for being in touch at a time when she might have thought Alex was about to come into some money, Alex ended up confessing to her mistrust. 'And now here you are, like my fairy godmother, making everything possible in ways I'd never even imagined. I hardly know what to say, apart from thank you, of course, which seems pretty meagre for such huge generosity – and obviously I'll find a way of repaying you.'

'Then you'll be repaying yourself, which is fine, if that's what you want to do. All that's important to me is that I take care of you in a way I haven't been able to up till now, hopefully without being too interfering.'

Alex smiled. 'I can't imagine you ever being that.'

Anna laughed and rolled her eyes. 'Best not to get Bob started on that,' she quipped. 'Anyway, I have to tell you if I'd known what a difficult time you were having in your teens I swear I'd have risked Gavril's threats and come to find you then. The only reason I didn't was because it didn't seem fair to tear you away from the people you loved, and who loved you.'

Alex's eyes drifted. 'Yes, I think they did love me, in their way,' she commented, almost to herself.

'Oh, I'm sure they did, and we've a lot to be grateful to them for, because we know how much worse your upbringing could have been.'

Alex nodded. 'I'm definitely a whole lot better off than most of the children I come across, that's for sure.'

Anna cast her a glance. 'Are you thinking of Ottilie?' she said quietly.

'And others, but yes, of Ottilie. You've seen her, you've felt for her too, so you understand, don't you, that no matter what, I can't just up and leave? At the moment, I couldn't even do it for a couple of weeks.'

'Of course not,' Anna replied. 'But Christmas isn't

here yet – and dare I say, she's not yours, Alex, so one day, when you've got her sorted out . . .'

'She's three years old, and if she is suffering in the way I fear, then the damage has already been done. So what would you have me do, leave her for someone else to cope with, and then someone else, and then someone else again? She has no other family, so that's what her life will be like if she goes into care. At least if I'm here, seeing her regularly, giving her some small sense of stability, of self-worth even, she'll have someone to make her feel special.'

Anna's eyes were dark with concern as she regarded her. 'No, my darling, I wouldn't have you do that,' she said earnestly. 'I'm simply saying that you have a life too, so please don't forget it.'

Chapter Twenty-One

Over the following days, as they came to know one another better and discovered some amusing similarities in their ways and tastes as well as their looks, Alex could feel her trust building in Anna, and perhaps in herself too. She really didn't have anything to be fearful of, she kept telling herself. Anna clearly hadn't come with any intention other than to create a bond between them, and it didn't seem likely that she was simply going to forget her as soon as she returned to New Zealand. Nor did she, Alex, have to make any decisions right now about what she was going to do in the future.

The only real friction between them, if it could even be termed that, was caused by Alex's concern for Ottilie. If they'd had the same sort of confidence in their relationship as other mothers and daughters, there were occasions when they might actually have come to blows over it. As it was, Anna tried hard not to be too critical of how attached Alex clearly was to the child, but still regularly managed to point out that she was in danger of letting Ottilie take over her life.

'You can't just come here and tell me how to do my job,' Alex snapped one evening after she'd arrived home from dropping Ottilie off when she'd had another irritating and fruitless exchange with Erica Wade. 'I've been in this sort of situation plenty of times before, so please stop worrying.'

'I can't help it. I can see how much she means to you, and I don't want you to end up being hurt,' Anna told her.

Before she could stop herself, Alex cried, 'You might have thought of that twenty-five years ago.'

Anna flushed, and seeing the anguish in her eyes Alex immediately regretted the attack.

'I can take care of myself,' she mumbled. 'Now can we please leave it?'

Anna had accepted this, mainly because she didn't want to provoke a serious falling-out. From then on, however, she decided to start joining Alex and Ottilie as often as she could to see for herself just how close they were becoming. Though she remained concerned, and she and Alex continued to exchange words over it, Anna did find herself becoming a little more understanding. It would be the most difficult thing in the world to work with vulnerable children and not be affected by them, she'd always realised that, and now she was beginning to understand that in Ottilie's case it was downright impossible. She was so sweet and compliant, and clearly so happy just to be with Alex, that Anna simply couldn't begrudge her the pleasure and security of that when she was apparently so lonely at home, and possibly a lot worse.

Fortunately there had been no recurrence of the terrible state Ottilie had got herself into the night she'd stowed away in Alex's car. She seemed to understand now that it would make it difficult for Alex to take her out again if she was crying when Alex returned her to the house. Nevertheless, there

467

were always tears before they parted, and the awful bleakness in her eyes as Alex kissed her goodbye tore almost as painfully at Anna's heart as it did at Alex's.

On a day when Alex had no other commitments, she and Anna decided to go and visit Helen Drake. However, when Anna rang to make the arrangements the old lady asked them not to come.

'I'm glad you've found each other again,' she said on the phone, 'and I wish you well, but if you don't mind I'd prefer to leave things as they are.'

Stung, but not prepared to insist, Anna asked Alex to accompany her to the cemetery at Temple Fields where four members of her family were buried. When Alex told her about the times she'd been before, and the flowers that occasionally turned up on the grave, Anna went into the church to make a generous donation. It was her only way of saying thank you to the kind stranger. Afterwards they made a trip to Exmoor, where Alex's father was interred along with his parents. In spite of the cold and drizzling rain, they sat on a bench gazing out over the misted wilderness, talking about him and trying to feel his presence, both feeling certain they could.

Later, in the cosy warmth of a pub with a log fire burning in an old stone hearth, Anna continued telling Alex everything she could remember about Nigel, from how they'd met – at a small art gallery in Kesterly – to how instant and powerful their connection had been, to how overwhelmed with joy and pride he had been when she'd first put Alex – Charlotte – into his arms. Alex's emotions were in turmoil as she listened, full of regret and longing on the one hand, wishing she herself had more memories of her father, while horrified on the other to think of his last moments. No one should ever have to die that way, and knowing it had happened because of her made it feel so much worse.

The following morning, after nursery, they took Ottilie on a woodland walk through the arboretum a few miles out of town, where there were climbing frames and an obstacle course for children to play on. Alex had assumed Ottilie wouldn't want to swing in one of the tyres, having had a fall from one once, but to her surprise she was more than ready to try again. She loved it, and the sound of her laughter was as uplifting as it was infectious.

What wasn't at all enjoyable, however, was finding Ottilie's sweet little face watching them from an upstairs window as they drove away from the house on North Hill. She looked so lonely and sad that even Anna felt as though she was abandoning her.

The next day Gabby and Aunt Sheila came up to the Vicarage for a visit, and just as Alex had hoped, within minutes of meeting Anna their concerns that she might not be who she was claiming to be, or that she had some sinister motive for being there, were put to rest. Gabby, being Gabby, spent most of the time chattering on about her own childhood, seeming to forget that Anna might be more interested to hear about Alex's. On the other hand, Sheila appeared genuinely keen to hear about Anna's family in New Zealand, and how different life was down there. Anna was happy to entertain her with stories that made her chuckle and shake her head in amazement.

No one mentioned the terrible circumstances that had brought Alex into the Lake family all those years ago, nor did they talk much about Myra and Douglas. Alex only realised that when Gabby and Sheila were leaving, and Gabby pointed it out.

'I'm not sure whether to feel guilty about it or not,' she said, gazing worriedly into Alex's eyes.

Since she wasn't quite sure how to answer that, Alex simply hugged her.

'She's very nice,' Gabby whispered. 'I mean Anna. Though I have to admit it makes me feel a bit weird to think that you've got a mum now and I haven't.'

Still not fully able to think of Anna that way, though unwilling to say so, Alex told her, 'We're still family, us two, and that's never going to change.'

Gabby smiled. 'You said that before and I hope it's true, but I'm already scared she's going to take you away.'

Hearing their aunt coming down the hall, Alex said, 'We don't need to talk about this now. I'll come and see you next week and we can have a nice long chat then.'

Seeming happy with that, Gabby embraced her hard, and hugged Anna too before helping Sheila into the car and waving out of the driver's window all the way down the hill. As they disappeared from view Alex found herself feeling oddly lonely, as though they had left her for good, which was absurd, she knew, but it was hard to shake.

'Are you OK?' Anna asked as she returned to the kitchen.

Alex's head came up, almost as though she'd been startled. 'Yes, I'm fine,' she replied, managing a smile. 'Are you?'

'I think so. It seemed to go well, didn't it?'

Alex nodded, because it had.

'At least it took our minds off Ottilie for an hour,' Anna sighed, starting to wash up.

Though Alex bristled, wanting to point out that Ottilie had no such easy escape from her lot, she couldn't deny that it had been a relief to stop worrying about her for a while. 'I wonder what she's doing now,' she said, reaching for a tea cloth.

Casting her a wary glance, Anna said, 'It's probably best not to torment yourself with it. You'll see her tomorrow, and I'm sure she'll be fine.'

Hoping so, Alex said, 'You know, I keep remembering myself as a child trying to open a door and not able to reach the latch. She has a similar cupboard in her bedroom.'

Anna frowned. 'Are you saying you think they keep her locked in?' she asked worriedly.

Alex shook her head. 'I don't have any evidence of it . . . No, I don't think so, but what I'm pretty sure of is that it won't be as simple as lifting up a latch to rescue her, the way it happened for me.'

'Perhaps not in a literal sense,' Anna replied, 'but it could be said that you're already rescuing her.'

Alex was casting her mind back to the time she'd been trapped, trying to find, amongst her few, shadowy memories, one of the rector coming to save her. There was nothing, but what did move briefly into the light was the image she occasionally saw of a woman running down the stairs with a child under her arm.

'Are you absolutely sure it was the rector who found me?' she asked her mother.

Apparently surprised by the question, Anna said, 'It's what he told me, and I've never had any reason to doubt it. Why?'

Alex shrugged. 'It's just that I have this dream

471

sometimes, or flashback, I don't know what it is exactly, of a woman carrying me down the stairs. She's panicking, as if she's trying to get away from someone . . . I've always thought it was you, but I know you couldn't come back then, so maybe it's from a time before it all happened?'

Anna seemed baffled. 'I don't recall anything like that,' she responded, shaking her head.

'Maybe it's something I saw on TV that's stayed with me. You never know with these things how they'll crop up again.' Then quickly pushing the brooding aside, she said, 'So how about going online to find out if Bob's reposted his epic video yet?'

Laughing, Anna said, 'For how long he's taking to complete it, epic is probably the right word.'

In the end it wasn't until the following day that Bob finally managed to upload his finished masterpiece, by which time Anna and Alex had returned home from Kesterly with crunchy baguettes and a wicked slice of cheesecake to share for lunch. It hadn't been their intention to bring Ottilie with them – Alex never brought the children in her caseload home – however, when she'd taken her back to North Hill after nursery earlier she'd been unable to get an answer from inside the house.

'Heaven only knows where the blasted woman is,' she'd grumbled as she'd buckled Ottilie back into her seat (though secretly she couldn't help feeling glad that Ottilie was able to spend more time with them; at least then she knew where she was and what was happening to her). 'We can't go anywhere in all this rain so we'll have to take her to the Vicarage with us. I'll bring her back later when I go to see Tawny Hopkins.'

Though their plan had been to sit and watch old Pooh and Paddington videos, at least until Ottilie fell asleep, when Anna announced that Bob's email had arrived inviting them to a screening of the premiere of *Te Puna* the movie, as he put it, Alex found herself keen to watch that instead. If Ottilie got bored they could always turn it off and go back to it later, but as usual Ottilie seemed happy simply to be with them.

From the first shots of the opening sequence of 'the movie', featuring stunning aerial views of the Bay of Islands, Alex could feel herself being transported to what looked like paradise. The way the camera gently soared and dived around the turquoise-blue coves, seeming to skim the translucent coastal waters and ride the waterfalls, made her feel as if she were flying like a bird.

Then came a mix-through to some lively scenes of Keri Keri's main street lined with towering palms and bustling cafés.

It was nothing like she'd imagined, but there again until lately she hadn't imagined it at all.

As the music faded and the images changed to show sumptuous citrus orchards either side of a sun-drenched road, Bob began a voice-over. 'Here we are making the drive out to our house, which is about eighteen k, or roughly eleven miles from town. Shelley is with me, my lovely daughter, and she's doing the driving.' As the camera panned to an open-faced, pleasant-looking woman, Ottilie said, 'Shelley.'

'That's right,' Anna laughed, smoothing a hand over her hair.

Alex was smiling too as Shelley turned to the lens. In a slightly husky voice she said, 'Hi Charlotte.

Welcome to New Zealand. I'm hoping to be doing this drive with you before very much longer. Hi, if you're watching, Anna. We love you, and we're all so happy for you.'

'She's so sweet,' Anna murmured.

Alex couldn't be sure whether she felt jealous of Shelley for having been a part of Anna's life for so long, or moved by how genuinely warm Shelley seemed. She guessed it was probably a bit of both.

'See here,' Bob was saying as he panned to a lofty set of gates they were passing, 'these belong to one of our wealthiest neighbours. You can't see the house from here, but it's an old Tuscan monastery that he had deconstructed, shipped over and rebuilt on his own private clifftop. It's quite something, I can tell you.'

There was a mix-through then to the driveway of another house, followed by Bob saying, 'Here we are at Te Puna, which is our home. It's just around the bend here. Te Puna, by the way, is Maori for deep well. The waters we're on are where the stingray and dolphin come to mate. Here we are now, this is the beautiful home that Anna has created for us.'

Alex's eyes rounded as the most exquisite pale grey weatherboard house with wraparound verandas and white Georgian sash windows came into view – with a stunning backdrop of pure blue ocean.

'It started out as a traditional Kiwi villa,' Bob was explaining, 'but over time we've been making it our own. I always say that we're a little touch of Raffles away from Singapore, with all our lovely palms and wicker furniture around the decks. From most of them we have gorgeous views of the bay, which is where I keep the dive boat. OK, Shelley and I are going to get out of the car now, and take you to meet some other members of the family.'

As Alex turned to Anna, Ottilie said, 'Shelley.'

Laughing again, Alex tightened her arms around her. 'This is a good programme, isn't it?' she said, as Ottilie's head rocked back against her.

Ottilie nodded and sat Boots comfortably on her lap to watch some more.

The next scene opened with a close-up of an enormous lobster sizzling on a barbecue before pulling back to show a relaxed, friendly-looking group milling about the deck with beers, glasses of wine, or soft drinks for the kids. They were all healthily tanned, Alex noticed, and the sky above them was pristine blue.

'Shelley's in charge of the barbie today,' Bob announced into the mic.

Shelley smiled at the camera and waved a fork.

'She's preparing a little fellow that Rick, her brother, brought up this morning. She's going to serve it with Anna's homemade macadamia butter, and a fresh green salad picked earlier from our vegetable garden where we grow everything from artichokes to strawberries to . . . well, you name it, I expect we have it. We also have chickens and ducks for eggs, obviously a ready supply of oysters, scallops and mussels from the bay, and Anna's enormous larder packed full of all the dried foods you can imagine. So we're always pretty much ready to feed about a dozen people if they drop in by boat, which they often do. If you don't know it already, Kiwis are big dropper-inners.'

Alex glanced at Anna and wasn't sure whether she felt proud or slightly overawed by the amazing life she led.

Anna smiled and rolled her eyes, as if downplaying the magnificence on view.

'OK, so now we come to my son, Rick,' Bob announced, going in for a close-up on a tall, slender man in his mid-thirties who had a much darker shock of the same luxuriant hair as Bob's, and even deeper blue eyes. 'Rick is our family's top creative director, in that he's the only one,' Bob had a little chuckle here while Rick cast a pitying glance at the camera, 'and he spends most of his time in Auckland, or Sydney, and occasionally Beijing.'

'Hey, Charlotte,' Rick smiled, holding up his beer. 'Believe it or not I can speak for myself, but as Dad's just told you the most interesting bits about me I'll make do with saying how happy we all are that Anna's found you. We're also really looking forward to you coming here so we can show you around, and hopefully impress you with our very different way of life to the one I expect you're used to over there. Not that ours is better, you understand, just another way of doing things.'

'I'm taking you over here now,' Bob was saying, as he walked the camera through the party, 'to meet Sarah, Anna's best friend from way back when, and Sarah's niece, Katie, who's engaged to Rick. Here we are, ladies, your chance to say hi to Charlotte.'

Alex immediately liked Sarah, whose rosy face was as round as it was smiley. 'Hello, my darling,' she said affectionately. 'I can't tell you how much it means to us that we're being able to greet you like this. Knowing your mum for as long as I have, I can tell you it's all she's ever dreamt of, being with you again one day, and Bob told me on the phone last night how happy she is. It lights me up just to hear it; to meet you would be even better. Come soon, angel, you have a family here just waiting to get to know you.'

'Lady,' Ottilie said, pointing at the screen.

'A lovely lady,' Anna told her softly.

Ottilie turned to look at her and broke into the sweetest little laugh.

Touched by how much she seemed to be enjoying herself, Alex hugged her again and swallowed a lump that had lodged in her throat as she looked back at the screen. Katie, Rick's fiancée and Sarah's niece, was in shot now. She was very slim with boyishly cut white-blonde hair, large brown eyes and a smile that, to Alex's mind, didn't quite seem to reach them.

'Hi Charlotte,' she said, waving an airy hand. 'Really good that Anna's found you. Everyone's talking about it and hoping you'll come soon. It'll definitely be a change for you from Blighty, so be prepared. I love it here myself and wouldn't ever go back.'

Realising she was speaking with an English accent, Alex said, 'How long has she lived over there?'

'About ten years, I think,' Anna replied. 'She turned up with a friend during a gap year, fell in love with the place, and stayed.'

'So how long have she and Rick been together?'

'Mm, eighteen months? Obviously they've known each other a lot longer, with our two families being so close, but they were involved with other people until a couple of years ago. Ah, here's Shelley's husband Phil, with the kids.'

Hearing the pride and affection in her mother's voice, Alex turned to the screen as Anna's step-grandchildren spoke in unison, saying, 'Hi Charlotte, welcome to New Zealand. We're really looking forward to meeting you.' They grinned. 'I'm Danni, and I'm ten,' the lithe little blonde bombshell informed her. 'I'm Craig and I'm eight,' her curly-haired brother added.

'And I'm Phil and I'm thirty-eight,' their father quipped. 'Hi Charlotte. Welcome. They do a mean barbie in this house, so you need to get yourself over here.'

'Do you water-ski?' Danni asked.

'We do,' Craig told Alex.

At that up came a sequence showing both children whizzing round the bay on their skis, with Phil driving one boat and Rick the other. In voice-over, Danni said, 'We usually do this every day after school. It's one of our favourite sports, but Craig's really good at rugger too and I'm into dancing. I also love my horse, Diesel. If you come I'll take you out for a ride on him. He's very gentle.'

'And I'll teach you to dive if you like,' Craig chipped in, 'I mean if you don't already know how to do it. Mum said you might, because you live by the sea, but it's a lot colder over there so you might not.'

'Look,' Anna whispered and nodded towards Ottilie, whose eyes were like saucers as she watched the children cutting wild swathes through the water.

'Look,' Ottilie whispered to Boots, and held him up.

Stifling their laughs, Alex and Anna returned to the screen as the images changed to some kind of county fair and Bob said, 'I'm going to finish up with some additional flavour of our wonderful North Island. What you're seeing here is some footage of last year's Waimate Show, beginning with our very own Danni on Diesel. There she goes clearing the final jump, and now here she is picking up yet another prizewinner's cup. Now we have Craig parading one of the prizewinning lambs, and a real beauty she was too. Aha, here are a couple of babes on the dodgems, big kids the pair of them.' Alex laughed when she realised it was Anna and Sarah. 'Ooh! That looked nasty,' Bob gulped, as someone rammed their car into them. 'NZ's answer to road rage. Here we have a few of the sideshows for those of us who like to win big.'

Alex laughed again as Bob himself held up a sorry-looking plastic toy.

'Woof,' Ottilie said.

'That's right, it's a dog,' Alex told her.

'And of course no little taster of our wonderful country would be complete without showing you the All Blacks nailing the World Cup and touring it round town.'

By the time the sounds of cheering crowds faded into silence and the video was over, Alex felt so caught up in the world she'd been watching that it almost came as a shock to find herself in the Vicarage, with its tightly shut windows and dismal grey skies outside. She glanced at her mother and could so easily see her amongst her family in the video. She belonged there, far more than she did in this dingy, old-fashioned kitchen that had never seen a lobster or hosted the making of macadamia butter in its entire life.

Noticing that Ottilie had dropped off in her lap, she rose carefully from the chair with her cheek resting against Ottilie's head and began to rock her back and forth as Anna shut down the computer. Then, realising her mother was waiting for a response, she smiled as she said, 'It looks wonderful, nothing at all like I was expecting. I can understand why you're so happy there.'

Anna's smile seemed both knowing and troubled as she dropped her eyes to Ottilie and smoothed a finger over her cheek. 'I suppose it's time to take her home,' she said quietly.

Alex nodded, and making sure Boots was tucked safely into Ottilie's bag, she carried them out to the car. What was wrenching at her heart more than anything, she realised, was the guilt of knowing that the future, whatever it contained, was looking so much better for her than it was for Ottilie.

Alex and Anna spent that weekend viewing flats, most of which made Alex's head spin simply to walk through the door. She'd never dreamt of being able to live in such luxury. It was on the first floor of a glossy white Georgian town house with not one, but two bright and airy bedrooms, a newly fitted high-quality kitchen and a seriously grand, part-furnished sitting room with French windows on to balconies that looked straight out to sea, that Anna came to a decision. When an embarrassed Alex tried to point out that it was way beyond her means and that they really should go now, it appeared her mother wasn't listening. She declared the flat to be perfect, and ignoring the shock and protest on Alex's face she informed the agent that she'd bring a banker's draft to his office on Monday morning to cover the deposit and six months' rent starting November 1st.

'We'd also like to take an option on a further six months,' she added decisively. 'Just in case,' she informed Alex as they left, 'you think I'm trying to pressure you into moving to New Zealand by Easter.'

Having no idea how on earth she'd manage to pay the rent when the first six months were up, Alex decided simply to go with the flow for now and worry about it when the time came. After all, she'd have a second bedroom she could let out, so there was one answer already.

With the apartment sorted it was time, Anna declared, to indulge her long-forgotten, but suddenly resurgent passion for shopping. Since it wasn't a national hobby in New Zealand the way it was in England, she explained, she was determined to make the most of it while she was here.

Alex found it breathtaking to watch how much it thrilled her mother to spend, spend, spend, like she was a millionaire. Apart from the crazy number of presents she bought for everyone back home, she kept piling Alex up with more clothes, shoes, jewellery and make-up than Alex would ever know what to do with. She even offered to buy gifts for Ottilie, but Alex cautioned against it – she had no idea how Brian Wade would react, but she really didn't think he'd approve.

After exhausting themselves at the mall, they then rounded the weekend off with a dinner for Tommy and his wife Jackie, a large, energetic woman with vibrantly dyed red hair and as warm a heart as Tommy's. They arrived at the Vicarage bearing two bottles of Cloudy Bay that made Anna swoon with delight, and four albums of their own memorable two months in New Zealand, thirteen years ago.

In no time at all they were chatting away about the many different places in the world they'd visited, making Alex realise, with some embarrassment, that

481

she really needed to get out more. She was enjoying listening though, since it was offering her an even greater insight into her mother, and not only her, but the man who she, Alex, might one day get used to thinking of as her stepfather. Though that particular title often rang warning bells for someone in her position, finding that she had one of her own who seemed to be a model version of the species – gentle, humorous, not to mention extremely generous – was every bit as intriguing as the prospect of one day going to visit him.

It was towards the end of the evening that the conversation, almost inevitably, turned to Ottilie as Tommy asked how she was.

'Much the same as usual,' Alex replied, with a quick glance at her mother. She hoped Anna wasn't going to mention anything about her being too close to Ottilie, or it could end up ruining a lovely evening. 'The medical assessments can't happen soon enough though,' she added, 'for both her and her mother.'

'What about the child's inflammation?' Tommy prompted.

'I checked her myself when we were at nursery on Friday,' Alex said, 'and it's pretty well cleared up.'

'So could it have been whatever the doctor called it?' Jackie asked.

'Vulvovaginitis,' Alex provided, interested to realise that Tommy had told his wife about Ottilie. 'Yes, it could, in fact I'd prefer to think that it was, because the alternative is somewhere we really don't want to go.'

Jackie's expression was grim as she glanced at Anna and shook her head in dismay. 'You just never know where bad things are going to happen, do you?' she sighed. 'And to think of what that bloke does for a living. He's with kids all the time, so it makes you wonder if any of them are safe.'

'To be honest, it's about the only thing that's helping me to trust him,' Alex told her. 'If anything was going on at the school something would surely have come to light by now, if not through one of the parents, then one of the teachers.'

'It reminds me of a case, years ago,' Tommy said, picking up his wine. 'It was a chap who drove buses for kids with special needs. A kinder, gentler soul you never wished to meet; he'd do anything for anyone, went out of his way to make sure his passengers were properly taken care of, even used to remember their birthdays. Turned out he had a little boy at home, Euan his name was, eight years old, and what that animal had been doing to his own son . . .'

Anna shuddered. 'Why do you say it reminds you of Ottilie?' she asked worriedly.

'I suppose because he worked with kids, and it took us over a year to get any evidence of what was actually going on with the boy. We suspected it after an incident at school brought him to our attention, but delivering actual proof, or enough to persuade the courts that he was in danger, turned out to be next to impossible.'

'What about the boy's mother?' Jackie protested. 'Didn't she know what was going on?'

Tommy shook his head sadly. 'Even if she did, poor woman probably didn't understand. She had the mental age of a ten-year-old and though she loved her son, she had no more idea of what it meant to be a mother than she did of what it was to be a right-thinking person.'

'So what happened to the little boy in the end?' Alex dared to ask.

Looking as though he wished he hadn't started the story now, Tommy said, 'I want to tell you he was taken into care, but I'm afraid he was taken to the graveyard. The father killed him, I suppose to stop him from talking, then he went to the police and confessed.'

Alex's face had turned white.

'It's not going to happen here,' Tommy assured her. 'We've got the paediatrician's report coming this week, and the psych on the mother . . .'

'Yeah, what about Ottilie's mother?' Jackie came in. 'Where's she in all of this?'

Alex sighed. 'It's a very good question, but all I can tell you is that it never seems to be on this planet. It might be helpful if I could find out what sort of medication she's on, because I swear she's drugged out of her mind half the time. Her doctor admits to prescribing sleeping tablets, but as you can get just about anything online these days, I have to wonder if she's self-prescribing.'

As they sat with the bleakness of that, Jackie turned to Anna and said, 'I don't expect you imagined being caught up in anything like this when you came to find your daughter.'

Anna's smile was weak. 'Not really, no,' she admitted, 'but what matters is that I support her in any way I can.'

Alex glanced at her gratefully as Jackie nodded.

'She's going to miss you when you've gone back,' Jackie commented. 'How much longer are you staying?'

'Until the weekend,' Anna replied, looking at Alex. 'Then we're hoping she'll come to us for Christmas.'

Not wanting to think about the parting, or to say anything to disappoint her mother, since a lot could happen between now and then, Alex simply smiled as though she was keen on the idea of the visit, which under other circumstances she might have been, and got up to make some coffee.

What's going to happen to you, Ottilie? she was thinking, as she gazed at the odd-looking picture pinned to the fridge. It was one Ottilie had done a few days ago, at nursery, when Janet had asked the children to draw an animal that scared them. Most had come up with various forms of jagged teeth, or claws, saying they were lions or tigers, or savage dogs, but Ottilie had simply drawn a line then scribbled all over it. When Alex had asked her what it was, she'd pushed it away and hidden behind Boots.

If only she could persuade Ottilie to talk a little more, she might be able to get some idea of what was going on, not only in her mind, but in that wretchedly dismal house on the hill.

'I'm going to give Ottilie her bath now,' Brian Wade informed his wife. 'Do we still have the cream the doctor gave us for her inflammation?'

Erica was staring at the night-black window. The big yellow eye had been watching her for over an hour, the entire time Brian had been inside it with Ottilie. It had stopped now; even the afterglow was fading.

Brian shifted Ottilie on to his other arm. She was pale, limp with exhaustion, unable to hold up her head. 'Did you hear me?' he prompted irritably.

Erica had no idea why he was asking her, when he was the one who applied the cream.

485

As he walked on through the kitchen and out into the hall Erica's gaze dropped to the bank of knives in front of her, blades buried, handles inviting. Wrapping her fingers around one, she drew it slowly from the block and turned it over in her hand. She imagined plunging it into everyone she hated, all those who were screaming inside her head. She envisaged blood spurting up the walls, dripping from the lights, pooling on the floor.

Her gaze returned to where the unblinking eye was slumbering, invisible in the darkness. Tomorrow, or the next day, she would climb inside it and try again to destroy its evil brain.

Chapter Twenty-Two

It was on Wednesday morning while Alex was at the Pumpkin with Ottilie that Scott Danes rang from Northumbria.

'Hope this is a good time,' he said in his brusque northern way. 'I've got some news you're going to want to hear.'

Anxious not to be overheard, Alex said, 'Bear with me one second,' and kneeling in front of Ottilie she whispered, 'This is an important call that I have to take. I'll just be in the office, OK?'

Ottilie's glum face turned towards her, and she started to get up.

'It's all right, I'll look after you,' Chloe said, putting an arm around her.

'I won't be long,' Alex promised.

By the time she reached the door she could still feel Ottilie's eyes following her, and had to force herself not to turn round. If she did, she knew she'd go back for her, or at least stay in the room where Ottilie could see her. Maybe she should stay anyway, because these last couple of days Ottilie had been even more withdrawn than usual, and Alex didn't want to make her feel any more insecure.

So, settling herself in a far corner, she gave Ottilie

a wave as she returned to the call. 'OK, with you,' she told Scott Danes.

'Great. This is pretty interesting stuff,' he began. 'It turns out that Jill McCarthy, deceased mother of Erica Wade, was a card-carrying member of the officially diagnosed paranoid-schizophrenic brigade.'

Alex's heart gave an unsteady beat.

'As you probably know, the condition can be hereditary, so Erica could also be at risk.'

Oh God, please don't let it be the same for Ottilie.

It explained so much about Erica, though, and instantly made Alex fearful of ever leaving Ottilie with her again. There would be nothing she could do until they had another official diagnosis, of course, and even then Brian Wade might challenge it . . .

He'd have a serious fight on his hands if he did.

'Now we come to Erica Wade's stepfather, George McCarthy,' Scott Danes ran on. 'And this is where it gets even more interesting. The real father snuffed it around the time Erica was born, by the way, but he wasn't with the mother then anyway. Back to stepfather George. He committed suicide twelve years ago while serving a twenty-five-year stretch for the sexual, physical and mental abuse of Jill's only daughter, namely Erica. The length of the sentence will tell you how bad it was. I can send details if you like, but believe me, it doesn't make for easy reading.'

Knowing that nothing in that category ever did, Alex said, 'I'm going to need it anyway, so if you can attach whatever you have to an email . . . Did you come up with any psychiatric reports on Erica either as a child, or later?'

488

'Not so far, but that's not to say they don't exist, I just haven't had a lot of time to go digging. I'll stay on it though, and get back to you with whatever I find.'

'Thanks, I really appreciate it. And if you can manage to come up with anything on Brian Wade . . .'

'Don't worry, I've been trying, but nothing's come to light on him yet that sets him apart from any other guy on the block. Only child of schoolteacher parents, both practising Christians, both long since skipped off to the Elysian Fields. Got a 2:1 in English at Manchester, started teaching at a primary school in Hull a few months after graduation, moved to Leeds a couple of years later which is presumably where he met Erica, who was a teaching assistant at the same school. They got married at St Mark's in Scarborough, had a baby boy four years later, which is about the time they moved up here, to my neck of the woods. The rest you know.'

'That the baby boy died when he was three years old while Erica was pregnant with Ottilie. No suspicious circumstances surrounding his death, or none that came to light at the time. She's now neglecting Ottilie terribly in an emotional sense, and her husband, though he must know that, doesn't seem to want to do anything about it.'

'Which, in itself, gives me cause for suspicion, but you're the expert here, what do you think?' Scott asked.

Recalling the story Tommy had told about the school bus driver and his mentally deficient wife, Alex was about to reply when she spotted Ottilie trotting towards the door. Smiling to see Anna coming in, she said to Scott Danes, 'I'm going to put my thoughts in an email so we have everything on record. Meantime, you've given me some vital information today. Thanks very much.'

Ringing off, she sat watching Ottilie's face coming alive with amazement as Anna began blowing bubbles from the pot she'd brought with her. Chloe was clapping her hands to burst them, and gently encouraged by Anna Ottilie joined in. The sound of her laughter wrapped itself so tightly around Alex's heart that she wondered if she'd ever heard anything so lovely. It didn't seem as though Ottilie had ever played with bubbles before, and the look of sheer surprise and joy on her face when Anna gave her the wand to blow some too almost made Alex want to cry. How lovely it was to see her looking happy when she'd been so sad these last few days.

Pulling herself together, Alex quickly rang Tommy to brief him on the call from Scott Danes, then rang the psychiatrist's office to report what she'd learned about Erica Wade's mother.

'The relevant documents are on their way,' she told the secretary. 'I'll send them on as soon as they arrive, just please tell me that Mrs Wade's appointment hasn't been cancelled again.'

After checking, the secretary said, 'No, she's still booked in for Friday.'

'Good. If it changes, please ring or text and let me know.'

As she ended the call her mother came to sit with her, still laughing at the way Ottilie was gaining so much pleasure from making Chloe and a few others go chasing after bubbles. 'Such a simple thing,' she sighed, unbuttoning her coat.

'And it's brought such a lovely big smile to her face,' Alex added, feeling her insides twisting with dread of what the next forty-eight hours might bring. How terrible it was going to be for Ottilie, being subjected to a virginity test. She could hardly bear to think of it, yet it had to happen. 'So how did you get on with the estate agent?' she asked Anna.

Anna beamed. 'Everything's set for you to move in at the beginning of November. So I think we should start making a list of what you're taking with you from the Vicarage. That way we can draw up another of what you're going to need.'

Alex's answer was cut off by a scream. Her eyes flew straight to Ottilie who was already running towards her, chin wobbling as she tried not to cry. Alex scooped her up and held her close, feeling her little frame shuddering as Chloe, still in the midst of a fracas, angrily scolded a curly-haired blond boy for being so mean.

'He knocked Ottilie's bubbles right out of her hand and now they're all over the floor,' she cried indignantly as Janet stepped in to sort them out.

'All right, all right, I'm sure it was an accident . . .'

'No it wasn't, he did it on purpose and I think he should say sorry.'

As a helper came along to wipe up the mess, Anna whispered to Ottilie, 'Don't worry, I've got a secret bottle in my bag that we'll keep until we go to the park.'

Ottilie lifted her head, her eyes shiny with tears as she looked at Anna – her very own fairy godmother.

Anna smiled. 'I wonder if we can take Chloe to the park too,' she said. 'We'll have to check it's all right with her mummy first, but if it is, shall we do that?'

Ottilie nodded and gasped on a sob as Alex used a finger to wipe the tears from her cheeks.

'Shall we get Boots for you now?' Alex suggested. 'Then you can take him to listen to the story before we go.'

With the drama effectively over and children gathered round for the next instalment of *The Gruffalo*, Alex and Anna gratefully accepted some tea from another helper and sat down again.

'You seem worried,' Anna commented. 'Is it something I should know about?'

After taking a sip of her tea Alex recounted the call from Scott Danes, her eyes on Ottilie as she spoke, her mind racing ahead to what it could all mean. 'Something I keep coming back to,' she said in the end, 'is the way paedophiles are known to prey on people, usually women, who are weak, often mentally challenged, to use them as a kind of cover for their perversions.'

Anna's revulsion was curling her lip. 'Are you saying you think Ottilie's father . . . ? You are, aren't you?'

Alex said, 'I don't know for certain, but it's starting to bear the hallmarks.'

'So what are you going to do?'

'The only thing I can do. Take her to see the paediatrician tomorrow, get the report and hope with every fibre of my being that I'm wrong.' She turned to look at her mother.

'Will the paediatrician be able to tell for certain?' Anna asked.

Alex's heart sank as she shook her head. 'Not necessarily,' she replied. 'I mean, obviously a virginity test in itself will be conclusive, but there is more than one way of breaking a hymen. And if there's no penetration involved in the abuse, it's almost impossible to prove that something's going on.'

Anna's eyes went down, and as Alex turned back to Ottilie she decided that all she could do for the next twenty-four hours was at least try to carry on hoping that she was wrong.

Later that day, having spent the best part of the afternoon with Ottilie and Chloe, Anna and Alex were back at the Vicarage drinking a glass of wine each as they prepared dinner. Mattie was due to arrive at any minute with a short list of potential judges for *Mulgrove's Got Talent*, and a much longer list of budding hopefuls from amongst their friends and neighbours. Since the contest had the promise of providing a hilarious run-up to Christmas, Alex felt sorry that Anna wasn't going to be around to enjoy it too. Or to help her move into her new flat, which was still seeming slightly unreal, or to lend her some moral support when things came to a head with Ottilie, which they were almost certainly going to do in the next couple of weeks.

How empty the Vicarage was going to feel once Anna had gone, and how silent her world with no one to talk to, at least not in the way she'd lately been opening up to her mother. She was dreading Anna going, but it was best, she kept telling herself, not to think about it any more than she had to.

Alex's mobile rang at the same instant as the front bell chimed. 'I'll get the door if you get the phone,' Anna announced, putting down her tasting spoon.

Digging her mobile from her bag, Alex's heart lurched when she saw who was calling.

'Mr Wade,' she said stiffly as she clicked on. 'I hope everything's all right with Ottilie.'

'Yes, she's fine, thank you,' he retorted, 'but of course she's the reason I'm calling. I've managed to snatch a few hours off school tomorrow, so I'll be able to take her to the paediatrician myself.'

Thrown by the unexpectedness of it, Alex found herself momentarily lost for an objection. 'Well, that's very good,' she finally managed, while thinking it was absolutely not good at all. However, as Ottilie's father he had every right to take her – indeed, it really ought to be him, and his wife, so what grounds did she have to try and deny them? Unable to dredge any up, she said, 'You know the time, I take it, and where to go?'

'Two o'clock at the Kesterly Health Centre.'

She wanted to ask if he really meant to go, or if this was an eleventh-hour attempt to stave off the inevitable, but for the moment she had no choice but to take him at his word. 'Are you still able to accompany your wife on Friday for her appointment?' she asked.

'Actually, that might prove a little difficult now, but I'm still trying to juggle things around.'

'It's very important for her to make it,' Alex told him abruptly. And deciding just to come out with it, she said, 'I've learned today that her mother was a paranoid schizophrenic, so if she has mental health issues too we need to know.'

There was a moment's awful silence before he said, 'I hadn't realised you were snooping into my wife's family history.'

'There wouldn't have been a need if you'd told me yourself that Jill McCarthy was your mother-in-law's name and that she was mentally afflicted. Instead, it seems you chose to overlook the obvious, that it was your wife who was making the calls to the school accusing you of killing your son.'

Mattie blinked in astonishment as she came into the kitchen.

'In fact,' Alex pressed on, 'I'd go as far as to say that you've been extremely negligent when it comes to telling me the truth about your wife, which leads me to ask: what exactly are you trying to hide, Mr Wade?'

As the phone went down at the other end Alex almost threw her own against the wall. Instead, she rapidly scrolled to his number and pressed to reconnect. It didn't surprise her that he failed to pick up, but it didn't do much to calm her temper either – or her fears of the damage she might just have done.

'I'm sorry,' she told Mattie, who was always uneasy with displays of emotion, 'I've got a very difficult father on my hands at the moment.' To her mother she said, 'Apparently he's going to take Ottilie for her appointment tomorrow.'

In spite of her concerns about Alex's closeness to Ottilie, Anna looked no happier about that than Alex felt. 'I don't suppose you can insist that you do it?' she enquired tentatively.

Alex shook her head. 'He'd just better turn up, is all I can say, because if he doesn't . . .' If he didn't, what was she going to do? She was already dialling Tommy's number. If Brian Wade thought he was going to stop Ottilie from seeing a paediatrician, then he was soon going to find out that the very minute she heard he hadn't shown up would be the very minute an Emergency Protection Order would be slapped on his daughter.

She couldn't bear the thought of Ottilie going into care; with all her heart she wanted to be able to look after her herself, but she couldn't, and if her father was doing anything to harm her she absolutely had to be got away from him.

She only hoped that her outburst a few minutes ago hadn't sent Wade into some sort of panic, because if anything happened to Ottilie between now and tomorrow she would never *ever* be able to forgive herself.

Brian Wade was sitting on a chair next to Ottilie's bed holding a copy of *Paddington Helps Out* in one hand, and Boots in the other. Ottilie was beneath the duvet, wide-eyed with incomprehension as she watched her bear and fought the urge to reach out and rescue him.

'So now, you understand, don't you,' her father was saying, 'that there's nothing to be afraid of. You only have to do as you're told and everything will be all right.'

Ottilie's eyes darted to his face and back to Boots.

'Do you understand?' her father insisted.

Ottilie quickly nodded.

'Do I have your promise that you'll behave as I tell you?'

Again she was quick to nod.

'Boots is listening, and he'll be with us, so if you break your promise he'll know and then he won't want to be with you any more. You don't want that to happen, do you?'

Ottilie shook her head and started to put out her hand.

'Ah, ah, he's not ready to come back yet,' he declared, moving Boots out of reach. 'He wants to listen to the story here on my lap.'

Obediently, Ottilie pulled her hand back.

Wade's head tilted to one side as a thought

seemed to occur to him. 'You know, I do believe Tiger wants to listen too,' he said, 'so I think we should let him, don't you?'

Ottilie's lower lip started to tremble.

'Oh now, he's going to think you don't like him if you look like that, and we can't allow that, can we?'

Ottilie tried to swallow.

'OK,' her father said a few minutes later, sitting comfortably with Boots propped against Tiger. 'We're ready, so I hope you are too.'

By the time the story ended and he left Ottilie's room she was fast asleep, her bear snuggled in next to her and the book back on its shelf. His cheeks were flushed, and his hand trembled slightly as he closed the door.

As he passed Erica's room he paused and listened. There were no sounds coming from within. He hadn't expected any, given the number of pills he'd watched her swallowing earlier. She took no care of what they were, never checked a label or even measured a dose.

It would be the easiest thing in the world to send her off into a sleep from which she would never awaken. No blame would be attached to him; the online orders were all in her name, placed from her computer and delivered to this address. She had her own bank account that he transferred small amounts of money to each month, enough to cover the cost of groceries that were also purchased from her computer, and the few extras she might need, such as pills. Ottilie's clothes and several of her toys were ordered and paid for the same way. Of course he bought some of them himself, as any father would who wanted to treat his little girl.

Going on to his own room he sat down on the

bed and put his head in his hands. Alex Lake's words were beating a vicious tattoo in his brain. 'What are you trying to hide, Mr Wade? What are you trying to hide?'

Everything, was the answer. Absolutely everything, but his secrets were like prisms: each time he managed to cover an image, another would appear, then another, then another. At the heart of them all were the faces of children with names long forgotten, if they'd ever been known – except there were those he remembered well, such as his son, Jonathan, and now his daughter, Ottilie.

Erica was in the shed. It was morning – the air outside was chill and damp and pouring in through the smashed window like a watery soup. It was clinging to her hair like tiny crystals, dampening her skin and settling in filmy layers over the computer and photographic equipment so carefully polished and stored.

Boots.

Of course it was the password. So simple, so obvious. Why hadn't she thought of it before?

She was delving deeply into the yellow eye's brain now, plucking out pictures, stories, emails, whole websites, like digging cockles from shells. As a child she used to find cockles in rock pools; she'd kept one once and called him Harry. He wasn't much of a friend, but she'd cried anyway when her stepfather had crushed him.

She used to cry a lot, but then she'd learned not to.

Ottilie was learning that it did no good.

Ottilie was here, frozen in images, moving in videos, packed into files, folders, albums, downloads, uploads . . . She even had a fan page.

Erica hummed as she copied it and sent it on its way to her own computer.

A fan page!

Ottilie had fans.

Ottilie probably had no idea what a fan was, much less that she had any.

Alex Lake could be termed a fan, couldn't she, though not in the same sense as those who belonged to Brian's club.

Where was Brian now?

She'd lost track of the time, maybe she shouldn't be here any more. If he found her . . . What would he do?

She hiccuped loudly, a sharp, staccato sound that punctured the air like pellets from the gun her step-father used to own. He'd shot her once, her mother too.

She hated her mother.

It didn't matter what Brian might do; it was too late now anyway.

Alex clicked off her phone and heaved a troubled sigh as she looked at her mother. 'Well, at least we know he took her,' she declared, 'but apparently the paediatrician's been called out on an emergency, so she's going to ring me tomorrow.'

Anna was looking as worried as Alex, but relieved too that at least Ottilie had been taken to her appointment. 'Did the nurse give you any indication of how it went?' she asked.

Alex shook her head. 'Not really, just that Ottilie was very good and didn't cry, and that her father was most respectful and concerned about what was happening.' With a dubious roll of her eyes she opened the fridge to take out some wine. Her mother always enjoyed a glass around six, and it seemed she was falling into the habit too.

This evening was to be their last together before Anna flew home on Saturday. Because the flight was leaving so early it made sense for her to spend the night before at a hotel close to the airport, so it was her intention to start out from Mulgrove around two tomorrow afternoon. Alex was dreading it, they both were, but there was no way Anna could stay any longer. The invitations had already gone out for Bob's sixtieth birthday party, and over eighty people had replied to say they were coming. Besides, Alex had to return to full-time work on Monday.

They'd spent most of the day at the retail centre on the edge of town, browsing furniture stores and kitchen shops while trying not to worry themselves sick about Ottilie. It was over a salad at Bella Pasta that they'd decided it would be best for Anna to leave without saying goodbye to her. They didn't want to make a fuss of it, in case it upset her and left her with a fear that Alex might do the same. Simply disappearing didn't feel like much of a good alternative, but as they'd agreed, it was the least traumatic way of letting go.

Anna hadn't voiced the suspicion that she might not see Ottilie again, but it had been there between them, large and real and as inescapable as the dread of where Ottilie might end up. If she was removed from the family home then it might not be possible for Anna to visit her the next time she came to England. It would depend on her carers and whether or not they considered it to be in Ottilie's best interests.

'But of course, as her social worker, I'll have a say

500

in it too,' Alex had assured her mother, 'so don't let's look on the black side yet.'

Anna had forced a smile, in much the same way as she was forcing one now. 'It's a funny thing about children, isn't it?' she said. 'They work their way into your heart and are filling it up before you've even noticed.'

'It's lovely that you care about her,' Alex replied. 'I'm not sure anyone else has in her short little life, at least not in a way that's good for her.'

'Apart from you, of course.'

Alex nodded. 'Apart from me.' She couldn't put into words how deeply she cared, nor would she try. It was hard enough to think of the times that lay ahead when Ottilie might be wondering where she was and not understanding why she didn't come, without struggling to express it.

After filling two glasses with wine and tipping a bag of nuts into a bowl, she sat down at the table and watched her mother opening up the computer. They were about to embark on their last call to Bob together; after tonight they would speak to one another through Skype, feeling the thousands of miles between them while technology brought them together. The time difference meant that everything would have to be prearranged – no more spontaneity or exchanges of idle thoughts, only forced exuberance and promises to be in touch again soon.

After a lifetime of being without her mother, two weeks of getting to know her wasn't anywhere near long enough. She could feel an awful, engulfing sense of loneliness coming over her, which was foolish, she knew, and even childish, but she couldn't help it.

'It's still a bit early yet,' Anna said, when Bob didn't reply. 'I'll try again in a few minutes.'

501

As her eyes came to Alex and Alex saw her tears, she felt her own starting to burn. They laughed and hugged and reminded each other that they'd promised not to cry, but it was a promise they both knew they'd never be able to keep.

In the end Bob's call managed to get them laughing in a way that lasted a while after they rang off. Alex could feel how torn her mother was between a longing to return to her husband and the desire to prolong her stay – perhaps until she could take her daughter home with her.

Alex wasn't sure that day would ever come, but on the other hand she wasn't going to rule it out.

It was gone midnight before they finally exhausted themselves talking and went off to bed. Though Alex felt sure she'd be unable to sleep, to her amazement, when she woke up, she realised it was morning and past the time she usually rose.

She found her mother already in the kitchen, warming bread in the oven and scrambling eggs on the stove. How wonderful it was to be this spoiled; how awful it was going to feel when she came down the stairs tomorrow to find no one there.

'Did you sleep?' she asked, going to pour herself a coffee.

'Better than I expected to,' Anna replied, passing her own mug for a refill. With a sigh, she said, 'I keep wishing you could come and stay the night at the hotel with me, but I don't want you making that long drive back after we've said goodbye.'

'I wouldn't mind,' Alex told her.

'Maybe not, but I would. And besides, it would mean taking two cars to the airport today, which is a bit of a nonsense. Then I'll have to go off to the terminal at five thirty in the morning, even more of a nonsense. So it's best that we stay with our plan to say goodbye here.'

Alex went to put her arms around her. 'Thank you for coming to find me,' she whispered.

'I'm so glad I did.' Anna smiled tenderly. 'You've grown into a wonderful young woman. I feel so proud of you, coming through all that you have and turning out as smart and capable as you are.'

Alex's eyes twinkled. 'That sounds like me,' she said teasingly.

'It is you,' Anna told her. 'I've watched you over these last two weeks and I've come to admire you almost as much as I love you. You understand, don't you, that I never stopped loving you?'

Alex nodded. 'Yes, I understand,' she replied, her eyes starting to blur.

'And I never will stop. From now on, I'll always be there for you, no matter what. Whether we're thousands of miles apart, or in the same country, nothing is ever going to come between us again.'

Thinking of Ottilie, Alex said, 'We must try not to let it, but sometimes . . .' She stopped as Anna put a finger over her lips.

'I know what's in your mind,' she said, 'but I promise you, things have a way of working themselves out. I know it's taken a very long time for us, but that's not to say it'll be the same for Ottilie.'

Wishing she could believe that, Alex turned at the sound of her mobile ringing. Both dreading and hoping it would be the paediatrician, she went to dig it out of her bag. Seeing that it was indeed the doctor, she felt her insides turning weak.

'Hi, Alex Lake speaking,' she said, clicking on.

'Hi Alex, it's Tina, Tina Gardiner.'

'Yes, how are you?' she asked.

'I'm good. Rushed off my feet as usual, but I know you're waiting for my report on Ottilie Wade. I'll make sure it's typed up and emailed over by the end of the day, but I thought you'd want an answer to your most pressing question right away.'

Alex could no longer breathe.

'I'm afraid she's not intact. The hymen's broken and the clitoris is responsive to mild stimulation.'

Alex tried to speak, but unthinkable images were blocking the words.

'Needless to say the father had an excuse for the hymen,' Tina Gardiner continued. 'Apparently she fell off a tyre swing about eighteen months ago and landed on a tent peg.'

The tyre swing. 'Do – do you believe him?' Alex managed to ask.

'Let's just say there are no scars consistent with that sort of injury, but as for proving he's lying . . . It'll take some doing and it'll also require Ottilie to go through more internal exams. Anyway, I'm sorry the news isn't good. From what I hear you've taken a special interest in the child, so I understand this will be a blow.'

It was more than that, it was devastating.

For the first time in her life Alex felt that she really, truly wanted to kill another human being.

'As I said,' Tina Gardiner continued, 'a full report will be with you by the end of the day, or, if I'm being honest, it could be Monday or Tuesday before you get it now. Sorry about that, it's just the way things are.'

After thanking her, Alex rang off and as the grotesque imagery of Ottilie and her father loomed at her again, she ran to the bathroom to be sick.

A while later her mother was dabbing her mouth

with a wet flannel as her heart pounded wildly in her chest. 'I've just realised something,' she said weakly. 'The day I first met Ottilie at her home and I asked what games she wanted to play she said 'not tyre'. At least that's what I thought she said, but she's never shown any signs of being nervous about going on a tyre swing while she's been with us. You'd have thought she would, if the fall was what injured her so badly, but the only thing she never wants to see or have anything to do with is a tiger, which sounds like tyre, especially the way she says it.' Her eyes went to Anna's. 'She doesn't actually know what a tiger is, because when she saw one in a jigsaw puzzle, and then I showed her one at the zoo, she had no idea it was an animal with stripes.'

Suspecting where this was leading, Anna's revulsion showed.

'She was happy if I called it Tigger, just not tiger,' Alex went on, starting to feel nauseous again.

'So what are you going to do?' Anna asked hoarsely.

Alex was trying to make herself think clearly. 'Obviously report it to Tommy,' she replied, 'then we'll have to speak to Brian Wade ourselves . . .'

'But knowing what you do, can't you take her away now?'

Alex shook her head. 'We still have no proof, but at least the paediatrician seems to be on our side, which isn't to say another one will be, and there's no doubt that Brian Wade will demand a second opinion, possibly even a third.'

Anna seemed at a loss. 'Well, I guess there's always a chance he's telling the truth,' she ventured weakly.

'I only wish I could believe that, but I'm afraid I can't.' Alex glanced at the time. 'I have to pick Ottilie up and take her to nursery. She's going to be with me all day, until her parents get back from her mother's psychiatric assessment.'

'Jesus Christ,' Anna murmured helplessly, 'that poor child hardly stands a chance, does she? A mother who's crazy and a father who's very probably one of the lowest forms of human life . . .'

'Not very probably, he is,' Alex insisted. 'There's no doubt in my mind about that, and what's more, I'm going to prove it.' Already the implications of exposing the deputy head of a primary school were starting to present themselves, but she was far from daunted. 'If it's the last thing I ever do,' she declared forcefully, 'I'm going to make sure that sly, evil bastard never lays a hand on her again.'

Chapter Twenty-Three

Brian Wade was digging and digging, turning over huge spadefuls of earth, throwing them on to a pile that was already almost to his waist. He knew Ottilie was watching from an upstairs window and perhaps Erica was too, but he didn't care. Since Thursday's visit to the paediatrician he'd been trapped in a paralysis of fear, not knowing what to do or where to turn. This morning, as he was getting ready for church, it had come to him. He must create a hole large enough to bury the evidence of his shame, a grave for the proof Alex Lake was seeking.

She'd come on Friday, as usual, to collect Ottilie for nursery, but he'd sent her away. She hadn't gone easily, had put up a terrible fight, but not so terrible that he hadn't won in the end. Ottilie was his daughter; if he wanted to take her to nursery himself, he had every right to. The fact that he hadn't turned up at the Pumpkin had taken little time to get back to Ms Lake, because she'd been banging on the door again within the hour, demanding to see Ottilie for herself.

He'd allowed it, briefly, then had sent Ottilie back to her room.

'Are you taking your wife for her assessment today?' Alex Lake had thrown out the challenge with such contempt that even if he'd been in any doubt before, which he hadn't, he'd have known then that the paediatrician had already confided her findings.

Ottilie had fallen from a tyre swing on to a tent peg. For heaven's sake, it happened, and it was tragic, but it couldn't be helped.

'You know my wife has difficulties about leaving the house,' he'd thrown back at Alex Lake. 'She can't do it, she's an agoraphobic . . .'

'She has far worse problems than that and you know it,' Alex Lake had cut in. 'You're using her, trying to hide behind her, but it's not going to work.'

'If you'd let me finish I could tell you that I'm going to see the psychiatrist myself,' he growled, but nerves were diluting his indignation, making him sound pathetic and weak. 'I need to tell him about her, explain what's happened in her past, the reasons why she's the way she is now.'

'It's her he needs to see, not you.'

'I'm aware of that, but . . .'

'You're stalling again, Mr Wade, trying to prevent us from doing our jobs, but let me tell you this, nothing you do is going to save you from what you've done to your daughter. There is nowhere, *nowhere* in the world you can hide from that. Do you hear me? I don't care who you are, or what kind of defence you put up . . .'

He'd slammed the door on her then and stood against it, his pounding heart deafening him as he'd waited for her to drive away. It had taken a while longer for her to go than he'd expected, but in the end she'd had no choice but to leave.

She'd be back though, there was no doubt about that.

It was Sunday afternoon now. He wondered if she'd been told that he had gone to see the psychiatrist. Even if she had, the doctor couldn't – at least shouldn't – have divulged what had been said, because the official request was for an assessment on his wife, and he'd only spoken about himself. He'd hijacked the appointment and told the doctor, pleaded with him to understand that what was happening to him, the things he did, weren't his fault. He was one of nature's victims, an otherwise normally functioning person with a terrible mix-up in the chemistry of his brain, a wrongly wired circuit that allowed no change to his default system. Everyone had urges, some much stronger than others – his weren't as bad as many others he knew of, and he'd swear before God that he'd never touched a child that wasn't his own.

Had he detected disgust and loathing in the psychiatrist's eyes? Certainly it had been there in Alex Lake's. Occasionally his wife looked at him that way too, when she was in a sane enough state of mind to look at him at all. He knew she saw her stepfather in him, but he was nothing like that oaf, who had been evil through and through. A sadist, a lecher, an abuser in every sense of the word, and his demented wife, Erica's mother, had been no better. Though they'd died before Erica came into his life, he'd sensed from the start how fragile, how deeply scarred she was by the upbringing she'd been forced to endure. He'd pitied her, and wanted to protect her, so he'd taken her up, married her and given her a new start in a new town.

She had much to be grateful to him for, including their children – and not forgetting, *never* forgetting, the secret he'd never told, that she, with her bare hands, had stifled their three-year-old son to death. If he hadn't stood by her over that she'd be in Broadmoor now, or some other establishment for the criminally insane. Ottilie would have been born there, and he'd have been forced to find another mother for his daughter.

As it was they were trapped here in this house, each of them suffering in their own way, unable to communicate with one another, or with anyone on the outside. It was their prison, their punishment, their own private hell.

The hole must be at least four feet deep by now. He was perspiring so badly that the air on his skin felt colder than it was, and sharp. Blisters were forming on his hands, his heart and lungs were burning with exertion. Pains creaked through his back as he righted himself. He was parched, trembling and so afraid that he could barely summon the strength to make himself walk.

He must do something with Ottilie before everything erupted around them.

Erica was watching from the kitchen window, a faint smile on her lips and a knife in her hand. She didn't look at the knife, or even particularly feel its weight; she simply held it and watched her husband's activities in a wistful sort of way as she listened to the voices in her head. Some were deep and echoey, others shrieked and whined, still others rasped and choked and mocked her in accents she didn't understand. Threading through them all was the song her stepfather used to sing, the haunting, chilling tune with its cruelly changed words: *Round and round the garden like a teddy bear, one step two step smash her on the stair.*

Sensing Ottilie standing behind her, she turned around and hissed like a snake. It was the way her mother used to hiss at her.

Eyes wide with terror, Ottilie scampered back down the hall.

Erica returned her glassy eyes to the garden. Brian was lumbering towards his studio now, his face bloated and muddied by his efforts, his shoulders sagging with the weight of all that he carried. Erica was certain this would be the first time he'd gone in there since Thursday, the day he'd taken Ottilie for her physical exam. Since then it had sat there like a chamber of horrors, slumbering in its space under the tree, its single yellow eye closed to business. Anyone who entered did so at their peril.

He must have noticed by now that the window was gone, and would no doubt guess she had smashed it again, using the garden spade he'd just left beside the freshly dug grave.

Now would be the time, she decided, to go upstairs and carry out the first of her little jobs for today.

Alex was standing on the front in Kesterly. Pounding waves were rearing off the sea wall behind her as she stared across the road at the smart white Georgian house that was to be her home from the beginning of November. It hardly seemed real: indeed, since her mother had left on Friday almost nothing had felt grounded in truth. It was as though she'd made everything up, from the tentative, awkward moments she and her mother had first laid eyes on each other, to the ache of standing at the Vicarage door watching her driving away. The feelings inside her then had been awful, far worse even than she'd feared, as the dread of not seeing her again rose up from the past to engulf her. She'd felt like a small child, shut in a cupboard, unable to get out and desperate for her mother to save her.

They'd spoken yesterday. Anna had rung from Dubai where she was changing planes. By now she should have landed in Auckland. Bob had promised to meet her there so he could make the short hop to Keri Keri with her, where no doubt other members of their family would be waiting to treat her to the kind of welcome that made Alex feel both envious and proud. She had no trouble imagining how delighted they'd be to see their stepmother, aunt, grandma. As Alex had found, she was the kind of woman who lit up people's lives, so why wouldn't they love her?

Looking around at the gloom of her surroundings as daylight began merging slowly into dusk, she felt almost burdened by the austere drama of the steel-grey estuary and forbidding sky. By comparison she saw the Bay of Islands as flamboyantly exotic, full of light, constantly warm. It was odd to realise that it was already Monday over there. Tonight had come and gone, and tomorrow was their today. Anna had said she'd take until Tuesday to recover from the flight, then she'd be throwing herself into plans for the party with the same sort of relish as Bob threw himself in for a dive.

Could their worlds possibly be any more different? Of course she'd known her own would feel drab and empty as soon as her mother left, how could it not when she'd wafted in like an artist's paintbrush, adding so much vibrancy and meaning to her daughter's drooping and dreary hopes, so many new dimensions to her dreams that she, Alex, was only just waking up to what her life could actually be like.

She'd made the mistake of saying that to Gabby when Gabby and Martin had come to Mulgrove earlier to pack up Gabby's old bedroom and transport everything down to Devon. The hurt and confusion in Gabby's eyes had made Alex feel wretched, just as she did now, remembering it. How could she have been so insensitive as to make everything Myra and Douglas had done for her seem colourless, maybe even worthless, now she'd been reunited with her real mother?

Before she'd left Gabby had said, 'I know Anna's much more glamorous than Mum, and younger too, so I understand why you think she's something special. I expect I'd feel like it too, if I were you, but Mum and Dad loved you, you know. And they did their best.'

Gabby was right, they really had done their best, and in her own way Alex would always love them for it, in spite of the difficulties they'd had. What they'd never been able to do, however, was make her feel as though she really belonged, but maybe that was as much her fault as theirs.

Never underestimate the power of a child's mind.

She remembered that from her studies, and she'd seen it, been stunned by it, so many times in her work that it was as though she was having to revisit the advice, the lesson, over and over again. Children could be as crafty and resilient as they could be vulnerable and needy, as well as manipulative to a degree that was shocking, sometimes even dangerous. The barriers they put up around them when afraid, or confused, or simply tired, could be immovable, and often took months, even years merely to start bringing down. Ottilie's defence was her silence, and yet her need to be loved, to bond with someone, anyone who was ready to show her kindness, had spilled over the barriers straight into Alex's heart.

All of the children in her care mattered to her, and she'd do anything in her power to help them, but from the very first day she'd laid eyes on Ottilie, in Dillersby Park, it had felt as though Ottilie was calling to her in some special kind of way. It was why she'd noticed her, sitting alone on the swing, and why she'd gone over to speak to her. Even as she'd watched her walking away she'd felt a connection to her that was as impossible to explain as it had been to ignore. In some curious way Ottilie had reached for her, and in that very same way, which was as incomprehensible as it was powerful, she could sense Ottilie's need now.

It was always there, whether at the centre of her attention, or waiting in the wings. She wondered what she was doing at this moment, whether she was alone in her room with Boots, or sitting at the top of the stairs trying to decide if she could come down. Perhaps she was somewhere with her father . . .

Alex couldn't think about that, she just couldn't.

She wanted to imagine Ottilie safely asleep with no awareness of all the terrible things that had happened to her. She wanted her to feel sure that she would go to nursery tomorrow. She wanted her to have all the right kind of love in her life.

As Alex got into her car she vaguely registered the sound of an email dropping into her phone shortly followed by another. It was Sunday, so they could wait until she got home, or even until tomorrow. So reversing out of her space she turned in the direction of North Hill.

This wasn't really on her way home, but for some reason she was feeling the need to drive past the Wades. She wished Ottilie could know that she was close by and that she was doing everything she could to make her safe. It wasn't enough though, was it? How much more neglect and abuse would that sweet little soul have to suffer before all the official channels had been gone through and her father had been proved a liar – before she, Alex, had the right to take her out of there? The answer should have been none at all, but it wasn't the answer she could give.

She had no idea what she was expecting to find when she got to the Wades; she wasn't even sure she was expecting anything at all, apart, perhaps, from a little glimpse of Ottilie's face at the window. What never entered her mind, even for a moment, was that she'd find every light in the house blazing. Something else she'd never seen at the Wades before was a silver Renault. It was coming out of the drive and turning down the hill, so perhaps it was simply someone who'd lost his way and used the open gate to turn round. It was too dark to see who was behind the wheel, but she felt sure it was a man.

Pulling into the drive, she got out of the car, and on reaching the front door she felt another bolt of unease to find it open. She stepped gingerly into the hall and called out, 'Hello? Is anyone here?'

As her voice faded into the silence she moved along to the sitting room. The squeal of the hinge grazed her nerves as she pushed the door open. With her heart in her mouth she peered inside.

Finding the room empty, she turned back to the hall and called out again. 'Mrs Wade? Ottilie, are you here?'

Still no reply.

'Oh God,' she murmured to herself. Something awful had happened, she just knew it.

Pushing herself on, she reached the kitchen and paused on the threshold. The back door was open and rocking gently back and forth in the breeze. It felt so eerie that she almost baulked at going any further. However, she wasn't giving up until she'd found Ottilie, and it seemed someone was outside in the shed, because there was a large yellow light glowing under the trees.

Going past the kitchen table she stepped out of the door and moved quietly across the garden. She could see the back of Brian Wade's head now, at a level that told her he must be sitting down. If he had Ottilie in there and was doing things to her . . . The surge of violence that charged through her spurred her recklessly on. She was at the window now. There was no glass; if she reached out a hand she could almost touch him. If he turned around he'd see her straight away, but he was too absorbed in whatever he was doing on the computer to register that he was no longer alone.

She looked quickly around the shed's interior, and felt a moment's relief to find no sign of Ottilie. She must be somewhere in the house, with her mother, or in her room. Why hadn't she shown herself when Alex had called her name?

Perhaps her TV was on.

Alex hadn't heard one, but maybe the door was closed.

Going back to the kitchen, she stepped inside and was about to make for the hall when she caught something at the corner of her eye. She looked down, and realising what it was she gave a gasp of pure horror.

Blood. A thick dark pool of it, seeping across the tiles from behind the table.

Starting to shake she took a step towards it, and then another. Suddenly she was sobbing with shock. Erica Wade was slumped on her back, glassy eyes wide open and a knife jutting from between her ribs.

Choking back the bile that rushed to her mouth, Alex tore out to the hall. 'Ottilie,' she gasped as she raced up the stairs. 'Ottilie! *OTTILIE!*'

Chapter Twenty-Four

Maggie Fenn was standing beside the table in her kitchen, eyes fixed on the TV screen where live pictures were being broadcast from outside Alex Lake's home in the village of Mulgrove.

'. . . the social worker in the case of missing Ottilie Wade,' the reporter was saying, 'is expected back here at her home any minute now. She's been at police headquarters again today, helping police with their inquiries, but so far there is still no sign of the little girl at the heart of the investigation. Naturally, three days into the search, the authorities are gravely concerned for her safety. As we saw earlier there's a forensic team currently at the Wades' home in Kesterly-on-Sea . . . In fact, I'm being told that we can go over there now . . .'

The picture switched to a shot of the sombre house on North Hill whose lower floors were clad in white tents, a bit like stiff petticoats, with a small number of police officers and blue-overalled forensics coming and going. 'Larry, what's happening over there at the moment?' the reporter asked.

Another voice began explaining as his face came into the edge of shot. 'It's very tense here at the moment, Andy,' he announced, keeping his voice low. 'As we know, all the activity is taking place at the back of the house, which for obvious reasons we're unable to gain access to . . . I think we can probably go to a helicopter shot . . . Yes, we can . . .'

At that point an overhead view of the Wades' back garden came on to the screen, though there wasn't much to see since a tent had been erected over most of it. 'The small building there to the left of the screen,' the reporter continued, 'is believed to be the shed, or studio, where Brian Wade allegedly carried out most of his atrocities.'

Maggie's hand was pressed tightly to her mouth.

Sophie, thinking of Alex and remembering her kindness, was sitting at the table in front of Maggie, every bit as riveted – and horrified and fearful for what the police were going to find in the shallow grave they were apparently in the process of uncovering.

'Do we know where Alex is at the moment?' Anthony, Maggie's brother, asked as he joined them.

'They showed her being taken into the police station again about an hour ago,' Maggie answered, 'but they said just now that she's on her way home.'

'Still no word from her?'

Maggie shook her head. 'I've left so many messages . . .' She broke off as the reporter said, 'We're just getting word through that a discovery has been made in the garden . . .'

'Oh my God,' Maggie murmured, not sure she wanted to hear any more. 'That poor, poor little girl.'

From the studio the presenter said, 'Larry, are you able to confirm what has been found?'

'Not yet, Erin, but as you can see, there's a lot of activity now . . . We're being asked to push back even further and at least half a dozen or more detectives have just gone in.'

'No, no, no,' Maggie muttered, knowing that probably half the nation was sharing her dread. 'Don't let it be her, please, please don't let it be her.'

As Anthony slipped an arm around her the reporter said, 'The coroner's already here, at the scene, which more or less confirms they've been expecting the worst. It's going to be a sad day for everyone if that little girl does turn out to be in the grave we suspect was dug by her father.'

'Do we know where Brian Wade is now?' the presenter asked over a static shot of the front of the house, where a small clutch of uniformed officers were keeping the press at bay.

'I believe he's still at Dean Valley Police Headquarters here in Kesterly,' came the reply. 'As we know he was charged on Monday with the murder of his wife, Erica, and remanded in custody following his appearance yesterday at the magistrates' court. Ordinarily he would have then been transported to the nearest high-security prison, but with the search for Ottilie still ongoing . . . One minute, Erin, something seems to be happening . . .'

The camera zoomed in tighter on the house as Detective Chief Inspector Terence Gould came out of the front door to speak to the press liaison officer.

'It would appear that some sort of statement is about to be made,' the reporter declared. 'Yes, I'm getting confirmation of that now. DCI Gould, who's leading this investigation, will be making an announcement in the next few minutes.'

'Larry, do we know if Brian Wade has been brought back to the house at all, since his arrest?' the presenter asked.

'No, I don't believe he has.'

'And no charges have yet been made against him concerning the disappearance of his daughter?'

'Not about the disappearance, but as we know several charges have been brought under the Sexual Offences Act as a result of information that came to light the day his wife's body was found at the house. We're also told that several more arrests are imminent in various parts of the country apparently directly related to this information.'

'Do we have any details yet on what the information is?'

'Only that it came in email form and that it suggests the existence of a nationwide paedophile ring of which Brian Wade is believed to be a member. There are rumours, and I have to stress that they are only rumours at this stage, that there was some footage contained in those emails showing pupils from Kesterly Rise Primary School at play. This is where Wade was deputy headmaster. Naturally, the parents and pupils of the school are being spoken to by police and counsellors. However, I'm told that no abuse was taking place in this footage.'

'And what about Ottilie? Is she shown at all in this footage?'

'We've been told that she is, and that the images are extremely graphic. The police have given no more detail than that.'

'It's probably the kind of detail most of us would rather never have to hear,' the presenter commented, grimly.

'I think that goes without saying . . . OK, it looks as though DCI Gould is ready to speak.'

The shot abruptly switched to show a large,

grey-haired man in his early fifties with shrewd, close-set eyes, pugnacious cheekbones and a voice that conveyed assured authority. 'I can tell you, with a mixture of regret and relief,' he began, 'that what we have unearthed here today is a quantity of what appears to be wilfully damaged computer and photographic equipment. This means that our search for Ottilie Wade continues, both here at these premises and in various further locations around the region.'

'What can you tell us about the driver of the silver Renault that was seen leaving the house on Sunday night?' someone shouted.

'We're still hoping someone will come forward,' Gould replied.

'Is it true,' another voice shouted, 'that the social worker involved in Ottilie's case has been suspended from duty?'

'Yes, I believe she has, but it's a matter for social services, not the police.'

'You are questioning her though?'

'Of course, and she is being most helpful. Now, if you'll excuse me . . .' And ignoring the barrage of questions that crowded in after him, he followed the liaison officer back inside the house and closed the door.

Maggie heaved a tremulous sigh. 'Well, at least they didn't find a body,' she said, 'though what that actually means for the poor little mite . . .'

'I still reckon he's offed her,' Sophie declared rashly. 'Have you seen the pictures of him? He looks dead creepy and like he'd definitely do something like that.'

'Question is, where's he hidden her?' Maggie said quietly.

'They're about to go to Alex,' Anthony informed them.

On the screen a reporter was saying, '. . . this looks like it's probably her returning home now . . . Yes, it is . . .'

The camera started to jerk and jump as a horde of reporters surged towards a dark grey BMW coming up the hill from Mulgrove village. As it pulled to a stop outside the Vicarage a handful of uniformed officers closed in to force the press back while a tall, navy-suited female detective with cropped dark hair and an unsmiling face stepped out of a rear passenger door. A moment later Alex emerged, looking haunted and scared and as though she might stagger under the weight of questions being loaded upon her.

'Do you hold yourself responsible for what's happened?'

'Could you have prevented it?'

'Did you know about the abuse?'

'Is it true you've been suspended?'

'Why are social services refusing to comment?'

'Poor lamb,' Maggie murmured with so much feeling that Sophie clung to her hand.

Flanked by the detective and a uniformed officer, Alex was ushered through the melee to her front door where she hunched away from the cameras as she fumbled with her keys.

In voice-over a reporter was saying, 'This is the third time in as many days that Alex Lake has been taken in for questioning, but whatever the outcome it's becoming increasingly clear that we're looking at another catastrophic failure on the part of social services, and perhaps in particular of the young woman we're seeing here.'

'How can he say that?' Maggie cried in outrage.

'He's a fucking jerk,' Sophie spluttered. 'She's brilliant. The best social worker I ever had and I've had loads.'

'Ssh,' Anthony cautioned.

Alex was disappearing inside the house now as the detective made her way back to the car and the presenter in the studio asked the reporter, 'Is it possible that Alex Lake might find herself charged with some kind of an offence too?'

'No!' Maggie gasped.

'I'm going to get all the kids she's cared for to tell those stupid bastards just how fantastic she is,' Sophie shouted.

Maggie put a comforting hand on her shoulder as they continued to watch. Sophie was missing Britney since Britney had gone to stay with an aunt, and now this with Alex . . . Sophie took things hard.

'. . . heard nothing from the police at this stage to suggest that they are intending to press charges,' the reporter was saying, 'but anything could happen in the next few days, or even hours.'

'Indeed it could,' the presenter responded gravely. 'Meanwhile, we're going over to our reporter, Emily Grint, who's currently outside police headquarters in Kesterly. Emily, what have you got for us?'

'Thanks Erin, well nothing new from the police at this stage, but I have someone here who works on the local paper and who's known Alex Lake for several years. Thanks for joining us, Heather. I'm told you'll be posting an interview on the *Kesterly Gazette*'s website later today that you did with a couple of Alex Lake's colleagues. Perhaps you can give our viewers some idea of what to expect from this piece?'

Heather Hancock was smiling pleasantly as she tucked a handful of her wiry red hair behind one ear and said, 'Well, basically, the social workers I spoke to, who are also from the Kesterly North hub where Alex Lake works, are claiming that she, Alex Lake, has always had an air about her as if she was too good for the job.'

Sophie cried, 'That is such bullshit! She is so not like that.'

Heather Hancock was still speaking. '. . . she's heavily involved in amateur dramatics in her home village, and so can't be relied on to put in the kind of hours or commitment she should for her day job. In other words, it's highly probable that some, if not all, of the children in her care are failing to get the attention they should.'

'Fucking bollocks!' Sophie spluttered.

'There's no way that's true,' Maggie murmured. 'Absolutely no way.'

'Tell me, is that the reporter who gave her play a bad review?' Anthony asked curiously.

'Yes, that's her,' Maggie confirmed, 'and if you ask me, she's got some personal axe she's grinding over there.'

Anthony didn't disagree.

'Have you managed to get any statements from Alex Lake's superiors at Dean Valley County Council?' the reporter was asking Heather Hancock.

Heather's eyes turned flinty, as though she'd just been accused of a dereliction of duty. 'Not yet, I'm afraid. As I'm sure you know, there's been a complete lockdown at the Kesterly North hub since it was discovered that Ottilie had gone missing. The people I've managed to speak to have come forward of their own accord, and off the record.'

Keeping her tone professionally neutral, the reporter said, 'One of my colleagues, in her interviews with Alex Lake's friends and neighbours, has found that everyone generally speaks very highly of her. But you're saying that doesn't seem to be the opinion of the people she works with.'

'I'm sorry, was there a question there?' Heather's tone was frosty.

'I'm simply wondering how you might account for this conflict of opinion,' the reporter responded mildly.

'I'm afraid I can't account for it, except to say that perhaps it goes some way towards confirming that she is far more focused on what goes on closer to home than she is on the needs of her job, which, let's never forget, involves some of the neediest and most vulnerable children in our society.'

'What's her problem?' Maggie blurted angrily.

'Indeed it does,' the reporter agreed, and turning back to camera she said, 'Just to recap, the interview can be viewed from four o'clock this afternoon on the *Kesterly Gazette* website.'

In the studio the presenter said, 'Thanks, Emily. We'll come back to you if anything changes there at police HQ. Meanwhile we're returning to the village of Mulgrove where Andy Besant is outside Alex Lake's home, Alex Lake, of course, being the social worker at the centre of this investigation. Andy, tell me, are we likely to hear from Alex Lake herself at any point?'

'I don't think so, Erin,' he replied. 'As you can see, the curtains are closed to prevent anyone seeing inside the house, and so far she's only opened the door to the police. I'm presuming they've given her a dedicated mobile in order to make contact with her, because she seems to know when they're coming. Certainly she doesn't open the door to anyone else, and there have been no signs of her speaking to anyone publicly yet. As you know, the director of Dean Valley social services has only given a very brief statement himself, saying that it wouldn't be appropriate for him, or any member of staff, to make a comment on the situation at this stage of the investigation.'

Going to switch off the TV, Maggie turned to Anthony, her eyes burning with purpose as she said, 'We have to try and help her. She's all on her own over there . . . OK, I know what you're going to say, that we're not certain about that, but the news crews have been outside her house virtually since it happened and have you seen anyone but the police coming and going, because I know I haven't?'

'Me neither,' Sophie declared firmly.

Though Anthony hadn't either, all he could say was, 'We've left enough messages . . .'

'But she might not be listening to them,' Maggie broke in heatedly. 'I mean, imagine the kind of calls she must be getting, thanks to the way the press are trying to blame her. Poor thing must be terrified to pick up the phone, never mind speak to anyone.'

'So what are you suggesting, that we go over there and knock on the door?'

'Definitely,' Sophie cried eagerly. 'I'll come too and if any of those reporters ask me what she's like then I'll tell them there's no way she'd ever hurt anyone, not in a million years.'

Maggie smiled at her fondly. 'You're right, she wouldn't,' she agreed, 'but no one's actually accusing her of hurting the little girl, it's neglect they're trying to pin on her, or dereliction of duty, or whatever they want to call it, and I'm just not buying it. I've met her, I know how much you kids mean to her, so what we have here is one of those ghastly press witch hunts, trying to sensationalise everything to sell a few papers or get people tuning into their radio or television stations. In other words, let's blame the social worker, because they're always the ones at fault and they're usually the least well equipped to stand up for themselves. Anthony, as a lawyer, you must be able to do something.'

Though his eyes showed amusement at her faith in him, his tone was perfectly serious as he said, 'Leave her another message, and meantime I'll try to find out what I can about this Heather Hancock and the social workers she claims to have interviewed. If I can knock some holes in that, it might at least help to relieve some of the pressure of responsibility the media is trying to pile on Alex.'

'Good,' Maggie stated approvingly, 'very good, and I think I'll try calling the police to see if they'll get a message to her, because I'm sorry, but I just can't bear to think of her being over there all on her own.'

Alex had unplugged the landline two days ago and switched off both her mobiles. The only phone she used now was the one DC Valerie Bingham had given her. Val was with CAIT – the Child Abuse Investigation Team – and was a detective Alex had worked with several times over the years. She'd always liked her, and nothing had happened so far to change her view.

Very few people had the number of this official mobile: Anna, Gabby and Tommy. They all rang regularly, but she'd soon found that the only person she really felt able to speak to was her mother. Anna had worried that she'd end up being hurt, but she could never have foreseen anything like this – and she'd come to love Ottilie too, so she understood, more than anyone, what all this was meaning for Alex.

So much, too much to bear.

Her mother would be coming soon. She'd already have been on her way if Alex hadn't insisted she stay for Bob's party. Even Bob wasn't asking her to do that, but the arrangements had been made, people were due in from all over, Alex didn't want everything to be spoiled because of her. But she really did want her mother here; so much that it was almost impossible to hold back the tears each time they connected on Skype and tried to make some reality out of the grainy, distorted images of each other. They only ever spoke briefly; Alex was afraid that the press might have a way of intercepting the calls.

They hadn't left her alone for a minute. They were outside the house all day and all night, knocking on windows, doors, creeping across the garden, targeting her with powerful lenses.

Gabby wanted to come and stay and kept saying she would, but Alex was against the idea. 'It's crazy here, horrible, awful,' she told her. 'You don't need to be a part of it.'

'Nor do you,' Gabby cried. 'It's not your fault. They can't blame you for this, it was that monster who should be hanged, tortured . . .'

'Gabby, please, I'm trying not to think about him.'

'I'm sorry, but I'm so worried about you. Why don't you come here? At least then I'll know where you are and that you're taking proper care of yourself.'

'If I do they'll find out where I am and then you'll be bombarded too. Besides, I have to be on hand for the police – and my bosses when they finally decide to speak to me.'

'You mean no one has yet?'

'Only Tommy. He's acting as a kind of go-between at the moment with my union rep, giving them all the information they need before they summon me in.'

'But they're going to stand by you? I mean, they know how good you are . . .'

'All they know is that a little girl who was under my care has gone missing after suffering the most appalling sexual abuse.'

'Yes, but you were trying to help her . . .'

'They're going to say I should have removed her from the home as soon as I had my suspicions, regardless of the fact that they know how difficult it is to prove something like this. They won't want any blame attaching to them or the department; it'll suit them quite well to lay it all on me if they can. Anyway, it isn't about me, it's about Ottilie.'

'Of course, I understand that, and obviously I'm as worried about her as everyone else is, but you're my sister so for me you come first.'

With a small smile Alex said, 'I'll be fine, honestly.'

It wasn't true, because she was so far from fine that sometimes she felt she could be losing her mind. Every minute of every day was eating her up with so much fear, guilt and horror that sleep had become almost as impossible as rational thought.

'Ottilie, Ottilie,' she wept softly to herself now, her hands clutched to her head as her heart tore in two. 'I'm sorry, I'm so, so sorry.' She took a breath, trying to make herself stop, but how could she when she was in the midst of such a terrible nightmare?

Her official mobile started to ring and seeing it was Val Bingham, she clicked on.

'Hi, just checking to see how you're holding up,' Val said kindly.

Alex used the back of a hand to dash away her tears. 'I'm OK.'

'Mm, you don't sound it. I hope you haven't put the TV on in the last hour.'

Feeling her stomach wrench as terrible images flashed through her mind, Alex replied, 'No, why?'

'Sky News have just aired an interview with the Sainsbury's delivery driver who first alerted your office to Ottilie.'

Since Alex herself had told the police that she suspected the driver of making the calls, the only surprise was that the press had taken this long to find her.

'She's claiming she called in three times before anything happened,' Val continued, 'and I'm afraid she – or they – have made it sound as though it was you she spoke to on each occasion.'

'It wasn't,' Alex said flatly.

'I know, I've seen the records, and once again I'm sorry the press are going after you like this.'

'Maybe they're right to. I mean, I should have got her out of there . . .'

'Alex, this is me you're talking to. I understand what's happened, I know how you were putting everything into place to rescue her, and that you didn't actually know for certain until Monday that he really was sexually abusing the child.'

Alex flinched, and tried to block the sickening

images from her mind, but it simply wasn't possible. She'd seen them now and would never be able to forget the way Ottilie had been shaken about like a rag doll, begging, sobbing and screaming for him to stop . . . They'd been linked from the emails Erica Wade had sent to her last Sunday, the emails she'd heard dropping into her phone as she'd got into her car at the seafront. She hadn't opened them until the following day, and had immediately sent them on to the police. Since then, Brian Wade had been charged under so many sections of the Sexual Offences Act that there couldn't be many left that didn't apply. How sick, depraved, monstrous he was that he could have filmed himself raping his own daughter; almost as bad was the fact that he'd then sold the footage on to others of his ilk.

'Ottilie's all I care about,' Alex said quietly.

'Of course, she's all any of us care about and we'll find her, I promise. Everyone's out there looking. If I was allowing you to watch the news you'd know that hundreds of people have turned out this afternoon to help search Dillersby Park and nearby Moorland Heath.'

'The park where I first saw her,' Alex murmured, almost to herself.

'That's right.'

'What about *him*? What kind of information is he giving you now?'

'It hasn't changed much. He's still saying that his wife stabbed herself and that he has no idea where Ottilie is, or who the silver Renault might belong to. But the phone records are showing that he made several calls on Sunday, presumably to tip off his fellow lowlife – sorry, club members. Police from various forces around the country are following up on the calls, a few arrests have already been made, but one chap is proving more elusive than the rest. There's a chance she's with him, but we won't know until we find him.'

Alex's head went down as a thick, burning bile rose to her throat.

'It turns out the hard drive of the computer we dug up from the garden yesterday is still pretty much intact,' Val continued. 'So we've got more details now of who was involved in this so-called club. If one of them has her, we'll soon track her down.'

'Yes, yes, I'm sure you will,' Alex said, having to swallow hard as more tears welled up from the fear and panic devastating her heart. If one of them did have Ottilie, what was to stop him passing her on to someone else, and then someone else and before they knew it she'd be out of the country . . .

Stop it, stop, stop! Don't do this to yourself. It's not real, nothing is, apart from the horror of it all.

'Moving on,' Val said, 'I've been chatting with your team leader, Tommy Burgess, again. He's very keen to make it known how highly he rates your professional abilities, and after the local paper ran the interview with a couple of your colleagues last night, he feels it's time for him to speak out.'

'But the powers that be have issued a blanket ban on anyone speaking to the press,' Alex objected. 'I don't want him getting into trouble for me.'

'You'll have to take it up with him, but frankly I think it's time someone other than your team leader and union rep helped you to fight your corner. The press are tearing you apart out there, quite unjustifiably, of course, but we know how they love to go for people in your position when things go wrong. You're the easiest and most obvious scapegoat.'

Since she blamed herself too, for everything, Alex had no words to defend herself. She'd call Tommy later and persuade him to see sense: there was nothing to be gained from him jeopardising his position when the department, the children, needed him far more than she did. Besides, it was all over for her now; they'd never give her back her job or let her near a child again after this.

'Further developments notwithstanding,' Val said, 'I'll stop by and check on you tomorrow. In the meantime, if anything else comes to mind, anything at all, you know how to get hold of me, day or night. Oh God, that reminds me, I've had a call from someone by the name of Maggie Fenn? She says she's a foster carer . . .'

'Yes, I know who she is.'

'Well, she's very keen to get hold of you. She said you have her number so please ring it, any time, day or night.'

'Thank you,' Alex said softly, already knowing she wouldn't.

'She also said,' Val continued, 'to remind you that her brother is a lawyer.'

Alex's heart clenched on a beat.

'It might not be a bad idea to have one,' Val said gently, 'or at least someone to advise you on how to handle the press – and your employers when the time comes.'

'Yes, of course,' Alex said, her voice sounding as parched as her hopes.

As she rang off she was so close to losing it again that it took at least a dozen sharp, ragged breaths to get past it. What was she going to do? What the hell could she do apart from sit here and wait?

She went to put on some music to drown out the

clamour of the press outside, and to mask the sobs that were tearing through her conscience into her heart. She barely listened to what was playing, couldn't focus on anything apart from Ottilie and the way the world was folding in around her.

To the haunting sounds of one of her father's Gregorian chants she took herself upstairs. She felt safer there, less able to be spotted by someone creeping up to the house to peer through a chink in the curtains and twist whatever she might be doing into some sort of news.

What would they make of it if they saw she had Boots? she wondered as she picked up the bear. Even the police didn't know she had him – why would they when they had no idea he even existed, much less that Ottilie would never go anywhere without him? She should hand him over, she knew it, but she simply couldn't make herself.

'Ottilie,' she whispered shakily, and as a terrible, wrenching horror escaped her she pressed the bear to her face as though to stifle her grief.

It was Saturday now, almost a week since Ottilie had disappeared, and Maggie Fenn, like so many others, was still glued to the regular updates of the search. One of the most tragic and in its way repulsive parts of it, she felt, was the fact that it had turned out so few usable photographs existed of the poor child. This was how DCI Gould had put it in one of his statements, '. . . hardly any usable photographs . . .' leaving the public to imagine the content of those the police did have. Maggie couldn't allow her mind to go there. It was too terrible, too traumatic to think of such a tiny, defenceless girl being subjected to the perversion of a grown man, and that grown man her own father. Instead she focused on the two grainy shots they were managing to show of a solemn, waif-like creature with dark curly hair and a pixieish face.

The owner of the Pumpkin playgroup had been on earlier, talking about how worried they all were for Ottilie. She'd spoken out for Alex too. 'I've known her for a long time,' she told the reporter, 'and I've seen first-hand how good she is with the children. In Ottilie's case she used to bring her here herself, three times a week. That in itself goes beyond the call of duty. I know for a fact that she was doing everything possible to socialise Ottilie and encourage her to speak. And actually she was making some progress. Ottilie did speak to her, and anyone with eyes in their head could see that the child was absolutely devoted to her. Knowing what I do now, about Ottilie's parents, I'd say it was probably the first time in her life that Ottilie had felt what it was like to be loved in a normal, healthy way.'

'Did you ever meet Ottilie's mother?' the interviewer asked.

'No, she never came to the nursery. I believe she was an agoraphobic.'

From everything that had been reported over the course of this week, Maggie couldn't be in much doubt that agoraphobia had been the least of Erica Wade's problems. A mother with schizophrenia, a stepfather who'd been even more abusive than the man she'd gone on to marry; a serious drug addiction serviced, it seemed, by online pharmacies – and now a new inquiry had been opened up in Northumbria into the death of her three-year-old son, Jonathan.

Some news reports had claimed that Erica had

confessed to the killing in an email found, but never sent, on her laptop computer, which had been seized by the police very early on. An officer with Northumbria Police had spoken briefly about the contact he'd recently had with Alex over the matter, but very few details had emerged as yet.

The predictable troop of experts had been paraded into TV studios to discuss why the death hadn't been treated as suspicious at the time, and most seemed to agree that panicked, inexpert lifesaving techniques might easily have caused the bruising around the boy's nose and mouth. As for the motive Erica Wade might have had for killing her own son, apparently, according to the unsent email, it had been to save him from her husband's abuse.

Naturally this had immediately raised the question, had she done the same to Ottilie? And was this the reason her husband had killed her, because she'd once again deprived him of his own personal plaything? Whatever the answers, they still didn't seem any closer to finding Ottilie, and the vicious media attacks on Alex were showing no signs of letting up.

'Will you listen to this fool?' Maggie cried angrily as her husband and brother came into the kitchen. 'I mean, who is he, for heaven's sake, apart from some thug they've picked out of the Temple Fields estate who can hardly string two coherent words together. What the hell does he know about anything?'

Anthony and Ron watched in silence as Shane Prince garbled on about how Alex Lake was always coming round their way trying to snatch kids from their families. 'It happened to ours,' he snorted, hefting a gob of spit to the kerb, 'but we wasn't having none of it. We got rid of her right off, then she only went and called on the dudes what live over Cander Street. I'm telling you, man, she could have caused a riot that day, and it would have been us lot what was left to blame, when it wasn't nothing to do with us at all.'

'It's crazy,' Maggie declared, 'there's him saying she was always trying to take kids away and everyone else going on about how she didn't act fast enough in Ottilie's case. They can't have it both ways, or I suppose they can, just as long as it paints her in as bad a light as Brian flipping Wade himself.'

Going to pour two coffees, her husband said, 'I hear they've made five more arrests in connection with this paedophile ring.'

Maggie nodded grimly. 'One of them a local GP. Dr Aiden.' She shuddered with revulsion. 'He was Ottilie's doctor, apparently. They're saying it's why the Wades moved here, because *he* thought being in with the GP would keep Ottilie out of the system.'

Anthony and Ron looked every bit as disgusted, as Ron said, 'I take it there's still no sign of the little girl.'

Maggie shook her head, then threw out her hands. 'For God's sake, she has to be somewhere, though thank God it wasn't at the bottom of Moorland lake. They're still searching over that way, though,'

'Thanks,' Anthony said, as Ron passed him a mug. 'Good news from the *Kesterly Gazette*,' he told his sister, but before he could continue the phone rang and Maggie snatched it up.

'Hello, Maggie Fenn speaking,' she announced.

As she listened her eyes widened in amazement, and she turned excitedly towards her husband and brother. 'Alex, thank goodness,' she gasped. 'Oh my dear, I've been so worried about you. Are you all right? Well, of course you're not, but we want to help if we can. Please tell us what we can do.'

In a hoarse and very tired-sounding voice, Alex said, 'That's so kind of you, Maggie. The police gave me your message . . . I really didn't want to bother you, but I was hoping your brother might . . .'

'He's right here,' Maggie assured her. 'He'll know what to do. I'll pass you over.'

With an ironic glance at his sister, Anthony took the phone. 'Hi Alex,' he said. 'I'm really sorry for all you're going through.'

'Thank you,' she replied. 'It's been . . . It's . . .'

'Hell, I expect,' he came in gently. 'And worse, but like Maggie said, we want to help if we can.'

'Thank you,' Alex said again. 'I'd really appreciate that. The police are saying I ought to have someone.'

'Yes, you should,' he agreed, 'if only to help you deal with the press.' He didn't utter the words *they're flaying you alive*, but they were uppermost in his mind. 'I shall be here for another week,' he told her, 'in Dean Crown Court from Wednesday, but I can make myself free to meet up before that if it suits you.'

Her voice faltered with emotion as she said, 'I really appreciate that. My mother's arriving from New Zealand tomorrow, so maybe Monday or Tuesday?'

Casting Maggie a curious glance, he replied, 'As soon as you like. You tell me.'

'What?' Maggie mouthed.

He held up a hand as Alex said, 'Would it be OK if I came there on Monday afternoon? I'd rather the press didn't try to make something of you coming here.'

'Of course. Will you manage to get through without them following you?'

'I've no idea. Will it be a problem if I don't? I'm sure Maggie won't want them bothering her . . .'

'Don't worry about that, she can deal with it. You're our main concern right now, and it might help you in some small way to know that Ron and I have just come from the *Kesterly Gazette*. The editor has agreed to run a letter both online and in the paper from Ron and Maggie, detailing the occasions that you pointed out certain errors Heather Hancock had made in her reporting. They go on to suggest that she might bear a grudge for this, which she has serviced through the only bad review you received for your play – and of course through the interview with two of your colleagues, who very conveniently had to remain anonymous. The suggestion, obviously, is that they don't exist.'

'Actually, I expect they do,' Alex confessed, 'and I could probably name them, but I guess we all have our enemies whether we feel we've earned them or not. What really beats me about Heather is the fact that she's making me a priority when a little girl in her own area is missing.'

'This is precisely the point Maggie and Ron have made in their letter. So, shall we say two o'clock on Monday?'

'That should be fine. Thank you, and please thank Maggie for me too. She hardly knows me, but the way she's . . . Sorry, I'm getting emotional, so I'd better ring off, just give Sophie a hug, will you? Tell her I'm sorry I won't be able to see her for . . . for a while.'

As the line went dead, Anthony handed the phone back to Maggie and because Sophie wasn't in the room he said, 'You never mentioned Alex has a mother.'

Maggie looked thrown. 'Doesn't everyone?' she replied.

He cast her a wryly disapproving look.

'Did I ever tell you how much you remind me of Grandad when you do that? He was a lawyer too, of course. Anyway, I take your point, I didn't know she had a mother. So I take it she's over there with Alex?'

'No, apparently she's on her way here from New Zealand.'

Maggie's eyebrows rose. 'Well, I must say she's taking her time,' she commented.

'Careful,' he warned, 'you're on the verge of making the same mistake as everyone else, drawing conclusions without knowing all the facts.'

Chapter Twenty-Five

The strain of being interviewed by DCI Gould from CID, the lead detective in the case, was showing in Alex's face as she waited almost desperately for her mother to arrive. He'd come here, to the house, this morning, Sunday – exactly a week after Ottilie had disappeared – to talk through the investigation and find out if there was anything, just one tiny, seemingly insignificant detail she might not have told them.

With Val Bingham from CAIT sitting beside her she'd assured him there was nothing she could think of, but she'd be happy to go over everything again if he wanted her to. He did, and so for two solid hours she'd relived every moment she'd spent with Ottilie, from that first day in the park when she'd talked to her on the swing, to the brief glimpse Brian Wade had allowed her, just over a week ago, when she'd turned up at the house to take Ottilie to nursery.

Had she noticed anything suspicious in Brian Wade's behaviour then, the detective had wanted to know. Though she'd answered the question several times over the course of the past week, she answered it again, saying that yes, she had felt there to be something suspicious in his manner, but she couldn't be specific as to why she had thought so.

Had she had any reason to think while she was there that day that he intended to harm his wife? Not really, she replied, but he had made it clear that he wouldn't be taking her to see the psychiatrist.

She knew from Val Bingham that the psychiatrist had been interviewed, but she had no details of what he'd told the police.

'Did you ever see anyone else at the Wades' house, besides the family?' Gould wanted to know.

No, she hadn't, apart from the Sainsbury's driver leaving once, and the silver Renault that had pulled away as she'd arrived last Sunday night. *Who did that car belong to? Would the police ever find out?* She knew they were afraid Ottilie had been inside, but as yet they had nothing to prove it. 'On my first visit, Mr Wade told me that they didn't have many friends,' she said.

How many visits had she actually made to the home? How often had she seen Ottilie in the company of her parents? Had they ever talked about holidays they'd taken? Had either of them ever mentioned their son Jonathan? How had she found out about Erica Wade's mother? Had she ever told Brian Wade what she knew?

The questions had seemed endless, almost brutal in some ways, and unnerving. Though Gould hadn't treated her harshly, she could tell he wasn't a man to be on the wrong side of, which, thank God, Brian Wade was sure to be. As far as Alex was concerned, no amount of suffering would ever be enough for him.

Ride the tiger, Ottilie. There's a good girl, ride the tiger.

As they were leaving Gould said, 'Erica Wade's

body is being cremated on Wednesday. We'd like you to come along in case anyone turns up who you might have seen before, someone who might jog a memory.'

'Of course,' she said quietly. 'Will . . . Will *he* be there?'

'No. He's been taken to Eastbrook Prison where he'll stay until we're ready to press more charges.'

'You – you feel sure you will?'

'I do,' Gould replied with unshakeable confidence. 'He's done something with that little girl, I mean beyond what we already know . . .' He broke off as he registered her distress. 'Please don't think we're giving up hope of finding her alive,' he said more gently. 'He's given her to someone, we're sure of it, and we haven't yet exhausted the leads taken from his phone records and computer.'

After closing the door behind him Alex stood against it, listening to the journalists outside shouting their questions and seeming to get nothing in response. She wondered what they were making of him turning up here, at her home, on a Sunday. Did they think he'd come to tell her they'd found Ottilie, buried in a ditch, cast into a quarry, locked up in someone's cellar? Maybe they'd become excited by the possibility of him arresting her for the gross dereliction of duty for which they had already condemned her.

She could easily imagine the headlines, but didn't want to.

On hearing someone outside shouting her name, she hurried to put on some music. Taking her phone, she went upstairs to shut herself in the bedroom until her mother rang, an hour later, to say she'd just driven into the village so would be with her in a couple of minutes.

Now Alex was standing at the foot of the stairs, waiting for the double and triple knock to tell her it was safe to open up. She was shaking so hard it was as though all the emotions buried inside her were struggling to break free. She almost choked with relief as the knock jarred her senses and sent her rushing to the door.

Seconds later she was in her mother's arms with the door firmly closed again, and the feeling of safety, support, trust caused her to break down.

'It's all right, it's all right,' Anna soothed, holding her tight. 'I'm here now. Everything's going to be fine, I promise.'

'Oh God, oh God, oh God,' Alex gasped almost hysterically.

'Sssh,' Anna murmured, tightening her embrace. 'This has been so hard for you, so very hard, but they're going to find her, sweetheart, they really will.'

Alex pulled back to look at her, tears streaming down her cheeks as she tried to speak and found she couldn't.

'I know they don't know where she is right now,' Anna whispered, brushing the hair from Alex's eyes, 'but that doesn't mean . . .'

'She's here,' Alex sobbed wretchedly. 'She's upstairs.'

Anna's face stiffened with incomprehension before slackening with shock, as Alex bowed her head and wept. 'I'm sorry, I'm sorry,' she wailed. 'I know I shouldn't . . . I just . . . Oh God, what am I going to do?'

Still too stunned to speak, Anna glanced up the stairs.

'I can't give her up,' Alex cried, 'I just can't, but I know I have to . . .'

'Ssh, ssh,' Anna soothed, hardly knowing what else to say. 'Is she . . . Is she all right? I mean . . .' What did she mean? Right now she had no idea.

'She's fine,' Alex assured her. Her face crumpled again. 'And happy and safe. Oh God, I know I shouldn't have done it . . . I wasn't thinking straight, I just grabbed her and ran and the next thing I knew . . .'

Anna put up a hand. 'Tell me when you're calmer,' she said gently. 'I want to see her now.'

'Of course.' Alex started up the stairs. 'I told her you were coming, and her little face lit up.'

Anna smiled, mainly because she didn't know what else to do, and of course she was profoundly relieved to know Ottilie was safe. *But like this?* Following Alex on to the landing, she asked, 'How on earth have you managed to keep her hidden with all those journalists outside, the police coming and going . . .'

'You know how good she is,' Alex replied, glancing over her shoulder. 'She does everything you tell her, so if I say she mustn't make a sound when someone else is in the house, she doesn't. The worst is when I have to go out, but again, she just stays here quietly and waits for me to come back.'

Horrified, and knowing she needed to act, but not in what way, Anna said, 'And no one's searched the place?'

'They've had no reason to, I'm not under suspicion, at least not of . . . being involved in . . .'

Alex let the sentence hang, and not wanting to provide the missing words Anna followed her to the main bedroom where the lights were on and the curtains firmly pulled.

'Ottilie, sweetie,' Alex said softly, 'she's here.'

As Anna watched Ottilie look up from the painting she was doing on a sheet on the floor, she felt such a strange light-headedness come over her that she might even have swayed.

'N-Anna,' Ottilie declared, her solemn face breaking into a smile.

Alex looked guiltily at her mother, afraid she might think she'd put Ottilie up to the name, but she hadn't. It had simply come out that way.

'Hello my darling,' Anna said tenderly as she went to lift Ottilie into her arms. Kissing her velvety cheek, she inhaled her deeply sweet scent of baby talc and play paints. She'd missed this little girl a lot more than she'd expected to over the past week, the feel of her pliant little body in her arms, the sound of her sudden bursts of laughter, the knowledge that she and Alex were bringing some much-needed love into her life . . . 'You don't know how happy I am to see you,' she murmured into Ottilie's hair, 'at least I think I am . . . Yes, of course I am, but heaven knows what we're going to do.' She turned to Alex, wishing she knew what to say, but was still unable to find her way past the shock.

'I'll make some tea,' Alex said. 'You must be tired after the journey, so why don't you sit here with Ottilie?' She had no idea how normal words were coming out of her mouth, when her life was so far from normal now it might have slipped anchor and drifted away to a place that wasn't even on the map.

'Boots,' Ottilie said, stretching out an arm to pluck him from the bed.

'Oh, he's here too, is he?' Anna laughed, picking him up. 'I suppose that can only be a good thing.'

She turned back to Alex, who gave an uneasy smile. 'I grabbed a few things before we left,' she admitted. 'It was a bit random, but we're managing.' Her eyes moved to Ottilie. 'I'll tell you everything,' she promised her mother, 'but not until she's asleep.'

Setting Ottilie back on the floor, Anna took off her coat and dropped to her knees. 'So let's have a look at your painting, shall we?' she said, feeling a flood of tenderness in her heart as Ottilie mimicked her actions.

Leaving the door ajar Alex went downstairs to make the tea, thankful that her mother had stayed with Ottilie rather than come down with her. It wasn't that she was trying to avoid explaining her actions, it was simply that she didn't want Ottilie to be alone for a single moment longer than she had to be. She was even sleeping in the same room as her now, using the mattress she'd dragged in from Gabby's old bed. It made both her and Ottilie laugh with delight each time she bounced Ottilie into the centre of Douglas and Myra's giant bed with its antique brass frame and creaky springs. Ottilie seemed to love being snuggled up under the duvet with Boots on the pillow and Alex lying next to her reading a story, or encouraging her to read it too, or singing a song. Over the last couple of days Ottilie had started to sing along with her, making Alex's heart swell with pride as her musical little voice tripped out the words to 'I'm a Little Teapot Short and Stout', or 'Humpty Dumpty Sat on the Wall', or 'This Little Piggy Went to Market'. It was amazing how quickly she seemed to pick up the words, even with Douglas's classical pieces playing in the background.

She loved to take a bath too, sailing little boats that Alex had found in the attic or trying to blow bubbles from the circle of her forefinger and thumb.

She giggled uncontrollably when Alex wrapped her in a towel and tickled her to bits. The constant music made their voices inaudible, and the phone was close by in case the police needed to be in touch.

Alex couldn't deal with her conscience, because she didn't even know what it was doing. She could only focus on making Ottilie as happy as she could for as long as she could, while doing her best to coax her away from the terrible habits she'd learned from her father. They came up in ways that were as shocking as they were tragic, but Alex was careful not to make a big deal out of them. She simply explained, very gently, that it wasn't necessary for her to do those things any more to prove that she was a good girl.

'I know you're a good girl,' she would whisper as she smoothed her hair, 'because you're the best and bravest and most beautiful little girl in the world.'

'And Boots,' Ottilie would whisper back.

'Yes, he's a good girl too,' Alex would reply, and after a moment Ottilie would laugh.

'Not a girl,' she would say.

Alex knew that nothing had ever touched her as deeply as Ottilie's laugh, unless it was her trust, or sudden bursts of affection. She seemed so content here, so willing to accept this new way of life, bizarre and confined though it was, but why shouldn't she, after all she'd been through? She never mentioned her parents so Alex didn't either, though she knew a time would come when she'd have to. For now, she wanted nothing more than to let Ottilie be at peace and feel safe, and as they played together, or chatted, or drew, or sang, Alex felt such a depth to their connection that she couldn't imagine it being any stronger if Ottilie was actually hers. And one glance from those winsome dark eyes with their flecks of anxiety and shadows of memory was enough to bring out every protective instinct she'd ever possessed.

Yet she had to give her up, and she knew it. There was absolutely no way she could keep her, but God only knew how she'd be able to make herself let go.

'I've tried explaining things to her,' she told her mother later. 'I've said that she'll have to go to another home soon with other people who'll take good care of her, but she gets so upset. "Stay here, stay with you," she says, and I just don't have it in me to make her go. I mean, I know I have to, but then I think of how frightened and lost she'll feel when I walk away, not understanding why I've left her . . .'

Looking every bit as torn, Anna said, 'Perhaps we should come to that later. For now, I need you to tell me what actually happened. How she comes to be here at all.'

Pushing her hands through her hair, Alex took a ragged breath as she tried to cast her mind back to that terrible night. It wasn't easy; she'd done her level best not to think about it at all, but eventually she began reliving the moments she'd found Brian Wade working manically in his shed, and Erica's obviously dead body in the kitchen.

'I know I should have called the police right then,' she stumbled on, 'but all I could think about was Ottilie . . . I was so afraid for her and there was no sign of her. I dashed up the stairs shouting her name . . . At first I thought she wasn't there. Then I heard a scraping on the cupboard door in her room. I couldn't get it open, someone had obviously locked her in, but then I spotted a key on the floor. I tore the door open and there she was, terrified ... I don't know how much she'd seen of what had happened downstairs, I only knew I had to get her away from there. As I scooped her up I kept getting all these flashbacks to when I'd been shut in a cupboard at her age and how I'd waited for you to come . . . I started to feel confused about who I was, who she was . . . It was like she was me as a child and I was you . . . I know it sounds crazy, but it's how it was. It was only later that I remembered the dream about a woman running down some stairs with a child in her arms. I don't know if I was having some kind of premonition with that, it seems like it now, but at the time, as it was happening, it still felt like a dream. She was clinging to me so hard and I was terrified Brian Wade would come in and find us. It seemed to take an eternity to get to my car, then she remembered Boots so I put her in the car seat and ran back inside. That was when I grabbed a few other things too. I was sure Brian Wade was going to walk in any minute. I had no idea what I'd do if I saw him, but thank God I didn't.'

She took a breath and blew it out harshly.

Across the table Anna watched her, feeling for the horror she'd been through, while still trying to see how on earth they were going to resolve the situation she'd created. There were no easy answers; in truth she could come up with no answers at all. 'So what happened next?' she prompted. 'I take it you brought her here?'

Alex nodded. 'I was going to call the police, but then I couldn't bear the thought of them taking her, not yet. She was so afraid, and had already been through so much. Imagine what it would have done to her if I'd just handed her over to strangers. She's come to trust me, you know that, she truly believes I'll always be there for her, so I couldn't find it in my heart to let her down. I know it's completely wrong of me, I'm not trying to say it isn't, but it feels as though we belong together, and tell me, who else does she have? She's only three, for God's sake, and you've seen what spirit she has. In spite of everything that's been done to her, she's still trying to be loved, to have a normal relationship with someone . . . How, at her age, and given the abuse she's suffered, can she even know what that is, but somehow, on some level, she seems to, and she's having it with me. And with you, though I know I shouldn't drag you into this, and, I swear, I'm not trying to. I understand what an impossible position I'm putting you in. If you don't contact the police right away you'll become an accomplice, so I understand you have to do it . . .'

Reaching for her hands to try and calm her, Anna said, 'Yes, I do, but before that . . .'

Alex stood up, walked to the door and turned back again. 'I've ruined everything, haven't I?' she declared. 'I mean for us. I've been such a fool, but there's no going back from it now. I've had her for over a week, I've lied to the police, to my sister, Tommy, to everyone I know. The fact that she means the world to me, and probably really is better off with me, won't count for anything when they find out that I took her and that I've had her here all along. Even Val, the detective who's been so kind, will turn against me, and who can blame her? It's a crime to steal a child, even if her parents are Brian and Erica Wade.'

Trying to steady the moment, Anna said, 'I under-stand that according to the letter of the law you shouldn't have done what you did, but you, more than anyone else, knew what was going on in that house . . .'

'It won't matter, Mum, honestly. In fact, it'll prob-ably make it a hundred times worse, because I know the rules. I'm actually someone who's supposed to apply them, and if people like me start to disobey them what do we have?'

Not reacting to the fact that Alex had called her Mum for the first time, though loving it, Anna said softly, 'In this case what we have is a little girl who's been rescued by someone who genuinely loves her, who's safely asleep upstairs, who doesn't want to be anywhere other than where she is now, and who wants to wake up to no one else but you in the morning.'

Though Alex was grateful for her mother being so understanding, it left her feeling more tortured than ever. 'She's not old enough to have a say,' she responded, trying to stop herself breaking down. 'And even if she were, it still won't make what I've done right.'

'No, it won't,' Anna agreed sombrely.

'I'm sorry,' Alex choked, 'I'm so, so sorry. We're only just getting to know one another, we had so much to look forward to, and now I'll never be able to come to New Zealand . . . For all I know I'm going to end up in prison and what will happen to Ottilie then? They'll never let me see her again after this, and how is that going to help her? It was all I ever wanted, to help her, and I've made such a terrible, stupid mess of it.'

Taking her in her arms, Anna said, 'I think we both

553

need to sleep on this and talk again in the morning.'

'But don't you understand?' Alex cried. 'If you don't go to the police right away, you're going to be in almost as much trouble as I am.'

'Why don't you let me worry about that,' Anna said gently. 'You just go on up to bed now so you can be there if Ottilie wakes up, and I'll go and bring in my luggage.'

Though Alex hadn't slept particularly well, lying awake most of the night gazing at Ottilie's sleeping face while trying to steel herself to give her up, by the time Anna came in with some breakfast she was feeling clearer-headed than she'd expected.

'N-Anna,' Ottilie cried cheerily as Anna put a tray down on the end of the bed.

'And how are you this morning?' Anna asked with a smile. This dear, sweet little creature really knew how to get to her.

Ottilie glanced at Alex.

'Go on, you can do it,' Alex encouraged softly.

'I'm fine,' Ottilie announced and gave a breathy little laugh. 'Boots too,' she added, holding him up.

'Well, that's all that matters, isn't it?' Anna teased. 'Did he sleep well?'

Ottilie nodded and gave him a squeeze. 'He likes stories,' she declared.

'Really? Which is his favourite?'

Again Ottilie turned to Alex.

'I think you know,' Alex told her.

'Pooh and Piglet,' Ottilie stated and showed all her teeth in a cheesy little grin.

Giving in to the urge to hug her, Alex said to Anna, 'How about you? Did you sleep well? I heard you in the night.'

'I'm sorry if I woke you,' Anna said, coming to sit with them and running her fingers over Ottilie's cheek. 'You're such a beautiful, darling little girl,' she told her fondly.

'And Boots,' Ottilie replied. 'But he's not a girl.'

Anna laughed, and choked with feeling Alex drew Ottilie in more tightly. 'I'm going to see a lawyer this afternoon,' she told her mother.

Anna's eyes widened in surprise.

'He's the brother of a . . . a friend, I guess,' Alex explained, 'and he's offered to help.'

More amazed than ever, Anna said, 'Does he know . . . about this?'

'No, no, of course not, but I thought . . . Actually, I'm not sure what I thought. I suppose that he might be able to help me make the press go away, but that's just being naïve, isn't it?'

'Probably,' Anna agreed. 'For that you're going to need another major story to break.'

Alex gazed wistfully down at Ottilie. 'Then she'll be off the front pages and everyone will move on . . . Until she's found.' She swallowed hard, trying not to imagine just how awful that was going to be for them both.

Tilting Alex's face up to gaze into her eyes, Anna told her, 'I had a long talk with Bob during the night, and now I'm a lot clearer in my mind about what we need to do.'

It was a couple of minutes before two when Maggie Fenn opened her front door, and before Alex had a chance to speak she pulled her straight into an embrace.

'Come in, come in,' she urged. 'I'm so glad to see you . . . My goodness, everything you're going through, well, I can hardly begin to imagine. Why can't they just focus on finding the little girl and leave you alone, that's what I want to know.'

And why, Alex was thinking desperately to herself, hadn't she just brought Ottilie straight here? OK, it wasn't the right way to do things, but she'd be in a whole lot less trouble now if she had. And if anyone could give Ottilie a loving home, it was Maggie. Maybe she still could, except the last person the authorities would allow to make any suggestions about Ottilie's future after this would be her, the woman who'd abducted her. It would be abduction, wouldn't it, with a maximum sentence of seven years; not kidnap, please. Heaven only knew how long they might give her for that.

'Alex, hi,' Anthony Goodman said, getting to his feet as Maggie showed Alex into the cosy sitting room, where a fire was glowing in the hearth and rain was spattering the deep bay windows.

Taking his hand, Alex forced a smile. As she met his eyes she found herself remembering how attractive she'd considered him on the two previous occasions they'd met, and she still did. It wasn't only his looks, it was the aura he seemed to exude that was severe and yet friendly too. He was a capable man, confident, would know how to tackle problems head-on and sort them.

Except this one.

If he knew the truth about her, if either he or his sister did, what would they think of her then?

How she hated deceiving them. They were decent, kind people, who totally believed in her; if only it could stay that way.

For a while, as Maggie poured the tea she'd already set out, they talked about the search and the nationwide shock of so many arrests being linked to the same paedophile ring.

'They were saying on the news just now,' Maggie ventured, 'that they're about to add conspiracy to kidnap to the list of charges against Brian Wade.'

Swallowing her tea, Alex kept her eyes down as she said, 'I guess, in the end, at least as far as sentencing goes, it won't make much difference. The abuse itself is enough to send him away for life, and then there's the murder of his wife, of course.' She glanced at Anthony, the expert in these matters, and didn't receive a contradiction.

'Let's just hope they don't end up having to charge him with a second murder,' Maggie commented sadly.

As Alex winced, Anthony shot his sister a reproving look.

Maggie apologised, blushing. 'That was thoughtless of me. Please try to forget I said it.'

'It's OK,' Alex assured her. 'I expect a lot of people are thinking the same way.' Feeling Anthony's eyes still on her, she made herself look up. She wanted to try and make a quip about fishing, but nothing would come to mind. 'Are you on holiday?' she asked.

He raised an ironic eyebrow. 'Not exactly,' he replied. 'I'm trying a case in Dean Crown Court starting on Wednesday, so I've been here for a few days getting prepared.'

Remembering he'd told her that when she'd rung, she said, 'Is it serious?' and immediately wished she hadn't. Maybe these things were confidential.

'A robbery,' he replied.

She nodded, and tried to conjure something incisive or at least intelligent to say about robberies, and decided she'd probably stood a better chance with the fishing.

'I believe your mother's here?' he remarked, raising a foot and resting it on one knee.

She noticed how expensive his shoes were, and that his black jeans were of very good quality. Why was she even registering these things? Anything rather than get to the real point of why she was here, especially now there was no point at all.

'Go anyway,' her mother had said. 'If he's as eminent a lawyer as you say he is, he could turn out to be a very worthwhile friend to have.'

Alex had blanched.

'I'm not saying you're going to need one,' Anna had hastily added, 'but you never know. Besides, it'll do you good to get out, knowing that Ottilie's safe with me.'

What if, in her absence, her mother took Ottilie to the police? She might feel it was the easiest way to do it, to spare her, and Ottilie, the agony of having to say goodbye.

'Yes, she arrived yesterday,' she told Anthony. 'She wanted to come before, but it was her husband's birthday and they'd arranged a big party.' She took a sip of her tea. She needed to be more communicative than this, but she could hardly think what to say. Then her mobile rang and seeing it was Val Bingham she said, 'It's the police, would you mind . . . ?'

'Of course not,' Maggie insisted. 'We'll wait in the kitchen.'

'No, no really. I'm sure it's only to fix up a time to come and see me,' and clicking on she said, 'Hi Val, how are you?'

'I'm good,' came the reply. 'I won't ask how you

are, but something's come up that I think you should know about before it hits the news. The remains of a little girl have been found in Norwich, at the home of one of the paedophile ring. Don't worry, we know it's not Ottilie, they're way too far gone for that, but obviously we can't rule out the possibility that other bodies might be buried in the vicinity.'

Alex put a hand to her head. 'That's terrible,' she said weakly. 'Do you have any idea yet who the child might be?' Though she could feel Maggie and Anthony watching her, she kept her eyes lowered.

'No way of telling at this stage,' Val Bingham replied, 'but apparently she's female and would have been around six or seven years old. Forensics will come up with a more detailed profile in the next couple of days. Meantime, if there's anything else, I'll be in touch.'

'Thank you,' Alex murmured.

After ringing off she passed on what she'd been told, and added, 'It's a gruesome business, awful, terrible. It makes me wonder sometimes why I chose to go into child protection.'

'I guess it would be a love of children,' Maggie suggested drily. 'Which reminds me, I didn't tell Sophie you were coming today. I knew I'd never get her to school if I did . . .'

'That's good, I'm glad you didn't,' Alex broke in. 'It could create even more problems if my bosses found out I'd visited one of the children in my caseload while I'm under suspension. She's all right though, is she?'

'Absolutely. We're very proud of the progress she's making, but she's worried about you.'

Anthony said, 'How's the internal inquiry going?'

'I'm not sure. Tommy, my team leader, is dealing with everything at the moment. I'm not due to see anyone myself until Wednesday.'

'Do you have someone to go with you?' he asked. 'I think it might be wise to have some legal support.'

'I – I don't actually know anyone. I was going to ask Tommy to be with me, but . . .'

'You need some independent counsel. If I weren't going to be in court I'd go with you myself, but not a problem. I'll make a couple of calls. I'm sure we can find someone.'

As he left the room, Maggie smiled at her warmly and refreshed her tea. 'I'm glad your mother's arrived,' she said. 'It must be a tremendous relief to have someone to lean on.'

Alex didn't deny it. 'She's being especially wonderful considering that we've only just got to know one another,' she replied.

Maggie looked intrigued, so Alex told her the story, or at least most of it. She didn't mention anything about why her mother had left her when she was young; it really wasn't something she wanted to discuss. Just thank God no one from the press had got hold of it – she didn't even want to think about what the headlines would have said.

'OK,' Anthony announced, coming back into the room, 'the chap I've just spoken to is Jolyon Crane. He's a pretty big noise in Bristol, so not a million miles from here. Unfortunately he can't attend himself on Wednesday, but he's going to send someone he knows he can trust.'

'Thank you.' Alex managed to smile.

'Alex was just telling me about her reunion with her mother,' Maggie said as he sat down again.

He raised an interested eyebrow.

'I think I already mentioned that she lives in New Zealand, didn't I?' Alex said, realising how hard she was finding it to keep track of her thoughts. 'I'm hoping to go back with her when she goes.'

'When will that be?' he ventured.

'I'm not sure yet. I guess as soon as I can get away.'

'And will you stay there, in New Zealand?' Maggie asked.

Alex felt her insides tightening. 'I'm thinking about it,' she replied. 'There won't be anything to keep me here once I've been fired,' she added.

Feeling Anthony's watchful eyes on her, she put her cup down and said, 'I guess I ought to be going now, I just wanted to come and thank you for your . . . Well, for being so kind and now for finding me a lawyer.'

'It's the least we can do,' Anthony responded, getting to his feet.

Alex wasn't sure if she saw a look pass between sister and brother, but guessed something must have, because Maggie hugged her goodbye in the sitting room and left Anthony to take her to the door.

'I trust there's been no comeback from Heather Hancock since Ron and Maggie's letter was published,' he said, as they stepped into the porch.

'Not that I'm aware of,' she replied, 'but I've been advised not to read the papers or follow the news. I guess Heather wouldn't have been very happy about it.'

'I guess not,' he responded wryly, 'but petty grudges have always annoyed me, especially when they're used to hurt someone who's already down.'

Alex swallowed drily. She hated being the victim,

but understood that he was just being kind. 'Thanks for fighting my corner,' she said with a note of humour.

'My pleasure,' he told her, holding out a hand to shake. 'I'm not sure we'll meet again if you're off to New Zealand. If we don't, I wish you good luck with everything.'

Feeling an absurd and wretched sense of loss stealing over her, she said, 'Thank you,' and before she could become emotional in front of him she let go of his hand and went to get into her car.

In a wine bar, close to the seafront in Kesterly, Heather Hancock's fiery temper was flashing in her eyes as she said to Jason, 'I'm sorry, but you've got to know more about Alex Lake's past than you're letting on.'

'I don't get what makes you so sure there is more to know,' he countered.

Heather glanced at Gina, her best friend, Jason's brassy blonde wife and mother of his three brattish kids. 'He's hiding something,' she told her. 'I can tell, can't you?'

'Like what?' Jason cried, throwing out his hands.

'That's what I'm trying to find out,' Heather retorted heatedly.

He sat back in his chair, defeated. 'I don't know why you're asking me. I haven't spoken to Alex in weeks . . .'

'Another drink, anyone?' Gina cut in, waving out to a waiter. She really didn't want this to continue, mainly because she knew it would end up in a place she didn't want to be. God knew, she and Jason had had enough rows about Alex Lake since he'd decided to come back, and now with all this going on . . . It was like there was no getting away from the bloody woman. And she knew very well that Jason had texted and emailed her since all this fuss had blown up, trying to get over there to see her to make sure she was all right. It was so typical of him, wanting to play the hero, he was like it with everyone, but in Alex Lake's case he was taking it way too far. Or he would, given half a chance.

And as for Heather and that ridiculous bee she had in her bonnet about Alex Lake, which wasn't to do with being publicly corrected in her reporting, or having her reviews put down by some fancy lawyer. Well, it was probably that too, but what had long bugged Heather Hancock about Alex Lake was the fact that when she, Gina, had broken up with Jason, Heather had fully expected him to go running to her. Instead, he'd met Alex Lake – at a party Heather was also at, just to make matters worse – and before Heather the hotshot reporter had time to smooth on her lip gloss or flash her come-to-bed eyes, he'd disappeared off home with Alex, never to be seen again. At least, not at Heather's apartment. She'd always had the hots for him, ever since she and Gina had first met him; Jason, though, didn't feel the same about her. Just as well, or it wasn't very likely she and Heather would still be friends.

After the waiter had taken their order, Heather said, 'You know what I don't get, Jason, is why you're being so defensive about her. I mean, it's not like you're together any more, is it?'

Gina sliced her a look, knowing the jibe had been meant as much for her as for him.

'Look, even if I did know something, and I really don't,' he lied, 'there's no way in the world I'd be telling you, when all you want is to do her down. Ease up on her, will you? She's going through a rough enough time, what with the press constantly on her back and being suspended from her job. And I can tell you this much, she'll be worried sick over what's happened to that little girl.'

'Who might now be safely in care if she'd done her job properly,' Heather snapped. 'I'm telling you this, if that child turns up dead somewhere, which is looking increasingly likely, then as far as I'm concerned Alex Lake will be as much to blame as whoever did it.'

Gina's eyebrows rose. 'Well, I suppose we should at least be thankful you're not planning to accuse her of having done it herself,' she commented drily.

Though Heather looked as though she might have liked to, all she said was, 'I'm just telling you, there's more to Alex Lake than meets the eye.'

'And wouldn't you just love that to be true,' Gina smirked. 'Now, can we please change the subject, because, frankly, I've got better things to talk about.'

Heather eyed her nastily, but knowing she'd start coming across as obsessive or paranoid if she didn't let the subject drop she allowed Gina to start waffling on about the kids, the way she always did. Sometimes Heather wondered why they'd bothered staying friends when they had so little in common these days. She guessed it was habit – they'd known each other so long. Anyway, whatever it was, if Gina Carmichael was dumb enough to think she was rid of Alex Lake, then as far as Heather was concerned, she was even dumber than she looked.

Chapter Twenty-Six

'Nanna's come up with a new game for us to play,' Alex was saying to Ottilie, as she undressed her ready for her bath. Ottilie always called her mother Nanna now, and they'd found themselves slipping into it too. 'We're going to choose new names. Won't that be fun? Nanna will keep hers, but you and me, we can have any names we like.'

Ottilie was looking faintly puzzled, and tired after missing her afternoon nap.

'So what name would you like?' Anna asked, coming into the bedroom with a pile of Ottilie's freshly ironed clothes.

Ottilie looked around, and spotting her bear on the bed she cried, 'Boots.'

Alex and Anna laughed. 'But that's his name,' Alex pointed out. 'You have to have one of your own. So think of your favourite name in the whole wide world.'

Ottilie frowned with concentration as she raised her arms for Alex to slip off her vest.

'Shall I tell you what I've chosen?' Alex said. 'You're Lex.'

'Yes, but now I've decided to be Charlotte. Do you like that?'

Ottilie immediately nodded. 'Char-*lotte*,' she repeated, with a little jump.

Smiling, Alex asked, 'So who are you going to be?'

Ottilie's frown returned, then suddenly her eyes brightened. 'Chloe!' she exclaimed, jumping again and doing a little twist.

Alex and Anna exchanged glances. 'That's a very good choice,' Anna told her. 'So shall we call you Chloe from now on?'

Ottilie nodded, up and down, up and down. 'I'm Chloe. And you're Charlotte and you're Nanna.'

'Well done,' Alex praised, scooping her up.

'Or you can call Alex Mummy, if you like,' Anna told her.

Alex's insides tightened as Ottilie shouted, 'Mmmmummy!' and threw her arms round Alex's neck.

In many ways it was hard to believe that over a month had swept by since the night she'd brought Ottilie here, while in others it felt as though an eternity had passed. Each day had brought its own challenges, some greater than others, but somehow they'd overcome them and since the press focus had shifted to the other side of the country it had become much easier. The talk now was mainly of the Norwich-based member of Brian Wade's paedophile ring, at whose house a six-year-old girl's remains had been discovered. It had turned out to be one of five bodies buried in the same cellar, most of whom had been identified now, but not all, and similarities to the case of Fred and Rose West were coming up all the time.

It turned Alex cold to her core to think of Ottilie's father being in touch with such a man, and made her thankful beyond words that the Sainsbury's delivery driver hadn't given up after her first couple of calls to social services, or God only knew what fate might have had in store for Ottilie. As if it hadn't been bad enough already.

The general opinion these days seemed to be that Ottilie too had perished, and because she didn't have parents to keep her in the spotlight, or a media campaign driving the search, she rarely got more than a brief mention now. When she did, it was clear people were sorry, or mostly angry that the system had failed yet another little girl, but then they shrugged helplessly and moved on with their lives. What else could they do, apart from call for Brian Wade to be charged with her murder, which the police were apparently considering. Quite what Alex would do if he ever was charged she had no idea, but she wasn't going to torment herself with it. She'd just have to face it when it happened, if it ever did.

For now, they were taking each day as it came, always careful and anxious, but relieved to have the full run of the house again, and the garden if the weather was good enough. Because they weren't overlooked up here on the hill, it was easy to pop Ottilie into the car to take her for day trips to Exmoor, or Saunton Sands, or parks where Alex was unlikely to run into anyone she knew.

It was amazing, really, how little attention people paid them. Of course it would have been different if the photographs the police had issued of Ottilie had been clearer, but even so, Alex always put a hat on her when they went out, just in case. She knew Ottilie didn't like them much, but being as eager to please as she was, she never complained. Sometimes

Alex wished she would, if only to show that her fear of doing wrong and being punished in the horrific way her father had inflicted was starting to diminish. What a horrible, lonely, brutal life she'd had up to now. It was really no wonder that she never asked for her parents; in fact it was as though she'd blocked them from her mind completely.

Erica's cremation, three weeks ago, had turned out to be a far sadder occasion than Alex had prepared for, mainly because there had only been her and a handful of detectives to mourn her passing. Whether Brian Wade had asked to attend she had no idea, though given that he'd now confessed to the killing she guessed it was unlikely. Privately she wondered if the confession had been to avoid a trial when the press and public would go for him all over again, but since she'd never know, or care, she didn't give it much of her time. What occupied her more was dealing with the damage he had caused to Ottilie's tender young psyche. Though, on the face of it, she seemed to be coping well, her confidence was still very fragile and she'd lately started creeping on to Alex's mattress at night, curling up with Boots as close to Alex as she could get without actually touching her. As soon as she realised she was there, Alex would pull her in close and rub her back until she drifted off to sleep again.

Now the day had come for them to start packing for their departure. Gabby was about to exchange on the house, and because there was no way Alex, her mother and Ottilie could move into the flat in Kesterly, Anna had cancelled the lease and had, just today, booked their flights to New Zealand. Merely to think of it made Alex feel sick with nerves. Yet what else could they do? This had long been the plan, that as soon as the internal inquiry had finished with Alex, and the police had no more need of her either, she would go to New Zealand for a holiday, which in reality was to be the start of a new life for her and Ottilie.

It was crazy, impossible, they'd never get away with it and what would happen then?

'If we don't go, we will be found out,' Anna had told her firmly. 'This way at least we stand a chance of being together, as a family, the way we should be.'

'But she isn't ours.'

Anna's eyebrows arched. 'Really? Have you seen the way she looks at you, copies you, adores you? She depends on you, Alex, now more than ever, and who in the world can make her happier than you?'

'Someone will . . .'

'Like who? You've said yourself that you can't bear the idea of her going into care, being passed from pillar to post, never knowing where she belongs, possibly ending up being abused by other children, or out on the streets taking drugs and selling herself. That's the kind of life you could be condemning her to if you give her up now, and think of where it'll leave you if you do go to the police and hand her over.' She was shaking her head vehemently. 'I can't let you do it. I know you've made a terrible mistake, that you never intended it to turn out this way, but if you go to prison what good is that going to do Ottilie, or you, or anyone? OK, justice might have been served, but what's the point of justice if all it does is break a little girl's heart? And she is innocent in all this, Alex. Even if you don't consider yourself to be, you can never say that she isn't, and I know that the very last thing you'd ever want is to make her suffer.'

Of course it was the last thing Alex wanted, her whole purpose in life was to make sure that children didn't suffer, but to be doing it this way . . . 'What about Bob?' she'd protested. 'I can't believe he's really going to support this. I mean, if we take her there it won't only be me who'll be in trouble then, it'll be you and him.'

'We'll have to cross that bridge when – *if* – we come to it. For now, what's important, and makes me believe that it's all meant to be, is the fact that no one there apart from Bob of course realises that you are the social worker involved in this case. Of course they'll have heard about it, but it won't have been anywhere near as big a news story there, and I never told them it was the reason I was coming back here so soon. They think it was simply to go on getting to know you. I didn't want them to know the truth, because I didn't want you to be carrying that stigma around with you when you finally came to meet them. And they all think of you as Charlotte; I'm not even sure how many of them know, or will even remember your other name. And if that isn't enough for you, then surely Ottilie calling me Nanna of her own volition has got to be another sign that it's meant to be. And the fact that the police haven't begun to suspect you, another sign. Then ask yourself why did fate bring you together in the park that day? And bring me here to find you at such a crucial time? It's all falling into place, Alex – someone up there is on our side, I swear it, and all we have to do is go with it.'

Though it made a certain kind of sense, and it was everything Alex wanted to hear, she still wasn't able to make herself believe it could be that easy. 'But how do we explain Ottilie when we get there?' she'd asked. 'Isn't everyone going to find it odd that you've never mentioned having a granddaughter before?'

'I'll just feign surprise that I didn't tell them, and say I felt sure I did. It won't be difficult, I promise you. People over there aren't nearly as inquisitive or judgemental as people are here, you'll see. They'll take you and Ottilie straight to their hearts and in no time at all you'll be just like one of us. And think of the life you can give her there. She'll be safe and loved and grow up knowing that she matters more to us than anything else in the world. Doesn't she deserve that, after all she's been through? And don't we deserve to be together after all the years we've been apart?'

Even if her mother's arguments hadn't been so compelling, Alex knew in her heart that terrified as she was of going through with it, the alternative was non-negotiable, not for her own sake, but for Ottilie's. Either way for Alex, whether she was caught now, or at any time in the future, there was no doubt she would end up in prison. At least this way she was giving Ottilie a chance to be with the only two people she loved and trusted, without having to be anxious, or afraid, or hurt in any way again.

And if she was going to go along with the signs her mother was pointing out, and accept that they really were destiny at work, then she couldn't ignore perhaps the biggest sign of all – that Gabby had married a man with the surname of Lake. This meant that Phoebe's passport might possibly be usable for Ottilie. The only problem had been how to get hold of it, but even that hadn't proved difficult, because when Alex had driven down there last week Gabby had been called to the school to collect Jackson who'd felt unwell. So, presented with a golden opportunity to search for the passports, Alex had tracked them down and when she'd found them her heart had given an unsteady beat of shock. Not only was the surname in their favour, but it turned out that Phoebe's passport had been issued two years earlier, when she was three. And thanks to her dark hair she and Ottilie really weren't so unalike.

She still felt terrible for 'borrowing' the passport – she couldn't bring herself to think of it as stealing – but she kept reminding herself that when Gabby discovered it was missing it would be the easiest thing in the world for her to apply for another. As for what Ottilie would do for one in the future, well, they'd worry about that then. Their biggest concern now was getting her through airport security under the name of Phoebe Lake.

This was presuming they made it to the airport at all.

It was the morning of their departure. Ottilie was already in the car, singing a nursery rhyme to Boots as she tried to belt herself into the seat Anna had bought during a shopping trip to John Lewis a couple of weeks ago. She also had a trendy new buggy now, a few friends for Boots, and a very cute wardrobe of clothes.

Anna was outside with her, doing her best to fit the luggage in the boot, while Alex made a last-minute check of the house, wanting to be sure they hadn't left anything behind, particularly anything that belonged to Ottilie.

Tugging her mobile from the back pocket of her jeans as it rang, she felt her heart catch as she saw Anthony's name and clicked on.

'Hi,' she said, doing her best to sound casual and cheery. He'd rung a couple of times since the day she'd seen him at Maggie's, the first to find out how the showdown with her bosses had gone; the second to commiserate with the findings that had ended in her losing her job. 'Your timing is less than perfect,' she reminded him teasingly. 'We're just about to leave.'

'I thought you might be, so I'm calling to wish you bon voyage.'

Touched and surprised, she said, 'That's very kind of you, thank you.'

'In fact,' he went on, 'I could possibly do a little better than that and come to the airport to say it in person. What time is your flight?'

Starting to panic, Alex said, 'Uh, four fifteen, I think. My mother's in charge of it all, but honestly, you don't need to do that. We're already running late, so we'll probably have to whizz straight through and I'd hate for you to have a wasted journey.'

Sounding slightly crushed, he said, 'OK, I guess I'm a bit late with the suggestion anyway, and I know how stressful long hauls can be. Have you ever flown that far before?'

She laughed, as much with relief as nerves. 'I've only ever been as far as Spain, where I went with a group of friends to celebrate our graduation.'

'Then you're in for quite an experience. Are you stopping off anywhere?'

'Only to change planes, otherwise we're going straight through.'

'Well, I hope it all goes smoothly, and they've got some good inflight movies.'

'Actually, we've bought a portable DVD player,'

she told him, not adding that it was mainly for Ottilie, 'so hopefully we'll be well entertained.'

'Good. OK, I guess I'd better not hold you up any longer. Take care of yourself, won't you, and stay in touch.'

'I will,' she lied, while wishing desperately that she could, but she couldn't, and now really wasn't the time to start reading things into his friendship. Even if he was interested in her, which was highly unlikely, she'd just have to accept that it wasn't meant to be and get on with her life.

Things happened that way at times, she reminded herself sadly as she carried on checking round the bedroom. Opportunities came up, paths crossed, stars aligned, and depending what else was going on in a person's life the chances were seized or let go in ignorance of how they might have affected the future. So many things in her life could have turned out differently if she'd had some kind of insight into how her actions were going to impact on her later, or if she hadn't rushed into decisions without thinking them through. It was the same for everyone, and just like the rest of the world she had to try to make the best of the circumstances she'd created and hope it all turned out right in the end.

As she looked around the room, and realised she was seeing it for the last time, she was suddenly caught by a powerful wave of nostalgia. For days she'd been trying desperately not to look back, only forward, but now her mind seemed set in that direction. Apart from her first three years, and her time at uni, she'd only ever lived in this house and though she'd thought she was ready to say goodbye to it, she was finding that she might not be after all. She smiled wistfully to herself as a memory of her and Gabby bouncing on the bed as children materialised like a home movie; she could see them cosied up in the window seat listening to their father's stories, or raiding their mother's wardrobe for dressing-up clothes and high-heeled shoes. (Myra hadn't gone for stilettos in a big way, but she'd always had a couple of pairs, wrapped in tissue and still in their boxes, for special occasions.) She recalled the way she and Gabby used to stick towels up their jumpers to give themselves chests, and paint their mouths with lipstick or red liquor-ice. She could hear them laughing, shrieking, crying, whispering their secrets; the sound of their footsteps thundering along the landing and down the stairs; their teenage music blaring off the walls drowning out their father's medieval chants and boring classical stuff.

Suddenly, more than anything, she wanted to be back there where it felt safe and normal, uncluttered by the kind of fear that was troubling her now. Or did she? She didn't know, she couldn't tell, because her mind seemed incapable of thinking straight. She was caught between two worlds, trapped like a deer in headlights, unable to go back and afraid to go forward. Even if she were able to return to a time before all this had happened, before she'd known her mother, before Ottilie had come into her life, would she really go? It would mean that Ottilie would still be in that dreadful house with her crazy parents, and her mother would be in New Zealand longing for a daughter she bitterly regretted giving up. And she would still be longing for her mother to come and find her. So maybe their prayers had been answered; life had finally brought her and her mother together, at the same time as it had brought a lonely, frightened and damaged little girl to them too. They were being given the opportunity to rescue her in a way that her mother had never been able to rescue her, and now, regardless of right and wrong, life was sweeping them along into a future that only it could see.

She took a breath as though to clear her mind, and was about to leave the room when a text dropped into her phone. It turned out to be from Tommy and Jackie wishing her a happy holiday, and telling her not to worry about her car, they'd take good care of it until she came back. Having to swallow a lump in her throat she sent a message back thanking them not only for that, but for every-thing else too. Tommy had fought hard to save her job, and had only given up when she'd asked him to.

He'd been such a good friend and a great boss; she was going to miss him terribly.

Feeling herself drawn to the window she looked out to find her mother staring up worriedly, as though she'd somehow connected with her misgiv-ings. She lifted a hand to give her a reassuring wave, but at that instant she froze as she saw a car coming up the hill.

A fleeting panic crossed Anna's face as she turned to follow the direction of Alex's eyes.

Hardly knowing what she was doing or thinking, Alex tore out of the room and down the stairs. By the time she got outside Gabby was pulling up behind Anna's hire car. Anna was watching her in horror, seeming unable to move. Then suddenly she was stooping over Ottilie speaking words Alex couldn't hear, and as the rear passenger door closed Alex went to Gabby, trying to stop her coming any nearer.

'What are you doing here?' she cried, sounding strangely normal considering the panic she was in.

'I was afraid I might be too late,' Gabby replied, coming to wrap Alex in her arms. 'I know we said goodbye on the phone last night, but when I woke up this morning I realised I couldn't let you go without seeing you one last time.'

'Oh Gabby,' Alex murmured, squeezing her hard. 'You shouldn't have driven all this way just for that.' She hadn't told Gabby she was going for good – she even had a return ticket, because she had to – but it seemed Gabby had sensed it anyway.

'I had to come because there were things I should have said last night . . . I know I could have called this morning, but then I decided I had to tell you in person.'

Alex looked at her curiously, trying not to show her unease as Anna came to join them.

'I'm sorry if I'm making you late,' Gabby said to Anna, 'this won't take a moment, I promise.'

'It's OK,' Anna assured her, and giving her a hug she whispered her own goodbye and went back to the car where Ottilie was being as quiet as a mouse.

Bringing her eyes back to Alex, Gabby said, 'I know I probably haven't been the best sister in the world, but I wanted to tell you that I've always loved you, and growing up with you has been one of the best things that ever happened to me.'

As emotion rushed to Alex's throat she tried to speak, but Gabby hadn't finished.

'I'm going to miss you more than I can put into words,' she continued brokenly, 'and so will the kids, but I think you'll be happy in New Zealand and that's all that matters.'

'Oh Gabby,' Alex said tearfully, 'you're making

it sound as though we're never going to see one another again, but we will, I promise. I'll come back to visit, and you can come there.' She had to tell herself it might be possible, in time, or she'd never be able to leave.

Gabby smiled through her tears. 'Just know that I'll always be here for you,' she whispered shakily, 'and I mean always, no matter what,' and reaching into her bag she pulled out an envelope. 'This is for you,' she said. 'I always meant to give it to you, perhaps I should have said so before now, but it's yours and I want you to have it.'

Baffled, Alex looked down at it.

'It's post-dated for after the completion, but it's half the money from the sale of the house,' Gabby explained. 'It's been as much your home as it has mine, so it's only right . . .' She swallowed hard, but couldn't go on as Alex started to break down too.

'You don't need to do this,' Alex told her. 'It wasn't what your mother wanted.'

'It was what Daddy wanted, and it's what I want too.' She bit her lips as she tried to smile, then casting a quick glance at Anna's car she turned back to her own.

'Gabby,' Alex said, almost unable to bear this.

Gabby looked back.

'I love you,' Alex told her.

Gabby tried to smile. 'Go safely,' she said. Her eyes remained on Alex's, then in a voice Alex barely heard she added, 'Don't forget to send Phoebe's passport back when you're ready.'

As the words hit Alex's heart Gabby blew her a kiss and got into the car.

Gabby knew. Somehow she'd guessed and . . . And what? What was it going to mean?

Gabby was still watching her as she reversed the car ready to drive away. 'It'll be all right,' she mouthed, and moving off slowly, she started down the hill.

Suddenly Alex was sobbing. She wanted to go after Gabby. She needed to tell her again how much she loved her and how much this meant to her. She wanted to apologise for taking the passport, for putting Gabby in this position. She had to make sure she knew that no matter what, they would always be sisters, but Gabby was already turning into the village.

'Are you OK?' Anna asked, coming to put an arm round Alex.

'Yes, yes I'm fine,' Alex replied shakily. She'd tell her mother later, it would only alarm her now. 'It was just harder than I . . .' She took a breath. 'I should have given her the keys to the house. But it doesn't matter, I'll post them through the letter box, the way we arranged.' She inhaled deeply and turned to look at the Vicarage. It seemed to be watching her with Douglas's eyes, knowingly, maybe disapprovingly, but always lovingly. 'I guess I should go and lock up,' she said, certain if she didn't do it now she never would, 'then we can be on our way.'

Anna smiled, but as Alex looked at her she could see the anxiety in her eyes.

There was still a long way to go, and maybe they were only now starting to connect with the enormity of what they were doing.

They were on the plane now, sitting in a row of three close to the back of economy class, with Anna beside the window, Alex on the aisle and Ottilie looking very tiny between them. Her legs barely reached over the edge of the seat, but for her that was good, because she was so proud of her new flashing trainers that she could easily see them each time she lifted a foot to check if the lights had come on again yet. Her other source of fascination was the cabin crew, who were bustling up and down the aisle in smart red uniforms and neat boater hats. Some of them had paused to say hello and ask about Boots. As always she was holding on to him, though she'd dropped him earlier, as they were leaving security, and because she was asleep on Alex's shoulder they might not have noticed if an airport official hadn't picked him up.

Alex's heart was still racing from the shock of being tapped on the shoulder by a man in uniform who she'd immediately assumed was a policeman. He'd been so friendly as he handed Boots back, understanding what a nightmare it could be if a small child lost a special friend. Anna had stepped in to chat to him about his own children, while Alex had settled Ottilie back in her buggy. If he'd known, had even the slightest suspicion, how different their exchange would have been.

They'd fastened their seat belts quite some time ago, and the doors had long since been sealed, but for some reason the plane still wasn't pushing back from the gate. Minute after endless minute was ticking by. Alex could feel her skin prickling with sweat; she was desperate to find out what was happening, but too terrified to ask. She just knew that any minute now it would all be over: the doors were going to open, the police would stream on board and Ottilie would be plucked from her seat while she, Alex, was escorted away. She was so convinced of it that she could scarcely breathe past the fear of it, and she could tell that Anna was every bit as tense.

Looking down as Ottilie's head flopped against her arm, she had to choke back a sob as she lifted a hand to stroke her hair. She was going to miss her so much. The pain of it was already crippling her. She simply couldn't bear to think of being without her, of wondering every day where she was, how she was, and knowing she would never be told.

'I wonder why they're not saying what the delay is?' Anna murmured, the tremor in her voice seeming to shake through Alex too. 'They usually make an announcement, but I haven't heard anything, have you?'

Alex was so rigid she could barely reply, but then she lifted a hand and cupped it round Ottilie's face. As those beautiful solemn eyes looked up at her, so trusting and adoring, she could feel herself starting to break down. 'Are you OK?' she whispered raggedly.

Ottilie nodded. 'We're going up in the sky,' she told her.

Alex managed a smile. 'That's right,' she replied.

'But we don't have any wings.'

'No, but the plane does.'

'Wheeee,' Ottilie sang as she flew Boots as high as she could reach.

She's so happy, Alex was thinking desperately. *Please don't let it all come to an end for her now. She doesn't deserve it, even if I do.* Swallowing hard, she said, 'Would you like some juice?'

Ottilie shook her head and smacked a kiss on to Boots's nose before offering him to Alex to do the same. Then she flew him over to Anna and giggled when Anna blew a raspberry. She tried to do the same, and made a mess that Alex dabbed away with a tissue.

'Alexandra Lake?'

Alex froze as icy fear gripped her. They were here, it was finally happening, and now somehow, for Ottilie's sake, she had to make herself stay calm. She looked up, her vision so blurred by terror that she could hardly make out the person standing over her. 'It's OK,' she said, starting to unfasten her seat belt. *Oh God, Ottilie, I'm sorry, I'm so, so sorry.*

'There's no need to get up,' the person was saying. 'I think this is yours.'

Bewildered, Alex looked down at what he was holding.

'You must have dropped it,' he told her.

Stunned, but finally starting to register that he was a steward, not a policeman, she took the passport and looked inside. It was indeed hers.

'Hello you,' he said across her to Ottilie. 'And what's your name?'

Ottilie gazed at him wonderingly.

Alex was still so undone by the past few minutes that she was barely able to register what he was saying.

'Boots,' Ottilie suddenly announced, holding up her bear.

The steward appeared impressed. 'And isn't he a handsome lad,' he smiled.

Ottilie nodded earnestly.

'So are you going to tell me *your* name?' he prompted.

Ottilie looked at Alex.

Alex's head was spinning again as she realised they hadn't encouraged her to say Phoebe, which was on her ticket, for fear of confusing her.

Anna said, 'She changes her name sometimes, so I wonder who she is today. Are you going to tell us, sweetheart?'

Ottilie took a big breath and slapping a hand against her chest, she announced, 'I am Chloe. And this is Nanna, and this is *Mummy*.' As she said Mummy she tried to throw herself over the arm of the chair on to Alex's lap.

Laughing, the steward said, 'Well I think you have a very pretty name, Chloe, which is only right for a pretty little girl. And is our aeroplane taking you somewhere nice?'

Ottilie's eyes went questioningly to Alex. 'We're going to New Zealand, aren't we?' Alex responded.

'Zealand,' Ottilie echoed.

'Oh, so you've got a very long journey ahead of you,' he declared. 'Is it a holiday?'

Ottilie looked at Alex again. 'Actually,' Alex said, gazing down at her and loving her so much she seemed to be made of it, 'we're going home, aren't we, my darling?'

Ottilie nodded seriously. 'Going home,' she told him.

'Well, there's lovely. And it would seem,' he added, glancing out of the window as the plane started to ease back from the stand, 'that we're finally on our way. Are you buckled in nice and tightly now?'

Ottilie checked and nodded obediently.

'There's a good girl. I expect we'll find some nice surprises for you once we're in the air.' He smiled at her fondly. 'I'll be back soon, so don't go anywhere, will you?'

'No,' Ottilie promised in a whisper.

Somehow Alex managed a laugh, and wanting to hug her with all her heart, she turned to her mother, still not quite daring to believe that they really were on their way.

Anna smiled through her tears of relief, and her hand was shaking as she reached for Alex's. 'It's going to be all right,' she told her softly. 'Remember, it's meant to be.'

Alex looked down at Ottilie, who was watching them curiously. 'Yes,' she whispered shakily, 'yes, I think it is.'

Acknowledgements

I'd like to express the biggest thank you possible to Karen Hallam and Sarah Scully the social workers in child protection who guided me through the vital stages of this book. It's absolutely true to say that I could never have done it without them, and I especially thank Karen for finding the time to come to my home to help keep me on track. Also for her help in the field of Family Services I would like to extend a very warm thank you to Gill Briggs. (Because of how complex the child protection system is I have taken the liberty of simplifying it now and again in order to move the story along.)

I would also like to thank Sean Goodridge of the Child Abuse Investigation Team who helped me to set the research in motion and who lent much support along the way.

Once again my thanks go to Ian Kelcey and Gill Hall of Kelcey and Hall who advised on the legal aspects of the case. And to Carl Gadd for yet more invaluable backup.

I would also like to thank Sharon Barton for sharing her knowledge of private fostering, and my wonderful GP Helen Lewis for advising me on hallucinogens and tranquillisers.

My thanks and great affection also go to my editor

Susan Sandon and my agent Toby Eady, two people who quite simply make my world go round. Thank you for believing in me and thank you for your incredible support. Last, but by no means least, I'd like to say a huge thank you to the amazing team that takes the book from me, prepares it for its new life in the world at large and then delivers it to you, the reader: Georgina Hawtrey-Woore, Averil Ashfield, Rob Waddington, Jen Doyle, Sarah Page, Louise Page, Simon Littlewood, Diana Jones and the fantastic sales and marketing teams both here in the UK and around the world.

Getting to know

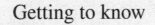

Read on for exclusive content including an insight into *No Child of Mine*, all about Susan and her links to the charity Breast Cancer Care

It probably won't surprise you to learn that this wasn't always an easy book to write. I'm sure at times you didn't find it easy to read either. Little Ottilie's story touched me deeply in its creation, perhaps more than any other book I've written.

Thank you for staying with her and Alex. Abandoning them, which would have been the less challenging option, would have felt as though we'd abandoned all the children who experience the same sort of tragedy in their lives. None of us would want to do that, though it's true we'd often like to bury our heads in the sand and pretend it's not happening.

My decision to tackle this difficult subject came about because of how frequently we see social workers being lambasted in the news. Sometimes this will be deserved, but more often than not we don't get to hear the whole story. Therefore we have no idea how bureaucracy, inflexible rules and regulations, manipulative adults, might have made it all but impossible for them to act even when their instincts are telling them they must. I didn't meet a single social worker during my research who didn't care passionately about the children in their caseloads; Alex herself is based on one of them (though I must stress that Ottilie's case is purely fictional).

Indeed, because this is fiction I have been able to make some good finally emerge from the horror of Alex and Ottilie's situation and to show that love can turn up in the most unexpected of ways.

It is, of course, a huge pity that this doesn't happen for far too many children, but I felt it was extremely important to try to leave you, the reader, with a sense of hope in your hearts.

Having said that, it might interest – and perhaps please – you to hear that there is a sequel, already written, entitled *Don't Let Me Go*. Obviously I won't give anything away here, but I hope you'll agree that there needed to be more.

Once again, I thank you for choosing to read one of my books, especially this one. It matters a great deal to me what you think of it, so if you would like to be in touch please don't hesitate. You can reach me through the contact link on my website – www.susanlewis.com – or on the Official Susan Lewis Facebook page: www.facebook/susanlewisbooks.

I was born in 1956 to a happy, normal family living in a brand new council house on the outskirts of Bristol. My mother, at the age of twenty, and one of thirteen children, persuaded my father to spend his bonus on a ring rather than a motorbike and they never looked back. She was an ambitious woman determined to see her children on the right path: I was signed up for ballet, elocution and piano lessons and my little brother was to succeed in all he set his mind to.

Tragically, at the age of thirty-three, my mother lost the battle against cancer and died. I was nine, my brother was five.

My father was left with two children to bring up on his own. Sending me to boarding school was thought to be 'for the best' but I disagreed. No one listened to my pleas for freedom, so after a while I took it upon myself to get expelled. By the time I was thirteen, I was back in our little council house with my father and brother. The teenage years passed and before I knew it I was eighteen…an adult.

I got a job at HTV in Bristol for a few years before moving to London at the age of twenty-two to work for Thames. I moved up the ranks, from secretary in news and current affairs, to a production assistant in light entertainment and drama. My mother's ambition and a love of drama gave me the courage to knock on the Controller's door to ask what it takes to be a success. I received the reply of 'Oh, go away and write something'. So I did!

Three years into my writing career I left TV and moved to France. At first it was bliss. I was living the dream and even found myself involved in a love affair with one of the FBI's most wanted! Reality soon dawned, however, and I realised that a full time life in France was very different to a two week holiday frolicking around on the sunny Riviera.

So I made the move to California with my beloved dogs Casanova and Floozie. With the rich and famous as my neighbours I was enthralled and inspired by Tinsel Town. The reality, however, was an obstacle course of cowboy agents, big-talking producers and wannabe directors. Hollywood was not waiting for me, but it was a great place to have fun! Romances flourished and faded, dreams were crushed but others came true.

After seven happy years of taking the best of Hollywood and avoiding the rest, I decided it was time for a change. My dogs and I spent a short while in Wiltshire before then settling once again in France. Perched high above the Riviera with glorious views of the sea. It was wonderful to be back amongst old friends, and to make so many new ones. Casanova and Floozie both passed away during our first few years there, but Coco and Lulabelle are doing a valiant job of taking over their places – and my life!

Everything changed again three months after my fiftieth birthday when I met James, my partner, who lives and works in Bristol. For a couple of years we had a very romantic and enjoyable time of flying back and forth to see one another at the weekends, but at the end of 2010 I finally sold my house on the Riviera and am now living in Gloucestershire in a delightful old barn with Coco and Lulabelle. My writing is flourishing and twenty-six books down the line I couldn't be happier. James is still in Bristol, with his boys, Michael and Luke – a great musician and a champion footballer! – so I believe James and I are what's called very happy LATTES (Living Apart Together – don't quite see how that acronym works but I'm told that's what we are!)

It's been exhilarating and educational having two teenage boys in my life! Needless to say they know everything, which is very useful (saves me looking things up) and they're incredibly inspiring in ways they probably have no idea about.

Should you be interested to know a little more about my early life, why not try *Just One More Day*, a memoir about me and my mother? The story then continues in *One Day at a Time*, a memoir about me and my father and how we coped with my mother's loss.

1.What made you want to become a writer?

It's something I instinctively felt would happen one day, though I didn't do much about it until I began working in TV drama. Editing scripts, pulling together storylines, dreaming up characters and their backgrounds was something I enjoyed so much that when an agent suggested I turn one of my projects into a book I decided to give it a go. That book was never published, but the bug had bitten and the rest, I guess, is history.

2. Describe your routine for writing and where you like to write, including whether you have any little quirks or funny habits when you are writing.

I have a study at home that overlooks a beautiful spread of lower Cotswold countryside where I aim to be by ten each morning, through until six or seven in the evening. For a long time I wrote seven days a week taking a break only when I was so exhausted I couldn't do any more. Now, I pace myself a little better by doing only five or six days, but even that is pretty gruelling. I don't have any quirks particularly, but I do have a very bad but thoroughly enjoyable habit of drinking a glass or two of wine when I read back over what I've written during the day.

3. What themes are you interested in when you're writing?

I'm always interested in the strange or terrible things fate inflicts on innocent people and how courageously (or not) they strive to overcome it.

4. Where do you get your inspiration from?

The most obvious source of inspiration is life itself. Added to that there are certain authors I find very inspirational in the way they write, such as Lionel Shriver; Jodi Picoult; Anita Shreve; Susan Howatch and Irène Némirovsky whose book, *Suite Française*, played a very big part in my own book, *A French Affair*.

5. How do you manage to get inside the heads of your characters in order to portray them truthfully?

It's all done through imagination, I guess – I can't think that there would be any other way.

6. Do you base your characters on real people? And if not, where does the inspiration come from?

Very occasionally they're based on people I meet, but as a real character is so highly complex it would only ever be one or two aspects of them. I guess you could say that personality traits are perhaps more inspiring than actual characters.

7. What's the most extreme thing you've ever done to research your book?

I once allowed myself to be locked up in a Filipino jail when researching *Last Resort* – that was pretty scary, and it didn't smell too good either!

8. What aspect of writing do you enjoy most?

I enjoy it all, especially when exciting and pivotal things happen that I hadn't seen coming!

9. What's the best thing about being an author?

For me it would definitely be doing the second draft when all the really hard work is done, and the smoothing out is underway. After that comes a lovely freeing time when I hold onto the book before giving it to my editor – this is a period when there is no pressure at all, or anxiety about whether or not she is going to like it. That begins the moment I send it from my computer to hers.

10. What advice would you give aspiring writers?

Probably that you have to be serious about writing to make it work, not simply think 'I'm going to write a bestseller' or 'I'd write a book if I only had time.' It takes a huge amount of dedication and belief in yourself; if you have that then I think the best advice I could give is pay great attention to your characters and who they are, and don't forget to listen to them. It's uncanny how often they'll help out when you find yourself stuck.

11. What is your favourite book of all time and why?

There are many books I could list here, but I'm going to settle for *Suite Française*, because it's the only book I've ever finished reading and then gone straight back to the beginning to read it again.

12. If you could be a character in a book, or live in the world of a book who or where would you be?

I wouldn't mind being one of Georgette Heyer's heroines back in Georgian times, but as they didn't have much in the way of anaesthetic then, perhaps I'd rather be Claudine in my own book, *Darkest Longings*.

and

I lost my mother to breast cancer when she was thirty-three years old and I was nine. This was back at a time when women, even doctors, spoke in hushed tones about the dreaded Big C. Nothing was discussed, no counselling offered; there was even a kind of shame attached to having fallen victim to this terrible disease.

Luckily, all that has changed. Today someone is always there to offer advice and support to those who need it, or simply to lend an ear if all that's required is to talk. Many of these people are doctors, nurses, or members of the healthcare professions; but just as many are women who selflessly give up their time to be there for those in need. Stephanie Harrison of Breast Cancer Care is one of these very special people, and it is because of her that I have become associated with this extremely worthwhile organisation.

Read on to learn more about Steph in her own words...

In June 2008, I was sitting in my doctor's office hearing the words 'Stephanie, you have breast cancer'. As those words reached my ears I felt like I'd been kicked in the stomach, and for a moment or two I sat in a daze of numbness and shock. I then heard, 'Is there any history of breast cancer in your family?' to which I replied 'No, but trust me to start a new trend'. Everyone in the room laughed, and I decided from that moment on I would try to fight this disease with humour.

At my diagnosis I received all the information I would need about treatment, lifestyle and aftercare, which was provided by Breast Cancer Care. At that time I had no idea just how important this organisation and its staff would become in my life. Subsequently they gave me so much help and support throughout my fight with cancer. I consider myself very fortunate that I was offered their support because now I realise it really is second to none. What I didn't realise at the time is that not everyone is aware of the support they offer. Therefore I decided to help raise awareness for this amazing charity by choosing Breast Cancer Care for my own fundraising activities.

It seems odd to say that my life has got better since being diagnosed with breast cancer, but in a lot of ways it has. It has focused my mind and made me realise life is short – that old cliché 'life is not a dress rehearsal' is so true. Seeing that this disease has no respect for age, colour or creed was a real eye-opener for me and it made me realise I had to do something to help others who would hear this devastating news. So I set out on my path as a fundraiser for BCC. During this time I have been overwhelmed by the love and support of so many people and their willingness to help me, as well as by the support of those at Breast Cancer Care. I have met so many amazing people, many of whom have become good friends and some of them have changed my life in more ways than they will ever know. One of those people is Susan Lewis.

In the spring of 2011 I was given a copy of the first part of Susan's autobiography *Just One More Day* and it changed my life. I wasn't sure reading a book about someone dying from breast cancer as I approached my 3rd annual mammogram would be a fun thing to do, but how wrong could I be. From the very first few lines I was hooked and I spent the next two days laughing and crying as I experienced all the ups and downs of Susan's family's lives; a family being torn apart by illness and secrets. Three things struck me immediately. One was how well written it was. Then I wondered how Susan wrote so effectively from the point of view of a child. I was also overwhelmed by Susan's honesty. By the end of the book I was so moved that I had to speak to Susan and tell her how it affected me. The mother/daughter scenario she described got me thinking about my own mum and just

how important this book is and on so many levels. I have since read many of Susan's novels, and last year the wonderful *One Day at a Time*, the second part to Susan's autobiography. Every book is not only a joy to read but also a learning experience about life. The first time I met Susan I realised I was in the presence of a kind, caring and truly genuine human being and working with her is one of the greatest joys of my life. I am proud to call her my friend and know that we will do wonderful things to help Breast Cancer Care help those who suffer from this life-altering disease.

Being told you have a life-threatening illness totally puts your life into perspective and makes you realise just what is important. It is also one of the scariest things any of us will ever have to face but with the love and support of others we can hopefully make the lives of those diagnosed in the future a little easier. It is a joy and an honour to represent Breast Cancer Care and the wonderful work they do.

There are more than half a million people in the UK
today who have been treated for breast cancer and
every year another 50,000 or so – including around
300 men – hear the devastating news that they have the
disease. They'll probably feel frightened and confused
– and their family and friends might need help too.

Breast Cancer Care is just a phone call or mouse
click away for anyone affected by breast cancer. Their
free helpline and information-packed website offer
a friendly ear and expert guidance to anyone dealing
with the turmoil of this life-threatening illness. Across
the UK, they also provide skilled emotional and
practical support through a range of confidential, face-
to-face services, helping people every step of the way.

Their unique strength lies in the way they combine
their understanding of people's experience of breast
cancer with the clinical expertise of their team of
specialist nurses. They care because they've been
there, and they know how to help.

Breast Cancer Care helpline:
0808 800 6000

Breast Cancer Care website:
www.breastcancercare.org.uk

Read my story...

To find out more about my family's experience with breast cancer then you can read *Just One More Day* and *One Day At A Time* – two memoirs that will hopefully make you laugh as well as cry! For some they may prove entertaining trips down memory lane; for others they will hopefully show how fortunate we are to be living in the times that we are.

Available at your local bookshop or online

Can you *ever* be free of your past?

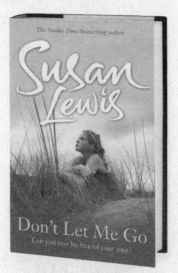

Charlotte Nicholls has a secret that haunts her.

She and three-year-old Chloe have left their home
and friends, and are now building a new life for
themselves elsewhere.

All Charlotte wants to do is to forget the past, to blot out
what went before, and to look only to the future.

At last she and Chloe feel safe.

Then, suddenly, their nightmare returns, and Charlotte finds
she has no power to prevent what comes next…

Out in hardcover 14 Feb 2013

Also by Susan Lewis
LOSING YOU

Lauren Scott is bright, talented and beautiful. At eighteen,
she is the most precious gift in the world to her mother,
and has a dazzling career ahead of her.

Oliver Lomax is a young man full of promise, despite the
shadow his own, deeply troubled, mother casts over him.

Then one fateful night, Oliver makes a decision
that tears their worlds apart.

Until then, Lauren and Oliver had never met, but now they
become so closely bound together that their families are forced
to confront truths they hoped they'd never have to face, secrets
they'd never even imagined...

Also by Susan Lewis
NO TURNING BACK

Eva Montgomery is at the peak of her career when she is viciously attacked by a stalker. While still traumatised, she makes the biggest mistake of her life – one she can never turn back from.

Sixteen years later, Eva has managed to rebuild her life in a way that seemed impossible after the attack. Her home in Dorset, high on the cliffs overlooking the sea, is as elegant as she is, but bears none of the scars. To an outsider, her world seems perfect in every way.

Then the past invades the present – with shattering consequences.

Hurt, frightened and confused, Eva struggles desperately to put right the terrible mistake she made sixteen years ago and finally break free from a past that nearly destroyed her.

Also by Susan Lewis
STOLEN

Lucy Winters' parents have always been there for her. Loving, gentle and kind they have given her everything she could have wished for. Now, estranged from her husband, she has moved to the country to take over their thriving auction business. The moment she begins to prepare for her first sale she knows she's made the right decision. And she dares to hope that at last she is living the life she has always dreamed of.

But then, quite suddenly, her world is thrown into turmoil. She discovers a shocking truth, one that forces her to question everything she has ever known. And it becomes frighteningly possible that the very people who should have protected her are the ones who have betrayed her in the most devastating of ways. Can she ever forgive them? Can they ever forgive themselves...?

Also by Susan Lewis
FORGOTTEN

When Lisa Martin and David Kirby were forced to part, they never dreamed they might one day have a second chance. Many years later, they meet again and it is clear that, despite everything that's happened to them, they are still the big love of each other's life. And nothing is going to keep them apart this time around. But then they are faced with a shocking truth.

However, David won't be defeated. In spite of knowing this is a battle they can't win, he decides to fight anyway, in the only way he knows how. When Lisa discovers what he intends she's horrified. Yet, through a chink in her fear, she can see the logic of what he's suggesting. But can she bring herself to help him...?

Also by Susan Lewis
THE CHOICE

Nikki Grant is only twenty-one when she discovers she's pregnant. Despite her parents' disappointment and anger, she welcomes the news with joy. The baby will complete the happy home she shares with the man she adores, Spencer James.

Baby Zac arrives and is perfect in every way. And with Spencer's career taking off they are ready to make the big move to London. And then, on a day like any other, Nikki suddenly finds her life turned upside down by tragedy. As she becomes evermore embroiled in a world she cannot escape, the love between Nikki and her son is put to the kind of test no mother should ever have to face...

Also by Susan Lewis
LOST INNOCENCE

When Alicia Carlyle returns to the home of her childhood after the tragic death of her husband, she is hoping to put the past behind her. But first she must come face to face with the woman who nearly destroyed her marriage and tore her family in two – her sister-in-law, Sabrina. Their enmity runs deep, but Alicia is determined to make a fresh start for herself and her two children, Nathan and Darcie, and to heal her fractured relationship with her beloved brother.

However, just when it looks as if they might have a chance at a brighter future, Sabrina's fifteen-year-old daughter, Annabelle, accuses seventeen-year-old Nathan of a crime he insists he didn't commit. And once more the two families are locked in a battle that is fraught with mistrust, betrayal and lies – a battle that threatens to destroy them all...

Join

Susan Lewis

online